WAYNE'S ANGEL

A novel by

RON W. MUMFORD

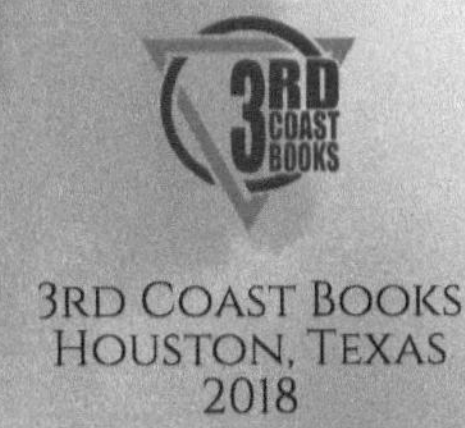

3RD COAST BOOKS
HOUSTON, TEXAS
2018

3rd Coast Books
11111 West Little York Rd., #222
Houston, TX 77041

www.3rdCoastBooks.com

ISBN's

Perfect Binding — 978-1-946743-09-1
eBook/.MOBI — 978-1-946743-10-7
eBook/.ePub — 978-1-946743-11-4

Project Coordinator — Rita Mills
Editor & Collaborator — Faye Walker
Text Design — Deena Rae
Cover Design — James Price

Printed in The United States of America

CONTENTS

ACKNOWLEDGEMENTS

When a writer sits down to create a novel it is a time of loneliness, solitude, reflections of past experiences of his or her life and a time of absolute joy in perfecting their story-telling art. They go to a place that I call "Out There," where they meet their characters, deciding which will play major or minor roles in the adventure, giving them separate voices/personalities and developing the story line that each will follow in their own individual way.

And, there are doubts. Doubts of whether the story is good enough, real enough and worthy of a readers time. Doubts are either verified or authenticated by a list of wise advisors who encourage or correct the writers work. Here is my list of advisors who I thank to the utmost and appreciate so very much.

Faye Walker, Ph.D., my trusted editor who not only corrected the punctuation but verified storyline breaks and added an insight into realism. My literary agent, Leticia Gomez of Savvy Literary, who believed in the work and placed it with a publisher through skilled knowledge of the publishing industry. Barbara Pennington, M.A., who created the cover art for *Wayne's Angel* that perfectly took us to *Out There*.

I also want to acknowledge people who read the original manuscript and wrote their honest opinions of what they read. Rita Mills, Publisher of New Era Times, T. Kent Atkins, Ph.D,, Phillip Hatfield, Certified Zig Ziglar Speaker and author of *Carried by Angels*. Pastor Michael Perron of Summit Life Church, and Pamela K. Ott.

And finally, kudos to Scott Easterwood, talented musician, singer and arranger of "The Only Love Song" that ends the book and available on YouTube. The song was written by my great friend, Belinda Davis-Wright, J.D., I truly believe it takes a woman's heart to help men discover what love is. And to my encouraging sister, Donna Easterwood who always tells me, "Brother, this is bound to be a best seller!" Above all, Thank You, Lord, for giving me the words…You are the greatest writer.

INTRODUCTION

Many literary scholars have tried to define the genre of Wayne's Angel. Some call this book Mainstream fiction, others have said it is Fantasy, Action-Thriller, Romance and may be Spiritual fiction. Whatever your genre of choice is, you will find it in this book and I'll let the reader decide. After all, we all have free choice and free will.

In a contemporary setting around the beautiful lake and Galveston Bay area where the NASA Command Center is located near Houston, Texas, the journey ultimately leads to another dimension where few mortals have been—Between, a place of reflection and preparation, then to Betwixt, when demons hang out.

Don't let the demons and demonesses scare you. Some are absolutely hilarious, all are deceiving, some are gorgeous and others are what you may not expect. They tempt you with the world's pleasures and try to confuse you about the truth.

Wayne Tyler is a lady-killer, very talented singer, musician, impersonator of both rock stars and C&W headliners. He's also a vagabond that has never learned what true love is or had any meaningful relationships in his life other than one-night stands. At least not until he meets Abby Hawkins, who really loves him and wants Wayne to write her a love song. Wayne can't find the words. After he is falsely accused of sleeping with Abby's free-spirited sister, Bella, he thinks the only way back to Abby is to learn what love is.

That's the set-up for this far out journey to other dimensions. Wayne's angel, Gordon (as in Guardian) let's Wayne choose his destiny. He can go back to being drunk and fourteen feet under water in Galveston Bay; he can choose to face seven demons or he can call upon the name of the Lord. Wayne has no idea who the Lord is and chooses to face the demons. Their prize is his soul. Wayne's prize is to know what love is so he can write Abby that song. But there are no guarantees of any kind...

Fasten your seat belts! You've never been on a ride like you are about to experience...

WAYNE'S ANGEL

1

Hank — We Sang in the Moonlight

Like many men, Hank Hawkins always compartmentalized events in his life and dealt with them head-on, one at a time. He'd been an aggressive linebacker on his football team in the school for boys in Clear Lake, Texas, but when the coming-of-age call of fun, travel and adventure overshadowed his thirst for knowledge, he joined the Marine Corps when he was eighteen during the end of the Vietnam war era. He was off to see the world.

After two tours in Vietnam as a member of a Marine Recon unit, he had experienced enough horrors of war and sought peace in his life. For the remainder of his six-year enlistment, he trained other Marines in San Diego and spent a lot of time on weekends in the fading hippie haven of San Francisco. His love of eclectic music kept him going back to his temporary escape from the military and the pictures of death buried in his mind.

The evolving phantasmagorical music scene in the 70s and 80s touched his soul and mesmerized the demons in his mind. He wasn't exactly the center of attention when he frequented his favorite bars in the Bay Area but tended to stand out with his Marine haircut. That was just fine with Hank. He was there for the music and the last of the free-spirited flower-child ladies, not the long-haired draft-card-burning self-proclaimed poets that seemed ever present in the San Fran bars.

After commuting for months to his hideaway on the bay, Hank had made no friends whatsoever. He was the establishment in the minds of the young know-it-all liberal government antagonists and was pretty much blackballed from conversation, relationships and even as an opponent in the familiar political debates fueled by Sangria wine and a touch of LSD.

These free-spirited, undisciplined, irresponsible voyeurs amused Hank. He was okay with who he was and chuckled about some of the far out drug-enhanced points and counter points brokenly offered up by the egotistical politicos who only wanted to be heard, noticed and pursued by some of the scantily clad, bra-less hippie chics. Most of these would-be orators made no sense at all. Their logic was scattered and unplanned at best.

But sometimes even they got lucky with a little help from their friends: mind-bending drugs, alcohol and the constant reminder through song and poetry that they were living in the last days of the Age of Aquarius, the age of free love. Janis Joplin and Jimi Hendrix were gone, Linda Ronstadt was just coming into her own and as Bob Dylan said, "The times, they are a changing …"

Halfway through an evening, most of the foul smelling poets could barely walk much less continue ranting on their pointless points of view. That's when Hank began to be noticed since he was one of the only half- way sober, semi-conscious males in the bar, short hair or not.

In 1979, with only months to go before he was released from active duty, Hank took another trip up to San Fran. He dropped in to The Enchanted Cup, a remnant, die-hard hippie hollow bar with some great music. He had rented a cheap room two floors above the establishment while he was there for the weekend.

The "Cup" as it was called, was retro in design with a small stage for the singers, artists and orators and was surrounded by bean-bag chairs. No two tables were alike, concrete floors, and old Chianti wine bottles with melted candles enhanced the black-light, day-glow peace signs and bubbling psychedelic spirals on the black walls. It was a dark, dreamy nostalgic setting that only appealed to a select few. Not your high traffic happy, go-lucky bar.

Immediately, Hank's eyes were fixed on a waitress across the room. He was mesmerized. The world seemed to stand still for a moment and the only movement in the room was her gentle, flowing swagger, beautiful green eyes, long brown hair and a siren's call for him to meet her.

Completely out of character, Hank stood up from his table, walked across the room to her and said, "I'm Hank. Would you be my waitress?"

She smiled at him. "I'm Abigail. I would love to be your waitress."

Tough guy Hank, 6'2", 195, had never experienced a moment like this. It was as though Cupid was using his heart as a pin cushion. He tried to get a grip on his infatuation but to no avail. He couldn't take his eyes off of Abigail's black hip-hugger, bell-bottomed slacks, purple crop-top and the band of flowers holding back her long brown hair. Her eyes pierced his very soul and melted any attempt for him to retreat.

"What cha drinking, big boy Hank?" she said with an aloof, flirting eye.

"Sangria."

"Great choice. We have the best Sangria on the bay. Where ya from?"

"Houston, via San Diego. I'm in the Marines if you couldn't guess."

Abigail smiled and turned to go to the bar. She returned with a glass of Sangria and placed a rose on the table in front of Hank. He didn't know what to think or say.

"What's with the rose?" Hank was stumbling for words.

"It's to heal your heart and memories," she said.

"How do you know that my heart and memories need healing?'

"Because you're a Marine. My big brother was a Marine. He didn't make it home …"

Hank had no words. Abigail's demeanor seemed to change from her usual smiling free spirit to one of deep thought.

Later, she returned to his table and said, "Hank, you've brought back some memories of my own. I don't want to be alone tonight. Where are you staying? I'm off at two …"

"Two floors up. I'll wait for you here."

Hank passed the night away watching Abigail make her rounds with very little conversation between them. He watched her every move, trying to figure out what was going on in that beautiful mind of hers. She was so different, so simply beautiful, like no other he had ever met. He didn't have lust in his heart for her, but whatever it was he was feeling was completely foreign to him. No experience had ever been like this one. Hank asked himself, *Is this what love is?*

The Cup was having an open-mic night. A lady singer stepped up on the stage and began singing a Gale Garnett song from the 60s, "We'll Sing in the Sunshine" …

The words to the song had an almost prophetic message as Hank drifted into the lyrics …

We'll sing in the sunshine,
We'll laugh every day,
We'll sing in the sunshine,
Then I'll be on my way …
My daddy he once told me,
Hey, don't you love you any man.
Just take what they may give you,
And give but what you can …

What seemed like a millennium finally turned into two in the morning. Abigail walked over, grabbed Hank's hand and said absolutely nothing. They walked up two flights of stairs to Hank's room and closed the door behind them.

What followed was a night of gentle pleasure, long soft kisses and unbreakable embraces. Hank and Abigail were healing each other in the only way they knew how. They became one, sharing their hurts, their hearts, their passions, their histories and their love.

At some point just before dawn, Hank drifted off into sleep, continuing to dream of the night, the lady and the moment. When he awoke, Abigail was gone. She left a note for him on the dresser which read:

Dearest Hank,
We sang in the moonlight,
Now I must be gone …
You're a good man!
Always, Abigail.

Hank knew in a moment that Abigail had been listening to the song earlier that night. Maybe the words were the reason for her bold move.

Hank returned to The Enchanted Cup for the next two nights looking for her, but Abigail didn't show up. He asked the owner of the Cup where she was, where she lived and how he could get in touch with her. Chip, the owner, said that Abigail had been a mystery to everyone there. No one knew where she lived, she had no phone, no friends, no contact information. Because the waitresses worked for tips, Chip didn't even know her last name, no one did. Everyone simply knew her as "Abigail." In desperation to find her, Hank made a couple of more weekend trips to San Francisco before his time in the Marines ended. He searched everywhere for her. His heart was breaking. He placed ads in the ever-popular "Personals" in the local rag sheets. He had to find her, but she was gone. Maybe forever.

Finally, Hank decided that he could only retain the memories of his one-night, one chance-of-a-lifetime soul mate. The images of her kisses, her fragrance, the note and her introduction to love would never be far from Hank's mind. He kept Abigail's rose as a treasured reminder of the greatest love of his life, the greatest night of his life.

Two months later, Hank returned to civilian life and headed home to Kemah, Texas, to see what else destiny had in store for him. His heart was still in San Francisco. Maybe he could discover it again in Texas …

At 5 a.m. as Hank was sitting on the balcony of his two-bedroom condo overlooking Clear Lake, he watched the sunrise over Galveston Bay, reflecting on the past as he looked at the announcement of The University of Houston, Clear Lake Campus, Master's Degree ceremony later that evening. He brushed his long gray hair out of his eyes and twisted it into a pony tail. It had been thirty-four years since that memorable night with Abigail and tonight was going to be another special occasion in his life.

In all the time that followed, he had never found another woman to take her place, no other woman that stole his heart and no other woman had taken his breath away …

[illegible] [illegible] [illegible] [illegible]
[illegible] on the [illegible] [illegible] [illegible]
[illegible] [illegible] [illegible]
[illegible] [illegible] [illegible]
[illegible] [illegible] [illegible]
[illegible] [illegible] [illegible]
[illegible] [illegible] [illegible]
[illegible] [illegible] [illegible]
[illegible] [illegible]

2

THE LETTER — DEAR MR. HAWKINS ...

Kemah, Texas, on Clear Lake was a laid back, seaside community built around the NASA Space Center just outside of Houston and the booming fishing business on Galveston Bay that contained a rare mix of red neck fishermen, construction workers and the affluent, intelligent NASA engineering community. Where there is beautiful water and affluent people, there are boats, lots of boats, of every size and purpose. Kemah had floating boat docks, enclosed boat storage with dockside valet service, boat lifts that accommodated the weekend pleasures of the high society Houston oilmen, business owners, land developers, and the highly paid NASA astrophysicist and engineering crowd.

Along the boardwalk in Kemah there were great seafood restaurants that attracted people from all over the world. Commercial fishing boats docked right at the businesses and off-loaded their catch. The oysters, giant shrimp, red fish, flounder and speckled trout that people ordered from a variety of side-by-side restaurants, had been swimming in the Gulf of Mexico just hours before delivery.

As Hank continued reminiscing, waking up, drinking his coffee, he thought about his past career in the Marine Corps when at age twenty-four he had decided that there wasn't much opportunity of employment for a behind-the-scenes. black-ops veteran.

Back then, Hank had a destination but had no plan. He had saved most of his money and it wasn't like he was broke. While in San Diego he had seen job openings for licensed electricians in the Houston area, so he just chose that as a new profession, went through an apprentice program and the opportunities became limitless. During the week days, he worked construction in the refineries and on weekends installed electronics on the many yachts, pleasure and fishing boats on Clear Lake.

During all the years of hard work, Hank knew that he needed a dream to keep him going. His passion had been music, freedom, happiness and people, even though he was a bit of a loner. How could he put these seemingly intangible, almost unreachable elements together and mix them into a dream and a way to make a living at the same time?

Hank took another sip of his hot coffee and chuckled as he remembered driving back from San Diego when he was chilling out one night in the Arizona desert during his drive home. It was such a quiet, serene place. Surely his dream would appear to him if he thought hard enough. As he awoke from sleeping in the back seat of his Camaro, his dream came to him in a single word: "Tequilaville," a good-time, fun place with great music, food and drink. He knew absolutely nothing about the club business.

Hank was really laughing at himself now, after all these years. He had taken this omen or dream seriously, with eager anticipation when he was younger. He feared nothing in life then, had plenty of time to make this dream a reality and took off on his second day of driving home absolutely pumped. He drove with a dream and a goal. Now he had to figure out how to make it happen. So far, after all these years, he'd never figured it out.

Life in his 60s was fairly routine, but Hank wasn't unthankful. His business had grown to the point of never having to work construction again since the boat owners around the Lake kept him busy. He knew just about everyone, everyone knew him and called him with any work that needed to be done from installing expensive radar units in the larger yachts and sailboats to repairing electrical connections or putting in ship-to-shore communications on weekend pleasure boats. The sun over Clear Lake was now peeking above the horizon even though Hank had no urgency about starting his day. He was lost in his memories, counting his blessings when he got an early morning phone call from his life-long BFF, Robbie Cantrell, a woman in her fifties, very attractive, tall and thin with short blonde hair. They had been friends from the first time they met but never even held hands.

"Did you get your suit?" Robbie was always checking on Hank.

"Yeah, I did. Just sitting here thinking about the journey to get to this day. What's up with you, Robbie?"

"I'm excited, too. Are we all going to do something afterwards to celebrate? I was thinking Turtle Club. Is that okay?"

"Sounds good to me. I'll see you and Bella at the commencement around 5:30 tonight if that's good. Bella is coming, isn't she?"

"Are you kidding! Like mother like daughter. She wouldn't miss it. See you then …"

For years, just to break the monotony of work, Hank would pop in to some of the landmark clubs on Clear Lake to get ideas for Tequilaville. He made a few friends, had a fling or two, but no woman could compete with the thoughts and memories of Abigail. He still pined for her to the point that no one could compete with the ghost of another. Most of the women he met over the years had no chance of a long-lasting relationship with Hank.

Maribelle's was a tough biker bar just across the channel from the restaurant district in Kemah on Clear Lake. Its clientele consisted of bikers, strippers, young and old, blue collar, white collar, anyone who sought an element of danger and excitement in their lives while getting loaded watching Maribelle's famous wet T-shirt competitions on the weekends. The strippers got ample competition from NASA lady engineers who had had just a little too much to drink and got into the moment. They would willingly flash their boobs at the insistence of the very vocal, rowdy crowd and took first place more often than the uncaring strippers who made a living flashing and strutting their stuff half naked. Bella had won a couple of competitions herself, much to her mother's disapproval.

Maribelle's was always packed on the weekends. There was plentiful security on premise since bikers and astrophysicists rarely exchanged ideas in the same way and a few short-lived fights would break out adding to the excitement. The hard rock music was loud, open-aired and the booze and good times flowed freely. Hank had let his hair grow long so he blended right in during that period of his life.

The other landmark club was The Turtle Club, located right on the water of Clear Lake, referred to as "The Lake" by locals, which opened up into the Gulf of Mexico. Locals could drive into their huge parking lot off NASA Road 1 or boat owners could pull their cigarette boats and yachts right up to the Turtle's private dock, tie up, go in for drinks and food and speed off again into the night. Tying your boat up at the dock at the Turtle Club was at one's own risk. Many of the larger boats were owned by the inexperienced elite and they would often gently crash their crafts into other boats while docking. For some reason it didn't seem to matter and people just got along and called the dents in their shiny boats "whisky bumps." Getting along with the diverse crowd in the Clear Lake area was the unwritten law. Chilling, flowing, drinking and having fun was at the top of the menu.

Hank took all of this in to figure out how to make Tequilaville unique but as yet had no idea how to do this. He had rented an old, inexpensive warehouse and, over the years, begun to store unused materials that he collected. Furniture, restaurant equipment, chairs, tables … the accumulation of materials grew over the years and all was paid in full from the beginning. Now he had to find a location on the Lake. He was going to use his GI Bill to buy it when a great location came on the market, but so far, it hadn't happened.

Sooner or later he was going to have to get going. The morning was slipping away. Rarely did Hank sit and reminisce, but today was special and he couldn't tear himself away from his memories. He thought about that day when the letter arrived about twenty-four years ago …

During his early days on the Lake, Hank often let his mail pile up and spent most of his time writing bids for extra work. He'd quickly sift through the junk mail and file-thirteen all the letters and grocery ads that he thought to be unnecessary. It was a Saturday morning and one letter had caught his attention. The return address was: California Child Protective Services, County of San Francisco, San Francisco, CA.

He'd never forget that day … Hank had no idea what was in the contents of the envelope but memories of Abigail led him immediately to rip open the letter. A thousand thoughts ran through his mind; *Why would I be getting a letter from Child Protective Services? Is Abigail reaching out to me from San Francisco? Can our love have another chance?* He was shaking as he carefully pulled out the letter:

Dear Mr. Hawkins,

In 1980, eight years ago, a Ms. Abigail Greene, an unwed woman originally from Wisconsin, living in San Francisco at 2110 Boa Street, Apartment 11, San Francisco, gave birth to a female child named Abby Gale Greene. On the birth certificate, authenticated at San Francisco County Hospital, Ms. Greene listed the father as Hank Hawkins, employed by the U.S. Marine Corps in San Diego, California. After an extensive search, you are the only "Hank Hawkins" listed as serving with the Marine Corps in San Diego during that period of time. This is why we are contacting you.

Ms. Greene had custody of her daughter for six years until she was involved in a fatal car accident. She was pronounced DOA on March

30, 1986. With no known living relatives, Ms. Greene's daughter, Abby Gale Greene, was placed in Foster Care by California Child Protective Services. She is now a ward of the State of California.

If you believe that you may be the birth father of Ms. Abby Gale Greene, please contact S. Bain, Case Worker, Case # 5234688 at the following number ...

Hank remembered the lump that had formed in his throat before he got half way through the letter. He fought to keep his emotions intact. The address, 2110 Boa Street, was the address where he had rented the room above The Enchanted Cup the night he met Abigail. He never knew that she had lived just down the hallway. No wonder she could have disappeared so quickly from his room that night. Now she was gone! He would never see her again. Hank remembered saying to himself, *Big boys don't cry!*

He also relished the memory of the moment when he found out that he had a daughter. His emotions exploded that day. He was terribly sad, yet jubilant at the same time. His hands were shaking, his mind was fried, he couldn't think. All the compartments in his head seemed to open at the same time. He was overwhelmed. His world had just changed in a big way. He was a daddy. He had an eight-year old daughter named Abby, and there was no doubt. Now he had to do the right thing; get his daughter and bring her home. Nothing else mattered ...

At this point in his recollections, Hank walked back into the condo to get his second cup of the new day.

In 1988 Hank had booked a flight to San Fran, not even knowing whether the Cali CPS officials would see him. He bought his first suit for the meeting to make a good impression and a new pair of shoes since he only owned two pair of work boots and three pair of cowboy boots. Hank hadn't worn shoes in years and still didn't.

Back then, the one thing that was racking his brain was trying to figure out how he was going to handle this new situation in his life and why Abigail never told him ...

Of course her last name was Greene, he thought, she had the most beautiful green eyes ... oh those beautiful eyes ... I wonder if they'll let me have Abby? Is my place an appropriate home for an eight-year old little girl? I'm not married. I don't know anything about raising a child, much less a little girl … When will she need a training bra and who is going to tell her about Aunt Matilda visiting every month? How do I enroll her in school? Who is going to take care of her in the afternoons after school? What little girl sizes of clothes and shoes does she wear? This scares the hell out of me! He finally admitted to himself, I'm not sure I can do this, but I have to. I am Abby's birth father. Nothing is going to keep me away from her … or is it?

Then Hank remembered calling Robbie Cantrell so many years ago. Robbie was a widowed, single mom that lived two condos down from his. She had a twelve-year old daughter at the time, and Hank had asked her to help him out. Robbie had given him the best advice in the world when she told him, "You raise a daughter one day at a time. Everything else will work out …"

The phone interrupted his memories, "Speak of the devil, Robbie, I was just thinking about something you told me years ago."

"I couldn't think of what it could be, I've told you so many things over the years. Right now I'm telling you to get going. I can see you from my balcony. What kind of cake do we need for tonight?"

"Uhhh … Chocolate Devil's food?"

"Hank, that's for birthdays. Remember that I've baked that cake every year for ages. Tonight is festive, not a birthday. How 'bout French Vanilla?"

"Good choice."

"Fine, I've already ordered it at Heaven Bakery. Can you pick it up?"

"Sure, what time shall I … ?"

Back to his memories, refusing to get going, Hank remembered the first call and every detail of the conversation with the California CPS.

"Child Protective Services, may I help you?"

"Yes, this is Hank Hawkins in Kemah, Texas. I got a letter from you. I need to speak with S. Bain. The file number is 5234688."

"Mr. Hawkins, I will need your contact information first." The receptionist pulled up his file number and glancing over it said, "And then I need to know more about why you believe that you may be the birth father of Abby Gale Greene?"

"Because I know I'm her birth father. I can tell you anything you want to know. How is she doing? Is she okay? When can I see her? I can be there this afternoon. I've already booked a flight …"

Hank gave the receptionist his contact information and stayed on the phone for over half an hour answering questions about his knowledge of

Abigail Greene, which wasn't much. He hardly knew her. Finally, Mrs. S. Bain picked up the conversation.

"Mr. Hawkins, we have given you all the information we can at this time. You cannot see Ms. Greene until your paternity tests are done confirming that you are in fact the birth father, we do an F.B.I. check on you, work with Texas CPS to see where you live, talk to your references and make a final determination for custody. Plus, you will need an attorney for the custody process if our ruling goes in your favor."

"Okay, Mrs. Bain, I'll be there tomorrow at 10 a.m. How long does this process usually take?"

"No less than six months, Mr. Hawkins. You have to be patient. We are very protective of our children …" Click.

At 10 a.m. the next morning, twenty-four years ago, Hank remembered the receptionist at the Cali CPS offices calling his name.

"I'm here!"

"Mr. Hawkins, please go down the hallway to your right. Mrs. Bain is in room 223."

"Have a seat, Mr. Hawkins. I have forms for you to fill out later, but first I want to do a thorough qualifying interview. Just part of our procedures.

"Mr. Hawkins, tell me about your family. Tell me about your mom, dad, brothers and sisters, and are you married with any other children?"

"None of the above," Hank remembered saying to Mrs. Bain.

"I beg your pardon? Could you be a little more specific?"

"I have no known family, no mom, no dad, no siblings and never been married."

"We'll need to go a bit farther into this, Mr. Hawkins. What do you mean that you have no mom or dad?"

"Long story short, Mrs. Bain, the story I was told in the orphanage back in Houston, was that some firemen found me in a basket outside their fire house one morning and passed me on to the State. I'm not even real sure when my correct birthday is because I didn't arrive with a birth certificate. I was never in foster care. I just grew up and went to school at a State school for boys. I've brought the file that they gave me when I turned eighteen to verify this."

"Mr. Hawkins, after you were of age, didn't you try and track down your parents? Any brothers and sisters?"

"No. When I came of age and left the orphanage, I joined the Marine Corps. That's why it's so important for me to get custody of my daughter. I understand what she's going through. I understand her loneliness, I understand her fears and her lack of belonging."

Mrs. Bain was taken aback by Hank's compassion and intensity.

"Tell me about how you met Abigail Greene …"

Back to reality, Hank's nostalgia was interrupted by another phone call, "This is Hank!"

"Gunny, what's the plan for tonight?" It was Tito Chavez, a thirty-two-year old 5'7" former Marine, karate instructor and one of Hank's small circle of Lake friends. Tito had a small local dojo and was a fifth degree Black Belt.

"As usual, Robbie has the program planned for tonight, Tito. Ceremony at six at the University of Houston Clear Lake campus, reception dinner afterwards, same location, then we're all going over to the Turtle Club for a little celebration. You in?"

"It's a big day for you Hank. Of course, Mary and I are in. See you there, Semper Fi!"

Diving back into his memories, Hank recalled the greatest night of his life. He was completely open and honest talking to Mrs. Bain about the encounter with Abigail, her disappearance and how he sought to find her for so long before giving up hope and moving back to Texas.

"So Mr. Hawkins, you didn't even know Abigail's last name?"

"No Ma'am. I just knew that I loved her. I pined for her. That's the reason I never married if that makes any sense to you. You see, Mrs. Bain, I never knew what love felt like until I met Abigail and that's the truth."

"We'll need you to go down the hall and give blood samples for paternity verification before you leave, Mr. Hawkins. We're using something new called a DNA test. It's only been around for four years and is 99.99% accurate. We'll also be conducting an F.B.I. check on you. Do you have a record of any felony or misdemeanor violations that you would like to tell me about? Any bankruptcies?"

"Not that I know of."

"Then I'll contact you when we are further into the investigation. Give me at least a couple of months before checking back with me, Mr. Hawkins, but feel free to call after that. I'll try and keep you informed."

"Mrs. Bain, before I leave, can I see a picture of Abby?"

"I truly wish that was allowable, Mr. Hawkins. At this stage, it's against the rules. Just be patient."

"Can I have a picture of Abigail?"

"Mr. Hawkins, there was no picture on her obituary. That was public record. I can tell you that she never married. The accident report was also public record. Do you want a copy of that?"

"Was Abby in the accident?"

"No."

Hank remembered that Mrs. Bain didn't extend her hand to end the interview.

"Mr. Hawkins. I shouldn't be saying anything about this. I want to leave you with something to think about."

"Sure, Mrs. Bain. Hit me with it. I'm gonna need lots of time to think about things …"

Mrs. Bain took in a long breath and let it out slowly. Hank remembered the troubled look on her face. What she told him he would never forget."Abby has been … how do I put this? A bit of a problem child. After the accident, Abby was placed in foster care with a family we thought we had screened very carefully while we sought her next-of-kin. Without going into detail, Abby set fire to the foster parents' house a short time later. Police found her walking the streets. We immediately took Abby to some of our psychologists to find out why she had set the fire.

"Abby was completely silent and withdrawn with the psychologists and gave no information. Before her mom's accident, she had above average grades in school, especially in mathematics. She seemed to make friends easily and was a happy little girl. After the fire, she was totally different. Introverted, no friends and a complete loner. The final psychologists' conclusion was that they thought she may have been abused by her foster father. That's why she is now a ward of the State of California. With no evidence, there was no prosecution, but we immediately removed her from the foster program. Oddly enough, Abby does not cry, either about her mom's accident or the situation with her foster parents …"

"That S.O.B.! I'll kill that sorry no-good!" Hank interrupted. He couldn't contain his anger and that rage had never left him. He felt that way to this day.

Hank returned to Kemah with more than he wanted to think about. He was emotionally exhausted, but the thought of Abby kept him going. He wondered if she looked like her mother. Even before he met her, he loved Abby's spunk, a trait that had surely come from him.

3

ABBY — A MAN JUST KNOWS

...

Blasted phone! Hank thought to himself.

"Hey bro, what's up for tonight?" It was another friend of Hank's, T-Bone. No one knew him by any other name. T-Bone was 6'7", 285 and had almost become a member of a notorious motorcycle club, MC, in San Antonio until he had to kill someone during his initiation for entry into the MC. T-Bone, 34, thought he was tough in his younger years but just didn't have the stomach for senseless killings so he had to relocate and become a ghost for a while to escape the wrath of the other MC members. In fact, T-Bone was a big, bad, gentle giant that now worked on a shrimp boat in Kemah.

"T-Bone, how ya doing?"

"Same ole, same ole, man. It's a big day for you tonight and I wanted to know where I need to be."

Hank gave him the plans; their conversations were always short.

Back to Abby and his thoughts … Hank had forwarded all of the requested documents to Mrs. Bain, spoken to her many times on the phone and then he just had to be patient while the system took its course until he heard from her again.

Finally, Hank's phone rang with the call that he'd waited so long to get.

"Mr. Hawkins? This is Sara Bain with CPS in California."

"I'm here, Mrs. Hawkins. Is everything okay with Abby? With the investigation?"

Mrs. Bain could hear the concern in Hank's voice along with his anticipation of answers.

"Abby's just fine. We have some preliminary reports back from the F.B.I. and your service record. I see that you were a hero in Vietnam and received two Bronze Stars …"

Hank quickly cut her off and said, "No Ma'am! I was *not* a hero. I was just doing my job. The heroes were the ones that didn't come home or got the Medal of Honor."

"Nonetheless, Mr. Hawkins, you had a commendable service record and with a Top Secret clearance in the Marines, it made the F.B.I. check go very well. No problems so far."

"So where do we go from here, Mrs. Bain?"

"The best news is, Mr. Hawkins, the DNA tests revealed beyond a shadow of a doubt that you are, in fact, the biological birth father. How would you like to meet Abby?"

Hank's heart skipped a beat. These were the words he was yearning to hear.

"When? What time? Where? Of course I want to meet Abby! What do I need to do?"

"We would like to arrange a first meeting with Abby the middle of next month here in San Francisco. Before the meeting is set, we need you to sit down with some of our psychologists. They have questions about your experiences in Vietnam and want to get an idea of how you intend to support Abby, among other things.

"If and when we set the meeting with Abby, Mr. Hawkins, it will be no more than thirty minutes and under the supervision of a CPS agent and an employee of the orphanage whom Abby knows. There are no exceptions to our rules."

"Agreed, Mrs. Bain. Just tell me when and where. I'm ready. And Mrs. Bain, I knew all along that I was Abby's father. A man just knows …"

Hank arrived in San Fran on a Wednesday night, stayed at the same motel and arrived early at the scheduled meetings with the psychologists. He couldn't begin to imagine what they would ask him or what he would say.

"Good morning Mr. Hawkins, I'm Dr. Leena Shah, Cali CPS. Did you have a good trip out?"

Dr. Shah was of Indian descent, small build, attractive, wore a wedding band and had grown up in America as she later went on to explain.

"No complaints, Dr. Shah." Hank took a deep breath.

"Shall we begin?"

"Shoot."

"Tell me about your dreams, Mr. Hawkins. Do you have recurring dreams about your time in Vietnam?"

"Sometimes."

"Please expand. What are they about?"

"Sometimes I dream that I'm back there. No rhyme or reason to the dreams, I just dream that I'm back in that setting and can't figure out why."

"How often do you have those dreams?"

"Not often and they don't last long. I wake up and I'm back home."

"Do these dreams scare you, Mr. Hawkins?"

"No. More than anything else they confuse me as to why I'm back over there, but they don't scare me."

"Do you ever have night sweats or talk in your sleep?"

"Only when the AC goes out. Houston's hot and humid. As for talking in my sleep, how would I know that? I'm asleep."

After each question, Dr. Shah wrote notes on the legal pad in front of her and she was quick to follow up with the next question on her list.

"Your military reports show that you were a small arms expert. Do you own a fire arm?"

"Yes. I've got a pistol for personal protection. I've got a license for it."

"Where do you keep it?"

"In my night stand. But if Abby comes to live with me, I'll be sure to lock it up."

"Good answer, Mr. Hawkins. Are you a hunter?"

"Well, Dr. Shah, since I, too, grew up in an orphanage, I really didn't have anyone to take me or teach me how to hunt or fish. So, no, I'm not a hunter and don't want to be."

"Why's that, Mr. Hawkins?"

"First, because I work at my own business on the weekends and don't have time to hunt. Second, to be perfectly honest, Dr. Shah, I'm just not that much into killing anymore."

"Do you still have memories of killing, Mr. Hawkins?"

"Of course I do."

"How do they make you feel?"

"They don't make me feel anything. I had a job to do and I did it. I was a good soldier and obeyed orders. I can't completely keep things like that out of my memory, but I don't have to dwell on 'em either."

Hank remembered becoming uncomfortable, digging up old memories from a time he was trying to forget. He knew the questioning had just begun, and he really needed to think before answering each one.

"Mr. Hawkins, you state that you've never been married. Do you have a girl friend or a significant other in your life?"

"Not really."

"Why not?"

"I guess if I could answer that, I'd have your job," he said, smiling. "I can't explain chemistry, Dr. Shah, can you?"

She smiled, giving both of them a break from the monotony, and then she asked, "Do you ever have encounters with women?"

"What do you mean encounters? Are you asking if I'm gay or fool around sometimes? The answer is I'm not gay and yes, I fool around sometimes. Just never met *the one* if that makes any sense."

"How often do you have these encounters?"

"You got me there, Dr. Shah. I don't make notches on my bed post and don't keep track … Probably not that often."

"Once a year, a month, more encounters than that?"

"I've already answered your question, Dr. Shah. I'm not uncomfortable talking about sex, but I don't dwell on it either. Could we move on?"

Dr. Shah wrote for a couple of minutes on her forms then asked, "Do you have any kind of a spiritual life? If so, what denomination are you, Mr. Hawkins?"

"I'm usually working on Sundays, doctor. I don't really belong to any church, but I do believe there is a higher power than myself. Sometimes I even pray."

"To whom do you pray?"

"God, I guess."

"Which god?"

Hank had a feeling that Dr. Shah was probably of the Hindu faith, and he knew nothing about it. He took a moment to reply, then he said, "The One in heaven?"

Dr. Shah took her time writing in her tablet. It gave Hank a little pause and he was already feeling the stress of the questioning.

"Mr. Hawkins, I know this may be difficult for you but could you tell me about how you met Abigail Greene?"

Hank easily searched for the little compartment in his mind labeled "Abigail." It was not one that he opened very often but not one he was fond of opening even though his memories of Abigail were the best he had ever had.

"I needed to put some space between my military life and begin to experience civilian life," Hank mused. "I made several weekend trips to San Fran and loved to hang out in small venues with great music. That's when I discovered The Enchanted Cup on Boa Street. That's where I met Abigail. She was a waitress there."

"How did your relationship begin?" Dr. Shah continued to make notes.

"It began when my world stood still at the very moment I laid eyes on Abigail. I asked her to be my waitress, we talked some, then at the end of the night, she said that she had some memories of her brother who didn't make it home from Vietnam and she didn't want to be alone. When she got off work that's when we went to my room two floors above The Cup and, as you've explained, Dr. Shah, conceived Abby.

"I knew from the first phone call from CPS that I was the father. Abigail was a light in my dark life. She taught me how to love in a single night. And, Dr. Shah, it had nothing to do with one night stands or getting laid or lust. Abigail just had an abundance of love to give, and I guess she noticed that I needed some. I learned to love that night. That's the only way I can describe it. Our night was so special, so loving with a tenderness that I have never experienced. It's as if our souls bonded. She said that she didn't want to be alone that night and that's how our night began."

"Touching story, Mr. Hawkins. Do you have any idea why Ms. Greene never told you about being pregnant?"

"I guess that's the mystery, Dr. Shah. Abigail was, herself, a mystery to everyone. I tried for weeks, even months, to find her again but no one even knew where she lived or what she was about. Another mystery is that she lived in the very building where the Enchanted Cup was located."

"In your conversations with her that night, did Ms. Greene tell you anything about her background? Her past life? Her family?"

"Yes. We talked about everything that night. We bared our souls to each other. She did tell me some things about her childhood and made me promise never to reveal them. I can't tell you anymore than that, Dr. Shah. I hope you understand that a confidence can never be broken …"

"Admirable, Mr. Hawkins. I do understand. But it would be helpful to understand more about the environment where Abby grew up. Did she tell you about her present life in San Francisco?"

"She did tell me that she didn't have a boy friend, didn't sleep around and that this night together was completely out of character for her. That's why I knew I was Abby's father."

"And you believed her, Mr. Hawkins?"

"I believed every word that came out of her sweet mouth that night, Dr. Shah."

The meeting with Abby was arranged for the next day.

"Remember, your time with Abby will last only thirty minutes," Dr. Shah said, "Then we'll take her back to the orphanage and you'll have to return to Texas."

Hank remembered the sleepless night before meeting his daughter. He was stressed to the max but knew he had to appear relaxed in order to make Abby feel the same. The moment arrived. He was back at CPS and took another deep breath …

"Let's quickly go over some things, Mr. Hawkins. Abby will be accompanied by a Ms. Jessica Wilde. Ms. Wilde is an employee of the orphanage and knows Abby very well. It's important for Abby to be with someone she trusts as she's going to be apprehensive also. We want to make Abby feel secure."

"Of course, Mrs. Bain. I understand."

"Mr. Hawkins, please don't be disappointed if Abby is stand-offish. She's eight years old and has experienced some difficult situations with people she doesn't know. I told you earlier that she doesn't make friends too easily. It would probably be best not to try and give her a hug or even shake hands with her. Give Abby her space and just follow her lead."

"Okay, Mrs. Bain." Hank remembered that landmark day and that his heart was exploding inside.

Then the moment happened. Jessica Wilde, in her mid-twenties, slowly walked around the corner of the office holding the hand of a shy little girl dressed in State-issued jeans, tennis shoes and a white knit, long-sleeved top. Abby clung to Jessica like glue.

Hank only thought that he was ready to meet his little girl. The moment he laid eyes on her, the world, for the second time in his life, stood still. Tears welled up in his eyes and for a moment, he had to catch his breath and turn away to compose himself. His knees were weak, his nose was running and he just stood there forcing back the tears. Abby looked like a 'mini-me' version of her mother. In an instant, Hank was in love again.

Abby stood in front of him, becoming even closer to Jessica and watched a former tough Marine trying to gather his courage. After Hank blew his nose, he turned to Abby, walked within a few feet of her and decided to meet her face-to-face. He squatted down to her level and said, "Hi Abby. I'm Hank. So glad to meet you."

Abby didn't reply. Jessica interceded by saying, "Abby, this is the nice man I told you about. Would you like to say 'hello' to him?"

"Hi." Abby didn't extend her hand but kept close to Jessica, like she was going to run at any second.

"Abby, you look just like your beautiful mother."

"Did you know my mommy?"

"Yes, I knew your mommy."

"Tell me what she looked like." Abby wasn't very good at trusting and didn't look at Hank when she spoke.

"She had long brown hair just like yours and beautiful green eyes. She always wore a band of flowers in her hair …"

When Hank began describing Abigail, little Abby's eyes swelled with tears, but she didn't cry. Hank figured he'd better change the subject. He could see how Mrs. Bain kept her eyes on Jessica to see if Jessica wanted to cut the meeting short.

"Are you going to be my new daddy?" Abby asked with a defiant look in her eyes.

Using all the restraint he could muster, Hank looked straight into Abby's big green eyes and said, "I *am* your daddy, Sweetie Pie." Hank was searching his mind for the right words to say. He didn't have to reason it out, his heart was doing all the talking.

It was too much for Abby to handle. She released her grip on Jessica and bolted down the hallway and around the corner with Jessica chasing right behind her. Hank just stayed in his squatted position not knowing what to do. He was beginning to learn about fatherhood, and he didn't have a clue how to proceed. The meeting had lasted fewer than three minutes. Hank immediately began to blame himself for saying the wrong things.

Mrs. Bain walked up behind Hank and placed her hand on his shoulder, trying to comfort him.

"Mr. Hawkins, don't be upset. I warned you this could happen. It's not unusual at all for first meetings to end abruptly. After all, we are dealing with an eight-year-old who doesn't yet have the maturity to deal with so many feelings at one time. Abby was overwhelmed. She had to re-group, if you know what I mean."

"I know exactly what you mean, Mrs. Bain. I think I need to re-group also. That's one of the heaviest moments I have ever experienced. I didn't know what to do or say …"

"When is your flight back, Mr. Hawkins?"

"Tomorrow at 11:30 in the morning. I need to get back in time for work. If I need to stay I will."

"The reason I asked about your flight time is because we at CPS are pro's at seeing children meeting their parents for the first time." Mrs. Bain motioned for Hank to stand. "Jessica is going to take Abby back to familiar surroundings at the orphanage, get her something to eat and probably urge a short nap. I'd suggest you do the same thing when you get back to your room.

"When Abby's had her nap, Jessica will talk to her, and answer any questions she may have. Then, one of two things will usually happen. Abby will either not mention meeting you and want to go play with the other children or she may want to talk to you again. Each child reacts differently. Will you be available to return here later this afternoon?"

Hank smiled. "In a heartbeat. And thank you, Mrs. Bain for being available. I know it's Saturday and your day off ..."

Sara Bain interrupted and replied, "We've all taken a special interest in Abby, Mr. Hawkins ..."

Hank interrupted her, "The word *special* is my favorite word in the English language. It's ironic that you use it to describe Abby, and I appreciate it."

Hank returned to his room and decided to take Mrs. Bain's advice. Once again Hank recalled waiting for the phone to ring ...

"Hey Hank, this is Bill over at Heaven Bakery, I'll have the cake ready about five this afternoon that Ms. Cantrell ordered. We stay open till nine. Will that be convenient for you?"

"I'll be there to pick it up, Bill, and thanks for the call ..."

A day he would cherish forever played the vision over and over again in his mind. He was back at his room in Cali that fateful day twenty-four years ago and he did get the call. He remembered every word, every second.

"Mr. Hawkins? This is Jessica Wilde from the orphanage. I'm sitting here with a pretty little girl named Abby. She wants to know if you could meet us in about twenty minutes. She has a question to ask you."

"Well, tell that pretty little girl I will be at the CPS offices in twenty."

Fifteen minutes later he was pacing at the CPS offices with a million questions on his mind that he thought Abby might want to ask him. He tried to put himself back to age eight and think what he would ask. He found himself in the state of *what do I do now?*

When Abby and Jessica walked up to him, Abby seemed different, more at ease, less defensive. She and Jessica were skipping, talking and laughing as they approached. This was a great sign and a real anxiety reliever for Hank. He smiled back at them and had no idea what Jessica and Abby had been talking about, but whatever it was, it was working.

Trying to make the meeting more informal, Jessica addressed Hank by his first name. "Hank, Abby wants to ask you a question."

"Hi Abby. What do you want to know?" Hank again kneeled down to Abby's eye level.

Abby fumbled around a little putting her words together but not losing her happy demeanor.

"Uh, what should I call ya?" Abby asked, looking off to the side.

"Well, you can call me 'Hank' or you can call me 'daddy.' What do you want to call me?"

"I've never had a daddy before …"

"And I've never had a pretty little daughter before. Do you think you could teach me about little girls?"

Abby finally cracked a little smile that made Hank's heart jump.

"Uh huh. I know all about little girls …"

"So what do you want to call me?"

"Can I call you 'Daddy Hank'?"

"'Daddy Hank' it is. What do you want me to call you?"

Abby smiled and looked up at Jessica for a little support. Hank saw Jessica nodding her head at Abby, saying, "Go ahead and tell him. It's okay."

Abby had a sheepish little grin on her face and said, "Can you call me 'Sweetie Pie?'"

That one took Hank for a loop. Completely out of the blue.

"I would love to call you 'Sweetie Pie.' So how did you come up with that, precious?"

Abby looked up at Jessica and said, "Can you help me? I don't know how to tell him."

Jessica gave Abby a little reassuring hug and said, "Sure you can. Just tell Daddy Hank what you told me. He'll understand."

Abby began to talk but started over a couple of times trying to express what she wanted to say.

"Cause … when people call me 'Abby,' they're just talkin' to me, telling me stuff … Sometimes, they're scolding me … When you called me 'Sweetie Pie,' I … uh, well uh …"

"You can say it Abby," Jessica broke in trying to give Abby time to put her words together.

"When you called me 'Sweetie Pie,' I knew you weren't just talking to me … you were loving me …"

As soon as the words rolled out of Abby's mouth, she began to cry and left the safety of Jessica's grasp, walked over to Hank, still kneeling, and wrapped her arms around him. They held each other and cried. The walls around their two hearts came down …

Sitting on the balcony remembering, Hank's eyes swelled up with tears once again. He looked around the other balconies to see if anyone was watching, especially Robbie or her daughter, Bella, who had become a big sister to Abby over the years. He blew his nose and wiped his tears. This was one compartment of his mind that he never wanted closed. It was the sweetest memory in his entire life, before or since.

4

FAST FORWARD
CHASING BAD BOYS

Abby grew up in a completely different age and had pushed and shoved Daddy Hank into the twenty-first century when she bought him a smart phone, taught him how to use it, somewhat, and programmed in some of his favorite songs for caller ID. "Sara", by Fleetwood Mac was his favorite song, so naturally that was her ring tone. It began to play on Hank's phone and was a welcomed distraction from his nostalgic morning.

"Sweetie Pie!"

"Daddy Hank, I need to talk to you about a couple of things before tonight. I'm pissed!" Abby was always direct in her feelings.

"What's wrong, baby?"

"You want the good news or the bad news first?"

"Let's start with the bad news and get it out of the way for the good news. Shoot!"

"My *older sister,* Bella," Abby was being facetious, "is bringing that asshole, Frank Jr., to the deal tonight. He's no good, rich, obnoxious, and treats her like a dog. He'll probably get drunk and blow the whole evening. She always chases the bad boys. Can you call her and talk to her?"

"You mean Frank Jr. of "Mutual Funz"? Hank identified people by the names on their boats. "Mutual Funz" was the largest yacht on the lake, owned by Frank Baggett, Sr., lead partner in a local investment firm and one of Hank's long-time clients. "I think I'll just let Miss Robbie handle that one. What's the good news?"

Abby was still steaming but took a breath to tell him about something she had discovered while working at L3, the name of a sailboat owned by her employer, Location, Location, Location Properties, Inc., the largest commercial/residential realtor in the area. "I found the property for Tequilaville! I'll fill you in on the details tonight, but we'll need to move quickly. You'll like it, I promise."

"Should I bring my checkbook?"

"No, I've already taken care of it. See you at 5:30. Are you as excited as I am?"

"More so, baby. What a big day. I'll meet you in the foyer of the auditorium."

Hank had worked so hard for so many years building a business and raising Abby that he had forgotten his dream of ever building Tequilaville. He never realized that Abby also needed a dream to keep her going and had adopted his dream many years ago. Hank was tired and had given up his youthful vigor for life and his dream. Abby had just begun and was determined to make Daddy Hank's dream come true. He was a good man and had given up his life, his freedoms and his dreams for her. It was her time to give back ...

The auditorium at University of Houston, Clear Lake was bustling with families and well-wishers, waiting to see their friends and loved ones walk across the stage to receive their Masters' Degrees. Hank's group had gathered and joined into the mix as each one showed up for the big event.

Hank was nervous and it showed as he greeted each person.

"Can we yell and clap during the big moment, Hank?" Robbie asked, trying to corral Bella and Frank Jr. or "Frankie" as Bella called him.

"I guess. Yell all you want."

As the ceremonies began and graduates lined up, the name the group had been waiting for was finally called out, "Abby Gale Hawkins, Masters of Business Administration, Accounting!" As she walked across the stage, Abby looked up as if to get her Mom's approval. She was wearing a band of flowers in her hair and carried her cap in a respectful way as the choir sang the usual, "Climb Every Mountain". Wearing flip-flops under her robe, she took the degree, got a quick picture made and returned to her seat. It had taken her many years of discipline, study and working a full time job as the L3 bookkeeper to exhale finally. This part of her life was over, a new one was about to launch and she could hardly contain herself to share the good news with Daddy Hank. She was going to make Tequilaville happen through sheer brilliance, timing and a little help from her friend, Hattie Lang.

"Sweetie Pie, I'm so proud of you." Hank gave her a big hug and loosened the tie around his neck.

"Daddy Hank, this has been part of the bad news. It's time for us to start a new life and have some good news. I can't wait to tell you about my plan."

After the on-campus buffet style dinner, rubber chicken and the usual amenities, they headed over to the Turtle Club for drinks.

"I'm buying," Hank said as he got the crowd all huddled up and headed for the parking lot. Big crowds were never part of their lives and their small group was more like family. Hank opened the door to his truck for Abby and took off his coat and tie.

With presents in hand, Robbie, big sister Bella, Frankie, Tito and his wife Mary, T-Bone, Hattie Lang and Hank arrived at The Turtle Club. Mike, the owner, was a friend of Hank's and seated them at the best table in the house overlooking the Lake. Before they went in, Hank gave Abby his graduation present, an envelope with a check for $10,000. He wanted to give it to her in a private moment.

"Oh, Pop, you didn't have to do that!"

"Abby, you paid your way on full ride academic scholarships through your undergraduate and post-graduate degrees. You've worked your butt off, lived in a one-bedroom dungeon for so many years, it's the least I can do. Use it any way you want. This is my gift to you. I love you, Sweetie Pie, and I'm so proud of everything you've meant to me all these years."

"I love you, too, Daddy Hank. You've been a good father, worked hard, took care of me, taught me, protected me, loved me and raised me in a loving home. You have no idea what I'm going to do with this money, and I can't wait to tell you."

Everyone was hugging Abby, giving her graduation presents, laughing and looking forward to a festive evening. Bella was having a hard time backing off and letting this be Abby's special day. She always liked to be the center of attention.

"Little sister, you've come a long way, baby! What's next in this exciting life of yours?" Bella said, getting her facetious jabs in to seize the moment.

Bella Cantrell, Abby's *big sister*, was dressed to the nines for the event and wore a low cut expensive dress showing as much cleavage as possible to attract Frankie's attention. She walked on six-inch heels and as always, was feeling really, really great about herself after her make-over day at the spa. Bella was pleasing to any man's eye with her olive complexion and thick black hair, and she used all of her beautiful traits for every advantage both at work as a realtor and at play. She had a Master's in fun and a taste for the good life.

"Big sister, you won't believe what I've got in store for my life. Thank you for being there for me." They hugged and Bella gave Abby a gift certificate for a day at the spa. Abby had never been to a spa or had a make-over in her life. Just wasn't her bag. Abby, like her mother, had always been a simple beauty and wore very little make-up. She could stop traffic just the way she was.

Hank ordered drinks and tequila shots for everyone to get the celebration going. Tito stood up and proposed the first toast then presented Abby with his and Mary's graduation present.

"Abby, we'll do the official ceremony at the dojo but I wanted to make this special. I have a gift for you and also one for Hattie." Tito slid the two presents in front them and waited for their surprised looks.

Abby opened the box and found a new ghee with a black belt wrapped around it.

She stood, bowed and replied, "Master Tito, this is truly an honor. Thank you for not giving up on me."

Tito returned the bow and said, "Abby, it is my honor to be your instructor. Hattie, congrats on your Brown belt. It shouldn't be too long before it turns black; keep working." Hattie also bowed but didn't want to take anything away from her friend and confidant, Abby, on her special day.

Hattie Lang, originally from Ohio, was a bean counter like Abby. She was not a real flashy lady but attractive. They'd met years ago when both did summer internships at the Government Accounting Offices (GAO) in Washington, D.C. They had remained close friends ever since. Abby had told Hattie about life on the Gulf Coast and when an accounting position became available at NASA, Hattie applied, got the job, and moved to Texas. Hattie was thin, tall and had silky, long red hair and, like Abby at her job with L3, sat in front of a computer all day crunching numbers. Neither had much of a wild side and took out their stress and frustrations at Tito's karate dojo to learn self-defense, sometimes aggressive self-defense.

Hattie was sitting next to Abby and gave her a greeting card. Abby opened it up, read it privately and smiled. Hank knew Abby so well and could tell that these two were up to something. What? He hadn't a clue, but something was up.

T-Bone then stood empty-handed and said, "Abby, my present is iced-down in the back of my truck outside. It's twenty pounds of the best Gulf shrimp known to mankind." Then T-Bone went into his *Forrest Gump* routine and finished by saying, "You can have baked shrimp, barbecued shrimp, butterfly shrimp, boiled shrimp …" Everyone applauded T-Bone's impersonations of the movie script, clicked tequila shots and threw 'em down. That gift represented about two days' wages for the gentle giant. Abby walked over to T-Bone, he bent down and she gave him a kiss on the cheek.

Finally Robbie stood up and walked around the table to Abby. She had been like a mother to her over the years. Abby carefully opened the white, heavy box and looked down on a beautiful, leather bound Bible with her name engraved on it in gold lettering. The inscription inside the front cover read, "To my other daughter, Abby. Every answer to every question you will ever have in life can be found in this book. Be Blessed on this special day. I love you, Robbie." There was no toast after this present.

Robbie had given Bella a Bible years earlier and doubted if Bella even knew where it was, much less had read any of it. Hank and Robbie had always been the "go-to" people for advice in their small circle of friends. Abby lived by the advice she was given, Bella challenged every piece of it she had ever heard from Robbie or Hank. If they advised her to zig, she would zag and often lived the consequences. Life raising Bella had not been easy for Robbie, but she was her daughter and she picked her up when she was down and got out of her way when Bella was on a roll.

Frankie had no time for Bible stuff and to get the party going again, reached into his pocket, pulled out a roll of bills, peeled off two C-notes and said, "Next time you're in Vegas, put these down on thirteen black at the roulette wheel …" Frankie was just flat out arrogant. He usually carried six to ten grand cash on him at all times so it wasn't as if he was making much of a financial sacrifice for his spur-of-the-moment graduation gift for Abby. He was a cornucopia kid raised with a gold spoon in his mouth and daddy's platinum American Express card in his wallet. He was a lot more interested in getting Bella back to his outlandish bachelor's pad to add another notch to his almost whittled-down bedpost than he was in celebrating Abby's graduation. It seemed Bella could hardly contain herself either. She would make tonight *her* night. Frankie would be a good catch for her future if she could reel him in.

As usual, Abby's insights and concerns about the night were happening. Frankie and Bella were getting completely bombed and both were making asses of themselves. Robbie asked Bella to come with her to the ladies room and shortly afterwards, Frankie and Bella left.

"Hey, let's take this party to my place," Robbie was trying her best to cover for Bella once again. "I'll put some coffee on, serve some great French Vanilla cake. Hank, you did pick up the cake, didn't you?"

Hank nodded, "Yeah, it's in the truck, probably melting. Great idea. Fine with me if it is okay with everyone else."

The party shifted to the comfort of Robbie's condo and everyone began to decompress. Back in familiar surroundings with friends, the chit-chat became more real than plastic and everyone was letting their hair down with conversations about "what now," "how's things" and catching up on everyone's lives. Around midnight, they said their final congrats to Abby and went their separate ways. Hank knew the night was far from over and that

Abby still had a few things on her mind. That sheepish little grin on her face hadn't gone away all night.

As Abby and Hank walked back to his condo, she took a quick detour to the truck and pulled out a roll of architectural plans she had brought.

"Daddy Hank, I'm going to hit you with a lot of information. Something that I have worked on for a long time. The schooling, the internships in D.C. and my time at L3 have all been part of this plan. Please let me finish before making up your mind on this, okay? Just trust me."

"I'm all ears, baby."

"Why do you think I work for L3?"

"Because you're a CPA and they pay you a lot of money?"

"Nope, not even close. That's why I lived in a dump for seven years even though I had the funds to have a better home. I was trying to learn their secret of success so I could make *our dream* come true."

"*Our* dream?"

"Pop, your dream became my dream, and today I'm going to make that happen. By Monday morning you'll become a paper millionaire."

"Hey, Abby, just what I've always wanted to be, a paper tiger. Go on."

Abby began by telling Hank what she had learned during her time in Washington with the GAO. While there, working side-by-side with Hattie, she had access to their files and out of curiosity pulled the file on L3 Properties.

"Do you know how the deceased founder of L3 Properties, Fitzpatrick Bone, became a billionaire, Pop?"

"Hadn't really thought about it, baby, but I have a feeling you're gonna tell me."

"I don't mean to give you a history lesson, Pop, but back when our own Sam Rayburn was Speaker of the House and the most powerful man in Washington along with his protégé, LBJ, the National Aeronautics & Space Administration, NASA, was conceived in order to launch the U.S. into the space race. Speaker Rayburn made sure the new facilities would be located in Texas. Ole "Fitz," as we called him, was working at the GAO offices as a clerk back then, saw the request for appropriations come through and knew exactly where the facilities would be located.

"Fitz quit his job, secured a number of wealthy investors, a few powerful congressmen and headed for the Gulf Coast with a checkbook to buy up all the land for pennies on the dollar and sell it back to the government at astronomical prices. Every piece of property along NASA Road 1 was owned by L3 at the beginning. They screwed local families and land owners with lowball offers of what was thought to be *worthless* coastal marsh land, then turned around and sold it not only to government, but to all the government contractors, hotel operators and every small business along what is now NASA Road 1. They robbed from the poor and made themselves rich."

"Was this legal, baby?"

"Absolutely legal, Pop. How do you think politicians get rich? They know what's going to happen before it happens …"

"I'm still listening for the paper tiger part, honey, and me being a millionaire by Monday. I can't wait to hear … and I do trust you, but forgive me if I'm a bit skeptical."

"Just a little more background before I get there, Daddy Hank." Abby's green eyes were flashing, her brilliant mind was racing. She had done her homework well. "Think about all of the people the government would be hiring for the space program and would bring to the area: scientists, physicists, astronauts, engineers, all highly paid members of this newly created city of Clear Lake. They would need homes, schools, supermarkets, fast food shops, and every service industry known to mankind.

"L3 Properties began working with their own architects, set up their own commercial and residential construction companies, formed a city council, wrote all of the zoning laws and began building homes, schools, hotels, and again soaked every land buyer in the area. They owned it all and controlled it all."

"Hats off to ole Fitz, baby. Seems to me that this carpet bagger got rich the ole fashioned way, he scammed the people out of their money. Now how are we going to build our dream?"

Abby reached for the architectural plans she'd brought with her and spread them over the kitchen table. As soon as Hank saw them, he knew the facility Abby was talking about.

"Aren't those the plans to the NASA Oceanographic building just across the point from the Hilton?"

"Yeah, Dad. It already has docks built for their capsule recovery boats and it's situated on ten acres of the most expensive lakeside property in Clear Lake, second only in value to the Hilton's property."

"Hasn't it been closed for the past few years? I mean that old single story building has been falling apart for years."

"Sharp, Dad. You'd know since you're on the Lake almost every day." The smirk came back on Abby's pretty face. "During our current administration, funding for NASA has been greatly reduced. Our astronauts even have to hitch rides to the International Space Station on Russian rockets ...”

“Yeah, I know,” Hank interrupted. “I work on many of the astronauts’ boats. That doesn’t set well with them; they’re embarrassed. So how much is the property worth? I’d guess about $5 mil.”

“Actually, the current valuation is $7.1 mil, Dad.”

“That leaves me out. I don’t have $7 mil, baby, do you?”

“Don’t need that much, Pop. This is where my friend Hattie Lang comes in. She just got an order from Washington to liquidate the property immediately on a bona fide first offer bid. She’s the one who will post it at one minute past midnight on Monday morning.”

“Baby,” Hank leaned back on the back two legs of his chair, scratching his head, “I’m going to ask you this again. Is what you’re planning to do legal? I’m too old to spend time in prison.”

“Completely legal, Dad. The key phrase here is *liquidate immediately on a bona fide first offer bid.* The government term *liquidate immediately* means sell ASAP without due diligence and the *bona fide first offer bid* means just that. Hattie said that the definition of this term is five figures plus a dollar with a cashier’s check or wiring instructions attached to the offer.”

“Abby, are you telling me that we can buy this $7.1 million property, the building, the huge paved lighted parking lot, the boat docks, all of it for ten grand plus a dollar?”

“Happy dream come true, Daddy Hank. That’s exactly what I’m telling you and it’s all very legal. Now we become the *Robin Hood* taking from the rich to give to the poor. And the poor are us. This is the new location for Tequilaville.

“You see, Pop, $7 mil is pocket change to the government unless it’s a campaign contribution going into one of the congressmen’s bank accounts. Seven million is like seven cents to them. They deal in billions and trillions these days. We may have one of the best governments in the world, Dad, but it’s also one of the most inefficient governments in the world when it comes to paying attention to little things like millions of dollars.”

“Baby, pardon my lack of excitement and playing the devil’s advocate here but whenever things seem too good to be true, they usually are. What’s the down side? You’ve always been honest with me and this is serious. Give me the details because this is scaring me to death.”

“Pop, like I said, Hattie will post the announcement on the internet at 12:01 Monday morning. I’ve already prepared all the paperwork including the bid and wiring instructions from the bank for our money to be forwarded. The nano second her computer receives our info, it automatically takes the bid off the screen, the land has been sold and it’s a done deal. I doubt seriously if anyone will be watching their screens at this time of the morning, no one but me, anyway. When opportunity strikes, we take it.

"The downside is that if L3 Properties ever finds out that I slicked 'em, I'll be blackballed from the entire country. I could probably find a job in Timbuktu if you know what I mean." Abby began to giggle. It was getting late.

"So you're gonna have to quit your job, huh? What about the taxes?"

"Dad, let me worry about taxes. I'm a CPA, remember? As far as quitting my job, well, let's just chalk that up to the fact that we're both free spirits and never fit well into the pin-striped suit community. This is our shot at freedom, good times, a lot of fun and making our dream come true.

"I'm leaving these plans for you, Dad. We can scrape the old building and leave the foundation with all the plumbing ready to go. The foundation is in good shape, I checked. Now you just need to put your vision of Tequilaville onto that foundation. That's where we start."

Hank got up from his chair without looking at the plans and walked out to his balcony. The Lake was glimmering with reflected lights from boats and businesses encircling the water. He grabbed a beer from his ever present patio cooler and lit up a cigarette. *Was this a great opportunity or was it his downfall?* It was hard to dampen the spirits of Abby, especially on this great day of hers, but a million thoughts were again racing through his mind. Abby followed him out and sat down in one of the patio chairs.

"You're gonna put that bid in with me or without me aren't you, baby?"

"Pop, you remember when I got you that smart phone and almost forced you to use it?"

"Yeah."

"Now I'm pushing you into never giving up hope on your dream. All that I ask is that you trust me. I know what I'm doing, Daddy Hank."

"Do you know anything about running a bar? Mixing drinks? Planning food menus or hiring staff? Do you know anything about building that facility and how to finance it? There's so many things to consider here, Sweetie Pie …"

Abby went back inside and pulled her Master's Case Study out of stacks of paperwork entitled *Tequilaville* walked back onto the patio and gave it to Hank.

"I've planned it all. Why do you think that it took me so long to get my Master's? This case study was the basis for my thesis and I got an 'A' on it. I even know how much we'll have to spend on ice every day. Take a look at it when you have time. I haven't left anything out."

Hank downed the rest of his beer and lit another cigarette. After a few moments of uninterrupted silence, he looked over at Abby. "I've got one last question. What's Hattie gonna want out of this?"

"Free drinks for life!"

Hank began to laugh. The idea that this was about to happen finally hit him. He pushed aside his fears, his anxieties, his concerns and remembered something that Abigail had told him years ago, *"Just flow!"*

"Let's do it, Sweetie Pie. I'm in!"

At that very moment before any celebration could take place on their new venture, Abby's phone began to play "Wild Thing", her ring tone for Bella. It was 3 a.m.

"Bella, are you okay?"

"Oh god! Oh god! Help me sister. I think we've OD'ed."

"Bella, where are you?" There was a long pause, "Bella! Tell me where you are. We'll come get you."

Abby could hear Bella breathing and stumbling for words, "Frankie's place. Don't bring Mom …"

"Stay with me Bella. We're on our way!"

Abby put her phone on mute and looked at Hank.

"Pop, Bella's at Frankie's place. They've OD'ed. We've got to get over there. I know where he lives …"

"Run down and wake up Miss Robbie. She's going with us. I'll call Frankie's dad; I've got his cell number. I'll have him meet us there with one of his doctor clients. Hurry!"

All three hopped into Hank's truck and took off into the night. Robbie was completely freaking out but stopped long enough to offer up a quick prayer for her daughter. Hank put in a call to Frank Baggett, Sr..

"Hello. Who is this?"

"Mr. Baggett, this is Hank Hawkins. We're on the way over to your son's house. He and a friend of ours just OD'ed. You may want to bring a doctor and meet us over there ASAP. I haven't called the cops …"

"My god! Thank you. I'm on my way. If you beat me there, the security code at the gate is 77777."

Frank Jr. lived about three miles away. Hank, Abby and Robbie pulled up into the circular driveway of the palatial residence and quickly headed for the front door. Robbie led the way. Abby had tried to stay on the phone with Bella but hadn't been able to get a response from her for the past few minutes. They had no idea what they would do when they got inside. Robbie turned the knob of the front door: it was unlocked and the alarm was disarmed.

"Bella! Bella!" Robbie was running all over the huge house trying to find them.

Hank and Abby split up and began going down the different hallways, trying to find the bedrooms. None of them had ever been in the house and were completely disoriented.

Abby cut down one hallway and saw an open door, smelled the stench of vomit and rushed in. There was Bella, completely naked, unconscious, lying on the floor on one side of the king-sized bed. Her face was smeared with mascara, a bloody mucous was dripping out of her nose and she had traces of white powder all over her cheeks. Frank Jr. was in the bed, also naked, foaming at the mouth, seemingly unconscious. Abby threw a blanket over Bella, pulled the covers over Frankie and began shouting.

"They're in here. Follow my voice. Help me!"

Robbie had previously worked in a crisis hotline center dealing with suicidal kids while getting her RN degree and had training in drug OD's. She kneeled down beside Bella, lifted her head, cleared the vomit from her airway and started mouth-to-mouth on her until finally Bella gurgled, showing signs of life. Hank was working on Frankie, still showing no signs of life when Frank Sr. and his doctor friend hurried into the bedroom.

"My god! Is he dead?" Mr. Baggett yelled.

The doctor rushed over and took Frankie's pulse and reached into his bag for a hand-held ventilator.

"I've got a pulse." The doctor pulled Frankie upright and started an IV and continued ventilating him.

Hank and Abby stood there taking in the chaos while Robbie and the doctor, who was switching back and forth between Frankie and Bella, did what only they knew to do. It wasn't the doctor's first rodeo with OD cases and Robbie had been there herself. Out of the corner of his eye, Hank saw Frank Baggett Sr. put a bag containing about a quarter kilo of cocaine in his pocket and wiped the unused lines on the night stand into the trash basket, which he quickly handed over to his limo driver.

After half an hour, both Frank Jr. and Bella were breathing normally. The IV's were working. Another hour passed and the doctor told them that Frankie and Bella should be okay with some sleep and fluids.

"Mr. Hawkins," Frank Sr. said, having barely spoken the whole time, "I want to thank you for saving my son's life and keeping it quiet. I sincerely hope the girl will be okay. I won't forget this."

Hank nodded back to Frank Sr., picked Bella up in the blanket wrapped around her and carried her out to his truck. Robbie and Abby led the way and opened the truck door for Hank to gently place Bella in the back seat. Once they got back to Robbie's condo, for the next few hours, they hovered over Bella and drank cup after cup of coffee saying very little. It had been a long night for everyone.

No explanations or excuses were necessary. They were family. A few hours later, Bella woke up with Abby sitting on the bed next to her. Hank and Robbie were in the kitchen making more coffee.

"Hey, wild thing, how ya feeling?" Abby asked, stroking Bella's head.

"Not so good. What happened?"

"You just about out did yourself last night, big sister. Ever heard the term *bite the dust?*"

"That bad, huh? Did I really almost bite it?"

"Yeah, you did."

"Where am I?"

"At your mom's house …"

"Oh god, did she see me at Frankie's?"

"Yeah. But don't worry Bella, she's your mom, she's seen you naked before."

"I was naked?! Oh god, I'm so embarrassed! How's Frankie?"

"He'll make it, that asshole! Are you ever going to learn? You've gotta stop chasing the bad boys, big sister."

"Yeah, right … Did you bring my shoes and clothes? I paid over fifteen hundred dollars for that ensemble. Who else saw me naked?"

"Sister, you need to spend some time with yourself and think about your demons. You could've died last night, for real."

"No lectures, Abby, Frankie just bought some bad coke."

"Bella, seriously, is there such a thing as *good* coke? I mean you don't know who cut this stuff or what they put in it. Cocaine begins by soaking leaves in kerosene. Everyone knows that; it's on TV. When was the last time you went to a bar and ordered a shot of kerosene? And, it's not like 'blow' is made by a pharmaceutical company. Maybe you should stick to Diet Coke."

"Abby! You deal with your demons, I'll deal with mine. Don't lecture me. I'm hungry."

Abby laughed and shook her head. "Miss Robbie! Bella's awake!"

Bella took a quick glance under the covers to make sure she was dressed and discovered that Abby had put her in a pair of her Mom's PJs. As Robbie walked into the room, Bella slid down into the bed and pulled the covers over her head. She was embarrassed and didn't look forward to this inevitable conversation. Hank and Abby were tired beyond belief and headed for the door to get some sleep.

"Daddy Hank, when you have time, read over the business plan that I gave you. I'm sure you'll have more questions."

"I will, Sweetie Pie. Call me tonight."

"Will do. Pop, nothing's a done deal until I get confirmation on the sale of the land. I'll call when I know."

5

TEQUILAVILLE
DREAM MAKERS

At 7 p.m. Sunday night, Hank put in a call to Abby.

"Did you get some rest, Pop?" Abby spoke first.

"Some. Been reading over your business plan for Tequilaville and I have a million questions. I talked to Robbie earlier and Bella is doing okay."

"Thank God for that. I figured you would have questions. Where do you want to start?"

Hank had made a long list of notes and began flipping the pages of his spiral notebook. He put his cell phone on speaker.

"Do we have the money for the build out?"

Abby figured that Daddy Hank wouldn't dive too deeply into the pro forma financial spread sheets listing every line item of the project that she had prepared.

"Yep! But the first rule of business is never use your own money. *If* we get the land, we can borrow up to fifty percent on it, which is about $3.5 mil. That should do it, don't you think?"

"Abby, you know me. I don't like to borrow money and be under a cloud of debt. Plus, my vision for the club is fairly simple. I don't think we'll need that kind of dough, do you?"

"I know you pretty well, Pop. I've been doing a lot of behind the scenes work."

"You mean *secret stuff* you hadn't told me about?"

"Pop, I prefer to call it *due diligence*. I know your simple tastes and have already gotten with a trusted architect friend to do some basic drawings on the club along with estimations of what it will cost once we demo the old

NASA Oceanographic building. I've also gotten some ballpark bids on the work and have done an inventory of all of the materials that you've been storing in that warehouse for years."

"Bottom line, Abby. How much to build out?"

"About $800K, depending on how big a Tequilaville sign you want to put up." Abby chuckled. "I'm calling in some big time favors, Dad, and offering a career move to some of our favorite and most trusted family members. The $800K budget means we won't have to put up all the land as collateral. Between the two of us, we have that much in our own accounts and can pay the loans back if everything goes south. We'll still own the land and can secure our futures by selling it."

Hank paged over to the "Personnel" section of the plan, took a swig of coffee and resumed his questions.

"Abby, tell me about how Tito Chavez is working into our plan. You have him down as a paid employee who's over *Food and Beverage Services.* I thought he had his own dojo and was doing okay."

"Master Tito is a great karate master, Pop. The problem is, he and Mary are about to go bankrupt. Too many self-defense schools in the area, too little money to go around.

"Then, I figured you would've put Tito over security," Hank said with a muffled laugh.

"Scroll down on the plan, Pop. I'm putting T-Bone over security. He can't make a living on a shrimp boat forever, and I don't think anyone wants to tangle with him. Master Tito can be a great back up.

"A few months ago I attended a Zig Ziglar restaurateur conference here in Houston. The number one place that employees can steal from you is at the cash register behind the bar where every drink and food order is recorded and paid. Cash can be hidden in a heartbeat, Pop. We can trust Master Tito and I have other plans for him as you'll see later. He's got a gazillion cousins in about every skilled craft line that we need. One of his cousins even built Frank Jr.'s place and you saw how beautiful it is."

"As long as you're not part of the security team, baby, black belt or not."

"I'm the CFO and fifty-fifty owner, Daddy Hank. I'll handle the money. You're the CEO and over the entertainment. It's all your dream how Tequilaville will look inside and out. You supply the heart, I'll supply the beat."

"How many occupants did you plan for, Abby?"

"Tequilaville won't be as large as nearby Scout Bar, which seats about eight hundred guests. I'm figuring about three-fifty to four hundred tops, including patio seating. If we can keep it half full for four nights per week,

Thursday through Sunday, my figures show we can each net about $200K per year after all expenses and taxes are paid."

"I can live on that, Abby, but there sure are lots of 'ifs' and 'maybes.'"

"That's the risk we take, Daddy Hank. Is your dream worth it?"

"I told you earlier that I was in, Abby. So what do we do next?"

Abby went through a start-up check list, step-by-step, what had to take place once the land was secured. They could be operational in nine months if there were no hang-ups. They were both aware that there are always 'hang-ups.'

"So you heard from Miss Robbie on how Bella is doing?"

Hank let out a long, audible sigh. "Yeah. Robbie said that she had a long talk with Bella and believed that it went in one ear and out the other. She asked us to say a prayer for her."

"As much as I love Bella, she'll do her own thing until it brings her completely down, Pop. While you're at it, say a prayer for us. I'll call you just after midnight to tell you if we got the land."

At five minutes past midnight on Monday morning, *Sara* began to play on Hank's phone.

"We got it Dad! It's a done deal. Hattie Lang called me a minute ago, literally, and said we own the land. Ownership docs should be done in two days."

Reality began to set in with Hank and overpowered his thoughts of celebration.

"Congrats, baby. For some reason I feel a freight train is going to bear down on us and I don't know from which direction. We should be celebrating, but I've got a bad feeling. Don't mean to throw a wet blanket over all your work …"

"Get some sleep, Pop. We'll fight the battles as they come. We're paper tigers now, remember?"

By Friday, after Abby had secured the $800K loan at the bank, the news was out on the quick and silent purchase of the land. Abby got an inter-office call from her boss, Gerald Bone, grandson of the founder of the company. It was the call she'd dreaded.

"Be seated, Abby," Bone said with a hostile tone in his voice. "I think we have a few things to talk about. Tell me about how you got that NASA land for your dad, a Mr. Hank Hawkins."

"Oh, I was up late, saw the bid come across the computer from GAO and just put in a 'what the hell' offer. Never thought I would get it so I just gave it to my Dad as an early Christmas present."

"Sure you did, Abby," Bone said facetiously. "Why didn't you get the property for L3. You are an employee, remember?"

"Oh, it was after hours, my own time, not company time when I put in the bid."

"Word around the Lake is that Mr. Hawkins is going to build a club on the property named Tequilaville. Know anything about that?"

"Wow, I wondered what he would do with that property. What else do you know that I don't, Mr. Bone?"

Gerald Bone was seething mad. He could barely contain his anger and maintain his countenance as Abby sat in front of him cool as a cucumber, which just made him madder.

"Well, I'll tell you a couple of things I know, Ms. Hawkins. First, I sit on the City Council. You'll never get a permit to construct that building and open a drinking establishment on that land. We don't need more clubs in Clear Lake, not good for our community reputation. And secondly, Ms. Hawkins, you're fired! Security will accompany you out of the building."

Abby was expecting this and she was not going to cave in, sit there and take it without giving Gerald Bone a piece of her mind. She stood up, leaned over his desk to look him right in his eye.

"You got slicked, Gerry! I learned it from the best, your grandfather, ole Fitz." Abby's green eyes were blazing. "I got the building permits yesterday and there's not a damn thing you can do about it. You'd have to shut down the Hilton to stop me since we're under the same zoning laws.

"As far as getting fired, great! I'll file for unemployment. One last thing, Gerry, if you can't contain your vindictiveness and want to cause us more trouble, just remember, I keep your books! I know every underhanded, closed-in scam deal you've done for the past ten years, and I've got a photographic memory when it comes to numbers. Don't mess with me!"And P.S. Bone, if one of your security goons lays a hand on me, I'll take it as an act of aggression and break their arms!"

Abby turned and stormed out of Bone's office, not even stopping by her own. Her two-inch heels clicked as she strutted, with head held high, down the corridor. She'd packed up the night before expecting this event to take place soon after the deal was done. To add insult to injury, her first stop after leaving the building was the unemployment office.

Finished filling out the forms for unemployment, Abby called her Dad. "Pop, it hit the fan! Bone fired me and told me we would never get the building permits. I reminded him about my photographic memory of all his accounts. He's another one of the world's assholes. I gave him a piece of my mind before I left and it felt so good."

"Whoa, baby. Slow down. Are you okay?"

"Of course I'm okay. I'm a CPA with a Master's degree, a black belt with a Marine daddy. It doesn't get much better than that. Let's have a drink, Pop. I need one."

"Sounds like you're either feeling your oats, baby, or you're scared to death."

"I'm feeling … Uh, I don't know how I feel, Pop. I'm either relieved, stupid or just beginning to experience my freedom and right now I don't know which. It's like Bella said, I'm 'facing demons' that I had no idea were there. It does scare me. I've never gone without a paycheck in my life or a job to go to in the morning."

"Let's meet at The Turtle. I'm calling the family to join us. Maybe we can finally celebrate and tell everyone what's happening, baby. Take a deep breath and breathe. The battles have just begun. Put on your armor, Sweetie Pie!"

Hank texted Robbie, Tito and T-Bone to meet at The Turtle later that evening after work. His phone began chirping.

"Gunny? Tito."

"What's up? Can you make it tonight?"

"Wouldn't miss it. Can I bring one of my students from the dojo, Scott Wood? He's run local restaurants, set up the sound system at several of the clubs and has a band. His experience in the club business can help us a lot. He's a good guy and I trust him."

"No prob, Tito. Bring him, we'll need all the help we can get. See you there."

Tonight would be more than a celebration to kick-start their dream, it would be their first planning meeting. Again, Hank's phone rang.

"Mr. Hawkins, this is Frank Baggett. How's Bella doing?"

"She's much better, Mr. Baggett. How's Frank Jr.?"

"Besides making a complete, embarrassing fool out of himself, he'll live. Thanks again for your help and discretion in this matter. I heard you bought the old NASA Oceanographic location and are turning it into a club named Tequilaville. Congrats!"

"News travels fast around the Lake, Mr. Baggett. Abby put most of it together."

"I told you at Frank Jr.'s house that I wouldn't forget what you did so I have a proposition for you. Are you open to discuss this right now? I think you'll like it!"

"I'm all ears. Shoot!"

"I'm buying "Mutual Funz 2", an older, larger sixty-five foot Hatteras. It's going to need all new wiring, installation of some updated radar and Commo equipment that I've purchased and new interior, exterior lighting. Plus, I'm going to need a permanent docking facility to park it. It won't fit where I have my other yacht.

"So here's my deal for you Mr. Hawkins. If you'll do the updates on the '2', *pro bono*, I'll put in $100 grand for your dock facilities at Tequilaville. But I want a permanent, private, floating dock there for my new yacht rent free. What do you say?"

Hank hesitated a second or two so as not to appear too eager and finally said, "Not to be nosey, Mr. Baggett, but how did you find out about all of this so quickly?"

"It's my business to know what goes on here. I'm also on the City Council. Your daughter's former employer, Gerald Bone, tried to recall your work permits and I got a call to vote on it. I cancelled out his vote so your permits are in order. Another thing before you make your decision, you can use me as a reference to get your liquor license from the State as long as you and Abby continue putting your investments with my firm. So your decision is … ?"

"I know we're not your largest clients yet, but you've done well with our little nest eggs so far. I say you've got yourself a deal, Mr. Baggett. Congrats on the new boat. When do you want me to send my crew over to start on the '2'?"

"Next week. I'll have my assistant email you the details."

Later that night the family assembled at The Turtle. Abby was still a bit hyper so Hank ordered a round of beer to cool the situation. Everyone was feeling the pressure of entrepreneurship and career changes. Big risks, and they hoped, big rewards, but there was so much to be done over the next nine months and there was no time to spare.

"Abby, pop in another $100 grand to the building funds for the boat docks. I just made a little deal with Frank Baggett, Sr. He's going to park his new boat at Tequilaville. His form of payback, if you know what I mean."

"I'm not sure I even want to know the details, if you know what I mean. So where do we start?"

Robbie Cantrell stood, held up her mug of diet Coke and said, "We start with a prayer and a toast to Tequilaville. Lord bless this place and our efforts."

Before all the small talk began to cut the tension, Tito introduced Scott Wood to everyone. Scott was 40ish, tall, slender and always had a smile on his face.

"Scott, Tito speaks highly of you." Hank was always careful before admitting new people into the family. "Your resume says you've run some area restaurants, went to San Jac College studying sound equipment, arranging music and have a band. What's the name of your band?"

"It's called *South*, Mr. Hawkins ..."

"Call me Hank. Everyone does but Tito and he calls me *Gunny*, it's a *Semper Fi* thing between us. Ever been in the military?"

"No sir, I mean, Hank. Never been much of a fighter. I joined Master Tito's dojo for fitness reasons and to add some discipline to my life."

"That's fine, Scott. We've got enough fighters in the family. What we need now is some help with entertainment. That's my area. What's hot around the Lake these days?"

"Everything's hot for a time, Hank. What's your play list? What type of music are you thinking about?"

"R&B, 70s and 80s Pop with a heavy dose of C&W. No rap, no heavy metal. I want the music to be entertaining, friendly and have a range of tastes that will keep people coming back. Sort of a retro, 'yesterday once more' atmosphere where people will feel comfortable. This isn't a family club, it's a fun-on-the-lake type of club. How's that for a music menu?"

"Hmmm ... easy to say, hard to do, Hank. At first glance, I'd say to bring in different types of bands but other clubs in the area are already doing that and can probably pay higher prices. Booking bands has a lot of drawbacks such as scheduling, different booking agents and fees, not to mention dealing with many egos and personalities. My idea would be to audition a house band that can play a little bit of everything with a diversified, talented vocalist. That's going to be the trick, finding one."

"Tell me about your band, Scott. It's called *South*?"

"*South* plays a little bit of everything from ZZ Top to Willie Nelson. We've been together for over ten years and the guys in the band are great musicians. They can play by ear, jam or read music. I sing, play rhythm guitar and keyboard. If you want, when we get to that point, we'll audition just like everyone else, but my main area is running the sound equipment, song arrangement and lighting."

"What about planning drink and food menus, Scott? Tito's gonna need a little help. What're your thoughts?"

"To keep things simple. We're here to sell drinks mainly. That's where we make our money. Kitchen equipment is expensive. You could have a big covered cooker on the patio with brisket, chicken, hamburgers and link sausage along with an oven in the kitchen for pizza. You'll need a walk-in refrigerator for storing beer and veggies with a deep fry area in the kitchen. That's as simple as it gets and cuts down on the chef staff. Drink menus are easy. We'll come up with some original drink names and promote them. Got any ideas in this area, Hank?"

"Obviously we're promoting tequila. How about *Tequila-Ritas?*"

Tito chimed in, "That can also be the name of our waitresses. I've got lots of cousins to fill this area. They're cute, of age and they're honest, plus they need jobs. I'll manage them, hire them and fire them if necessary. My responsibility."

"Scott, I like your experience and your enthusiasm. Want to work for me?" Hank asked.

"I was hoping you'd offer me a position, Hank. I'd love to be a part of a start-up."

Abby put down her second mug of beer, looked over at Scott and said, "This isn't a start-up. It's the beginning of building a dream. We're dream makers here."

"Abby, do you have room for Scott in the budget?"

"We do now since you made that deal with Mr. Baggett. Scott, I do the payroll around here. You're now our new creative director. Welcome to our dream world. You start working with Tito and Hank as of tomorrow." Abby extended her hand and called for another toast.

As the night continued, Abby gave Daddy Hank the appointments she had set up with her architect friend, Terry Bailey of Bailey and Associates, so Hank could put his visions into drawings for the club. She passed out "To Do" lists for each person with instructions and a timeline to accomplish their nine-month Grand Opening date.

Tito's cousins in the different crafts had were ready to submit bids so all that needed to be done was get the drawings for the entire building, patio, boat docks and parking areas from Bailey & Associates and begin the demolition of the old NASA building.

"Enough business for one night," Hank said. "One more round and we're outta here. Big day tomorrow. The dream begins."

Over the next eight months the newly acquired property became a buzz of activity. There were problems and solutions. Robbie's prayer was being answered day by day. The group grew to trust each other through their hard work and discipline to Abby's plan. They were on target, on plan, with little time to worry about the small stuff. Tequilaville was becoming a reality.

6

WAYNE TYLER
VAGABOND: A WANDERER

After auditioning all the local bands, Hank and Abby chose *South* and Scott Wood agreed to be a fill-in singer but insisted that they audition other vocalists. The parking lot was full of applicants as workmen installed the large, hot purple script sign that simply read *Tequilaville*. It was three weeks before the grand opening.

Hank, Abby and Scott Wood sat behind a table at the far end of the dance floor in front of the stage. *South* played the arrangements for the vocalists as the buzz of activity by the workmen and wait staff continued. Listening to the singers audition created a fun atmosphere for everyone and was an extra little perk of working on the weekend. Scott had prepared a score sheet with qualities they would need to choose the right singer.

Wayne Tyler pulled into the parking lot in a beat-up van. The tail pipe and bumper were held up by pieces of wire and the tires were bare. Nonetheless, he got out of the van with an air of confidence and strolled around the property to get a feel of the place before going inside. Dressed in boots and jeans, wrapped in arrogance, Wayne was far from being an average singer and musician. He was very talented, very skilled at his profession and he knew it. Just under six feet tall, Wayne had a slender build, sandy brown hair and charismatic turquoise eyes. Wayne Tyler was an Adonis by most any woman's definition.

He walked around back and saw a sixty-five-foot Hatteras, "Mutual Funz 2", stationed at a private floating slip with a sign that read *Reserved*. He walked out on the long connecting pier that appeared like it could dock most of the boats on the lake. The smell of smoke coming from the covered cooker on the patio area gave him an idea of the food menu. Wayne was no stranger to clubs but, so far, he was very impressed. He sensed that someone had dumped a lot of money into this place, and he hadn't been inside yet. The music from inside echoed onto the back patio. Wayne listened to several singers audition and so far he hadn't heard anyone that he considered to be in his league. He could tell that the back-up band could play practically any of the songs on his own diversified play list. That gave him ideas for his own audition.

Wayne walked in from the back door of the club as workmen continued all the menial tasks. The club had a good feel to him and he didn't want to make his usual self-centered entrance yet. The walls inside were constructed of weathered, unfinished wood where individually lighted posters of some of the great entertainers hung around the perimeter of the main bar area. Entertainers such as Buddy Holly, Stevie Ray Vaughn, Willie Nelson, Elvis Presley, Eric Clapton, Santana, Jimi Hendrix, Jeff Beck, Ray Wiley Hubbard, Delbert McClinton and Jerry Jeff Walker complimented the retro, yesterday-once-more atmosphere that Hank wanted to capture. Old guitars, kerosene lanterns, and hub caps hung on the walls, and the front end of an old Ford 150 truck blasted through the wall on one side of the club. Classic records and a host of music memorabilia accented the rest of the wall space. There were also pictures and gold record replicas of Barbra Streisand, Aretha Franklin, Dolly Parton, Celine Dion and Whitney Houston. The floors were polished concrete except for the hardwood dance floor in front of the large and wonderfully lit stage area that reminded Wayne of some of the clubs that he had played in Gruene and Luckenbach, Texas. There were several small side rooms, which he guessed were for bachelor and bachelorette parties, and no two tables or chairs even came close to matching. Hanging from the ceiling over the dance floor was an over-sized mirror globe with reflective lights all around it adding to the ambiance of the dance floor. A six-foot brass replica of an armadillo, the unofficial State Animal of Texas, hung over the bar.

The rustic-looking hardwood bar was located near the back of the main club, facing the stage and nailed down barstools ran along the entire length. Behind the bar was the kitchen area that opened up to the outside patio area. It appeared to Wayne that Tequilaville could probably handle a big bar room brawl and emerge with very little damage. He had seen a few of those in his entertainment days.

He walked over to an old, beautiful, bubbling Wurlitzer jukebox just to see what type of music it offered. The records were extremely well-known, hard to find classics and ranged from Edith Piaf, the Little Sparrow of France, singing her heart wrenching song, "Mon Dieu", to Lee Marvin singing "I was Born Under a Wandering Star". Wayne could tell that someone had given lots of thought and time to finding these old records and they probably hadn't come cheap. The play list was beyond phenomenal.

Finally, Wayne looked at the enclosed control area for sound and lighting. It was first class equipment. The sound and acoustics were well balanced and Wayne hoped the owners would hire someone who knew how to operate the instrumentation. He was all about looking and sounding great. He went back out the back door to his van.

Meanwhile, Tito was instructing his nieces how to be great Tequila Rita waitresses, T-Bone was standing at the door making sure only pertinent auditioners entered the club when Robbie and Bella came in to see the end of the auditions and get some of the great food that Hank was preparing for the staff and musicians.

"Have you decided on your lead singer?" Robbie asked, looking over at Bella who was socializing with everyone in the club in her usual manner.

Hank looked at Scott and Abby to get a reaction before answering. Both gave a thumbs down.

"Not yet. We still have a couple to go. Grab some food and help us out," Hank said with a grimace.

Wayne Tyler walked in the front door carrying a Stratocaster and an old, beat-up classical acoustic guitar. He carried a small duffle bag of props and sheet music and walked over to Hank and company to put his name on the list. He wanted to be last.

"I'm Wayne Tyler. I'd like to audition."

"You're the last one today, Wayne. What type of music do you play?" Scott asked.

"A little bit of everything."

After two more singers tried their luck, Hank called Wayne's name.

"Good luck, Mr. Tyler, give it your best shot." Hank was actually getting bored of the auditions. Everyone sounded pretty much alike and opening night was closing in on them.

Wayne walked up to the bandstand, took off his baseball cap and shook hands with all the guys in *South,* then handed out sheet music which they quickly glanced over and discarded. He pointed to the different pictures lining the walls of the club and after a little more conversation, Wayne turned his back to the crowd, put on some heavy black glasses, flipped up the back of his collar, and turned back around to face the audience. When he broke into a Buddy Holley song, "Peggy Sue", the workmen and staff stopped what they were doing.

From Buddy Holley, the next picture hanging on the wall was Stevie Ray Vaughn. Wayne put on a flat-top, straight-brimmed hat with a solid silver Indian-type hat band and played some hot blues on his Stratocaster, doing his impersonation of SRV. Next he moved on to Willie Nelson, singing "Angel Flying too Close to the Ground", accompanying himself on his beat-up, classical guitar. By this time, every worker and staff member in the club had stopped and gathered behind Hank, Abby and Scott. Wayne Tyler was a show stopper.

In a medley of songs that continued to follow the pictures around the club walls, Wayne did various impressions of every artist, looking, playing and sounding just like them. He could play guitar like Santana, Clapton, Hendrix and Beck with such skill that no one could believe he wasn't the original.

Switching from electric to acoustic guitar, Wayne quickly slid them behind him and got behind the keyboard and went into his version of Jerry Lee Lewis singing "Great Balls of Fire", then with a quick prop to rhinestone glasses did his impersonation of Elton John singing "Saturday:. Next was his impersonation of the King, Elvis Presley, singing "You Ain't Nothing but a Hound Dog", complete with all the moves. The Tequila Ritas were screaming and dancing in the aisles.

Wayne ended his medley with Jerry Jeff Walker's "London Homesick Blues" (Going Back to the Armadillo), which Hank considered the unofficial State Song of Texas. *South* was getting into the session and were just as amazed as everyone else. Tequilaville was rocking!

At the end of the last song everyone was clapping, whooping, laughing and whistling, shouting "Encore! Encore!" Hank looked at Scott who was looking at Billie, *South's* keyboard player, who gave him a thumbs up. No one had ever heard such a display of singing, guitar playing, exact impersonations, and showmanship. Scott motioned to Hank with a nod of approval.

"Sweetie Pie, what do you think? Abby? Abby! Honey, are you with us?" Hank hadn't seen that star-struck look in her eye since she was eight years old. Abby was completely mesmerized and slow to respond.

"He's the one, Pop! He's absolutely the one!"

"Scott, have you ever heard of Wayne Tyler?" Hank asked.

"Never. But it won't be long till everyone's heard of him. We've got a star on our hands, and I can make him and Tequilaville great! Signing Tyler would be like signing a whole slew of bands. He could do a different impersonation every night of the week and pack this place!"

During all the celebration, T-Bone walked up behind Hank and whispered to him to have a private conversation. They walked out to the patio area.

"I know him, Boss. I remember him well. Ten years ago Wayne Tyler went by the name Tom Wayne. He played at a little club called *Jeckyl's* just outside of San Antonio. He was the one that I was supposed to whack to gain entry to the MC."

Stunned, Hank walked out near the pier. T-Bone followed him.

"What happened, T-Bone? What'd he do to get a contract put on him?"

T-Bone reached back in his memory to put his words together. "Well, Tom Wayne, back then, was fooling around with one of the MC members' ole lady. The member found out and assigned me to take him out. I refused, couldn't do it, so

the MC torched the club and this guy, Tom Wayne, took off to the UK, we heard, and no one's heard from him since. That's the short version, Boss."

"Thanks, T-Bone. You just earned your keep around here. I appreciate you coming to me with this. I've always said that if something is too good to be true, it usually is, so I'll deal with it from here. Don't say anything more about this to anyone, understood?"

"Understood, Boss."

Wayne's medley audition had lasted almost forty-five minutes. As he stepped down from the stage and wiped his forehead with a handkerchief, he looked exhausted. Abby was still in a semi-trance as Bella moved through the crowd of well-wishers to get Wayne's attention.

"Hi, I'm Bella. Hank and Abby Hawkins, the owners of Tequilaville, are like family to me. I hope we can get to know one another very soon," she said with a flirtatious grin.

"The pleasure is all mine, Bella. So glad to meet ya. Let me have your number and I'll call when I get settled into town."

Abby caught Bella's eye with a look that could kill giants. Bella didn't care and acted as though she didn't notice the piercing eyes pointed her direction from her *little sister.*

Wayne walked over to a table and sat down, grabbed a bottle of water and waited for the obvious decision by the owners.

"Abby and Scott, it's obvious that this guy, Wayne Tyler, is your decision for our vocalist. Correct?" Hank asked.

Both heads nodded, and Scott gave Hank a big thumbs up.

"Last I heard, this is my area. I've got final say on who we hire. I want to talk to this guy before we make up our minds." Hank looked concerned.

"What's to talk about, Pop? He's in a league of his own," Abby said, still star struck.

"But why haven't we ever heard of him? Scott, what's your take?"

"Hank, I'll admit, it's a mystery. There's no way the music world or someone in it has never heard of him. Right now, I'm searching for a word that goes beyond *fantastic.*"

"Pop, he's left me speechless also. There's just something about him …" Abby couldn't take her eyes off Wayne.

"I noticed, sweetie. I noticed. I'm going to sit down with him alone if you two don't mind."

Hank motioned to T-Bone to hang close by and walked over to the table where Wayne was cooling off.

"I'm Hank Hawkins, co-owner of Tequilaville." Hank put on his poker face for the talk with Wayne. "Quite a performance you just put on. Everyone's impressed."

"I gave it my best, Mr. Hawkins. Has your group made a decision yet?" Wayne was very confident in asking for the decision preemptively.

"I've got a few questions for you first if you don't mind, Mr. Tyler. Where've you played and why haven't we heard about you?"

"Mr. Hawkins, I've been singing, playing and studying my craft for over twenty years. I've jammed with most of the people that I did the impersonations of. Well, almost everyone. I never met Elvis Presley; he was a little before my time."

"You didn't answer my questions, Mr. Tyler."

"Oh, I've played the Texas circuit: Luckenbach, Gruene, Billy Bob's in Fort Worth, clubs on 6th Street in Austin, a couple of clubs in San Antonio. Then I got the itch to go to London where I jammed with Eric Clapton, Jeff Beck and played a few clubs there for several years."

"Uh huh, Mr. Tyler. Tell me about San Antonio and a club named *Jeckyl's*."

"You heard about that, huh? I played there for a while, the club burned down and I went to London. That's pretty much the long and short of it."

Hank kicked back in his chair, pushed the old cowboy hat back on his head, looked Wayne right in the eyes and said, "Yep, I'd say that's the short of it. Truth is I heard you had to get out of town. You fooled around with a biker mama and they put a hit out on you. Is that true?"

"Uh … uh … Mr. Hawkins, you obviously know someone who knows me. Yeah, I had to take off. I made some mistakes and it cost me a career. Women are attracted to me and I took advantage of it. I can't say that I'm a saint, but I am who I am."

"Had trouble keeping your Wranglers zipped, huh? So where are you now, Mr. Tyler? I can see why you didn't sign a recording contract; you'd be looking over your shoulder in every venue, waiting for that guy from the MC to take you out. Am I getting close?"

Wayne was past squirming. He respected Hank for being up front with him and decided to lay it all on the table. He finally realized that he wasn't a shoe-in for the job, and he needed it desperately.

"That was the main reason, Mr. Hawkins. The other reason was that when someone signs a recording contract, it's about two inches thick. The label owns you. They tell you where to go, what to wear, what to say and keep you on the road for 360 days a year. The money is great but not the life. The thing in San Antonio just helped me to realize it. That's the total truth. If you're going to hold my past against me, then I'll just say adios, no fuss, no bother and go my way."

"Mr. Tyler, I'd like to introduce you to T-Bone. He's my head of security. T-Bone, shake hands with Mr. Tyler."

T-Bone towered over Wayne as he stood up from his chair to shake hands.

"Wayne, this is the man in the motorcycle club who was given the hit to take you out!"

Wayne pulled back quickly.

"Don't worry, Wayne. T-Bone obviously didn't accomplish his assignment from the MC. As a matter of fact, he declined the hit and was never admitted into the club. You're safe now."

After fumbling for words, Wayne looked up at T-Bone and said, "I guess I owe you my life, Mr. T-Bone." Wayne took a little sigh of relief and sat back down in his chair. T-Bone didn't reply.

For several minutes Hank just sat in front of Wayne sizing him up, saying nothing, making a few mental notes and, quite frankly, waiting for Wayne to start sweating about the job. Hank could see that Wayne was talented but was he trustworthy? It was obvious by the reaction of the crowd, not to mention the look on Abby's face, that Wayne was a lady-killer but could he be humbled into becoming part of a hard working family? Hank didn't want Scott to start publicizing someone who would be gone in a week or two.

"How bad do you want this job, Wayne?" Hank never minced words when it came to business.

"Mr. Hawkins, since meeting my killer, no offense meant, Mr. T-Bone, today is the first day in many years that I know that someone isn't trying to kill me. I've learned my talents from the best and have worked hard to perfect them but I couldn't use 'em. I had to drift from place to place when my fifteen minutes of fame were right around the corner, always just out of my grasp.

"You want to know how bad I want this job? To me this represents freedom, it represents a new start and I'm pushing forty. I haven't had a stable life for so long I don't know what the word means. I admitted that I wasn't a saint, but I'll do the best I can. I can't just change overnight and I won't promise you any more than that. I'll give it my best shot, Mr. Hawkins, you have my word on that."

"You're an exceptional talent, Wayne. By the way, is Wayne Tyler your real name?"

"Real name, got the birth certificate to prove it, Mr. Hawkins."

"Here's my deal, Wayne. I do want you to come with us but until now I haven't had any hard and fast rules. I'm making some up as I go. Want to hear 'em?"

"All ears, Mr. Hawkins."

"First, since you are such a Willie Nelson fan, he said something to his own band years ago that I never forgot. He told them, 'If you're wired, you're fired.' I don't allow druggies working here at Tequilaville. Are you a junkie, Wayne?"

"No, sir. That's the truth. I take a drink every now and then but I'm not an alcoholic either."

"Second, what you do on your own time is your business. But if it ever interferes with my business, like fooling around with someone's ole lady and an irate husband decides to torch my club, I'll have a big problem with that. Are we clear?"

"Perfectly clear, Mr. Hawkins."

"Finally, and hear me well. You see that little brown-haired, green-eyed beauty sitting over there?" Hank pointed at Abby.

"Yessir."

"That's my daughter and co-owner, Abby Hawkins. She writes the checks around here. Stay clear of her. Do you understand me, Mr. Tyler?"

"Stay clear of Miss Abby Hawkins! I am very clear on that, Mr. Hawkins."

After another brief pause, looking Wayne directly in the eyes, Hank reached across the table and offered his hand.

"Wayne, we're like a family around here. We work hard, we're honest and we're all about new beginnings. This club is our dream and you're welcome to be a part of it. We open in three weeks. Why don't you go over and meet Scott Wood and his band members. We'll need your contact info, and I'll talk to you soon about the details. And by the way, call me 'Hank.'"

Abby got up from the director's table and made a bee-line to Bella, grabbing her by the arm and leading her out to the back patio.

"We need to have a little sister-to-sister talk, Bella."

"Get your hands off of me, little sister! What's wrong with you?" Bella tried to pull away but Abby's grip was firm.

"Stay away from Wayne Tyler! He's our business, not yours." Abby was in no mood for rebuttal.

"Abby, you don't tell me what to do! Who I can and can't see. And, please, don't pull any of that karate crap on me either. I bruise easily."

Abby shook her finger right in Bella's face, said nothing else and walked away. She cut a wide path back into the club, grabbed her purse and burned rubber in her late model SUV as she stormed out of the parking lot.

Bella remained on the patio long enough to smoke a cigarette, making gestures in the air, then walked past Robbie, saying, "That little bitch can't talk to me that way, sister or not! What the hell's wrong with her, anyway, Mom?"

"Bella, did you see the look in Abby's eyes?"

"What look, Mom? I guess I missed it."

"Bella, daughter, you need to take the time to notice what others are feeling and stop concentrating on yourself all the time. Abby's in love or at least she thinks she is. Couldn't you see that?"

"Mom, all I could see was her finger in my face. I won't stand for that, little sister or not. Get my drift?" Bella stormed out of the club.

7

NOVA
SEEKING THE SORDID

Robbie looked over at Hank holding her arms out as if to ask, *What's going on with our daughters?* Hank shook his head and resumed overseeing all the commotion for preparation of the grand opening that was catching up with them day by day. During the next couple of weeks, Wayne Tyler and *South* rehearsed for opening night, getting their songs and music coordinated, Abby got *Tequilaville's* web site up and sent out emails to over four thousand friends and clients that she, Hank, Scott, and Tito had accumulated over the years.

Stress levels were running high as Friday night's kick-off event was less than a week off. Hank and Abby didn't know if anyone would show up, too many would show up, if their docking facilities and crew could handle all the boats pulling in and or just how their staff would adjust to the big night. So many questions with absolutely no answers. Both had their life savings tied up in *Tequilaville* with no guarantee of success and wondered if their dream would become their demise.

Competition for entertainment dollars around the Lake was stiff. Hank was completely unprepared for the onslaught of radio and TV advertising that competitor clubs launched just before his grand opening. Advertisements for special drink pricing, new bands being showcased, no-cover charge weekends and wet T-Shirt contests continued 24/7 for days.

Abby's checkbook was working overtime paying for all of the neon beer and tequila signs decorating the walls of Tequilaville along with paying up-front for all labor, booze and supplies. There were no consignment deals for start-up clubs since the same vendors Tequilaville used also supplied the other clubs on the Lake. The bank account was next to nil. The first weekend of the grand opening would either make or break them.

There was no work scheduled the Sunday before the last week of preparation and it gave Hank, Abby and the rest of the staff some much needed down time.

Robbie gave Hank a call to check his temperature.

"Are you ready for Friday night, brother?"

"Robbie, as usual, I'm so glad you called. I'm freaking out. The opening is on April 11th and it's still cold and rainy. Not many boats will be on the Lake."

"I figured you were a little anxious. One day at a time. Remember me telling you that?"

Hank was sitting out on his patio and looked over to see Robbie sitting on hers. They waved at each other.

"Have you got time to come over, Robbie? Got a couple of things on my mind."

"Be right over."

As soon as Robbie entered Hank's condo she could see the anxiety in his eyes and the wrinkles on his brow. She gave him a big hug, patted him on the back and said, "Let's talk. What's on your mind, as if I didn't know."

"N'ah, it's not just the opening I'm concerned about. What happens will happen. I'm worried about the little cat-fight between Bella and Abby a couple weeks ago. Abby's been completely silent about it and I have no idea what went on. I didn't ask her and she hasn't said anything. Has Bella talked to you?"

"Of course she has. Bella's an open book and very out-spoken about her life and emotions. She tells me everything."

"Well?"

"Hank, you can't tell me that you didn't see the look in Abby's eyes the first time she saw Wayne Tyler. It was pretty obvious to everyone."

"I noticed."

"After Wayne's audition, Abby literally dragged Bella out on the patio and told her in no uncertain terms to stay away from Wayne, like she was staking her claim to him. That's one of Bella's pet-peeves, to be told what to do. I can't even tell her what to do and I'm her mother."

"I'm not completely blind, Robbie. I suspected that and even told Wayne to stay clear of Abby during our little chat before signing him. I know a little more about him than you do. He's going to be good for business if he stays and complies with my rules, but you and I both know he's a heartbreaker. I don't want Abby's heartbroken. It's that simple. "

"Hank, love is never simple, is it? Abby's in love-at-first-sight with this guy. She's love struck."

"And he's going to hurt her and I can't allow that, Robbie. I love her too much."

"Hank, as much as I'd like to tell you that you can still protect Abby, you can't. She's a grown woman. I've never known her to act this way and that's all the more reason that you have to stay out of her way and let her make her own mistakes or she'll take some of that wrath out on you. Believe it, Hank, love is blind and sometimes it's deaf. Neither me, you nor anyone else can tell her anything at this point. She won't listen and she thinks she's in love. Just be there to catch her when she falls. That's all a daddy, or a mother can do."

They both sat there in silence for a few minutes. Hank was smoking one cigarette after the next trying his best to figure out what to do.

"Robbie, don't you get upset when Bella gets into bad relationships, like with Frank Jr.?"

"Of course I do, Hank. She's my daughter. I don't want to see her hurt. But that's the difference in personalities between our two daughters."

"What do you mean?"

"Hank, as much as I wish this wasn't true and I've done my best to teach her, Bella is a player. I know my daughter. She has fun, does her own thing but doesn't get caught up in the emotions of a relationship. Unfortunately, she handles her life style just fine. She must've gotten those cheating genes from her dad. He cheated on me more than once. I don't believe Abby is capable of dealing with a player like Wayne Tyler either. He's going to break her heart and I just pray Abby can get past it."

"Robbie, I've already forbid Wayne from seeing Abby. What now?"

"But you haven't and cannot forbid Abby from seeing Wayne, now, can you?"

"When you put it that way … I guess I can't. But I don't want Wayne coming between Bella and Abby. They're too close to lose each other."

"They won't. If one gets hurt, the other will be there. It's a *girl thing*."

"Robbie, I'm truly sorry to hear what happened with your hubby. You never talked about him to me."

"Hank, when I say 'Bella got her daddy's genes,' you have no idea. I've never told Bella or anyone else the truth about him. I've carried a lie and a shame around for many years. I need to get this off my chest, but first, what I'm about to tell you, you have to swear to carry to your grave, brother. You can't tell anyone, much less Abby and especially Bella."

"I swear. Want a cup of joe to get started?"

"Just put on a new pot. I'll try and give you the short version, Hank." Robbie took a deep breath, filled her cup and curled up with a little blanket on the chaise on Hank's patio.

"Two years after Bella was born, my husband, Bobby Cantrell, and I lived in a little West Texas oil field town out in the middle of nowhere. My parents lived there along with two of my dad's brothers, Uncle Gailard, the local sheriff, and Uncle Lynn, the only minister in the town. Bobby was the insurance guy and struggled to make us a living in a town of twenty-eight hundred where everyone knew everyone, their business and their comings and goings.

"One morning Bobby was *selling* insurance to a local housewife when her roughneck husband came home early, caught them in the act and beat Bobby to death with an eight-pound sledge hammer. Uncle Gailard got the call from the husband, had a little talk with him and his wife, rolled Bobby's body up in a blanket, put him in Bobby's car and drove out to one of the canyons just outside of town. He blew out one of the front tires, started the car, put it in gear with Bobby's body in the front seat, and rolled it off the cliff. The car hit the bottom of the canyon, burst into flames, destroying any evidence of the beating, then Uncle Gailard called me to come pick him up. That's when he told me what really happened. Bobby's death certificate said 'auto accident' and no autopsy was ever performed."

Robbie's lips were pursed as she garnered the courage to tell the rest of the story. Hank was being a good listener and never interrupted her.

"Now my parents and both my uncles are dead, and the only three people left alive to know the truth are me, the couple and now you. They're not going to say anything since murder charges would be filed against the husband. I got the insurance money, sold our little house, loaded up our car and Bella and I moved as far away as I could get, here to Clear Lake. Like it or not, Hank, that's West Texas blind justice. I've lived with this lie ever since. I enrolled in nursing school, worked five years in a nursing home and then started my home health business." That's why I can never give up on Bella. She has her dad's genes but she also has mine. I'm praying that mine will win out one of these days."

Hank had no idea where Robbie got her strength and he was glad when she finally broke down, laying her head on his shoulder. He sat still, holding her close.

"Hank, brother, thanks for listening," she said in between sobs. "You're the only man I've ever trusted in all these years. I'm blessed to have you as my best friend."

At 8 a.m., Friday, April 11th, Hank put in a call to Abby and woke her up. She'd been at Tequilaville late the night before making sure their credit card machines, cash registers and every area of her accounting office was working correctly.

"Happy Birthday, Sweetie Pie! What a big day." Hank was thankful that the sun was shining and an unusual south wind off the Gulf of Mexico had warmed up the Lake for their grand opening.

"Thanks, Daddy Hank," Abby said a bit groggily, "but please, no birthday party today. We have way too much to do. Are you ready?"

"Ready as we're going to be, baby. I'll see you over there in an hour or so …"

Normal hours for the club were going to be 5 p.m. until 2 a.m., closing at midnight on Sundays. But today, Friday, was an exception. Abby and Hank decided to open early, around 11:15 a.m. to draw some of the NASA lunch crowd. The cookers on the patio were smoking and it would be a good way for the wait staff to walk in their new boots and get into the weekend slowly. By 9:15 a.m., all hands were on deck. Tito had the bar stocked and his wait staff, including the dock boys, assembled. He instructed them on how to stop serving obviously inebriated guests and to make sure they had a friend to drive them home, or get T-Bone involved. He'd get them a cab and pay the fare. It was important to Hank to maintain a good reputation as a responsible club owner. Plus, he didn't want to get sued.

T-Bone was going over last minute details with his beefed-up security team which included putting on some local off-duty law enforcement to direct traffic and keep order. He had a wad of $20s to pay taxi fares later in the night and had arranged with a cab company to have several cabs camped out at Tequilaville beginning around midnight. T-Bone wore a shoulder holster holding a licensed-to-carry 9mm Glock tucked inside his coat. Scott Wood was doing last minute sound checks even though the band would not start playing until half past six. He would sing for a couple of hours to open up for the main attraction, Wayne Tyler, who would hit the stage at 8:30. It was going to be a long day, and everyone hoped people would show up.

Hank sauntered into the club, noticed the huge "Grand Opening" banner hanging just below the big purple Tequilaville sign and was a bit uncomfortable wearing starched jeans, starched snap front shirt, his best cowboy belt and buckle, lizard boots and an old cowboy hat pushed down over his gray ponytail. Tito walked over to him.

"Enjoy, Gunny. We got this. Everything's ready."

Abby was right behind him carrying her ever present back pack, wearing red boots, studded jeans and a crop-top that showed her muscled mid-section. She wore a band of daisies in her long brown silky hair that immediately made Hank think of Abigail.

"Let's make some money, Pop! I'm a bean counter ready to start countin'," Abby said in a festive mood, speaking with a giggle in her voice. It was her birthday and the grand opening of their dream. She strutted back to her almost hidden office, just behind Hank's table, where all the accounting and book keeping was done. Her door had a big "Private-No Entry" sign on it with double locks.

Tucked back in the left far corner facing the stage was a semi-circle booth with a white plaque reading "Hank's Table-Reserved" which gave him an overall vantage point viewing all areas of the club, including the dock area outside. From his table, Hank could also stop unauthorized people from entering Abby's office. Next to the booth were several glass sections, on either side of the bar area, providing sunlight during the day and a Lake and patio view for customers during the evening, adding a special ambiance of twinkling lights shimmering off the Lake.

By 11:15 a.m. that morning, the parking lot was full of mostly curious NASA people dropping in, not only for lunch, but to get a glimpse of the club they'd witnessed being constructed for the last nine months. Boats from all over the Lake began docking with more curiosity seekers and within half an hour, the patio was filled to capacity. No one was buying a lot of booze but their food business was going ballistic. The stellar jukebox was cranked up and coupled with the friendliness of the lovely Tequila Rita waitresses, the atmosphere was just like Hank had imagined … A lakeside, good-times bar. Scott Wood walked over to each and every table with his perpetual smile greeting customers and telling them about Wayne Tyler and the big band event later that evening. He was not only a singer, sound man and arranger, Scott was *the* good-will ambassador of Tequilaville. The opening was working out well. Now if it would just continue into the night and the weekend to follow.

By 7 p.m., Tequilaville was at the point of chaos. Traffic was stacked up along NASA Road 1, boats were jockeying for position to get a spot at the T-ville docks, and it seemed like most of the party goers on the Lake were headed for the grand opening.

Scott and *South* cranked up to begin the night's entertainment, welcoming everyone to Tequilaville and prepping the crowd for the main attraction. Very few people had even heard of Wayne Tyler and tonight would tell the tale of his debut. Finally 8:30 rolled around and Scott introduced Wayne Tyler. No one paid much notice to the announcement and continued to laugh, have a good time and drink … lots of drinking!

Robbie, Bella, Abby, Hattie Lang, and every friend they had were anxiously awaiting Wayne's first session on stage, especially Abby. She was still mesmerized by him and it was plain to see as she took a break from counting all the money they were raking in.

"Hey buckaroos, I'm Wayne Tyler and I'd like to play a few songs for you!"

South agreed that Wayne should begin with Jerry Jeff Walker's "London Homesick Blues". The crowd loved it when he let loose with "Great Balls of Fire", banging on the keyboard, getting in character to keep the moment going. Next was a medley of Stevie Ray Vaughn songs, tearing up his Stratocaster, along with his impersonation of the legend. He followed, without pause, with Elvis' "You Ain't Nothin' but a Hound Dog", shaking his hips and driving the women absolutely out of their minds. A pair of lady's panties came sailing out of the audience and landed on the stage. All eyes were on Wayne Tyler. His first set debut was without description. He had everyone in the palm of his hand. Booze sales went nuts. Abby's eyes were gleaming, along with every other woman's in the club.

Bella looked at her mom, Robbie, who was standing by the table dancing up a storm. She couldn't help herself. "He's good, Mom. I hope I can keep my paws off of him."

"Off limits, kitten. He's Abby's!"

"I'm not a kitten anymore, Mom. I'm a lioness and I'm telling you right now, if Abby goes after that wild stallion, he'll rip her apart. No woman is going to tame him! You can go to the bank on that one."

Wayne's set even had Hank cranked up. "By gosh, Robbie, that boy's the best I've ever seen or heard. Look at this place! No one's ever rocked the Lake like Wayne. Damn, I'm proud of him! I think he's just nailed down our success and he's making the dream come true … on Abby's birthday."

Scott took a break from the sound booth and walked over to Hank.

"I'm recording this grand opening live, making some CDs and DVDs of tonight, Hank. We need something in the gift shop besides Tequilaville T-Shirts, coozies and bumper stickers. They should be ready by next week. We're gonna sell tons of 'em. I've never in twenty years in the music business seen anything like this. Just look at the people, Hank, look at them! We're a hit!"

Meanwhile, Abby was in a trance. Completely and totally engulfed in infatuation, a visitor in a world she had never experienced. Periodically throughout the night, she would emerge from her office, grab a guy friend out of the audience who she knew to be a good dancer, drag him directly in front of the bandstand on the dance floor to do her thing to get Wayne's attention.

Bella leaned over to Robbie sitting at Hank's table and whispered, "Mom, I didn't know little sister had moves like that. I'm impressed. She's shakin' her booty!"

Robbie leaned back to Bella so Hank wouldn't hear and replied, "Abby's making her move, baby. She's going after her man, and I don't think Hank is happy at all."

"I noticed the look on Mr. Hank's face, Mom. I also noticed that Wayne isn't paying Abby any attention. A girl knows these things …"

The chaos only intensified at Tequilaville over the next two nights. Tito was wearing a path to Abby's office taking cash and credit card receipts and stashing them in the safe embedded in concrete in the floor. T-Bone kept an armed guard in her office at all times. Hank got congratulatory calls from the other club owners around the Lake since it was obvious that T-ville and Wayne Tyler topped the weekend charts and everyone knew it.

Unknown to Abby, each night when the band stopped playing there were several women waiting in their cars in the parking lot for Wayne to emerge from the club. He had his pick and every evening made some lucky woman's dream come true, at least for a night. In his back pocket he had so many business cards and phone numbers from just three performances on the stage that all he needed was a place to stash his clothes, which he did in a nearby pay-by-the-week motel. Sleeping arrangements were never a problem. At least he felt that he was keeping his part of the bargain with Hank and thought nothing of his erotic escapades. Wayne was back in his element.

At 4:30 on Monday morning, Abby was still in her office counting the money and getting the deposits ready for later in the day when the banks opened. Hank and T-Bone never left the club before Abby was finished and always walked her to her SUV. Hank peeked into her office and saw rows of bills, bound in rubber bands, all denominations stacked in neat piles on her desk. Credit card receipts were also bound and totaled. She was plugging in the final numbers to her Excel spreadsheet when Hank entered.

"How'd we do, Sweetie Pie?"

"What a birthday present, Daddy Hank. I've never counted so much cash in my life!" She looked tired but happy. "We did about $250 for the weekend."

"Thousand?!"

"Two hundred and fifty thousand bucks, Pop. We killed it!" Abby was beside herself in disbelief but the numbers didn't lie. "If we can keep just half of this going every weekend, have a great Memorial Day and 4th of July holidays, we may be able to pay off our bank loan by the end of the summer. "We're good to go in the bank account and I'm pleased, not only as your loving daughter and partner but as your CPA."

"Sorry we didn't have time for cake, Sweetie Pie. I guess it wasn't much of a birthday for you. I did get you a card." Hank handed Abby an oversized card and told her to read it later.

"It was a great birthday, Pop! Thanks for the card. I'm completely bushed. Going straight home and going to bed … Alone!"

Just after noon the next day, Abby's phone began playing *Wild Thing*.

"Hey, little sister, got time for some lunch and girl talk?"

"Absolutely, Bella. What about Classic Cafe in forty-five? I've got to stop by the bank."

After they ordered, Bella began the conversation. She had a property to show about an hour later. "Great opening, huh?"

"Better than great, sister. We killed it."

"Abby, I've got to admit, you've got some moves on the dance floor. You shook your booty good, girl. I like my new *coming of age* little sister. Welcome to my world of having fun. Where'd you learn to dance like that and how's the romance going with Wayne?"

Abby didn't respond right away. Now she knew why Bella wanted to have lunch, to catch up on her love life and all the details.

"I took dance lessons and there's not much of a romance, Bella. I couldn't get Wayne to notice me. It's like I didn't exist. But I think I know why …Am I not attractive, Bella? I want your honest, brutal opinion."

"Sister, you have a simplistic beauty that I envy. There, I finally said it. You're beautiful inside and out and any man with half a brain would be blessed to have you in his life. Key word here is half a brain. Not someone who just lives for the moment but a man that will honor a woman like you. You're the prettiest woman I know besides my Mom."

Bella took a bite of her club sandwich, washed it down with her glass of lime and water and sighed. Abby's eyes teared up and she realized just how much she really loved Bella, always had. They'd been so close for so many years.

"Abby, were you out there in the club when that girl threw a pair of panties on the stage?"

"No, but I heard about it."

"Okay, little sister, here's where the girl talk begins. The panties incident, what did that tell you?"

"I guess it told me that some girl chose a bad time and place to change her underwear." Bella almost choked on her sandwich and began laughing.

"You are so funny, little sister. Maybe you could audition as a comedian. Let me fill you in. What that act showed was that Wayne can have any woman in that audience. Those girls were in a feeding frenzy and Wayne was the main course. Get my drift?"

"Bella, Wayne just needs a good woman to straighten him out. I'm that woman. I knew from the minute I laid eyes on him, before he sang, played or performed. He's the one I've been waiting for. I can't explain why, I just know it."

"Are you blind to what's going on Abby? Wayne's going to rip your heart out, and I don't want to see you hurt. I love you, sister!"

"Thanks, Bella. I'm not completely stupid. I've got a plan, as always, you know me. Next Sunday night I'm making my move. I'm putting an end to his sleeping around."

"You'd have to pull a *Bobbit* to do that little sister."

"Maybe not. I think I'll just love him through it. Wish me luck."

"You're going to need a lot more than luck! Guard your heart. That's your big sister's best advice."

The following weekend was much like the opening. The crowd on the Lake continued to favor Tequilaville over the other clubs, due in large part to Wayne Tyler, who brought the ladies into the club in droves. Where there's women, there's men who show up with their boats, their toys and their cash.

The success of Tequilaville was unprecedented and beyond everyone's wildest expectations. All the employees were happy making money and Hank was getting used to his new surroundings, taking a break from electrical work and settling in to being a club owner. The only one not completely happy was Abby, but she had a plan to make that happen and it was about to unfold.

Late Sunday night, just before last call, with a thinning crowd consisting mostly of friends and a few hangers on, Abby walked onto the stage, spoke briefly to the band and grabbed the microphone.

Pointing into the corner she said, "Daddy Hank, this one's for you …"

Prearranged, Scott Wood relieved *South's* keyboard player and opened Hank's favorite song, "Sara", by Fleetwood Mac. Wayne just backed off and played rhythm guitar. He had no idea what was taking place and was just as confused as everyone else.

No one had ever heard Abby sing but no one was going to stop her either. With a low-toned, raspy voice, she got into the lyrics and carried a pretty good tune. She was making her move and sending a message to Daddy Hank. Abby had changed up the words to the song.

"Wait a minute, Daddy, Stay with me a while

Said you'd give me light, but never told me about the fire

I'm drowning in the sea of love, where everyone would love to drown

And now it's gone, doesn't matter anymore

You've built your house so trust me, Daddy, trust me."

The usual buzz in the room came to a complete stop. Bella and Robbie were sitting in the booth with Hank and looked over at him to see his reaction. He sat steel-faced trying to prepare himself for what he knew was coming.

"I think I met my match … Wayne was s-i-n-g-i-n-g

And u-n-d-o-i-n-g, and undoing … Undoing the laces, Undoing the laces …"

Hank looked away. He was getting Abby's message loud and clear and he didn't like it. He remembered what Robbie had said to him just weeks ago, "You can keep Wayne away from Abby, but you can't keep Abby away from Wayne …"

Abby continued her song, her message …

"Said Daddy, I'm the poet in your heart

Never change, never stop …"

When Abby finished the song, she stepped down from the stage, walked over to Daddy Hank's table with a determined look on her face and asked everyone if she could have a private moment with her Dad. Robbie and Bella slid out of the booth and walked over to the bar. Bella knew that something was going down but had no clue.

"Pop, I just wanted to tell you how much you mean to me and how much I love you." She began to sniffle. "I know I'm the poet in your heart, Daddy, and always will be, but I need a poet in my heart. There's a hole in it that you can't fill … Do you remember telling me about the first night that you met Mom and how the world stood still?"

"Yes, baby, I remember."

Abby was softly crying now and couldn't hold back. In between sobs she gathered her words, trying to put them in a row.

"In my whole life, Daddy Hank, that has never happened to me. I couldn't understand what you felt when you told me about meeting Mom and the world standing still. Now I do. The moment that Wayne walked into Tequilaville, my entire world stood still, completely frozen, and I couldn't understand what was happening to me. I just knew he was the one, good or bad. There was no reason to it, Pop."

Hank now had a tear in his eye and reminisced about the night he had met Abigail. Abby had nailed the feeling down perfectly in her words.

"And now, Daddy, the hard part. It's time for me to undo the laces and try to fill that part of me that's missing in my life. I'm taking Wayne home with me tonight and I don't want you to say a word."

She wiped the tears streaming down her cheeks, reached over and gave Daddy Hank a long, hard hug and kissed him on the cheek. Hank held Abby tight and said nothing.

Abby walked over to Tito, told him to give the cash receipts to Daddy Hank, walked back up to the stage and grabbed Wayne's thin, black leather tie and led him out to the parking lot. On the way, Wayne glanced over at Hank, who just turned away.

Bella, always demanding the last word, faced her Mom and said, "Bold move! This is going to be interesting …"

8

EMOTIONS
I'LL KILL YOU!

Wayne awoke the next morning to the smell of bacon and eggs frying in the kitchen of Abby's comfortable but simple home. It was a morning-after situation that he'd avoided with all of the other notches on his bed post. He was a firm believer of no good-byes, 'I'll call you later' or 'By the way, what's your name again?' He hated the confrontations and had always left early in the morning from all of his other one-night-stands. Now he found himself in a situation he didn't know how to avoid or even if he wanted to avoid it.

As he lay in Abby's bed thinking, waking up, Abby came into the bedroom dressed only in a robe and handed him a cup of coffee. She never wore much make-up so Wayne wasn't completely repelled by her tossed brown hair and being a bit vain himself, felt uncomfortable for her to see him all disheveled.

"Thanks for the coffee, Abby. You're an angel."

"Wait till you taste my bacon and eggs with biscuits and honey, Honey, you'll feel like a new man." Abby smiled a sheepish sexy little smile, not too sure of herself and what she would say next. They hadn't talked much the night before and she was a novice at one-nighters. She didn't have a clue what was going on in Wayne's mind. "How do you feel after last night?"

Wayne stuttered and searched for words, "Uh, I feel great but I gotta tell you, Abby, I'm a bit confused."

"About what? I'm not the first girl that took you home, now am I?"

"To be honest, Abby, you're the first girl that's taken me home after her Dad, not to mention my employer, forbid me to see her. Did you see the look in Hank's eyes when we walked out together last night?"

"I figured he'd said that. Why do you think I sang a song to him and had a talk with Daddy Hank before I made my move?"

"You made a move, alright, Abby. I'm just wondering why. I mean, last night was wonderful and special, just very unexpected …"

"Daddy Hank thinks there's no man in the world good enough for me, Wayne. He's always been the man in my life and probably isn't willing to give that up to anyone. But even though he's a wonderful man and father, he can't be everything to me. I told him that."

Wayne got dressed, sat down at the small bar area in the kitchen while Abby served up breakfast. She was looking at Wayne with puppy dog eyes, a look that he was very familiar with as she watched him eat.

"And do you think I can be the one to give you everything that's missing in your life? You hardly know me, Abby."

"You're right, I don't. Tell me about Wayne Tyler. Where'd you grow up, who were your parents? What made Wayne who Wayne is?"

"I really don't want to go back there, Abby. It's not a pretty picture."

"I've got skeletons in my closet, too, Wayne. I burned a house down when I was a little girl!"

"Ooh! So you were an evil little kid, huh?"

"No, just abused in a foster home, but that's my story. Tell me yours. I won't judge you."

"Okay, you asked for it. I'll give you the short form. I was born in Austin, Texas. My dad was a drunken construction worker who came home bombed every night. He slapped me across the room for the first time when I was four. My mom would try and protect me by taking his blows before he got to me. Both of us feared him. One night he killed a man in a bar room brawl, went to prison and I never heard from him after that."

"What about your mom, Wayne? Is she still living?"

"She raised me by herself until I was twelve years old. Her name was Tara. She worked two jobs and eventually came down with cancer. She didn't have insurance or money to pay for treatment so State health workers would come by our apartment and give her shots of morphine to ease her pain but her pain and suffering got worse. I couldn't stand to hear her cry out in the night so I hit the streets, bought some morphine from a drug dealer and gave her a full syringe shot of it. I held her in my arms as she passed on…" Wayne sniffled, tears forming in his eyes.

"By then I mostly became a street kid and hung out near 6th Street where all the clubs and musicians play in Austin. I didn't want to go home, too many bad memories. I met an old black blues player named Mr. Elroy who taught me how to play guitar and somehow took me in when my mom died. We literally lived in a one room shack in the poor section of town, not far from 6th Street. I never knew when they buried my mom, I wasn't at her funeral and had no clue how Mr. Elroy kept me in school without the Austin authorities finding out. We just went to my apartment, got my clothes and left to go back to his shack."

Abby wasn't going to interrupt Wayne's story. She knew first-hand how difficult it must have been for him to tell it. She poured him another cup of coffee and he continued. His story just made her love him even more. They were kindred spirits.

"Man, could that old man play a guitar and sing the blues! He was living it. That's where I got my passion for music. We'd play after I got home from school and I'd go with him to some of his gigs on 6th Street when he wasn't playing for tips on the street. Everyone loved him and so did I. He was like a Mr. Bo Jangles, a grandfather to me and read to me out of his old battered Bible. I learned a little about the Bible but what I really wanted to learn was to play and sing his songs.

"Abby, what was odd about the whole encounter with Mr. Elroy was that I never saw him sleep. He gave me his bed and it was always clean. Sometimes I'd wake up at four in the morning and he would be sitting in his broken down rocking chair reading from his old Bible, sometimes out loud.

"One day right after I graduated high school, I came home and he was gone. His things were there, his guitar was there but he was just gone ..."

"Wayne, I feel so bad for you. How'd you survive? How did you live after that?"

"I started playing his gigs in some of the little clubs where they knew him. Of course they'd known me from an early age since I would stand outside while he played before I came of age to enter the clubs. I met all the club owners and knew them by name. Mr. Elroy taught me his songs, his music and I had to support myself. Eventually, I signed up for junior college to pursue a degree in music but I guess that survival was more pressing than my call for education. I dropped out before I finished my second year and began playing gigs full time. The people liked me and I made a living. In short, that was my childhood. Not a pretty story, but I survived and later went to London to learn more music and returned home and here I am ..."

"Wayne, did you ever get any therapy for what happened in your childhood?" Abby was deeply involved in his story and admired him to have the courage to tell her. She realized he had never shared this with anyone.

"Yeah, Abby, my therapy was all the shots of tequila and mugs of beer that people would buy me. My therapy was the applause of the crowd when

I sang and played. Everyone went crazy and the ladies especially liked me. They would buy me things and take me home …"

"So, Mr. Tyler, you pretty much fell into a lifestyle as an American gigolo, huh?"

"Pretty much."

"Wayne, has anyone ever loved you?"

"Yeah, my mom loved me and Mr. Elroy loved me. Beyond that I can't remember much love since. As a matter of fact, Abby, I'll tell you right now, I don't really know what love is … So there you have it, the story of Wayne Tyler. That's the best I got. Want to kick me out now?"

"Thanks for opening up to me, Wayne. Your story is heart breaking. No, I'm not kicking you out and this isn't an ultimatum. We had a night. I'd like to get to know you and you're welcome to stay or you're welcome to leave. Your choice."

Wayne put his fork down, took a long drink of coffee, sighed and looked straight into Abby's eyes.

"Let's get back to the 'why,' Abby. Why me? Why now?"

"I've got my reasons, Wayne. I happen to believe in you."

"And, what do you believe?"

"I believe that you' re a very talented singer and musician who's never had his fifteen minutes of fame. I believe you've had a tough life and been running from all the pain of it. I also believe you can start over, right here, right now with me."

"So you want to 'fix' me huh, Ms. Smarty Pants?" Wayne said jokingly, trying to lighten up the conversation.

"No, I don't want to 'fix' you. I just want to be with you and help you realize your gifts and talents."

"And how are you going to do that?"

"I've got some ideas. Do you ever write your own songs, Wayne? You know, singing and performing your own material. Seems like your life's had enough ups and downs to make for some really interesting songs. Scott can do the arrangements and *South* can back you up."

"So you're taking me in like some stray dog that needs a home, huh? You don't strike me as a tree-hugging 'save the animals' type." He handed his cup over for Abby to fill up again, hoping that he hadn't offended her. He smiled as he talked.

Abby laughed. "Nope, not me. I'm just offering you a new direction and someone to share it with. No obligations."

"What an offer. A bed, breakfast and a future. Great concept, pretty lady. I've never been much of a song writer and don't have a clue what I would write about. Got any ideas on that one?"

"Of course I do. Write a new song *for* me or *about* me. I'll be your inspiration." Abby giggled with a bit of a blush.

"Abby's song, coming right up! Give me about five minutes to jot it down. It'll be a big hit!" Wayne was being facetious and Abby loved it. They laughed together while she started to put the dishes in the sink.

Abby reached over, gave Wayne a peck on the lips and presented him with a key to her front door.

"Wayne, Rome wasn't built in a day. You're welcome to stay or to leave. If you leave, please lock up and just put the key under the front door mat. I'll understand. If you decide to stay, you may want to check out of that flea-bag motel you're staying in and move your stuff over here.

"I've cleared out room in the spare bedroom closet for you. I gotta get dressed and take care of some things. If you're here when I get back," she gently kissed him on the cheek, "Great. If you're not, I'll see you at Tequilaville on Thursday."

"No, wait, Abby! You can't put this on me. We've got to talk a little more before you leave."

A million things were going through Wayne's mind. The night had been special and he knew there was something different about her. He'd never known the compassion and loving nature that Abby had shared with him. She had bared her soul, her body and her affections, and he was having a difficult time trying to comprehend this woman and his situation.

"Baby, you're special. I know that. What I don't know is what I'm feeling and if I can handle this…"

"Wayne, I'm not too good at being tactful. But I'm not trying to trap you either. My home can be like a prison to you or it can be a palace. Either way, the door's not locked and you have a key. I don't know too much about relationships, especially one as complicated as this could be. I just want to give it a chance at a better life for both of us."

Wayne held her in his arms and said nothing for a couple of minutes, thinking about what could be, what had happened the night before and the consequences if their relationship didn't work out.

"Okay, Abby. I'll move my stuff in and give it a try. But I want to make one thing clear. I don't know if I can do this in a way that suits you. I've been a loveless vagabond most of my life…"

"Wayne, do you remember that old Al Wilson song entitled, *The Snake?*"

"No, I don't remember that one, Abby."

"The song's about a lady that found a half frozen snake, took it in and nursed it back to health. When the snake recovered, it bit her. She asked the snake why and he said, 'You knew I was a snake when you took me in.' I know who you are now, Wayne, I just don't know what you can become and you don't either. "There are things that a relationship can take and things it can't. I guess we'll have to test our limits. Your limits of being in a monogamous relationship and my limits of tolerance. That's all I can tell you. You're free to stay and I'm free to kick you out. Incidentally, I'm cooking a pot roast for tonight. Bring your appetite, big boy. Then, we'll sing in the moonlight…"

For the next two weeks Abby walked two feet off the floor. She was happy, giddy, enjoying her new infatuation, hoping that this undefined relationship would turn into love and that Wayne would turn from his hedonistic ways. Everyone noticed the change in her 'driven' nature. Her smiles and laughter were noted by all her friends, sometimes to the point of being sickening. Abby was enjoying every second of her new life with Wayne.

More and more people were coming into Tequilaville during the four days that they were open each week. Spring was turning into summer and all the fun that Clear Lake brought to its visitors. The club continued to be a huge success as Wayne and *South* became the main buzz on the lake. Scott Wood had the new CDs and DVDs of their grand opening on sale in the gift shop and sales were booming, adding an extra stream of revenue for the club that no one had anticipated.

Hank kept an eye on Abby and she made a special effort to let him know just how happy her life had become. Hank still hadn't warmed up to Wayne and kept him at arm's distance, letting him know in no uncertain terms that Hank Hawkins was still the hoss and the boss of Tequilaville.

Bella was at work when her phone rang. "Hattie! How's life at the Space Agency?" she asked in her usual commanding voice.

"Did you hear about the explosion in the lunch room at NASA? Can't wait to give you details. Let's have lunch, *The Dutchman* at 11:30 a.m.?"

"Great, see you there, Hattie. Was anyone hurt?"

"Some hearts were broken … I'll tell you about it over lunch."

Bella couldn't wait to hear what happened inside the Top Secret Space Agency lunch room. Things that happened inside NASA usually stayed at NASA since everything was classified.

After they ordered their seafood salads, sitting next to the glass walls overlooking the channel that led from Clear Lake into Galveston Bay with a constant stream of boats coming and going, Hattie began her story.

"Bella, I'm not going to mention any names but it's important for me to pass this on to you for Abby's sake. I know how much you care for her."

"What does Abby have to do with NASA?" Bella mused, waiting eagerly for all the details.

"Yesterday," Hattie took a drink of her lemon water, she never drank alcohol, "I had lunch with my little 'lunch bunch' consisting of four of us girls at NASA. One of the girls couldn't wait to tell the rest of us about her new boyfriend, Wayne Tyler. Half way through her lurid love story, her best friend, also sitting at the lunch table, broke into tears, then literally attacked her best friend because she, too, had a story to tell about her new found love and you guessed it, it was Wayne Tyler. He'd slept with both of 'em. It was a cat-fight of biblical proportions … the fur was flying!"

"Oh my, Hattie. Was either girl physically hurt?"

"Not physically. Hey, these girls are NASA engineers and astrophysicists, not fighters. Only their hearts and friendships were shattered. It was pretty tragic.

Since Wayne is living with Abby and obviously cheating on her. I thought you'd want to know."

Bella was embarrassed for Abby. It showed by the expression on her face sitting in front of Hattie. Bella's appetite seemed to go away. She had to come up with a plan to save her sister from any further embarrassment or heartache.

"Thanks for the heads-up, Hattie." Bella looked out the window at the boats passing by. "Abby's somewhat naive at relationships and she's absolutely blind to what Wayne is doing to her. She's way too smart not to know what's going on with Wayne and his wandering eyes but for some unknown reason, she's not doing anything about it and that's what worries me."

"You think Abby knows?"

"Of course she knows. Any woman can smell the perfume of another woman's scent, cut through a man's many excuses and see all the tell-tale signs. Abby's too analytical not to notice. She just refuses to kick him out. She's being way too tolerant and I've got to help her."

"How? Are you going to tell Abby what I told you?" Hattie had no clue what was going on in the worldly mind of Bella but she couldn't wait to hear her plan.

"Hattie, it wouldn't do any good. Abby's not going to listen to me or anyone else. For some reason Wayne's special to her. She told me that he made her world stand still. She's going through that blind and deaf stage in her love affair."

"So what's your plan?"

Bella was undecided whether to tell Hattie the details of her plan. She didn't want it getting back to Abby or anyone else. Finally, she decided to give Hattie some insight.

"The only person Abby couldn't tolerate Wayne sleeping with is me!"

"Bella, you wouldn't! She'll hate you!"

"Watch me!" Fire was blazing from Bella's eyes. "I would if it'll save my little sister's heart from being ripped out of her chest. I care nothing about Wayne and I can take the heat. Abby will eventually get over it, but I've got to stop this charade in its tracks before she's permanently damaged. I want Abby to love again but not with a gigolo like Wayne Tyler. She deserves better than that."

For the next two weeks Bella watched Wayne's routine, his coming and going, when he was at Abby's house alone and when he left. She already knew Abby's structured routine very well and had a key to her home. They'd exchanged keys years ago. Bella began planning her moves to save Abby.

After rehearsing with *South* at the club and getting ready for the weekend, Wayne drove his old van back to Abby's place. As he steered into her drive way, he noticed his clothes tossed out on the front lawn along with his suitcase and other personal items. Abby's SUV was there so he knew she was at home.

He had no idea what was going on and thought that maybe she'd found out about one of his little one-nighters from a few weeks ago. He took a deep breath and walked into the house.

"Are you re-arranging furniture today, honey?"

"Don't you 'honey' me you sorry no-good, cheating, narcissistic, hedonistic, gigolo son-of-a-b ... !"

"Whoa, whoa, Abby. Slow down! And leave my mother out of this. I don't even know what some of those words mean. You got time to tell me what this is all about?"

"Here's what this is about!" Abby held up an earring that she'd found in her ruffled bed that she knew belonged to her sister, Bella.

Wayne was caught completely off guard. He had no idea whose earring Abby was holding up or its significance.

"Are you mad about losing an earring, baby? I'll buy you another set if that'll make you happy. Why are my clothes out on the front lawn?"

"Because I'm kicking your sorry ass out of my house!" Abby was livid and hurt.

"Abby, I'm going to tell you the truth when I say I have no clue what's going on with you. Why are you so mad at me?"

Abby picked up a salt shaker in the kitchen and threw it at Wayne. He dodged it. One item after another came flying past his face. She wanted to take him out with some of her karate moves but was just too hurt and too furious to do it.

"It wasn't enough for you to fool around with some of the local chippies at the club, was it Wayne? You knew that I'd just look away and bear it like I have for the past few weeks, trying to make our relationship work. Do you think I didn't know about each and every one? Do you actually think I'm that stupid or oblivious to what's going on?"

"Abby, I told you I'd try, and I made no promises, remember?"

"Yeah, I remember very well. I remember every word of our conversation. I also remember telling you that I believed in you, that I love you and that I wanted you in my life. I remember kissing you, our long conversations, our intimacy … Didn't that mean anything to you?"

"Of course it does, Abby. I haven't slept with anyone else in two weeks. I'm trying to make this work! I'm not sure exactly what love is but when I figure it out I think it'll have your name on it. Now that's as close as I can get to telling you how I feel. Abby, I'm crazy about you and that's the truth."

"Then explain this!" She held up the earring again. "It belongs to Bella, my sister. I gave her these earrings last year for her birthday. So just how did they end up in my bed?!"

"Abby, I'll swear on a stack of Bibles that I have no idea how they wound up in our bed. I have not slept with your sister! You can either believe that or not. Why don't you just pick up the phone and call Bella and ask her?"

"Be careful, Wayne. Swearing a lie on a stack of Bibles could put you in danger of hell itself. And I wouldn't give Bella the satisfaction of a call. I'd almost expect that out of Bella but I would've never, in a million years, think that you could betray me by sleeping with my own sister. That's sick! "You've cut me in half and ripped my heart out! I have nothing left for you. That's the last straw. I can't ignore this, so get the hell out of my house and take your crap with you.

"Never, ever look at me again. Never call me, never text me, never get close to me or I *will* kill you and that's the total truth that's lacking in this conversation!"

"Abby, I got your message loud and clear but don't preach that heaven and hell stuff to me. I don't believe in it. Hell is right here and right now. The rest is malarkey. If that's the way you feel and won't believe anything I say, Adios. I'm outta here!"

Later that Wednesday night Bella got a call from her mom, Robbie.

"Hi Mom."

"I just had a conversation with Abby. She was crying her eyes out. Get your sorry butt over here, right now! I'm about to disown you!" Click.

Uh oh, Bella thought to herself, *here comes the heat.* She arrived at her mom's condo a few minutes later and knocked on her door.

"Mom?"

Robbie started slapping Bella with both hands the minute she closed the door behind her. Slap! Slap! Slap! Robbie was furious and unstoppable in her furious undaunted aggression toward her own daughter.

"I can't believe you'd do that to Abby!" Robbie screamed between the constant slaps. She didn't give Bella a chance to respond, talk or defend herself. She just kept up the attack.

"Mom! Listen to me! I didn't do it!" Bella was trying her best to defend herself, but knew she couldn't fight back against her own mother.

"Sure you did! I know you too well."

After repeated, unremitting blows, Bella was lying on the floor in a fetal position, reeling from Robbie's unrelenting rage. Her face was already beginning to swell and she was crying terribly; so was Robbie. A moment passed while Robbie re-grouped and walked away from Bella lying in the middle of the condo, Robbie accidentally kicked her foot into the coffee table. It was breaking her heart to even think about disowning her own daughter but even she had a line that couldn't be crossed and Bella had just crossed that line that no decent person should ever cross. Robbie was confused, exhausted, devastated and ashamed of her own actions and went over to sit down on the couch, burying her head in her lap, letting it all out, holding her foot. It was probably broken.

Bella cried silently on the floor, nursing her swollen face and trying to get a word in edgewise. She picked herself up, walked over to the couch and sat down beside Robbie.

"Mom, I didn't do it! I just made Abby think I'd slept with Wayne. I'd never hurt her like that. I had to save her and that's the truth!"

"You did sleep with Wayne and do not ever lie to me again, Bella!" Robbie was trying her best to stop the lying habits that Bella had displayed most of her life.

"Abby told me that she found one of your earrings in her ruffled bed, one of the earrings that she'd given you for your birthday last year. She was devastated and deeply hurt. Now how are you going to wiggle out of that one, young lady?"

"I put that earring in her bed, Mom, when both Abby and Wayne were away from the house so Abby would know exactly who it belonged to. I did it on purpose! I knew if she thought that I'd slept with Wayne, she would finally kick his sorry butt out of her house and her life. She knew about all the women he was cheating with but wouldn't do anything about it. Wayne continued to make a complete fool out of her and I had to stop it. I couldn't stand it any longer, Mom."

"You stopped it alright. When Abby called me a little while ago, she told me that she'd just now kicked him out. By the way, does Hank know?"

"Mom, no one knows except Hattie and she didn't know any details. I had to keep it a secret for my plan to work. Please forgive me, Mom! I love you and Abby and Mr. Hank so much ..."

Robbie was finally convinced that Bella was telling her the truth and reached over and pulled Bella close to her. They sat on the couch, crying, consoling each other as the night slipped away.

"Bella, please forgive your mother. I was judging you wrongly and that was worse than what I thought you'd done."

"So," Bella cracked a smile, looking at her Mom, "You're not going to disown me?"

"Well ... not today little girl! I'll always love you and I'll always be your mother, no matter what. You look terrible; does it hurt?"

"Of course it hurts, Mom. You know how easily I bruise. You're gonna owe me a facial at the spa to get rid of all these little anger marks you put on me. I probably won't be presentable to go to work for at least a week ..."

With that remark, Robbie and Bella were close again, despite the hurts and anger. Robbie vowed to Bella that no one would come between them ever again.

She hobbled over and got a wet washrag and wiped Bella's face, kissing her cheeks in between sobs.

"We've got to go down to Hank's place and tell him or he's going to hate both of us," Robbie said.

"Mom, do you think Abby called Mr. Hank and told him already?"

"Oh God, Bella, we can't take that chance. Come, go with me."

Bella helped her mom down the corridor to Hank's condo and knocked on the door, without calling ahead. Despite their knocking, there was no immediate response. Robbie could see Hank's truck in the parking lot and knew that he was at home.

"Hank! Hank! This is Robbie and Bella," she said repeatedly. "We've got to talk to you. Please answer the door."

Finally, they heard Hank's voice. "Now's not a real good time. We can talk later. Please go away."

Robbie looked at Bella. "This is not good, baby. Hank knows. He's gonna hate both of us until we talk to him and explain things. I'm worried about what he may do to Wayne, also. If he finds him, he'll kill him."

"How's your foot, Mom?"

"I think I broke it. Time for a quick trip to the ER, baby. Help me to the car."

At 3:15 a.m., Thursday, Hank was awakened by a call on his cell. Caller ID read: Clear Lake Police Department.

"Hank Hawkins."

"Mr. Hawkins, this is Officer LeGrano of the Clear Lake PD. I do some off-duty traffic control for your club and was doing a drive by and noticed someone sitting out on your back patio. I'm standing here with him now. He's pretty drunk and I can't let him drive. His license says his name is Wayne Tyler. As a courtesy, you can either come down and take responsibility for him or I can lock him up for Public Intoxication and Trespassing. Your call, Mr. Hawkins."

Hank thanked the officer, told him he'd be right down and would take responsibility for Wayne. He pulled on his clothes, grabbed his hat and headed toward Tequilaville. His anger became more intense the closer he got. He kept telling himself, *You can't kill him*, the officer would know. When he arrived at the club, he saw the officer's cruiser sitting in the front parking lot and walked around back to the patio area. The dock lights were on so it wasn't completely dark.

Hank viewed Officer LeGrano standing over Wayne who was plopped down in a chair in front of one of the patio tables with some car keys, a spiral notebook, a pen and about two dozen wadded up pieces of paper strewed around the floor of the dock. There was a half-full bottle of rot-gut tequila sitting on the table in front of Wayne. Officer LeGrano's description of Wayne was correct. Hank could see that Wayne was drunker than a nine-eyed skunk.

"Officer LeGrano, I'm Hank Hawkins, owner of the club. I'll take care of Mr. Tyler and make sure he doesn't drive. Thank you."

The officer left the premises, leaving Hank alone with Wayne.

"I should've had the officer charge you with littering. What's with all the wadded up pieces of paper?"

Wayne didn't want to look Hank in the face, grabbed the bottle and took another defiant drink and said, "Oh … I was just trying to write Abby a new song … couldn't find the words. Probably wasn't meant to be …"

"You're pathetic! You cheat on my daughter and think you can get her back with a song?"

Wayne knew how much Hank detested him, almost from day one. He slowly got to his feet, staggered in front of Hank with his feet spread wide apart to maintain his balance. He'd never been one to walk away from a fight and he knew there was going to be one.

"Hank, Abby didn't listen to me, maybe you will. I didn't do what she accused me of with Bella. That's the truth!"

"You wouldn't know the truth if it hit you in the face, which is exactly what I want to do right now!" Hank's anger was getting to the point of rage.

Wayne was still staggering but put both of his hands behind his back, raised his chin and said, "Take your best shot, Hank. You need it and I deserve it. Go ahead, hit me!"

"Don't tempt me, scumbag. You're not worth the skin off my knuckles."

"Then you're a yellow-bellied, spineless daddy who won't defend his daughter's honor. I spit on you!" Which he did.

That was too much for Hank to take. He sent a crashing right fist to Wayne's left cheek and nose knocking Wayne to the deck. Wayne tried to get up but couldn't as the blood gushed from his shattered nose. He'd never been hit so hard in his life and between the booze and the beating there was no use in trying to get up and take another blow from a man who was trained to kill. Hank yelled for him to stand up.

When it was clear that Wayne was done, Hank reached over and took his key ring off the patio table.

"I promised the officer that I wouldn't let you drive. I'm taking your keys. You can stagger back to whatever hole you crawled out of. Contact T-Bone to get your gear. You're fired! Now get the hell off my property and don't ever let me see your face around here again!"

As Hank returned to his truck, his right hand began to swell. *Damn, I probably broke it,* Hank said to himself and headed toward the emergency room at Clear Lake General.

Wayne finally picked himself up from the deck floor, wiping his gushing nose every few seconds. He wanted to run, to get away from people, life and bad situations. He was good at running, he'd been running for a long time, avoiding reality. For some reason 'Redfish Island' came to mind in his stupor-state. He'd been there several times on the boats of late-night partiers who just wanted a place to drink and have fun in the Gulf of Mexico. It was a favorite spot for many. He remembered the compass setting and knew it was only about fifteen minutes out in the Gulf.

Besides "Mutual Funz 2", there was a twenty-five-foot, red and white Sea Ray called the "Maui Blush" docked at the pier. It belonged to his bass player's dad who often tied up at the club. Wayne grabbed the bottle of tequila, staggered over and got into the boat. The keys were gone but that wouldn't be a problem. He'd hotwired his beat-up van many times when he habitually lost his own keys. He reached under the dash, pulled out some wires and fired up the "Maui Blush".

The night sky was clear and full of stars. There was a full moon that added light and pierced the darkness. The water was cold and calm as he putted his way out of Clear Lake, past the rows of restaurants, took a right when he got out into the bay and gave the boat more power. The sea spray felt good on his swollen face. Fifteen minutes later, Wayne could see the lights of a single, large sail boat anchored near Redfish Island which was a half-moon shaped, barren little island that barely showed above the surface of the water. No one had told him about the reef on the right side of the island.

As he reduced speed to about fifteen knots, Wayne heard the grinding sound of the shell reef rubbing underneath the fiberglass hull of the Sea Ray. The front half of the boat was up on the reef in about six inches of water. The back side of the boat was in fourteen feet of water. Trying to get off the reef, Wayne put the boat's engine in reverse and tried to dislodge it. No luck. The boat was listing to one side.

Ain't that great! What else can go wrong? Wayne thought to himself. He really didn't know where this little trip was going and now he was stuck. The lone sail boat was too far away to yell for help, so Wayne grabbed the bottle of tequila, sat down at the back of the boat and drank.

When the bottle was empty and he had no reasoning left, Wayne staggered up over the stern of the boat onto the ski ramp, threw the empty bottle as far as he could, then with a defiant gesture skyward, followed the bottle into the cold dark waters of the bay. The chill of the water took his breath away as he sank deeper into the murky depths. He really didn't care anymore, there was nothing to go back to and he made no attempt to save himself. Wayne would end his life on his own terms, no one else's.

Seconds after he entered the water, plummeting deeper into the cold depths, giving up his last breath, a tornadic water spout formed from a cloudless sky directly over Wayne's entry point into the water. Time on earth was instantly and divinely frozen as all time stood still. The hearts of every living creature on earth were immediately suspended between beats as the spout sucked up the soul of Wayne Tyler and delivered it to a place of reflection, judgment, trials and tribulations, a place called Between, located somewhere in the heavenly realms …

9

BETWEEN
BETWEEN LIFE AND DEATH?
HEAVEN AND HELL?

Wayne regained consciousness in a bright misty place that had no depth, nor height nor width. He floated in a mist that seemed to have no end. He was not wet or gasping for breath; he was completely sober and was temporarily blinded by the light that surrounded him. Wayne covered his eyes while curled in a fetal position. Slowly his senses returned.

"The light … too bright … I can't see!"

A figure began to form in the mist in front of him. Wayne saw a distorted image of a being that was over fifteen feet high, had hair like gold, eyes like flames, skin of shining bronze and a face like glazed porcelain. Wayne was immediately awe struck and scared almost to the point of death. The image spoke to Wayne in a thunderous, booming voice:

"Fear not! Your eyes will adjust. How do you feel?"

Tightening his fetal position, squinting, Wayne slowly lifted his head toward the voice.

"Who are you? What are you? Where am I?"

"My name is Gordon. You're … well … let's say that you are in a place called Between."

"A place called Between..? Between what? Am I dead?"

"No. You're very much alive."

Wayne looked around the white mist and squinted to make out the brilliant figure that formed before his eyes. He tried to feel the touch of his own arm with his hand to determine if this was a dream or even a bad nightmare.

"But ... where am I. I can't feel my body. Are you sure I'm not dead? Who are you? What do you want?"

"What do you want, Wayne?"

"I want to know just what I asked you ..."

"Fear not. All is well."

"Like hell it is ..."

"Truly, Wayne, you are not in hell ... yet."

In his defiant search for immediate answers, Wayne's fear began to subside somewhat. He was completely freaked out at his situation, his surroundings and the huge being with the booming voice looming over him.

"And what the fu…? What the fu..? Why won't my words come out?!"

"Blasphemies and vulgarities are not allowed in this heavenly realm. You'll have to search your vocabulary for other words, Wayne."

To get Wayne's full attention and help him focus on the questions, Gordon elevated his stature to fifty feet tall. Then, in an instant, he reduced his height to one foot tall and immediately resumed his normal fifteen-foot height. He reached out his hand to Wayne. He completely got his attention.

"Touch my hand!"

Wayne's mind was working overtime trying to comprehend the multiple changes in stature by the being who was speaking to him. The situation and setting did not compute in his mind and he couldn't imagine what was happening. Wayne reluctantly leaned toward the hand of Gordon and touched him. It felt like soft, burnished bronze.

"How do you feel now, Wayne?"

"When I touched your hand ... I felt ... I felt ... better. I feel ... I can't describe what I feel."

"Comforted? Warm? Loved?"

"Yeah, that's it! That's exactly how I feel ... I'm not dead?"

"No, Wayne, you're not dead."

"You said I'm at a place called Between ... between what? Life and death, heaven and hell? Day and night?"

"Very good, Wayne, You've described this realm perfectly."

"Are you some kind of space alien zombie that zapped me with a tractor beam and whisked me away and beamed me up with some sort of a gamma ray? What are you?"

"No, I'm not an alien as you describe. I am a servant to the Almighty."

"Like an angel or something?"

"Or something ..."

"I don't believe in all of that *Almighty*, angel stuff!"

"Belief is one of the many reasons you're here, Wayne. What *do* you believe in?"

"I believe in myself. I believe in reality. I believe in logic. This isn't reality or logical. You're playing mind games with me … It's some kind of a dream."

"Not a dream, Wayne. You touched my hand. How's this concept of reality working out for you?"

"Not logical, not real!" It seemed like all of the compartments of Wayne's mind were opened at the same time. He couldn't think straight. He was confused about his surroundings. Everything going through his mind was complete chaos.

"Wayne, logic has limits. Begin using wisdom and reasoning, they have no limits."

Wayne had no answers for Gordon, only more questions.

"What's your name again? Why can't I see you clearly? What time is it?"

"I told you, my name is Gordon. You'll see me clearly when you're ready to see me. And, as for time … Time is so relative, Wayne. Let's just say it's a time out for time. Beyond your mortal realm on earth, there is no time."

"Why am I here in this *between*? I'm having trouble wrapping my arms around this *no time* thing. I can't imagine that."

"Pay no attention to time. At this moment, throughout the entire universe, time remains frozen. Even on earth, everything is standing still. There are no heartbeats, waves splashing, wind blowing or birds flying. They are all suspended until you make certain decisions, Wayne, decisions about your life, or what's left of it."

"What's left of it?! What decisions? What are you talking about?"

Wayne was in a complete state of confusion, not knowing exactly where he was, what this giant of a being was and he still wasn't convinced that he was alive … or dead.

"What's the last thing you remember before coming to visit me?"

"I didn't come here … to visit you. I don't even know where *here* is."

"Think, Wayne. What's the last thing you remember before your divine appointment?"

Wayne began to turn and look at his surroundings, trying once again to make out the misty figure that was speaking to him. His mind flooded with questions. He had never heard of anyone talking about what he was experiencing. There was no sound basis to what was happening. He tried to remember.

"Uh … Let's see … I remember Abby kicking me out for something I didn't do. I, uh, remember trying to write her a new song to make up with her … I remember Hank flooring me and firing me. Umm, I got drunk on tequila, boated out to Red Fish Island …"

"Keep going, Wayne, all of it. Remember!"

"I remember feeling cold … wet. I remember darkness …"

"You've lived most of your life in darkness, Wayne. That's another reason that you're here. Keep thinking, remembering. Where were you just before you arrived here? Where is your body, Wayne?"

"My body?! Oh god, I'm trying, Gordon. I'm not sure that I want to remember this part."

"Wayne, your soul is here. Your body is where you left it on earth. Now think!

"My soul is here? I'm confused again. Just what exactly is my soul?"

"Your soul is who you are. It's your every thought, your every spoken word, your every action and experience in life. It records your gifts and what you have done with them. Your soul is like a DVD of Wayne Tyler since the second of conception, a record of every moment, every conversation and every occurrence in your life. Your soul never dies; it is immortal."

"Immortal? I didn't know that. Hmmm … Now, my body? Where did I leave my body? Oh god … I'm starting to remember."

Wayne curled back into his fetal position as thoughts closed in on reality. He wasn't willing to face facts, and he wasn't willing to face Gordon.

"Let me help you out. Does the word *suicide* come to mind?"

"Shi … Oh shi.., I mean shoot. Bad move on my part. So you're saying that my body is fourteen feet under in the Gulf of Mexico? That's where I left it?"

"Go ahead and say it, Wayne. You were about to end your life."

"Okay, I'll say it, *suicide*! I got drunk, depressed, feeling sorry for myself …"

"Why did you feel sorry for yourself?"

"Just a lot of things piling up."

"What type of things, Wayne? Things that you brought upon yourself?"

"Probably. Isn't that the way *things* happen?"

"You tell me, Wayne."

"I'm tired of talking to you! I'm tired of answering all of your questions that seem to have no answers. I don't even know what's happening or where I am."

"You can return to earth anytime you want, Wayne. You have free will and free choice."

"Some choice … I have a question for you, Gordon, or whatever your name is … Does everyone who attempts suicide come here?"

"Divine appointments are made only by the Divine. It's not my call. I can't tell you any more than that."

Between became dimmer as Wayne remembered negative details of his life. Light and darkness in his present realm seemed to be determined by positive and negative thoughts and comments. Wayne was at the point of complete confusion. He learned that he could escape this place but what would happen when he returned? Death? Life?

"Gordon, you've got to help me. I'm really back in that cold, black murky water aren't I? I'm shivering, I can't breathe. I'm under water. I'm dying, Gordon. I'm dying!"

"Do you want to die, Wayne?"

"No! Yes … I don't know …"

"At this point, the choice is yours. You'll hear me say those words many times—*free choice* and *free will*. You still control the destiny of your life."

"I'm a little out of control here, Gordon."

"*Control* is a key word. When you lose control, other factors run your life. You become like a pinball in a machine, bouncing off one life event to another. Some of these events ring the bell. Others send you down the hole. Does this sound familiar to you?"

"And that's where I am right now, at the bottom of Galveston Bay, in a deep dark hole. I'm about to die …"

"And you can't make up your mind whether or not you want to live or die, can you, Wayne?

"No, I can't."

Gordon gave Wayne a chance to gather his wits as he levitated in front of him, floating in the mist of Between. He was in no rush. There was no time.

"Do you want to continue now?"

"Continue this, uh, *time out*? How do we do that? I'm not familiar with the rules."

"There are no rules. You record them after everything you do here. Some rules you decide to live by, others you discard. Do you need rules, Wayne?"

"That's thought provoking, Gordon. You make life seem so simple. It isn't!"

"People, their thoughts, their decisions and their actions make life difficult. Life is really very simple, Wayne. You live, you eat, you do, you die. What's difficult about that?"

At this point Wayne was listening to every word Gordon spoke as if he was trying to help him organize and rationalize his thoughts, helping him to make decisions in his life, or what was left of it. His life was the part that continued to concern Wayne. It was the uncertainty of the unknown, of what was ahead, if anything.

"Wayne, you're here because you made a very bad decision, a decision that affects others, not only yourself. I'll contribute a new word to your limited vocabulary; *hubris*. It means exaggerated pride. Pride can be good, as in pride in your work and your life, or it can be bad, as in *pride* comes before a fall.

"Pride caused one-third of the heavenly angels to fall to earth as demons and it caused perfect beings in a perfect place, mainly Adam and Eve in the Garden of Eden, to introduce sin to all mankind. Pride is powerful, Wayne. Never forget that. It shakes the universe."

"So you called this *time out,* this *divine appointment* because of my pride?"

"That's one reason. We'll explore others in your life, Wayne. You bought yourself a ticket to *Between* when you jumped into the water and decided to take life and death into your own hands. "The Almighty is the giver and taker of all life. It isn't your right to end your own life or that of another. It is sin, but it's not unforgiveable.

"Oh, so now we're going to go over all my *sins*, huh? I can assure you that we'll be here for a long time. I can't remember them all. I don't even know which things are sins and which were just having a good time. Somehow, I have the feeling that you're going to tell me the difference …

"And, another thing, MR. BIG, let me remind you of your own words. You said that I have *free will* and *free choice*, now didn't you? *I* always choose my own path, and I'm not real sure I need you to redirect me! You're playing mind games with me again."

Gordon could easily see Wayne's defiant nature. Wayne was lashing out and fighting back, unwilling to be directed or to listen. This time out was about to have its own time out. Gordon decided to depart for a while to let Wayne think about his situation and cool down.

"Wayne, you seem so sure of yourself. Confidence, like pride, can be a good thing or a bad thing. I'm going to leave you here with your thoughts and your pride for a while. I hope they keep you company."

"No! Wait! Don't leave me here alone, Gordon! Where're you going and when will you be back? What am I supposed to do in the meantime?"

Gordon's huge image was gone at the speed of thought. He vanished in the mist. Wayne was completely alone standing, floating, surrounded by nothingness. He began to understand that lashing out at Gordon was not necessarily a good thing. He felt isolated, separated from life as he knew it and claustrophobic in a place without metes and bounds.

In his isolation, Wayne decided that he could not deal with all the compartments in his mind at the same time. He was there to make many decisions in all areas of his life, so one by one, he mentally closed the compartments and began to think on one thing at a time. His life: What a pile of peaks and valleys, triumphs and failures. He felt like a man looking at himself in a mirror and he wasn't pleased with what he saw. He had no family that was close, few friends, many admirers and others who hated the ground he walked on. He decided that, so far, his life had been a failure. After all, he'd made the choice to end it.

His loves: He hadn't any. He'd had more affairs than any ten men should have had but no love. Lots of sex but no intimacy, no commitment to anyone but himself and his pleasures. Wayne thought hard and decided that he probably didn't know what love was. So he was a failure at love.

Abby: Wow! What a special woman. Wayne reasoned that if he couldn't love Abby, he probably couldn't love anyone. She'd kicked him out of her life. He was a failure with Abby.

His gifts: He was an accomplished musician, singer and impersonator, but what had that gotten him? His fifteen minutes of fame? Never happened! Why not? He decided that this, too, fell into the failure column.

His beliefs: He had none. He believed only in himself and if this area of his life followed the others that he was reflecting upon, another failure. He couldn't even believe in himself. He remembered where his body was.

His contribution to mankind: This was heavy on his mind. Wayne had caused so much joy to those who had seen him perform but did that joy continue in his life and the life of others? Probably not! His talents and gifts had just led to many one-night stands causing hurt and heartache.

As Wayne came to these conclusions, the aura of Between became dimmer. He was lonely, lonely for people, lonely for life, lonely for purpose and lonely for love. The loneliness and isolation pierced him. But he'd always been an optimist. It kept him going. At the moment, Wayne couldn't see any light in his life as the darkness surrounded him and became dimmer with every gut-wrenching truth that appeared in his thoughts, in the mirror of his life that he viewed in his mind.

Wayne begin thinking, *Should I continue this gauntlet at Between? What will I face if I do? And what will happen if I choose to leave?* This look in the mirror of his life only led him back to confusion and indecision. Once again he was filled with fear.

Staring into the nothingness, Wayne began to see the image of Gordon walking on the mist toward him. Drifting, floating just behind Gordon was a huge door with singed edges and a golden door knob. It had to be twenty feet high. As he approached, Gordon's own brilliance added light to the darkened space.

"So glad you're back, Gordon. What's with the door?"

"I'll get to that later. I see you're doing the 'look in the mirror thing.'"

"How'd you know that?"

"Remember me talking about the soul, you know, the DVD of your life and your thoughts? I hear your thoughts, Wayne. So have you surrendered to your decisions?"

"Surrender? I'm an American, a Texan, a man. *Surrender* is not in my vocabulary. Ain't gonna happen, Gor-Don!"

Gordon chuckled, trying to lighten up the situation.

"Surrender is essential, Wayne."

"Essential to what?"

"Essential to feeling peace, essential to experiencing joy and to know what love is. You've been thinking about these subjects, haven't you?"

"Yeah. Don't know much about any of 'em. Do women have to surrender, too?"

"Yes, but their key word is *submission*. Mankind has always had trouble with those two words, for centuries, yet surrender and submission are the keys to a better life."

"I'll fight to the death before I surrender!"

"And it seems that you're going to have to do exactly that, Wayne. Now, I'll explain the symbolism of the door to you and what will take place if you decide to remain in Between."

"Great! Like what choice do I have? Put up with all of this nonsense or take a deep breath and hope I make it out of Galveston Bay? So what's the plan? Just who am I going to have to fight?"

Gordon explained to Wayne that the door was a final challenge which would come at the end of seven tribulations. Wayne was going to have his chance at being a non-surrendering warrior. Gordon explained to Wayne that he would soon face, in a public arena, seven demons.

"You've got to be kidding me! I can't fight demons. I don't even believe in demons, much less know how to fight 'em. Gordon, you're scaring the cra … uh, daylights out of me!"

"Wayne, at any moment, even during the tribulations, you can choose to return and leave Between. Just say the word. If you remain, this is what's going to happen. Call it another divine appointment."

"Oh my god! How do I fight a demon? What do they look like? How big are they? Will they kill me? What happens if they do? Where will I go?"

"You fight demons with the shield of faith, with the sword of the Spirit which is the Word of the Almighty."

"The only faith I have is in myself and right now that tank's pretty empty! And where's this sword I'm supposed to have? I don't know anything about sword fighting; that's ancient! Are these seven demons gonna kill me?"

"No, they cannot kill you, your soul is immortal and it never dies. It is not allowed by the Almighty. The demons are attempting to win your soul in battle and send it to Hades."

"OH SHI … … … ! Oh, I wish I could say that word! Please, Gordon, just this once. I'm scared to death. They can send me to hell?"

"No, they can't. The choice of where you spend eternity is your decision, Wayne. Fear is a great weapon of the evil ones. Do not succumb to fear but seek salvation. Be bold, be courageous!"

"Easy for you to say, Gordon. You're not going to be fighting 'em. I told you that I didn't believe in all this god-stuff and salvation-stuff. I don't even know what it is."

"Wayne, demons cannot claim your soul if you make the right choices. They're cunning, they're deceiving, they can even appear as angels of light. Nothing about the evil ones has any truth to it or good in it. They are one hundred percent evil. Remember that. I'll be your trainer before the battle. I'll get you ready."

"How long do we have? Is this going to be like a boot camp to learn to fight?"

"Again, Wayne, there is no time here. As for a boot camp and teaching you to fight, you said, in your own words, that *you would fight to the death.* Remember saying that?"

"Yeah, but … but … I wasn't referring to fighting demons. I mean, I don't know how to do that. You're going to train me to fight demons, right?"

"In a word, *yes*! As best I can …"

"What do you mean by, *as best I can?*"

"Wayne, without faith in the One True Almighty, without wisdom and without the Sword of the Spirit, about which you have no clue, I can only try to guide you in the fight, to be the trainer in your corner and give you advice between rounds. I can't fight it for you. But I will tell you this:

"Everything I tell you, about yourself, the demons, their strategies, you will remember clearly and have immediate access to. This training will help you in the battles."

"Tell me again what happens if I choose not to fight, Gordon. I'm having a real tough time with this!"

"Back to Galveston Bay, fourteen feet under, lungs full of water, you're drunk, no will to live, defeated. And I'll tell you this Wayne: your soul will be on its way to Hades, even without a fight. You're here at this place called Between to fight for your own soul. And I just told you the alternative to not facing the demons. What's your decision? I need to know, right now!"

10

LEGION
WE DO NOT FIGHT AGAINST FLESH AND BLOOD

Wayne felt that the weight of the world was on his shoulders. He had a choice to make, but there was no choice. He could either return to Red Fish Island, to certain death and be cast into Hades for all eternity, a place he didn't even believe existed, or he could fight unknown opponents without any guarantee of the outcome. If he lost, the destination was the same as being returned to the depths of Galveston Bay. But could he win the battle? And if so, how and what happened then?

"I have one last question for you before I make my decision."

"Quickly, Wayne! What is it? I'll answer it if I'm allowed."

"Why should I believe anything you've told me so far? About demons, Hell and Hades, about choices, about eternity, about love and purpose?"

"I am a holy servant of the Most High God. I am incapable of telling a lie. What I have told you in our conversations is the absolute truth."

"But how do I know this, Gordon? Not good enough for me."

"Wayne, I was present during creation. I was present when I, too, had a choice to make of whether to join the fallen angels, to follow the brilliance and the beauty of Lucifer, called the Son of the Morning, the fallen Archangel now named Satan. I saw the creation of the entire universe. I witnessed the downfall of mankind in the Garden of Eden, I have been in the presence of the Almighty. I have been a part of everything in the history of the world."

"Okay, impressive credentials, Gordon. But again you're asking me to believe in something *I* haven't witnessed. Give me more, Gordon. Give me a sign."

"Wayne, do you remember the unseasonably cold winter in San Antonio when the temperature dipped to twenty degrees?"

"Oh yeah. I was living in that dump one-bedroom apartment that I called 'the dungeon.'"

"Do you remember the elderly black man who knocked on your door selling candy that cold winter morning?"

"Yeah, I do. He was wearing a flannel shirt and thin pants, but he had no coat and no socks. He was shivering. How'd you know about that?"

"You gave him ten dollars for two pieces of candy, a Baby Ruth bar and a Butterfinger. Then you went to your closet, pulled out an old coat, a knit cap, a pair of socks, a pair of gloves and gave it to the elderly fellow, didn't you, Wayne?"

"Yeah, he was freezing and I felt sorry for him. It made me feel good that I did that. Plus, I gave him the last money that I had. Cool that you know about that, Gordon, but so what?"

"That elderly fellow was me, Wayne. I came to see you."

"That was you?! Can angels do that sort of stuff?"

"Angels often visit humans on earth disguised as mortals. Now what happened two days later? Think."

"Uh, let's see, oh, I remember, I got a check in the mail from a gig that I thought had stiffed me."

"It was for $2500, right, Wayne?"

"Yes. I used it to buy my ticket to London, to get the heck out of San Antonio. Some biker had put out a contract on me for fooling around with his wife. So how's that a sign, Gordon?"

"Few things happen without a reason, Wayne. That money got you away from the hit man, T-Bone, and gave you a new life, another chance. The Holy Spirit convinced T-Bone that it was wrong. T-Bone had never killed anyone."

"I don't know about the Holy Spirit stuff, Gordon, and I don't want to go there. This whole thing here at Between is almost more than I can take. But I'll admit, you told me some things that no one could've known about. No wonder T-Bone hates me ..."

"T-Bone doesn't hate you, Wayne. As a matter of fact, he prays for you almost daily. You've become an essential part of the income stream there at the club. Abby, Hank, Tito and his wife Mary, not to mention the guys in the band, all depend on you. That's how your bad decisions affect the lives of others."

Wayne tried to digest the new information Gordon had given him about his past. He couldn't deny what the angel had told him. It was true to the last detail. As much as he tried to refute it, he couldn't, the evidence was concrete. He had asked for a sign and Gordon had delivered.

"For the time being, you've made a good case, Gordon. But can I defeat the demons and if so, what's in it for me?"

"When you face your challenges head-on, Wayne, there is always hope. You can be victorious and I'll explain how. As far as what's in it for you: the reward is life, love and an eternity in such wonder that mankind cannot envision it."

Wayne was looking for hope, any hope. His will to survive began to take over his mind; it was strong and something to hold on to. If there was a chance, he'd take it. When Gordon mentioned the word *life,* Wayne quickly answered.

"Okay, let's fight the demons, Gordon! That's my decision. I hope you know what you're doing because I have no idea what to do. Let's get on with it."

The aura of Between became brighter. Wayne was no longer in the darkened mist. He was in the center of the brightness of hope. His attitude became one of learning, dependence on Gordon to teach him, of trying to trust; but the fear of the unknown was still present.

"Good decision, Wayne. I'll make the preparations. I must leave for a while. While I'm gone, be thinking of any more questions you may have."

Again, Wayne was left with his thoughts. Again, he felt the isolation and the anxiety of facing the unknown. He stared at the door with the golden door knob that remained suspended in the mist and wondered what significance it would play.

A short time later, Gordon returned.

"Wayne, would you feel more at ease if I reduced the size of my stature?"

"N'ah. I'm kinda getting used to you looming over me, Big Guy. I've thought of more questions before we get started."

"Go ahead. It is important for you to be as prepared as possible. Demons will use any doubt that you have against you. Doubt weakens you and can cause them to be victorious over you."

"In these battles, can the demons hurt me?

"Yes."

"Will I feel pain?"

"Yes."

"But they can't kill me, right?"

"Right."

"Can I hurt them? Can I kill the demons?"

"No, but you can defeat them. You are not fighting against flesh and blood, Wayne. You're fighting evil spirit demons that have controlled your life for years. You have seven demons. Collectively, they are called Legion. Your decisions during the tribulations can cast them away from you."

"Oh, man! I'm more confused now than ever. This is freaking me completely out. I'm all ears, Gordon. I really, really need your help."

Wayne took a deep breath and waited, filled with fright and anticipation. Like a patient master, Gordon explained the strategies of the evil ones and how to overcome them.

"First, always expect the unexpected from demons. They know you better than you know yourself, Wayne. Demons know all of your buttons to push and how to manipulate you. They can appear as angels of light, apparitions of people close to you, and they will deceive you and tempt you. They wish you no good because they are completely evil. Remember this. Never succumb to anything they want you to do. By resisting them, Wayne, you defeat them."

"If they appear as other people in my life, how will I know the difference? Whether or not they're real?"

"Demons always have imperfections. Look at each one closely. They will have an ill-placed, but barely noticeable knot in their hair, or imperfections on their skin. Look closely at their teeth and smell their breath. You'll smell a foul sulfur odor. All are dead giveaways that you are being tempted and manipulated by a demonic force."

"I see what you're saying. Good info, Gordon. Give me more!"

"The Almighty put *right* and *wrong* into the hearts of all mankind from the beginning of time. Everyone knows the difference. Protect your mind and your heart, Wayne. Think before you act. This is part of the armor of the Almighty, the breastplate of righteousness."

"All of a sudden these battles don't seem so bad. If all I have to do is what's right, that's simple enough. I'll kick these demons' butts!"

"Be careful, Wayne. Even the holy angels don't challenge the powers of the evil ones. At best we can only say to them, 'The Almighty rebuke you!' Never, ever challenge them head on. I cannot begin to tell you the powers they possess."

"Gordon, every time I think I'm getting ahead on these tribulations you keep knocking me back. How am I going to win if I have no confidence in winning?"

"Remember that word *hubris* that I mentioned to you? Pride, overconfidence and dependence on self is just what the demons want. You can defeat yourself with little or no effort on their part. This is one of the many ways they trick you. They may purposely let you win a couple of challenges just to deceive you with the next one."

"Oh, so I have to keep my guard up, huh?"

"More so than you will ever know. Your soul is the prize that they fight for. Don't forget the stakes, Wayne.

"Okay, Gordon, you mentioned that I have to fight with faith. What is your definition of faith? I've got my own ..."

"*Faith* is a belief and a trust in what you cannot see."

"Gordon, you know my logical mind. How can I trust in what I can't see?"

"Can you see the wind?"

"Of course not. No one can see wind."

"Yet it is there. You feel it but cannot see it, right?"

"Yeah, Gordon, you have a point. But how can I trust my soul to something or someone I cannot see?"

"Because you cannot save yourself, Wayne. That's the surrender part I mentioned before. You have to call upon the name of the Lord for your salvation."

"Man! Gordon, I really wish you hadn't mentioned that word again. I told you, I don't surrender, remember? So tell me about being saved. How do I do that?"

"Wayne, this is the most important decision that any mortal can make in their entire lives and they must do it while they're living. You are still alive, even here in this heavenly realm called Between. Your decision determines where your immortal soul will spend eternity, either, in Heaven or Hell. The Lake of Fire was created for the fallen angels and was never a plan of The Almighty for His children to go there."Salvation has two parts. First, you must confess with your mouth, publicly, that the Holy Son of the Almighty, Jesus, is your Lord and Savior. You must call out to Him by name ..."

"Stop right there, Gordon. If Hell was not created for mortal man, then why would 'The Almighty' send people there?"

"People send themselves there, Wayne. It is the hope of The Almighty that none should perish but all should have ever lasting life in Heaven. When people reject the fact that Jesus died for their sins, past, present and future, and don't believe that He can save them, they reject salvation. This is the only unforgiveable sin and it is a *free choice* and *free will* decision."

"Okay, Gordon, what about me giving you the coat, the gloves and my last ten bucks? Doesn't that count for something?"

"Yes and no. The act itself shows that you know the difference between right and wrong. Your compassion proved that. But you cannot get to Heaven with good works or good intentions. This is the misconception of all of the other false religions of the world which are based on good works versus bad works. It is also one of the leading deceptions of the evil ones."

"Gordon, it would seem to me that suicide would be an unforgiveable sin but you said it wasn't. I mean, if a person ends his life, commits murder of self, how can that not be unforgiveable?"

"Remember I said that when a person calls on the name of The Lord that *all* of their sins are forgiven—past, present and future sins?"

"Yeah. So suicide can be forgiven if a person is saved, right?"

"Yes, Wayne. Suicide is a sin, a terrible sin with grave consequences, but it can be forgiven."

"So what's part two of salvation, Gordon? Explain."

"Part two is what mortals often call the 'Catch 22.' Which is believing in your heart that the Son of The Almighty can save you from all your sins and will guarantee you eternal life in Heaven. Here's the truth part, Wayne. Only The Almighty truly knows your heart and if you really believe this. You can't fake it."

"Then, Gordon, you've just completely blown your case with me! It's easy enough to 'call upon the name of The Lord'; anyone can do that. But *if* The Almighty truly knows *my* heart, He knows that I really don't believe in all this 'salvation' malarkey. I'm doomed before I start fighting for my soul according to your own words."

"As long as you are living, Wayne, there is hope."

"Now I'm going to be gut-wrenchingly honest with you, Gordon. I think you're the one doing the manipulation. You're giving me no way out. You're shoving me out to the edge of a high cliff with no direction but down. How do I know that you're not a demon?"

"Wayne, would a demon fight against himself? I do not manipulate, nor do I tempt. I speak The Almighty's truth. The decision is yours to believe or not to believe. To accept or reject. Do you want to continue or go back to Red Fish Island?"

Wayne held on to his defiance and unbelief because he really didn't believe. He felt doomed before he started and avoided mental disaster by clinging to any form of hope. Even his hope was fading fast with every explanation that Gordon gave him. He simply didn't believe and his vision of victory was becoming very dim.

"So, Gordon, you say that I have seven demons controlling my life. That seems like a lot for one person. Tell me about these demons and why they're concentrating on me."

"Don't flatter yourself, Wayne. There are millions of demons. Satan is the lord and master of them all. He, himself, mostly focuses on heads of state, people and governments that change the course of world laws, wars, and life changing events. And, Wayne, his demons don't have to work very hard to claim your soul. You've been helping them out with your hedonistic lifestyle."

"But it's my life, Gordon. So do these demons have names? How big are they?"

"You know many of their names, Wayne. Satan, who is called the Prince of this World, is a very smart manager of his fallen angels. They are organized into demonic duties to torment and tempt humans. These evil tempters go to and fro across the earth to kill, steal and destroy all hope, dreams and joy of every living creature. They attack mankind cloaked in the veils of Pride, Anxiety, Shame, Worry, Suicide, Lust, Drunkenness, Depression, Fear, Hunger, Pestilence, War, Famine, and Greed. Many have ancient human names that are recorded in history books.

"Names like *Ishtar* the queen of heaven, *Diana of Ephesus,* a fertility goddess, *Chiun,* a goddess of the stars. And, Wayne, make special note of the twin sisters and consorts of Satan's high counsel: *Asherah,* an ancient false goddess of the sea and *Ashtoreth.* You will surely see them. And beware of *Dagon,* lieutenant of lies." There is also *Chemosh,* the false god who brought King Solomon down. Then, Satan's high captain, *Baal, a.k.a., Molech,* the most feared demon of them all with the exception of Satan himself.

"As for their size, Wayne, they can appear as tiny insects small enough to crawl into your ear and plant thoughts into your mind. They can be microscopic organisms entering food, animals and crops to cause disease and pestilence or they can be a dark cloud of terror covering half the size of the Americas to rain down fear and corruption across entire nations."

"I can't fight against these, Gordon!"

"Of course you can, Wayne. Don't fear. Fear will defeat you before you ever begin. We haven't finished our preparations yet."

"So, Gordon, you've told me about my opponents. Who's on my team? Will I have any help?"

"The prayers of your loved ones will help you, Wayne. I've told you some of the people who pray for you; there are others that you do not know about."

"Like who?"

"Like Robbie Cantrell. Hank even said a prayer for you after he punched you out and felt bad about doing it. Abby has prayed more than once for you, Wayne. But there is One who prays 24/7 for you in an unutterable language …"

"Yeah? Who'd that be?"

"That would be The Holy Spirit, whose prime directive is to draw people to salvation. He is part of the triune God. He is The Almighty and the giver of all blessings and gifts. He gave you the ability to play a guitar, to sing and to impersonate famous voices. He is the One who delivered you from T-Bone and called him to salvation. He will be with you always and will never forsake you."

"Yeah, right. Here we go with that holy spook thing again …"

"Careful, Wayne! You're bordering on blasphemy."

"Yeah? Then who are you to judge me? Isn't judging others a sin? You're really beginning to piss me off, Gor-Don, and I can't believe you allowed me to say that."

"It is a bodily function, Wayne. Why do spiritual things irritate you so much?"

"Because you talk about a *loving* Almighty. If He *loves* everyone, why does He allow millions of people to die of starvation in Africa? To be raped and murdered, forced into sex, tortured and abused? Explain that one to me if you can or if you're *allowed* to give me the answers!"

"I will give you the answers. There is a devil in this world. I just told you about him. The Almighty has provided enough food for every living creature on earth, the animals and the people. When the demons get into the minds of these heads-of-state, warlords, these terrorists, drug dealers, pornographers, rapists and pedophiles, they steal the food, they torture and kill and rape because they have decided to do this. Free will and free choice, Wayne; everyone makes their own decisions. Then The Almighty comes along to turn bad into good. He doesn't cause this pain. The demons cause it and mankind goes along with it for their own personal gain. Like you, Wayne. That's the reason people blame The Almighty for their own sins, their own bad choices, all the evil that goes on in this world.

"There's another thing you should know, Wayne. The Almighty sees death differently from the way mortals do, especially the ones who believe in a hereafter. The Creator intercedes on the part of His suffering children. He brings them home to heaven through death and rescues them from the pain and abuse they are living. He brings them to a place of plenty, a place of safety, a place of love, provision, healing and peace. Life is short, Wayne, but eternity is forever. It can be a place of exaggerated pain or a place of super natural wonder. I hope you can get your arms around this. I sincerely do."

"So why didn't *The Almighty* just hit me with a lightning bolt and end this misery that I'm suffering? You said that I was 'bordering on blasphemy.'"

"Because The Almighty gave mankind His own traits and emotions. Anger can be a good thing if used properly to motivate you to find the truth. You can lash out at Him, shake your fist at Him and speak your mind to Him. He expects you to question Him and He will always supply the answer that you, personally, understand. But in His timing, Wayne, not yours."

With his anger subsiding Wayne realized that he was retaining every detail of information that Gordon had given him. His total recall was uncanny and his mind was clear. He began to focus on the imminent battles with an edge and determination that he had never experienced. His warrior spirit was piqued.

"What's next, Big Guy?"

"Now that I have explained the tactics of your adversaries, I am going to show you the field of battle. Demons are not allowed in this dimension of Between but they are allowed where we are going. Be warned and be aware, Wayne. Take my hand …"

"Oh cra..! Oh shi..! Oh my! I'm not looking forward to this, Gordon. Where're we going?"

"To another realm, a realm called Betwixt. That's where the demons are."

Traveling at the speed of thought gave no time whatsoever of seeing the sights, the universe or the other dimensions along the way. One moment they were engulfed in Between, the next they arrived at their destination which was an eerie location hidden in the heavenly realms where few mortals were allowed. Only souls and spirits could enter this place.

Holding Gordon's hand, hovering in mid-air, Wayne looked down on an immense stadium. The architecture resembled an old style Roman coliseum where Christians had been fed to the lions in ancient times, but much larger. At first glance it seemed to have the seating capacity of a modern day, world class soccer field. The arena was huge, daunting and for the time, it was empty.

"WOW!" said Wayne. It was all that he could say. His voice echoed around the huge structure. He was overwhelmed at the sheer size of this tremendous arena.

Wayne noticed that there were no lighting facilities and the field was divided into two distinct sides. One side had meticulously honed white marble seating with perfectly rounded edges. It seemed to glow with brightness and was perfectly shaped. The seating on the other side was just the opposite and appeared to be gorilla- cut from jagged, rough black slate that gave the impression of darkness and doom. The field of play between the two sides was equally separated and appeared to be grass; healthy and green on one side of the turf and choked and dying on the other half. The sides of the stadium were clearly drawn. It didn't take a Rhodes Scholar to figure out who was on which side.

In the center of the grassy area a levitating stage hung suspended, varying its height between ground level and at times rising to over two hundred feet above the field. It was round with a fifty-foot radius platform. When the stage rose, the two distinct sides of the seating areas also rose to keep spectators at eye level with the activities. For any participant on the stage, it was a long way down to certain death below. At present, the stage was completely bare and gave no foretelling of future events.

There was a huge open area around the fringes of the stadium and Wayne wondered how spectators to the event would arrive, who would arrive and which side they would choose. Even though there was ample lighting for attendees to see the events that took place, the sky above the arena was black as pitch.

Both Wayne and Gordon continuously scanned the perimeter for signs of demons. Suddenly, Wayne heard distant voices. The sounds were unclear and he couldn't make out what was being said but he did sense an evil presence coming closer to the arena.

"Do those voices belong to the demons, Gordon?"

"Yes. It's good that you experience this. Don't let it scare you. You are getting a preview of what is about to take place here at Betwixt."

"Tell me the rules again, Gordon."

"Like I said, there are no rules. The agenda will be set by the demons and they're making their plans as we speak. Just remember, Wayne, they cannot kill your soul, but they can claim it. That's the prize of the games."

"Yeah, I was afraid you'd bring that up again. Can you give me any insight about what you think they will do to me?"

Gordon took another quick glance around the arena. He could hear the demon voices getting louder. They turned into shouts of ghoulish shrieks, obscenities and almost audible sounds of blasphemous expletives. Wayne heard them also and it caused fear to enter his being once again.

"All the tribulations will take place on the elevated stage. Specifically, Wayne, that is your field of battle, not the stadium or the crowds. Demons can change the settings, all around, at will. The grass below can turn into a raging ocean. The sky above can rain down brimstone. The demons can create apparitions to appear to you as anyone they want. Like I told you, expect the unexpected and be prepared to deal with whatever is before you."

Wayne was concentrating on the surroundings of the arena, listening to the demon shrieks as they grew louder. He was trying to put a clear picture of what the area appeared to be before the trials began so he would notice changes when they occurred.

"Gordon. Give me some bullet points to remember. Give me some quick ammunition to fight."

"Three things to remember, Wayne. First, RIGHT and WRONG. Those are the keys to your victory. In every tribulation that you face, stop and think what is the right thing to do or say and what is the wrong thing to do or say. Right trumps wrong every time. It requires your patience, your wisdom and your discernment. That is your path to victory over the demons. If you do the right thing, Wayne, the demons must withdraw from that tribulation.

"Second, demons will try to trick you into thinking you are worthless. They will play upon your favorite sins and fears. They will tempt you into believing they are here to help you go on to bigger and better things and may offer you fame, riches and status. Don't believe it. Their promises are empty. They are here to claim you.

"Third, Wayne, every trial, every tribulation comes down to the decisions *you* make. Demons cannot make you do anything you don't want to do. Rebuke them! That is why your fate is in your own hands, not theirs. They can hurt you, they can rip you to shreds and they can make you feel pain, but they cannot put words in your mouth, They cannot dismember you, Wayne. You will enter this arena whole and you will leave this arena whole. You are in control of your immediate destiny, whatever it may hold."

"Thanks, Gordon. You're truly a comforting spirit, whether or not I believe what you say. You are giving me strength. I just hope I can use it."

"That is my mission, Wayne. Give thanks to The Almighty, not me."

"Yeah, one of these days, Gordon, If there are no rules, are there any referees to these tribulations?"

"You're the referee, Wayne."

"What does that mean? Can I call penalties where there are no rules? Can I call a time out? How am *I* the referee?"

"Wayne, you can call a time out to regroup any time you want to and I would advise you to do so, often. As for being the referee, I've already told you. You control your fate. You will decide the winner by the decisions you make in the arena."

"Hmmm ... I want to go over one last thing. What are my exit strategies, Gordon? Tell me again. How do I get out of here? How do I end these trials?"

Gordon could see the effect of his training with Wayne. This young, talented man was listening, he was being a good student, but he was still being belligerent, self-centered and full of pride. A healthy amount of pride in his battle strategies was a good thing. It would increase his confidence, and Wayne was going to need all the confidence he could muster.

"As the seven trials begin, you will have three exit strategies," Gordon replied in a still soft voice.

"One is to keep fighting and do not give up until the end of the tribulations.

"Two is to simply say, 'Send me back.' At that time you depart from this realm and from Between. Your soul rejoins your body in the present situation that is fourteen feet under Galveston Bay and you take your chances from there.

"Third, at any time during the tribulations, you can call upon the name of the Lord, Wayne. At that moment you will receive divine intervention, the trials end, the demons are vanquished and you will return to the safety of Between to face the last challenge which is the doorway that is awaiting you. All three choices are yours to make."

Holding Gordon's hand, hovering over the colossal arena, Wayne was looking deep into himself and his options. He didn't like any of them, but he couldn't escape them either. The shrieks of the demons looming ever nearer to his location, for the moment, didn't seem to bother him near as much as his thoughts that were calling to him.

"Gordon? I need some 'Wayne time.' If I let go of your hand will I fall to the field below or can I just walk around for a while? I need to think."

"You can let go, Wayne. You'll be okay. Take a moment, talk to yourself but don't tarry. The event has been scheduled and it will take place before long. We'll return to Between for you to rest before the trials begin. Let me know when you're ready to leave this field of battle."

Wayne let go of Gordon's hand and remained suspended in the air. He thought of checking out the bright, white marble side of the stadium and was instantly there. He felt the smoothness, the softness of the continuous marble seats. Sitting, thinking, his thoughts turned to Abby, that special woman who had shown him more love and compassion than anyone he had ever met in his life.

He thought about her smile, her gentle nature, her caring and the joy in her eyes when he was with her. If he couldn't muster a reason to keep living on his own, just maybe she was his reason to keep fighting, to face his challenges for the mere chance of ever seeing her again, holding her again. He yearned for her and he adored her. Oh, for the chance of kissing her once more and holding her soft hand. What a joy that would be. When he looked at her picture in his mind, there were no thoughts of lust, only love. He realized that he did love Abby. She, above all women, was his soul mate. If only he had realized that a few days ago. He wanted a second chance and he would fight to the death for that chance.

Just to get the feel of the arena, he thought himself over to the dark, jagged slate side of the arena seating and immediately could feel the rough edges where he sat. He detected a foul odor coming from the slate and left immediately in a thought.

He was now walking on the grass in the center of the field of battle. The green grass on half the field felt like a cushion under his feet. He experienced the openness of the field and felt relief as a man lying in a field of flowers gazing up at the dark night sky. It reminded him of looking over Clear Lake and seeing all the twinkling lights from the boats and the restaurants encircling the lake. Clear Lake was now his home and he loved living there. For the first time, he had a real home, a real job, a real family of friends and never realized it until this moment in suspended time and space. Everything a man could want was waiting for him back there and he longed to return to it. It was worth fighting for.

He thought about Hank, a good man who loved his daughter very much. Tito and T-Bone were also good men even though one had almost taken a contract to end his life. Robbie and Bella made life interesting; there was never a dull moment around either of them. Wayne wondered if they would accept him again if he was able to make it back and to explain himself to them. All he wanted now was their forgiveness and their friendship. He missed his new life. It, too, was worth fighting for the opportunity to get it back.

Last, just before leaving the arena, Wayne thought himself up to the stage hovering above the field. He looked down onto the grass below and to each side of the huge stadium. *Wow, what a trip it would be to perform on a stage like this*, Wayne thought. He could just imagine singing, playing his Stratocaster, doing his entire act and being backed up by *South* with Scott Wood on the sound board. Crowds cheering, multiple spotlights shining on them, what a tremendous fifteen minutes of fame that would be for any performer.

His mind was made up. He wanted to fight, he wanted to live. Wayne decided he had more reasons to see this through than any other person on the planet earth, even though he was not on it at present.

"Gordon, let's get back to Between and get some rest. I'm as ready as I'll ever be. I'm all in!"

11

BETWIXT
THE ARENA: WHERE LIGHT
MEETS DARKNESS

As the moment to begin the tribulations became imminent, Gordon went over final details with Wayne.

"Take special note of what I will tell you, Wayne. The demons can use apparitions of the dead and the living to deceive you in your arena trials. These apparitions may appear as people that you know, even historical people. And don't rely on logic because much of what is going to take place is only logical on earth, not in this special realm. Demons can twist the laws of gravity, of physics and of nature itself in order to confuse you. Quickly adjust, reason it out and adapt to the deceit. Again, choose right over wrong.

"Next, there may be people who are called to the arena through dreams and visions and are not necessarily apparitions, but souls frozen in time that will be present at the arena to give you support and encouragement. Remember, it was about 4:30 a.m. back on earth when time was frozen. If they do appear in the stands, these people are on your side and the sides will be clearly defined."

"Kinda like a 'home team' side and a 'visitors' side, Gordon?"

"Yes, but more like a bright side and a dark side.

"Finally, Wayne, you will be able to hear my thoughts and coaching throughout the trials. Listen and obey; but the choice is yours to do so. You may be able to hear the thoughts of people on your team, sitting on the bright side of the arena. You will not hear the demon thoughts but you will hear their shrieks and blasphemies. Shut them out of your mind."

"Will Abby be there?"

"Probably, Wayne, I can't say for sure. But I can tell you this … There will be mirror images of most everyone who attends the event. On the bright side they will appear godly and pure. On the side of darkness you will see the same faces who will look totally ghastly and will shout obscenities and show great support for the demonic activities against you.

"Wayne, you can use expletives at Betwixt but I must warn you, every little slip of your tongue will give them power over you. The demons will use your own words to accuse you before the Throne of the Almighty even during the trials. Choose your words carefully, Wayne. They will be used against you."

"Gordon, do you have any idea what the demons are planning for me? I mean, uh, I could sure use your insight."

"I don't know what they will plan, I can only guess. I've seen many battles like this, Wayne, and all I can tell you is what I've already said: Expect the unexpected. Demons know every word in every language in the world. They are cunning with their command of speech and will use it to deceive your train of thought. They will try their best to overwhelm you with visions, with words and with situations. Just take your time. Think and resist. Especially, remember your three exit strategies. That's the best insight I can give you."

Just as Gordon had predicted, seven demons, Chiun, Chemosh, Diana of Ephesus, Dagon, Asherah and Ashtoreth, the twin consorts of the hierarchy of evil, Ishtar, queen of hell and Baal, a.k.a. Molech, Beelzebub's captain, were the team of immoral corruption chosen by Satan himself to take the soul of Wayne Tyler in mortal combat. They spoke to each other in rhyme, psyching themselves up before battle, showing the others their Satan-given powers to impress their horrid positions amongst the unclean spirits.

Each appeared in many different forms simultaneously as they stood to give their terrible testimonials. They impersonated beauty, dragons, serpents, naked men and women engaged in illicit sexual positions, angels of light and at times, just to compress blasphemy into more blasphemy, they appeared as priests and ministers, shouting expletives, vulgarity and every evil thing. Each had to gain the approval of Baal before commencing their evil charades.

Chiun levitated down into the center of the meet sitting in a hot tub in the rear of a huge stretch limo bubbling with champagne with a touch of blood to add color to anything resembling purity. He wore a pimp hat with feathers on his head as several ghoulish nymphs performed unthinkable acts. He was the agent to the stars of fame and fortune, a demonic record producer, his ruse for the evening events.

"I am Chiun, god of stars. I'll win Wayne's soul with music bars."

He'll play with the best, his ego will crest.
When pride arises in many disguises
He'll crash and burn before he can turn
And choose the fame … into the flame.

The great masses gathered at the evil coven of the ghouls of hell spew their terrible bile all over each other as they cheered the rhetoric of Chiun. They craved the darkness of each other. The horrendous pep rally had just begun and was already heard in the depths of Hades itself.

Chemosh took over the ghastly center ring to show her evil power by appearing to be an angelic angel of light. Her aura constantly changed to every color known to mankind and a few man had never seen.

Chiun, silly god of stars,
Can you begin to see the scars
That I, Chemosh brought to bear
Upon King Solomon and his concubines there.
I'll expand Wayne's mind without a bound
And make him think he hears the sound
Of good, not evil, true and sweet
Then pull the rug from 'neath his feet.

Diana, goddess of Ephesus, floated into the center of the rally and appeared with an air of arrogance. Her face was like porcelain, her skin painted white with perfectly pointed teeth. She wore a flowing hairpiece of super thin live, almost unrecognizable poisonous serpents that made her hair appear to move on its own.

You other demons haven't a chance.
To force young Wayne into your trance.
I'll claim his soul through hurt and pain
Through boils and lesions, venom insane.
He'll feel the bite from hairpiece snakes
And cry for death, for heaven's sake!

Baal laughed and howled, giving his approval of Diana's plans. Next entered Dagon, lieutenant of lies and father to the Prince of Persia himself. Baal could hardly wait to be entertained by the next proposal. Dagon appeared as a typical earthly salesman wearing white shoes, white belt, hair going in all directions, mismatched vest, shirt and coat. His pants were high water and his shoes were scuffed gaudy snakeskin. He smiled a gloat of deceit.

> *I, Dagon, fish god of old*
> *Will confuse Wayne's logic and unfold*
> *A kangaroo court to present the lies*
> *Of man-made myths as he tries*
> *To sort out right and prove the wrong*
> *I'll test his facts of all the songs*
> *Of heaven and hell, I'll bend his mind*
> *And make sure he is left behind.*

Somewhat amused, Baal relished in the 'left behind' thing, to further a blasphemy against his number one adversary, Jesus, who claimed to be the total truth of all mankind. Then came the twin consorts, Ashera and Ashtoreth, two that Baal knew intimately. He drooled as they made their way to center court. They appeared as five foot tall twin fairies, each with six transparent wings. They were scantily dressed and revealed their women-like figures with not much left to the imagination. In their hands were bottles containing the nectar of the gods.

> *You pus-filled demon 'would-be's' watch!*
> *Our proven plan you'll never botch.*
> *He'll drink the nectar of the gods,*
> *He'll wreak his guts, his head will nod.*
> *We'll fill his blood with poison bliss*
> *Then bottle his soul with one foul kiss."*

Howls and shrieks could be heard almost at heaven's door. All the demons knew the particular fondness that Baal had for the twins. Not to show their approval could mean banishment from the pleasures of the earthly realm and into the pit. They showed their approval, looking at Baal to notice them. But Baal knew that the twins had been instructed by their immediate superior, Ishtar, the queen of hell, to set Wayne up for her pleasures with strong drink. Ishtar knew that lust was Wayne's favorite sin and that she would claim his soul with the pleasures of her body.

Ishtar descended into the center ring completely naked in all her ghoulish splendor. She had been present and had witnessed the scene when Satan had tempted the only perfect female ever created, Eve, in the Garden of Eden. Ishtar appeared as the image of Eve's perfect beauty, with only a scale or two visible to show her allegiance to her master. All went silent at her appearance.

> *You talk your chants and plan your win.*
> *Both high and low know I'm the sin*
> *That melts the mighty and the bold*
> *That make men hot and leaves them cold.*
> *I'll steal his heart and eat it up.*
> *I turn the bulldog to a pup.*
> *I turn their daylight into dark.*
> *I steal them from the angel's hark.*
> *Fornication and adultery's my game.*
> *And Ishtar, queen of hell, is my name.*
> *That no man dares to turn from me,*
> *I'll bump and grind his vision be.*
> *And once with me Wayne's had his whirl,*
> *He'll never look upon a girl*
> *That he won't think about the night*
> *I ravished him in sheer delight.*
> *I'll own his love, I'll take his soul,*
> *I'll burn him up and freeze him cold.*
> *I'll fill him deep with emptiness*
> *And make him yearn for one more kiss.*

Baal bowed before Ishtar and lusted for her. If he couldn't resist her, no mortal man could. All the other demons put their heads on the ground before her. She was the private property of Satan and had powers that even Baal feared and Molech feared nothing!

To end the final game plan of the demons of darkness, Baal waited for Ishtar to make her departure from center stage. Then, appearing as a huge, two-headed fire-breathing dragon about the size of the State of Alaska, he swooped down blowing balls of fire and streams of sulfuric acid throughout the masses of demonic spectators. The wind from his mighty wings scorched and boiled the faces of the lesser demons as they turned, daring not to look Baal directly in the face. He stood boldly before them so the other demons could see their commander. His orders were only reprimanded by the Prince of the World, Satan.

Baal was the *closer* of demons. He confronted his opponents head-on with his awesome appearance, his mighty strength, his heavy claws and razor sharp fingernails jutting out from hands mid-way on the leading edge of his mighty wings. He didn't finesse, he didn't deceive, he destroyed. A booming voice rang out from one of the mouths of the huge fire breathing dragon that bowed the heads of almost ten million demons who gathered before him.

Much ado over you, Wayne Tyler. Much ado over you!
Sinful mortal, sinful past,
Now the battle here at last.
Prince of Darkness, demon's pride
Here to take the life you hide.
Forceful fury in the mire
Taking you, Wayne, to the fire.
Easy victory, nothing hard.
You so willing, heart so scarred.
Now the moment is at hand,
No more waiting, no more sand,
Take the step now, turn and bob,
Then your very soul I'll rob.
See what good and evil waits,
As you enter through the gate.
Other choices, one for you,
Leave this place and death ensues.
Pick your poison, do it fast.
Breathe in deeply, it's your last.
Much ado over you, Wayne Tyler.
Much ado over you!

"The moment is here, Wayne. We must go to the arena. Don't let the demons overwhelm you."

Wayne was anxious, troubled and his confidence was fading even before entering the coliseum. Knowing that Gordon could communicate with him through telepathy gave him some comfort. He gathered what courage he had left and immediately they were at the vast, huge venue of the old Roman coliseum. The sides were clearly drawn between the bright and dark. Hundreds of thousands of images of people filled the stands, many having no distinct faces and just as Gordon had described, there were mirror images of the same people on both sides. Outside the boundaries of the arena vast amounts of people gathered. The numbers were as the grains of sand on a beach and couldn't be counted.

There was a murmur of conversation going on when Wayne arrived. He could hear so many thoughts of the spectators on the bright side but none were definable. A bright path in the grass led him up to the platform where Wayne took his lonely position. Presently, there was nothing on the stage. He anxiously awaited his fate and his demons. His knees were weak and he could hardly stand. Wayne was anticipating the worst of his fears.

Still at ground level on the platform, Wayne glanced into the bright side of the crowd, looking for a familiar face. His stare immediately focused on Abby sitting center, looking beautiful in her white linen robe that everyone on that side of the arena was wearing. She was surrounded by Hank, Robbie, Bella, T-Bone and Tito and his wife, Mary. Wayne could make out many of the faces of people that had crossed his path during his lifetime. Fellow musicians, people who had attended his gigs, waitresses, ladies of the night, past family members he hadn't seen in decades.

Seated on one side of Abby was a young, thirty-ish looking man with short hair. He had a white streak in his brown hair just above his right ear. Maybe it was a birth mark thing. Wayne didn't know who he was even with his new given ability to think clearly and recall the past perfectly. For some reason, the guy looked as if he'd been here before and was deep in thought. Wayne sent a little thought message to Abby:

"Thank you for being here, baby, but I wish you didn't have to be a part of this madness or witness what is about to happen ..." He got no response from her.

Gordon appeared to Abby, Hank, Robbie, Bella and the rest of their group. They were groggy as if awakened from a deep sleep.

"Fear not, I am Gordon, Wayne's angel. You have been brought to this arena in dreams to encourage and support him while he faces his demons. You will not be harmed ..."

Suddenly the grass on the arena field turned into a one-piece solid mirror. The dark sky billowed with beautiful rays as thousands of meteors blazed down from the skies above, lighting up the arena, crashing around the perimeters of the masses of people, shaking the ground when they hit. It was a fireworks display like no other ever seen. After the meteors burned out, a low-flying comet whisked over the length of the mirrored field, astonishing everyone, cooling off the heat caused by the fiery meteors.

From the meteor-lit sky above, wrapped in changing white billowing clouds, classical music became audible and increased in volume as one by one, the greatest composers of all time appeared from the clouds, sitting at their pianos, floating, circling around the entire arena and areas outside the arena. The music they played on their pianos and harpsichords was beyond magical. The sound was clear and booming. A supporting orchestra, numbering in the thousands of violins, cellos, harps and wind instruments began to play on the mirrored field below.

Johann Sebastian Bach led the procession from the sky, circling overhead, playing music from a concerto that had never been heard before by mankind. He was followed by Wolfgang Amadeus Mozart banging wildly at his piano as he smiled outrageously down on the audience. Then Ludwig van Beethoven appeared playing in perfect harmony with the others as they flew in circles around the perimeter of the vast arena sitting behind their pianos.

Giuseppe Verdi, Pyotr Tchaikovsky, Frederic Chopin, Antonio Vivaldi, Giacomo Puccini, George Frederic Handel and Igor Stravinsky rounded out the list of greats that entertained the crowd with their brilliant talents. Magnificent sounds touched the very souls of everyone present. The music was almost heavenly, it penetrated their very beings and left all spectators, on both sides, crying out for more. This near angelic display of musical talent was nothing like Wayne had expected.

Crowds on both sides looked up in complete awe as the group of composers circled in the sky above them, echoing their work, combining their unique sounds to every ear that would hear. The crowd and Wayne were mesmerized at the brilliance of the compositions of the masters of the music world.

Slowly, the sound of the mystical music diminished as each composer bowed to the crowd and levitated back into the clouds. Opening ceremonies were beyond anything ever seen on earth and were still continuing. As the composers withdrew and the music ended, there was a vacuum of silence that needed to be filled and quickly. The silence was deafening. The spectators were breathless. Their senses were filled to overflowing.

"Oh Gordon! The music is beautiful, beyond any words to describe it. How could this be bad or of demons. This is beyond imagination. What an honor to be present and hear this massive demonstration of the world's greatest composers!"

"Wayne, do not be deceived."

The platform began to rise two hundred feet above the crowds with Wayne on it. Once again his apprehension heightened even in the midst of the nostalgia that he had just witnessed. In stark contrast to the classical display, the platform began taking on the image of the stage at the Grand Ole Opry in Nashville. Standing center stage was Johnny Cash, backed by *South*, familiar faces from Tequilaville. Scott Wood was sitting behind the sound board smiling over at Wayne.

Cash began singing "Ring of Fire" and the dark side of the arena went nuts, spewing obscenities, acting like the out-of-control ghouls they were. Cash was joined by Buck Owens, Hank Williams, Patsy Cline, and Tammy Wynette.

George Jones joined in along with Merle Haggard and the legendary cowboy star, Gene Autry. Hank Williams began singing "I'll Never get out of this World Alive" and motioned for Wayne to join in. Wayne looked around the stage and saw his acoustic guitar and his Stratocaster placed on props just in front of the band. He grabbed the acoustic and walked over next to the C&W greats and began playing. At first Wayne paid little attention to the fact that the apparition of Hank Williams was slurring his words and barely able to stand up.

As honored as Wayne was to be standing on the same stage with Hank Williams, he just had a feeling that something wasn't right. He smelled liquor on the breath of the country legend and just passed it off since cowboys, booze and broken hearts all went together in the lyrics of some of their greatest hits.

The crowd below, on both sides, were getting into this real grass roots American music. C&W lyrics told so many stories of the blood, the guts and the beer of life.

Willie Nelson appeared and walked up to the microphone in front of this vast venue and began singing "Angel Flying Too Close to the Ground". Wayne joined in for back up licks and tried his best to keep up with the Texas legend. Willie played a mean ole classical guitar, battered from years on stage. From classical brilliance to the heart of American music was such a contrast. But no less attended to by all the people gathered.

When the apparition of Garth Brooks began singing "Friends in Low Places" the shrieks of the hideous visages on the dark side were matched evenly with the shouts of praise by the viewers on the bright side. Everyone loved Garth's songs. What no one realized was that Chiun was setting them up with the titles of the songs and the words that they contained, all having to do with wrecked lives, heartache and heartbreak. Baal watched as Chiun spun his demonic magic.

Then, out of nowhere, Charlie Daniels appeared with his big cowboy hat and blazing fiddle. Simultaneously, an image of a freakish leprechaun, also holding a fiddle, formed beside Charlie. They stood face to face as dueling fiddles playing "The Devil Went Down to Georgia".

As they played out the words to the song, their fiddles began smoking, then blazing with fire causing the crowd to yell for more. Both sides cheered for their contestant in the song. Harder and harder, louder and louder, Charlie played against the ghoulish musician who seemed to play stronger as the fiddles burned brighter. Unlike the words to the song, the horrid little demon rose up from the stage, played faster and stronger than Charlie Daniels' apparition, who couldn't keep up and with an explosion, Charlie Daniels went up in a puff of smoke, disintegrated and disappeared.

The rascal-looking leprechaun raised up his bow in triumph. Looking down on the dark side stands, he said, "That one was for you! Praise be to the evil that is. Too bad, Charlie, you've been smoked!"

The bright side of the stands grew dimmer, more silent and the white robed attendees cast glances at their demonic counterparts on the other side of the arena who looked like long-term junkies, tracks mapping their arms and wearing torn, wreaking clothes that smelled like they had been fished out of a dumpster full of garbage and had mildewed for six months. The darkness became darker, the sky turned from white, billowing clouds into dark thunderous clouds. Gordon could easily see the evil being spun and the strategy of the demons was becoming evident to him. But opening events and the deceit of Chiun to claim Wayne's soul had just begun.

The Grand Ole Opry stage vanished in the twinkling of an eye. The next event in Chiun's carefully planned scheme was about to unfold. Wayne, again, stood on an empty stage looking down on the crowds below. His soul was vibrant from the music. The thought of the great European and Russian composers coming together with the home spun original American music being played by the legends of C&W was a brilliant contrast and he was part of it. He'd played with Hank Williams and Johnny Cash.

"Gordon, if this is the type of challenges that I'll be facing, bring on more. This is one of the greatest times of my life. How can this be bad?"

"Watch the small details, Wayne. They're sucking you in. Be aware."

During the brief intermission, once again the skies boiled as the setting began to change. There was a huge rumble, then a bright, burning fireball blazed down from the darkness above, streaking down to the stage, lighting up the entire arena. A gigantic explosion shook the now elevated platform then dissipated to reveal the likeness of Jerry Lee Lewis banging on his piano, singing "Great Balls of Fire".

The arena rocked as Jerry Lee stood up, kicked his piano stool across the stage and shrieked out the words. As the Rock & Roll Hall of Famer finished his nostalgic set, the clouds above the arena began boiling once again to signal the next act. Wayne was dancing at the edge of the stage, full of anticipation and thinking that this had to be the greatest concert in history. From burning fireballs to fluffy clouds, the colors turned completely violet as did the ground beneath the stage. Vague at first, then becoming more audible, Wayne heard the sound of a very recognizable guitar. Out of the plum mass overhead, the apparition of Jimi Hendrix appears with his wailing guitar playing "Purple Haze". The stage was now set with modern lighting, lasers and pyrotechnics orchestrated with the tones and sounds of the music. *South* was there dressed in 60s and 70s bell-bottomed pants, psychedelic, tie-dyed T-shirts and each band member had exceptionally long hair. Hendrix's psychedelic music filled the air. The heavy beat strummed the bodies of everyone in attendance. Hendrix floated around the arena, booming out his mighty tune and reached out his hand for Wayne to join him in the air.

Grabbing his Stratocaster with wireless pickups, Wayne floated alongside Hendrix hovering in circles over the arena. Wayne was in complete hippie dress and shared the same state of mind as he blasted out a few runs, amazing the crowd with his musical talents. Wayne looked to his left. He and Hendrix were joined by more apparitions of rock and roll legends. Eric Clapton began wailing his own Fender guitar as they drifted into playing and singing the words to "Cocaine". The dark side participants were passing huge bags of cocaine around for the taking. Their faces had the white powder strewn across their noses and ghoulish mouths. The crowds below and all around the arena were completely enamored with the stars. The music dazzled, the performers amazed and the moment mesmerized.

As they swirled around the coliseum, the stage began to take on a new shape. It became a replica of the flat-topped, straight brimmed hat with a sterling silver, carved American Indian hatband, the trademark of the immortal Stevie Ray Vaughn, one of the greatest blues singers and guitarists the world had ever known.

Vaughn floated down to the top of the huge hat while spotlights came out of the sky following his descent onto the stage. He motioned to Wayne to jam with him as *South* played opening music, situated around the flat brim, just below Vaughn and Wayne.

Stevie Ray began to belt out "The House is Rocking". Truer lyrics couldn't have been more appropriate as spectators on both sides were clapping their hands, yelling and witnessing events that went beyond imagination. Bright side and dark side spectators were getting into the moment in different ways. Bright side participants, including Abby and friends were rocking to the purity of the talents they witnessed. Dark side attendees were shouting expletives to describe their feelings and checking each other out with lust, slugged with the effects of the drugs, as they sucked down mass quantities of alcohol, getting drunker, higher and louder by the minute.

Wayne had once jammed with Eric Clapton and Stevie Ray when he was hanging out late one night in a small pub in England. This moment was as if they'd remembered him and taken him under their wings. Wayne could play the blues with the best and at this very moment, he was doing exactly that. He loved every second of it. Now he was spotlighted on Stevie Ray's own stage before the largest venue in history, playing with his very own guitar heroes. Wayne was in his element, high on the music!

A booming voice reached into Wayne's mind, clearly the voice of Gordon saying, "Remember *hubris* and pride, Wayne. Listen to me!"

Wayne verbally shouted back, "Shut up, Gordon! I don't want to hear it. I'm in *my* element now."

Mentally talking to himself, Wayne exclaimed, *"I love it! I love it! I love this life!"*

As the words left his mind, he heard another thought with a clear distinctive voice that he recognized immediately.

"Yes, you do love it, Wayne. Much more than you could ever love me …"

Wayne took a quick glance down on the bright side to check on Abby. She was sad, Her robe not as bright as it had been. Her green eyes shed a tear as it slowly found its way down her cheek. He could see her disappointment and knew that he was blowing it with her again. But he couldn't do anything about the way she felt. He could only live his life and if there was any of it left, he'd try again later. Right now, whether he lived longer or not, Wayne was going to go out with a bang! He was in the middle of the greatest moment he had ever experienced, and he loved every second of it. He couldn't escape his passion.Once again he was up and down about how he felt about Abby. He couldn't love her because he'd even said to himself that he didn't really know what love was. But he yearned for her touch at the same time. For the present, Wayne decided to stay in the moment and fight his battles. He would think about his relationship with Abby after he found out if it was even possible. Whether he would live or die.

In mid thought, in mid song, wrestling with his emotions about Abby, Wayne saw a genuine magic carpet flying around the coliseum. The music, the band and the legends all pitched in to join Steppenwolf, who was riding the magic carpet, an ancient rug from the land of India with long flowing tassels. Steppenwolf's apparition was singing and wailing out his boomer gold record, "The Pusher Man", which contained some of the most blasphemous lyrics ever released by a record label. The song was a sign of the 60s when a generation rebelled and pushed decency to the limits. A time when sex, drugs and rock and roll were worshiped as gods unto themselves.

"G..D..the Pusher man …" caused the dark side demons to go crazy, crazier than normal as they thrived on every blasphemous word in the lyrics. They shouted it out at the bright side crowd in complete defiance of an Almighty God! Their god was Satan. They had no use for nor did they hold back from showing their allegiance and what they stood for, to kill, steal and destroy all that was righteous and good.

Steppenwolf swooped down and hovered the magic carpet in front of the hat-like stage and invited Wayne to step on board. For some reason, Wayne took a step back and declined the offer. Even Wayne had his limits and 'GD' was one of the few expletives he refused to use in his language. He didn't want to shout it out here at this tremendous event and he really didn't know why. Again, things just didn't seem to be right, and Wayne was having trouble putting what was right in one column and what was wrong in another. All of a sudden, in this situation it was very difficult to tell the difference.

The music wound down after his decision not to go for a ride on the magic carpet with Steppenwolf. Wayne was still standing atop the hat with Eric Clapton and Stevie Ray. As the clouds grew dark and the music ended, Wayne walked over to Eric and Stevie Ray.

"I don't know if you guys are real or created apparitions. But either way, I want to tell you what an honor it's been to play with two of my heroes in this phenomenal venue. I wish you luck, guys, I really do."

One by one Clapton and Stevie Ray extended their hand to Wayne without saying a word to him. He shook both of their hands. Both the legends along with the band just disappeared right before Wayne's eyes. He was left standing on an empty stage, alone. The lights were out, the concert was over and there was no cast party afterwards.

As Wayne glanced down at the two sides of spectators, he noticed that the dark side was darker and the bright side was dimmer. Had he failed the test???

"Gordon! I need to talk to you. Is the first trial over? How'd I do?"

There was no reply.

Wayne looked up to see a huge black limo floating down from the sky with a hot tub in the rear of it. It rolled up to the edge of the elevated stage, the door swung open and out stepped Chiun dressed in the most expensive suit Wayne had ever seen. A seven-carat diamond stick pin dominated the thousand dollar fiery red tie. Chiun had a perfect build, slick-shaven head with a silver goatee and mustache. Wayne couldn't tell his nationality. Chiun's almost flawless skin was tan, whether natural or sprayed on, Wayne couldn't tell; either way, it was perfect. He noticed a long fingernail on the pinkie finger of Chiun's left hand.

"Step into my office, Wayne Tyler," Chiun said, motioning Wayne through a huge oak doorway. The stage had transformed into an opulent, high rise office that looked over the Pacific Ocean and appeared to be in Los Angeles. "Have a seat at the conference table and let's talk contract."

Wayne was still wearing his tie-dye T-shirt and ragged bell-bottomed jeans. He felt particularly underdressed for this unexpected meeting.

"Who are you?" Wayne asked.

"You can call me Mr. Chiun. I am the god and the agent of the stars. Look at the walls and the plaques of all of my gold and platinum record clients."

Wayne gazed around the conference room. Hundreds of gold and platinum record plaques hung on the walls in quadruple rows all around. He stood in front of each one to see the name of the artist and the title of their hit song but noticed that the names and song titles were blurred.

"Impressive opening, Mr. Chiun. The meteor fireworks display was brilliant, the ball of fire thing with Jerry Lee Lewis was stunning and all the rest that went with the opening acts. So, uh … Why are the names of the artists and their hit song titles blurred out on the plaques?"

"Confidentiality agreements, Mr. Tyler. My client list is a closely guarded secret. I make deals that no one in the music business can make. I *guarantee* fame, riches, women, and popularity to all of my clients."

"And I bet you're going to offer me a deal, right, Mr. Chiun?"

"I like the way you get right to the point, Mr. Tyler. Yes, I'm going to make you a deal you can't refuse!" The demon chuckled and rocked back in his huge leather chair, sliding a two and a half inch thick legal document in front of Wayne along with a solid gold pen studded with diamonds on the clip.

"You can just sign the last page, Mr. Tyler. The fine print isn't that important."

"Do you really think I would do that? Who are you that you can you guarantee such things?"

"Because I have a *special influence* over most of all of mankind. I plant thoughts in their heads. I can make you a world-wide star, Mr. Tyler, in every nation of the earth. I make movie deals, television guest appearances, I handle all promotion, publicity and record/CD/DVD distribution worldwide. I'll even guarantee you a hundred million dollars over ten years, great venues, out-of-this world songs and as a token of my guarantee, which is all written in the contract, I'll give you an advance cashier's check right now for half of it, fifty million U.S. dollars. Do you like the way I talk, Mr. Tyler? Just sign the last page."

"So, Mr. Chiun, I'm finally speaking face-to-face with a demon. Somehow, you look different from what I imagined. Great ruse you're putting on here and, incidentally, what a great opening performance you created … I'm guessing that was your work, Mr. Chiun."

"Of course it was my presentation. Colossal, brilliant, wasn't it, Mr. Tyler? I'll do even more for you. This isn't a ruse. Surely you don't want to spend the rest of your days singing at the dump, Tequilaville? Sign the contract." Chiun made no mention of Wayne realizing he was a demon.

"That contract is way too thick of a document for me to read over right now. I'd have to let my lawyer look it over." Wayne was being facetious.

Chiun placed his open hand over the document and instantly changed it from two inches thick to a single page with large, easy to read type.

"Is this a better format for you, Mr. Tyler?"

"Yeah, Mr. Chiun, much better. I see that all I have to do for all this fame, fortune and women is just sign my soul over to you. Is that pretty much the gist of the deal?"

"You've got it perfectly, Mr. Tyler. I'm not here to deceive you. Your soul for ten years of fame, one hundred million dollars with fifty million up front. When you die, your soul belongs to me. Let's sign!"

"Can you also guarantee that I have ten years of life left, Mr. Chiun, god of stars? Last I remember, I left my body fourteen feet under the waters of Galveston Bay in Texas. Do you know about that?"

"Of course I know about that, Mr. Tyler. It was your reason to be here and to give me the opportunity to represent you to the world. I'll give you your much deserved fifteen minutes, or in this case, your ten years of fame."

"Uh, Mr. Chiun, you failed to answer the first part of my question, the guarantee of ten more years of life, remember?"

"On that part, Mr. Tyler, you'll just have to trust me. In the meantime, here's your check for the fifty million or would you rather have it in cash? Now, let's cut to the chase and sign."

"Ya know, Chiun, you cheap, conniving demon, I wouldn't sign a record deal like this when I was a young aspiring artist. Yeah, I had the talent, the voice and the opportunities from three different record labels. The reason I wouldn't sign then was because their contract was similar to yours, but without the guarantees of course. They wanted to own me. They wanted to tell me what to sing, how to play, how to dress, what I could say and what I couldn't say. They wanted to control my life and keep me on the road for 360 days a year so the record executives could cash in at my expense.

"I got into music because I have a passion for the music and the performance of that music; not the money, not the women and not the fame. To me those are just perks of a craft that I take seriously. The music is in my heart and soul. I can't breathe without it. I didn't go for a controlling contract then and I'm not going to sell my soul for one now. Not for all the money in the world. I'll take my chances at Tequilaville to find my purpose, develop my talents and cling to my passions. I'll hook my wagon to a different star, Chiun. No deal!"

"You're a fool, Wayne! Do you realize what I can do for you?!"

"Yeah, I do, Chiun. You can send my soul to hell, but it's not going to happen today. I rebuke you. Leave me!"

"So full of pride, Wayne. I'm going to leave my card with you. Call me when you want to make a deal, I'll always be around."

Wayne looked at the card. It read "Mr. Chiun, Star God, 1-666-SOULMAN."

Chiun returned to the limo as the office setting on the platform disappeared into oblivion. Wayne could hear the demon wailing as the driver drove the limo up and beyond the clouds. Chiun had failed and he knew that Baal would punish him in terrible ways known only to the evil ones.

"Wayne, call a time out! We need to talk before your next trial. This one's over." Gordon's voice was insistent.

12

AMAZING DISGRACE
ANGEL OF LIGHT

Standing on the empty stage with only his memories of such an amazing opening event, Wayne officially called a time out and waited for Gordon to appear. He didn't and it concerned Wayne. He was becoming anxious and full of doubt when he finally heard Gordon's voice speaking to him by thought.

"Let's talk, Wayne. Tell me how you think you did during the first trial."

"To tell you the truth, Gordon, I'm confused."

"Go on. Keep thinking and tell me what confuses you."

"Well … Uh … I really got into that opening. I mean, playing and singing with my heroes really got to me. And as for whether it was good or bad … . Mmm, it was fantastic, Gordon! How could something like that be bad?"

"Did you hear what Abby said to you, Wayne?"

"Yeah … She was right, too. I do love this life and my passion for music."

"Wayne, what you're searching for is balance in your life. The Almighty gave you your passion for music and the gifts that go with it. HE loves music, too. HE invented it. If you let yourself be consumed by it, well, it's like loving a great steak. One's good for you but if you eat nothing else, it can take away the other spices of life, the diversity of all the other delicacies all around you.

"Music is a great passion, Wayne, but there are others you can enjoy such as love, family, friends, seeking your purpose in life. Why would you want to throw these wonders from your life and stay so focused solely on one passion when you can have so many?"

"Good point, Gordon. I do get wrapped up sometimes. So you're saying that too much of a good thing is a bad thing, huh?"

"You're figuring this out. As for as how you did in the first challenge, I'll give you an overview if you want to hear it, Wayne."

"Go. I'm all ears. I could use the clarity."

"Appreciating the performances of such gifted people was not bad in itself. It was an experience very few souls have ever had, but it was meant to suck you into the moment, to make you yearn for fame and fortune. To your credit, it didn't work. Your pure devotion to your craft made you decide which was more important. You stayed true to your heart, Wayne, and that was a good decision."

"Thanks, Gordon. Any encouragement right now helps me a great deal. Hearing Abby's comment kind of grounded me while my thoughts were getting out of control. She *was* my balance during that first trial … What's next?"

"I can't say, Wayne. When you're on the platform, you're on your own. I can prompt you, but I can't make decisions for you. Just think, take your time and make good decisions while you're up there."

"By the way, Gordon, who was that guy sitting next to Abby with the white streak in his hair over his right ear? I don't remember ever meeting him and for some reason I got the idea that he seemed familiar with this place. Was I wrong?"

"You haven't met him … yet. He could play an important part in your future if you have a future. As for what you felt, you're very perceptive, Wayne. He has been here before, but that's another story. When you're ready, just say, 'Resume!' The next trial will begin."

Wayne took a deep breath, looked at his surroundings as the platform began to levitate once again when he said, 'Resume.' As he rose, he looked down at Abby, at Hank and all of his friends sitting on the bright side. They stared back at him with a glance of anxious anticipation. Dread consumed him.

Suddenly the stage turned into a white fluffy cloud. The sky turned to a beautiful blue and Wayne could hear what appeared to be a massive angelic choir, voices singing in almost perfect unison. The field below turned to millions of colorful flowers bringing a wonderful fragrance to the surroundings. Descending from the sky was an even brighter angel-looking, rather rotund, woman sprouting tiny fairy wings and crowned with a halo. She laughed like a grandma as she happily sang …

"Amazing disgrace, how sweet the sound
That created a little pixie pumpkin like me.
I once was thin, but now I'm fat
Was lost but now I'm where it's at …

"Chill out, honey child," said Chemosh, "I ain't here to claim your soul, I'm gonna take you on a happy trip. Now give Mama-Che a big hug!"

Wayne pulled back from the enormous laughing lady. She had to weigh about 395, very obese but very happy in her, uh, skin? Again, he was completely unprepared to deal with what was happening.

"First thing we've got to do is to get comfortable, Wayne. Help me take this halo off. It's blinding me. You've got nothing to fear from me, sweet thang. I'm here to help you figure things out." She laughed like she knew him and for the moment, his anxieties diminished slightly.

"Hey, little boy, let's change the scenery to something a little more fun."

Immediately the cloud-like stage turned into a venue resembling an American honky-tonk bar with a Cheesecake Factory located on one end. The place was empty except for a table with two chairs in the center.

"Have a seat, Wayne, while I fold up my little pixie wings and get into one of my favorite Hawaiian muumuu dresses to kinda match all those beautiful flowers down below and show off my pixie figure. Ha ha ha! How ya doing? Do you want to get out of those ole tie-dyes you're still wearing?"

Wayne was speechless but did *think* on some boots, jeans and a nice flannel shirt.

"You don't have to say a word, honey child. Just let Mama-Che chill you out a little. Hey, you want some cheesecake and beer? It's my favorite. I bet you prefer a good Texas bock beer. You look like you need one, child."

"I could use a beer … uh … Mama-Che, is it? But I'll pass on the cheesecake."

"I wish you'd try a piece. I invented cheesecake when I bet on Goliath, you know that giant who got into a big fight with little David and lost. I had to create something kind of *heavenly* for the payback and stirred up that recipe. I just love cheesecake and eat as much as I can. You should try it. It'll make you feel so much better and like I said, 'I ain't here to hurt you, child.'"

"So what are you here to do? And can I just call you Che? I'm more comfortable with that."

"Hey, baby, you can call me anything you want, just don't call me late for dinner … Ha Ha Ha!" Her laughter was contagious. Wayne was actually enjoying this funny girl who had such of a sense of humor. He never thought that he'd see a lighter side during these trials, but he found himself laughing with her and at her at the same time. She had such a unique personality, completely different from what he had ever dreamed.

"Are you a demon, Che?"

"*Demoness*, Wayne. I'm a lady! But don't start judging me, and I won't judge you. Is that a deal, little buddy?"

"Deal. It's just that I thought that I was here for judgment."

"Not from me, Wayne. I'm a *live and let live* sort of lady. Demons and demonesses like me get a bad rap from people because they just don't understand us.

"We made choices, too, that were based on our own reasons. That's why you're here, Wayne, to do the same. I'm going to help you explore your options and do it in an unbiased manner, unlike your friend, Gordon. Oh yeah, I know Gordon. We were best of friends until we chose different paths. I like him, but he goes his way and I go mine. Who do you think I lost the bet to? HA HA HA! Gordon didn't really bet, I just bet him and paid off when I lost … It was the honorable thing to do. He really is adorable but he doesn't like me much. His loss …"

"So when is the happy trip going to begin, Che?"

"Soon! Let me go back to my early career when my territory was in the Middle East; it's in the deep south of the U.S. now. Back then I was assigned to David. What a trip he was, Wayne. King David just loved to do battle, but battle wasn't my thing at all. Way too much blood and gore for me.

"One morning when David was about to get up and fight another war, I, Che, ever so gently kind of hovered down on top of him just before he awoke, placed my full little pixie body on top of his and that boy, like most men, thought he was having a heart attack, you know, like an elephant sitting on his chest?

"So he stayed home that day. I decided he needed another passion in his life other than war and killing so I arranged for a pretty young lady, Bathsheba, to accidentally crack her indoor bathtub and go outside for her bath. He laid eyes on her gorgeous body while he was on his balcony looking down at her and, whamo! He had a new passion in his life. Hey, the rest is history. What a fling they had. You've heard of them, haven't you, Wayne?"

"Seems like I have. So what happened next?"

"They had a slight mishap in the beginning, she got pregnant and being married to one of David's generals, things got a bit tense for a while. But as fate would have it," Che pointed to herself, "And you're looking at fate, Wayne, that would be me, Che, Bathsheba's husband got killed in the war, Bathsheba moved in to the palace and out popped Solomon about a year or so later. Solomon was a handsome kid and heir to the throne of his father, David."

"Che, I don't know much about history but you seem to be leaving out some parts …"

"Hey, sugah, this is my story. You weren't there; I was. Let me tell it my way, okay?"

"Cool, go ahead, Che."

"Well, Solomon was just another little rich kid with a gold spoon in his mouth. His daddy had defeated all their enemies and when Solomon took over the throne, he had more money coming in than he could spend. He built a big temple, he built cities, vineyards, wineries, had stables full of horses and chariots, and basically just became an over-achieving little workaholic.

"So, once again, Mama-Che to the rescue! I started putting thoughts in his good-looking head about having fun with his life and not just working it away."

"And what were the results of these little thoughts, Che?"

"Seven hundred wives, three hundred concubines. You do know what a concubine is don't you, Wayne?"

"Not really."

"They're mistresses. I mean, a guy of his wealth and good looks needed some diversions."

"And you supplied those little diversions, huh, Che?"

"Did I ever, Wayne. Solomon was the richest man ever on earth. I showed him how to add a balance to his life and to quit being such an anal workaholic. I mean, Y.O.L.O. Ba-by! You only live once. Grab everything life has to give and worry about tomorrow later since worry won't add a single day to your life.

"*Carpe Diem*, Wayne. Seize the moment! Eat, drink and be merry for tomorrow we die, Sugah! That little stud punkin was just answering the natural calls of nature and he even built a monument to me for freeing him of his inhibitions."

Gordon knew full well that Wayne didn't know the details of the story of Solomon and gave him a little insight. Telepathically, Gordon sent a message to Wayne.

"Tell Chemosh that Solomon later wrote that life was all vanity and that the beginning of wisdom is fear of The Almighty! Solomon died a lonely, misguided man."

"Uhh … what about vanity, Che? I understand even with all his toys, Solomon was unfulfilled and lonely when he died."

"But what a life he lived, Wayne. One that you, too, can live. But there's a little more that I want to show you. I told you that I was here to help you, darling."

"Is this the happy trip you were talking about, Che?"

"Absolutely. Let's fly to and fro around today's world, Wayne."

The plump pixie demoness took Wayne by the hand and flew from one part of the earth to the other, pointing out scenes along the way. Che was constantly talking to him, planting seeds of doubt in his mind but never forcing any of her views on Wayne.

"Wayne, in this big ole fun place we call Earth, there are about seven billion people, give or take a few hundred thousand since about a quarter million babies arrive every day and about that number of people die each day."

"That many die each day?"

"Yeah, Wayne, on the average. But here's some numbers to kick around. Of the seven billion people, about five billion have freely chosen not to be Christians. What does that tell you?"

"I haven't a clue, Che. Why don't you tell me."

"It says that everyone has freedom of choice and free will to choose their lifestyle and their beliefs. Most inhabitants of this world make other choices than to stay under the strict terms of this Almighty, His Ten Commandments and all of those *thou shalt not's*! There's just no room for enjoying life as long as there are no alternatives and most people decide *not* to believe in all these restrictions of life. Cheesecake and beer or fruits and veggies, sugah? No one's perfect, Wayne."

"So when you made your decision, Che, you decided on life on earth over life in heaven?"

"You betcha I did, Wayne. That's why demons have such a bad rap. All we did was to choose a time of fun and choices rather than to stay on the straight and narrow. Can you imagine how boring eternity would be just sitting on a cloud all day playing a harp? "And, yes, Wayne, there is an Almighty, I've been in His presence, but I couldn't live by all His rules. I chose to go with my leader, Satan. Since the odds are so great in his favor, I believe he'll win out in the end."

Again, Gordon's distinctive voice pierced into Wayne's confused mind.

"The path to heaven is straight and narrow. Few will choose it. The path to the lake of fire is broad. Choose carefully, Wayne. Life is short. Eternity is forever and hell exists!"

Wayne thought for a short while, then said to Che,

"I heard some preacher on TV that said Jesus died for the sins of all mankind so they could have eternal life. Did Satan ever die for anyone to prove his point of view?"

"Are you kidding, Wayne? Our master Satan is all about life, not death. He died laughing at the herd mentality of so many suffering Christians wanting to *take up their cross* and all the *longsuffering* noise mentioned in the Almighty's book."

"So you read the Almighty's book, huh, Che?"

"Of course I did! All the demons know every word in the 31,173 verses. It's just that we chose another way. I mean, *suffering* or fun? Duh, Wayne that's a hard choice, isn't it? You know, there're a lot of books out there, Wayne. You should read more and see the other choices they offer to religion and life. Don't be a pinhead!"

"OK, Che, answer another question for me about the dark side crowd."

"Shoot, honey child!"

"Why do all of these ghoulish mirror imaged *things* look and smell so bad. I mean, who would want to look like they do?"

"It's a Halloween thing, Wayne. See, in our realm, every day is costume day. We get to be anyone or anything we want to be. It's fun and the more realistic, the better. Right now, with all the shows and movies promoting *the living dead*, seems like this is the most popular costume of the year. Get my drift?"

"Uh … I guess I do, Che … Thanks for the happy trip with all the choices. You've given me a lot to think about without trying to sway my opinion. I really need to digest all of this and if you don't mind, I'm ready to get back, maybe even have a piece of cheesecake."

Wayne smiled at Che as she immediately changed course and returned to the platform high above the arena.

After a piece of the best cheesecake Wayne had ever tasted, he looked over at Che, feeling somewhat comfortable in the setting and still a little confused about his decisions. It was easy to see that boredom was no match for fun.

"Che, are all the demons and demonesses as nice and friendly as you are?"

"Oh, Wayne, we're similar to the mortals in some respects. Some are more tolerable than others if you know what I mean. Not all of us appear as fire breathing dragons looking to kill, steal and destroy."

"What about Baal? Tell me more about him."

"You don't want to mess with Baal, Wayne. Baal's a beast! He's the baddest of the bad except for Satan. He's the bogie man in your worst nightmare. I won't lie to you; he uses no tact or finesse when it comes to being Satan's number one captain and enforcer. He's brute force and brute power, unrelenting, plus, Baal carries a huge grudge. He has for thousands of years."

"Grudge?" Wayne asked. "Against who and why?"

"There was a battle of sorts when Elijah challenged the prophets of Baal. I mean, Baal actually had his own church at one time long ago. Elijah, The Almighty's man, challenged the prophets of Baal to some kind of ego match and Elijah ended up killing 450 of Baal's men right in front of Baal's entire church. It hacked him off big time and he's had a chip on his shoulder ever since."

"Che, if Baal is so bad and powerful, why didn't he just kill Elijah and get it over with?"

"That's what he planned on doing but the Almighty whisked Elijah up from the earth and hid him in heaven. Elijah was kind of like the first to be in the witness protection program. He never returned to earth and he never died."

"Hmmm, I didn't know that …" Wayne had never heard of anyone not dying."I really hope your decisions don't come down to dealing with Baal, Wayne, because I kinda like you. Hey, if you have more questions, here's my card. Call me anytime, honey child."

Wayne took Che's card. On it was written:

Mama-Che, Matchmaker of the Kings, Phone: 1-666-PIGSFLY

With a billowing laugh, the rotund image of Chemosh rose into the sky and disappeared. The stage turned to bare marble once again. The bar, the cheesecake area was gone but the wonderful taste of it still lingered in Wayne's mouth. The flowers on the field below uprooted and followed Che up into nothingness. The field became grass once again. Trial number two was over and Wayne had no idea why it had ever occurred and what the outcome of this tribulation was all about. He was back to confusion and wondered what would happen next. So far, so good.

The still of the moment was broken as Wayne heard Gordon's voice.

"Do you want to call a time out, Wayne?"

"N'ah, I'm getting a handle on the trials. It's not like these demons are ripping me to shreds as you led me to believe, Gordon. Hey, I met an old friend of yours, Che."

"She's no friend of mine, Wayne, nor is she your friend. She's misleading you with half-truths. There's so much more you don't know about her stories of life and eternal life."

"Just cool it, Gordon. I'll make up my own mind. Buzz off!"

Before Wayne had a chance to say another word or have another thought, he heard some new age, soothing elevator-type music playing. The platform was transformed into the plush setting of a high end day spa, complete with massage table, burning incense and beautiful pictures of sunsets and sunrises on the wall, giving him a feeling of peace and comfort. He was standing with his underwear on and a towel wrapped around him.

Appearing before him was a beautiful lady in green silk scrubs. She had flowing dark hair. There was something mystifying about her hair, because it seemed to move on its own, like being underwater, swishing and swaying with the currents.

"When's the last time you had a great massage, Wayne?"

"I don't think I've ever had one. Who are you?"

"I'm your massage therapist. My name is Diana. I'm from Ephesus."

Wayne had no idea where Ephesus was and didn't want to show his ignorance with this beautiful lady by asking.

"You're beautiful, Diana. Are you here to seduce me?"

"Not at all. I'm going to give you a massage like no other. Climb on the table and lie on your stomach. I'll get some spicy oils to rub on your body …"

Diana slowly rubbed the fragrant oils into Wayne's neck, down his back and onto his thighs and calves. Her hands were soft and strong. Wayne felt the tension in his neck and shoulders slowly drift away, breathed in the scented air and listened to the soft music. He was absolutely relaxed, enjoying every second of his first massage and thought, *So this is the reason all the ladies like to go and get pampered. I'll have to do this for Abby one day … if we have another day.*

"How's the rub, Wayne? Are you feeling sexy?"

"I'm loving it, Diana and yes, I'm feeling very sexy, are you?

"I stay sexy, big boy. Are you ticklish?"

"Only in certain places. Are you sure you're not trying to seduce me?"

"Would I do a thing like that?" Diana said in a soft sensual whisper.

She began gently kissing Wayne behind his ear, licking his neck, all the time continuing the massage. She pulled his towel down lower and lower.

"Why don't you turn over, lover. How about a little snifter of cognac? It's a great relaxer."

Wayne turned over on his back as Diana slid the towel from his loins. Wayne looked at her with lust in his eyes, temporarily forgetting that everyone on both sides of the stadium watched his every move. He was mesmerized by this beautiful lady with the self-flowing hair. She slowly reached for his hand and put his fingers in her mouth with a gentle sucking sound. He took another sip of the cognac and let Diana continue with her sensuous massage.

"Abby's watching! I, uh, I can't do this!" Wayne startled himself back to some semblance of reality. He sat up on the massage table.

"Lie down, Wayne. Nothing's going to happen. Who do you think I am, some tramp?"

"No, I certainly wasn't looking at you like a tramp, Diana. Forgive me if I gave you the wrong impression. But I would like to know more about you."

"I'll tell you more about me in a little while. I'd rather talk about you. After all, you're the reason we're all here. You're the star of the show. I just thought you could use some chilling out before the rest of the trials resume. So let's break the ice … What's your favorite sin, Wayne?"

"That's a pointed question. Why would I want to talk about that? I'm guessing you already know what it is. You're a demoness, right, Diana?"

"Let me put you at ease … I'm a spirit being. You couldn't have sex with me if you wanted to, and believe me, Wayne, I know you well enough to guess that you want to."

"I never said that, Diana!"

"But you were lusting after me in your mind. I know your special looks very well, Wayne. I've witnessed every woman you've ever slept with. I've seen you break hearts, commit adultery with married women that caused divorces, deflower countless virgins. I've been there every time you've lured women back to your apartment with promises of back rubs, tickling them, filling them with strong drinks and soft music to lower their inhibitions, telling them how much you love them, how unique and beautiful they are so you could conquer them and add another notch to your bedpost, Mr. Studly! Do you deny this?"

"I can't help it if women find me attractive. I don't like where this conversation is going."

"Can you help it when you wake up the next morning, can't wait for them to leave and tell them you'll call them then never do, Wayne? Can you deny the walks of shame these women endured returning home in front of all their friends, family and neighbors early in the morning wearing the same party dresses you took off beside your bed, the ones they'd worn the night before? Can you deny the guilt and dirty feelings that these women couldn't wash off with ten showers and a bubble bath? Let's face it, Wayne, you're a vagabond and a voyeur of world class."

"You're judging me, Diana. I thought I wasn't here for judgment. I confess my sins of lust; I'm just human."

"You're not going to be judged by me, Wayne. But you will start paying up for the pain you've caused. You've admitted that you're guilty. It's time to face the consequences of your favorite sin, lust!"

As Diana spoke, her hair began to take on a mind of its own. It grew longer, down to her ankles and began to spread out around her head. Wayne still couldn't focus enough to see that each tiny hair on her head was an ultra-thin, dark brown serpent with a mouth that enclosed tiny fangs, hundreds of thousands of them. Diana's eyes began to turn blood red as her anger increased.

"Have you ever heard the expression, 'Hell hath no fury like a woman scorned?'"

"Of course. Everyone's heard that!"

"Well, you wanted to know more about me. I *am* hell's fury! "

Diana's glowing red eyes hypnotized Wayne into a semi-conscious state. He could see and feel everything going on around him as he lay face up on the massage table but was completely helpless to move and at Diana's mercy. There would be no mercy from her.

As Wayne lay with only his briefs on, Diana began to prostate herself on top of him. She moved her face close to his face and moved slowly down his body as the thousands of tiny hair-like serpents began biting him, injecting their poison into every square inch of his skin. Wayne could barely feel the tiny, countless bites but he could see what was happening to him and had no control to stop it. One by one, the serpents struck, filling Wayne's body with venom.

"Say hello to my little friends, Wayne. Do you remember that line from the movie? I'm giving it a whole new meaning! How does it feel to be helpless?"

Wayne couldn't speak, he could only shake his head wildly while he drooled at the mouth, anticipating the pain of the bites.

Diana stood up and with a wave of her hand, every single tiny venomous bite turned in to a blood-filled boil, causing Wayne excruciating pain. He moaned and shrieked, still unable able to speak intelligible words. He had never felt pain like this, it consumed his total being.

"Before I'm finished with you, Wayne, you'll beg me for death, but death will not come. You're experiencing the fury of hell from Diana of Ephesus for all the pain and shame that you've caused womankind. I'm the pay back and this is for them.

"Next you'll experience their scorn and well remember that old saying. The scorn of women is on its way. Feel it, experience it and never forget it!"

Still under the hypnotic trance, Wayne watched helplessly as Diana hovered above him. His pain level was ninety-five on a scale of one to ten. She reached down and touched Wayne's foot. Thousands of black, desert venomous scorpions crawled down from her opened hand and quickly covered every part of his body. They were on his face, his groin, his legs and stomach. Their stingers poised, waiting for Diana's command to strike.

"Wayne, just say, 'Send me back!' That's your only escape to rid yourself of this harrowing experience. Say it or bear the consequences." Diana released his hypnotic state so that he could talk and feel.

"Gordon! Help me! Please help me! I'm in agony and it's about to get worse!"

Wayne looked down from the table to see the entire field below the platform crawling with serpents and scorpions, one on top of the other forming a carpet of living horror. The dark side was howling, shouting in unison to Wayne saying, "Send me back! Send me back! Send me back!"

In his agonizing condition, Wayne looked at the bright side of the field to see Abby crying out, reaching up to him, leaving her seat to fearlessly crawl out amongst the snakes and scorpions trying to get to him. It was no use, he was two hundred feet in the air, hovering on the platform above the stands. She couldn't rescue him this time.

Abby yelled up at Wayne, "I forgive you, baby! Don't go back! Don't go back!" Wayne glanced over at Hank, the tough former Marine. Surely Hank or Tito could help him. But Hank couldn't look anymore and turned away, feeling completely helpless. The sound of his excruciating pain and sheer horror that Wayne was about to endure was beyond his human comprehension.

Wayne yelled down to Robbie, "Help me Robbie! Please help me!" Robbie was a woman of faith and pretty tough but now she was crying, praying and trying to hold herself together. There seemed to be no hope.

At that moment, Diana nodded her head and the black deadly scorpions plunged their stingers into Wayne. He had a feeling of pain that could not be imagined. Wayne's howls and shrieks went off the charts. His entire body was consumed with boils and the venom of snakes and scorpions.

"That, my world class voyeur, is the scorn of women! This is your payback. How do you feel now?"

"Kill me! Kill me, Diana, you witch from hell. Just kill me now!"

"Oh, Wayne, I love it when you talk dirty to me! You're just putting another nail in your coffin."

"I'll die before I let you claim my soul by going back!"

"Wayne, you pitiful man, you said exactly what I knew you'd say. I've been punishing men for thousands of years and now it's your turn. I can't wait for the sheer pleasure of dishing out this pain 24/7, non-stop forever. A wicked man is always in trouble throughout his life." Besides, I can't kill your soul, it's eternal and I'm looking forward to claiming it. Come on, big man!

Your fans down there are chanting for you to 'GO BACK!' Just say the word. Say it now and rid yourself of this scorn and fury."

At his weakest point of life and writhing in pain, Wayne heard the voice of Gordon.

"Take the pain! Take the pain! This too shall pass. Fight, Wayne, fight!"

Wayne didn't know if it was the small degree of encouragement from Gordon, the bravery and forgiveness of Abby or his own warrior spirit coming to life but he stood up, brushing the scorpions from his face. His anger and will to live were kicking in at a time when he thought he had lost all hope. Anger was his motivation and his new found strength.

He staggered, grasped at the massage table and slowly got to his feet driven only by his own will to survive. He faced Diana squarely.

"I will not go back! I'll take your pain! And another thing, you ghoulish bit … you sorry no good whatever you are, I've got a word for you from a man, a warrior to give to all your vengeful, pitiful women accusers.

"It takes two to tango, baby! I was seduced by as many women as I seduced. The payback, the consequences of this lust belongs to them, too. Now stick this double standard consequence right up your as … your derriere. I rebuke you! Get the hell out of my face!"

"Who are you to rebuke me, pitiful Wayne? Your rebuke means nothing to me. You have no power, no faith and no redeemer. You're armed only with a tin shield, clinching your fist against God, defying the Almighty and demons alike. Suffer long. You are cursed!"

Diana waved her hand and the scorpions disappeared from Wayne's boil infested body. She stuck her finger in his eye inflicting one last wound as she howled and rose out of sight leaving Wayne sitting on the side of the massage table, reeling from the pain of the boils and the bites. His eye began to swell and the boils continued reeking horror on his body.

He was still there. He was still fighting. Wayne took the pain as it took his breath away. With his last ounce of strength, he tried to stand up again as he said in a weak voice …"Time out," and fell back on the table, unconscious. The third trial had ended and there was no victor, only losers and … justice was not done.

13

THE SHADOW OF DOUBT OBJECTION!

At the sound of Wayne's weak, "time out," Gordon suddenly appeared, hovering over him on the elevated platform. With his right hand raised high to the heavens above and his left outstretched downward toward the snake and scorpion-laden field below, Gordon waved them away with a single sweeping motion. The turf below returned to grass once again. The dark side crowd yelled in protest as the fifteen foot Guardian angel commandingly took over the situation to prepare Wayne for his next tribulation. Gordon looked down at the ghoulish dark side crowd below.

"Be silent, you beastly demons! Obey the command of The Almighty! Your time of judgment draws nigh."

The stadium and the crowd all around the venue became instantly silent. In the distance, where the coven of demons was convened, Gordon heard a deafening clap of thunder, signaling the demon's contemptuous, defiant disapproval of his command.

"I appeal to Jehovah Rapha, the God of Healing, to heal this man's soul." Gordon's voice boomed, authoritative and clearly heard by all.

In a heartbeat the boils, the venom and the scorpion's inflicted stingers vanished from Wayne's tormented body. The swelling in his eyes quickly subsided and his pain was gone as Wayne sat up on the massage table completely healed from the pain inflicted upon him by hell's fury, the demoness, Diana.

Wayne's senses returned to him slowly. His energy level was restored. He looked around him with a start of apprehension and saw Gordon standing next to him.

"That was a tough one, Gordon! Who healed me? Is she gone? I hate snakes and scorpions! The boils were so painful! Am I alive? Did they get me? How'd I do?" Wayne was almost to the point of babbling as his fears and anxieties returned, almost overwhelming him, dreading the next trial.

"You were healed by the power of The Almighty, Jehovah Rapha! The trial with Diana is over. You are still with us, she did not claim your soul and Diana is gone. You took the pain, Wayne, but how much can you take on your own? That's the question you should be asking yourself."

"Well … If you would, Gordon, say 'Thanks' to Jehovah what's-his-name for healing me. I really thought I was a goner. I've never been in that much pain in my whole life. That woman scared the hell out of me!"

"Good! She was trying to scare the hell into you."

"Hey, did you see Abby walking through that pit of snakes and scorpions trying to get to me to help? Wow, that's the bravest thing I've ever seen in my life. Honestly, I'm not sure I could've done that."

"Love overcomes fears, Wayne. Abby truly loves you and was willing to give her life for you. Greater love has no man … or woman. Remember this. You just witnessed the love of a woman for her man."

Back in his regular clothes, Wayne's comfort level begins to return as he inspects his arms and face for any signs of boils or bites. Gordon waved away the day spa setting of the platform and transformed it into a cabin setting in the mountains with roomy leather chairs and a roaring fireplace. Coffee perked on the stove. This setting, arranged by Gordon, came from Wayne's thoughts when he needed serenity in his life. It was a great place for a time out and to kick back before the next trial began.

"How do you feel now, Wayne?"

"A lot better! Could I get a cup of joe? Whew, this is like heaven here."

"You couldn't imagine heaven, Wayne, but I knew this would be a good place to regenerate your strength, settle your fears and begin to put some order in that mind of yours. Right now, you're pretty scrambled."

"Wouldn't you be, Gordon? Anyone would be scrambled after what's just happened to me. I mean, my gosh, you have eyes. You've been a witness to this …"

"Yes, I have eyes and I have been a witness to your tribulations. Can you believe your own eyes, Wayne? If you told someone what just happened to you would anyone back on earth believe you? How would you prove it?"

"Well, uh, by the boils … Mmmm, they're gone. Or by the bites … Mmmm, they're gone, too. I don't know how I'd prove it to someone else. They'd just have to see the passion of my story and believe it."

"Great point, Wayne, hold on to that thought. You're going to need it in your next tribulation. *Belief* is a very powerful word. It can determine your very destiny in life … and in death. But remember this, The Almighty has many documented stories recorded in His book. People either believe them or they reject them. Again, your choice."

Wayne took a sip of coffee and relaxed by the crackling fire. He took a deep breath, thinking of what was about to happen in his next tribulation.

"Gordon, now I know what you meant when you said to take time-outs. I don't think I could have made it this far without them."

"You keep using that word *I*, Wayne. And you're not going to make it very far on your own strength. Before long, you'll come to realize this. But you're still fighting. You'll decide what to do on your own. No one can make that decision for you."

"So what's next?"

"Your next tribulation is actually going to be a trial, Wayne. A court room setting."

"Oh, no! I thought you said I wasn't here for judgment. How's this going to work?"

"You're not here for judgment, Wayne. You will not be the defendant in this kangaroo court arranged by the demons. You'll be a jury of one."

"Okay, so who is the defendant and what's at stake?"

"Truth and belief will be on trial here, Wayne. You get to cast the only verdict on what you believe to be that truth and what your beliefs are. Those are the stakes, and they are high. The demons will be the prosecutors and present their twisted truths. I will be the defense attorney to rebut them and disprove them."

"So you're going to be present, Gordon? That makes me feel better."

"I will be present but it's not about feelings, Wayne, it is about your verdict and your beliefs. I told you that earlier. Before you will be blessings or curses, life and death decisions, destiny or doom …"

The words had hardly left Gordon's booming voice when the venue was changed to a weird and eerie courtroom scene. The platform began rising high above the stadium. Wayne sat in a jury box, by himself, with no other chairs present.

In front of him was a towering judge's bench made of solid gold with a pentagon and a goat head emblazoned on the front of the bench. Behind the empty judge's chair was a large, inverted cross.

To the left and right of the high bench were bronze statues of blind justice holding scales weighted heavy on one side, tilting the scales of justice, mocking any fair judicial system known to mankind. The blindfolds were dipped down under one eye of the statues.

Positioned below and on each side of the towering bench, acting as bailiffs, were the twin sisters and consorts of Baal, Ashera and Ashtoreth.

They wore skimpy, revealing uniforms with no tops but only Poncho Villa-type criss-cross bandoliers holding rows of shot glasses to cover their almost nothing-left-to-the-imagination full, sensuous breasts. They paraded around in front of the bench acting like cheerleaders to get the dark side crowd fully into the moment.

Lighting in the courtroom was provided by hundreds of bats holding oil lamps dangling from their mouths. The black bats were bunched into several gigantic chandeliers hanging from the ceiling.

The prosecutor's table was solid ivory with inlaid gold trim. A plush black leather chair on rollers was pulled up under it. The defense attorney's table was charred rough wooden planks with a burned out stump for a chair. The doors to the courtroom resembled swinging bar room doors leading out to a green marble hallway where the demons were buzzing their blasphemies, preparing their case.

The upper gallery was separated into a dark side and a light side with dark side participants sitting in red, thick theater-type seats, joining into the blasphemous chants led by the twin bailiffs. The light side gallery was seated on three-legged stools with no backs. They, for the most part, sat quietly offering only looks of encouragement to Gordon and Wayne. His gang was there on the bright side. Robbie's eyes were closed in silent prayer, Hank was doing a quick reconnoiter of the courtroom while Abby's eyes were fixed on Wayne alone. Bella was carrying on a conversation with the mystery man with the white streak in his hair as if she'd frequented this venue many times before.

Dagon, the hellish prosecuting attorney, made his grand appearance into the courtroom as he swung through the doors and walked down the aisle to the cheers of the ghoulish attendees in the gallery. Still standing, he took his position behind the ivory and gold table. The former chief deity of the Philistines, and reported father of Baal, wore a red silk suit and shirt with a black vest and a fiery black and red tie held in place by a diamond stick pin that must have been at least ten carats. He bowed to the crowd as if he were receiving an Oscar for his anticipated, great courtroom performance.

By contrast, Gordon appeared in his simple white linen robe and, without protest, lightly hovered over the burnt stump behind the defense table. The charred wood left no stains on his robe. The glory given to him by The Almighty added white light to his side of this kangaroo court of darkness.

When all the participants in the courtroom were in place, the judge, Amon, former god of Thebes in ancient Egypt, made his appearance in astonishing style as fifty cherub-like beings hovered around the edges of the courtroom trumpeting his heralded arrival. Amon descended right through the ceiling and flew around the room as if he were the king of the world on his day of coronation. He held out his hands, receiving the praises of the many demons, smiling down on them, nodding his head and making the signs of an inverted cross, acting like he was a pope giving blessings to his congregation.

His long flowing red satin robe trailed behind him as he circled the room. Amon wore a heavy solid gold diamond-studded chain with a downward facing pentagon star medallion around his neck, gold and silver bracelets hanging from his arms. Huge ruby rings accented each of his pointy fingers. He carried a gavel like his own royal scepter, its head a human skull containing red laser-like eyes and a handle like the femur of a human leg. On his head was a golden wig similar to the wigs worn by English judges on earth. On top of the wig was a platinum crown studded with rubies, sapphires, emeralds, and diamonds.

Slowly floating downward into his royal high, ebony judge's chair, Amon looked across the astonished crowd and said, "This court is now in session."

Judge Amon spoke to the court, laying out his deceitful agenda.

"Since there are no rules here at this 'other realm' court, I will give some guidelines or we'll all be here for eternity. I really want to be finished by beer-thirty if you know what I mean." The dark side gallery cheered. Gordon said nothing.

"Mr. Dishonorable, Dagon, as prosecutor, you will present three topics of your choice for the defense to prove. The burden of proof is upon Gordon, representative of his god. If Gordon cannot prove or disprove your points, Dagon, we will move to the next item on the docket and claim the victory for Satan, our high god! Are these guidelines clear to all parties? I love the word *party!*"

Ashera and twin sister, Ashtoreth began cheering and twerking the audience to get the party going.

The screaming and howling from the dark side gallery getting into a festive atmosphere finally subsided. Amon banged his skull-head gavel and said, "Order in my court! This court will come to order, but feel free to do a little partying in between. Now, Dagon, what are the three points you want to present for Gordon to prove or disprove? It's not like we haven't done this many times before."

Dagon rose from his plush chair, paraded around the courtroom displaying his elegance and began his discourse.

"Part one will be the proof of creation. Either evolution, intelligent design or creationism."Part two is the proof of salvation by crucifixion concerning any proof of a Son of the most high, this so-called god-man, Jesus, ever being present on earth. "Part three will be proof of the existence of a heaven and a hell. I believe these false claims, uh, these false doctrines, should be sufficient to convince our jury of one, Mr. Wayne Tyler, that all of this *Almighty* religious stuff is completely false and has no foundations for belief in any way, shape or form."

"I hope these points are acceptable to you, Mr. Defense, because these are topics that *will* be discussed. No rebuttal. Is that clear?" Amon proclaimed in an authoritative voice.

Gordon offered no dissent and nodded his head in compliance.

"Begin the prosecution's case, Dagon." Amon said.

Wayne sat in his jury box taking in all that was going on around him. Even he noticed the disregard for proper law proceedings and wondered how Gordon would respond to these questions that the entire world would like to know. He awaited with anticipation for both sides to present their case to him.

"I will, of course, begin with Charles Darwin's writings on evolution entitled, *The Origin of the Species …*"

"Objection, Your Honor!" Gordon demanded. "Dagon has stated incorrectly. Darwin wrote a *theory* of evolution which has since been disproven by mortal scientists as unfeasible and incorrect."

"Objection overruled! Continue Dagon." Amon relished his position of authority to strike down any rebuttal.

Gordon saw the futility of his objections. He knew they would all be overruled. He sat quietly, confidently, with no notes, awaiting his time to refute.

"As I was stating before I was so rudely interrupted by the defense …" Dagon smiled and again sought the praise and sympathy from the gallery, "I will continue with Charles Darwin. He stated that complex creatures evolve from more simplistic ancestors naturally over time or amoebas forming into higher creatures on the food chain such as mankind. Mankind evolved from monkeys to apes to cavemen and eventually into our modern man. Evolution in its simplest form. What do you have to say about that, Mr. Defense Lawyer? Prove that I'm wrong."

Gordon rose.

"Dagon, who created the amoeba if not The Almighty, creator of all living things? Both you and Amon were present during the creation. You both saw how The Almighty created the universe; Adam and Eve and every living entity in the universe. There was no evolution. Do you deny your own eyes?"

"Objection, Your honor! I move for that statement to be stricken from the record," Dagon shot back.

"Objection sustained. No record of the defense's answer will be written. Dagon, you have the floor, continue with your points."

"I present to the court the writings of Stephen Hawking, reportedly the smartest scientist on the planet when he stated that it is possible to create something from nothing and that, I quote, 'There is no god!' What do you have to say about this, Gordon?"

"First, evolution is an enabler for atheism. Evolution gives unbelievers a basis for explaining how life exists apart from a Creator. Evolution denies the need for an Almighty God to be involved in the universe and is the false religion of atheism." The Almighty created science. He loves scientists and has given them challenges to reveal His truths, written in His book, the Holy Bible, the number one best seller of all times with seven billion in print. For thousands of years scientists have tried to disprove one single word, one single fact that He recorded and they have failed."

"Objection, Your honor! There are a lot of books. Who can say which one states the truth of creation."

"Sustained. Continue Gordon with your weak rebuttals."

"The proof of creation is found in the first chapter, the first verse of His Word and I will quote: 'In the beginning, God created the heaven and the earth.'"

"Objection! This book of Genesis was written by a lowly sheepherder named Moses. What does he know about science?"

"Objection sustained. Expand on your answer, Gordon." Amon was confident that Dagon had tripped up the case of the prosecution.

"You're exactly right, Dagon. Moses was uneducated in the ways of science. So how did he know how creation took place when he was not there to see it nor did he have any idea how it was done if the Almighty had not told him what to write?"

Dagon had stop and think before giving his answer. There was a murmur in the courtroom. The party atmosphere became silent. Dagon was trying to figure out a way to wiggle out of this theory.

Dagon quipped back at Gordon, "Then, on the other hand, creation could have begun with the big bang! That's how the universe was formed, just like Hawking said, 'Something from nothing!'"

"Wrong again, Dagon. I would suggest to the court that you plant a thought in Mr. Hawking's mind to create anything from nothing. Lock him in an empty room and have him create, uh, have him create a tree or even an ameba. "If he cannot, we go back to Genesis. Verse one says the heaven and the earth were created on the *first* day of creation. Both were created before any other celestial bodies, stars, moons, galaxies or planets, were formed. If there was a big bang, then all the universe and everything it contained would be created in a mighty boom, all at the same time. It wasn't until the *fourth* day that the Almighty placed the sun, moon and stars in the heavens exactly where He wanted them and gave each one a name. Can you recite the names of the trillions upon trillions of stars, Dagon?

"The world can believe the Word of our *omnipotent* God. Wayne, that means *all powerful.* And the Word of our *omniscient* God, meaning *all knowing*, or the world can believe the illogically biased 'scientific' theories of fools! The fool says in his heart, 'There is no God.' His Word proclaims that people are without excuse for not believing in a Creator God. Anyone who denies the existence of God is a fool. The Almighty laughs at the collective wisdom of all mankind including, and I'll call them by name; Plato, Aristotle, Caesar, Socrates, Homer, Darwin, Freud, Einstein and Hawking. The fear of The Almighty is the beginning of knowledge, but fools despise wisdom and discipline. I rest my case on this first point, your … your, uh, *honor.* Dagon, do you have a reply?"

Amon clapped his gavel and called for a brief recess.

"Dagon, see me in chambers," Amon commanded.

The two demons gathered in chambers for a brief war counsel before facing the arguments of Gordon. Things were not going to plan.

"Dagon, Gordon is tearing you apart! You'd better come up with more convincing arguments on your next point. Why did you rely on mankind's theories in the first place? They're all shot full of holes and inconsistencies. You're here to plant points of doubt into Wayne's mind. He's not a student of scriptures in the first place and doesn't have a clue about the truth of creation. You're allowing Gordon to educate him right here in my courtroom. I won't allow it. Why didn't you object? I would have sustained your objection and silenced that, that, speaker of the Almighty!"

"Amon, you and I both know that we can't dispute the Word of the Almighty. We can only place doubt in believing it and twist the truth that is in it. What would you have me do?"

"Lie, Dagon! Create doubt in Wayne's mind but don't just sit there and let Gordon steam over you like a run-away freight train. Don't you remember all of your courses in Demon School? You've had centuries to study mankind and all of his weaknesses. Use them! Gordon destroyed you in there. If you can't do better on the second point than you did on the first, I'll call in a different prosecutor and banish you to the pit! Do you get my drift? No more fun in the sun for you 'cause the sun don't shine down there ...

"I'm going to change the setting of my courtroom, Dagon. Wayne isn't buying in to our extravagant sorcery. I can see it in his eyes. When we return from this recess we'll go back to straight, disciplined courtroom scenes. You will be in a suit, I will wear a black judge's robe and the gallery will remain silent. If necessary, whether you make objections or not, I'll hold the tongue of Gordon. Hit hard on your points, Dagon."

"It seems to me that Wayne's becoming weary of the arguments that I'm making." Dagon was observing Wayne also. "He's a pacifist, laid-back, non-confrontational, narcissistic type of person. He also has an affinity for Gordon since the guardian healed him from Diana's afflictions. I won't attack Gordon directly but with twists on the truth as you mentioned, Amon."

"I agree, Dagon. Do the best you can in there. I have a plan for after the *juror's* decision, whatever Tyler decides. Make your case and leave the rest to me."

During the recess there was no communication between Wayne and Gordon. Wayne was weary of the arguments. Gordon remained standing and was silent. Wayne bent over in the jury box and held his head in his hands awaiting the next round of arguments. When he looked up, the courtroom had changed in an instant. The bat-like chandeliers were now simple chandeliers, the bronze statues held balanced scales and the blindfolds were in place. The twin sister bailiffs were dressed in conservative deputy uniforms and the gallery was silent. This former kangaroo court now looked like a court of law.

Amon appeared on the bench looking like a real judge and Dagon entered to take his place at the prosecutor's table without fanfare wearing a three-piece suit and a determined look on his face.

Amon began, "This court is now resumed. State your next point of proof, Dagon."

"I submit to the court and to the defense that there is no proof of the *Son* of the Almighty ever being born, no proof of his crucifixion, death and supposed resurrection and certainly no proof of the lies of salvation that he promised. The burden of proof is upon you, Gordon."

Gordon stood facing Dagon and replied, "The Almighty wrote in His Holy Bible, which is inerrant and infallible ..."

"Objection! Hearsay! There are millions of books in this world along with many other holy books that have been written. Your contention that this *bible* is inerrant and infallible has not been proven. Besides, it plagiarizes the words and thoughts of books written before it."

"Sustained! Prove your point, Gordon or admit you have no proof." Amon pointed his skull gavel with the laser red eyes straight at the guardian.

"I submit to the court Exhibit A, Twenty-four thousand hand-copied original manuscripts and scrolls of the Old Testament." Gordon raised his hand. Dusty stacks of scrolls appeared before the twin bailiffs, "And Exhibit B, twenty thousand original hand-copied manuscripts and scrolls of the New Testament." More scrolls appeared, filling the entire area before Amon's bench.

There was a low-humming buzz in the courtroom from both sides of the gallery as dust from the ancient documents clouded the air.

"Amon and Dagon, you've both read these manuscripts. They're standard reading at your Demon School. All demonic followers know every word contained in these compilations of scriptures."

"Objection!"

"The Almighty overrules your objection. I'm not finished!

"Every word contained in these ancient books, written in Syriac, Latin, Coptic, Hebrew, Greek and the Aramaic languages, are the same. Proof of their accuracy is contained in the discovery of the Dead Sea Scrolls in 1947, recorded by archeologists and heralded as the most important archeological find in centuries. The next most documented original manuscript is *The Iliad,* by Homer, with only 623 manuscripts."

"This proves nothing but the existence of old, dusty books. Five billion people on this earth don't believe the words written in these scrolls, they are, themselves, hearsay." Dagon shot back in defiance of the irrefutable evidence Gordon had presented.

Wayne sat up and paid attention to the exhibits Gordon produced even though he knew nothing of ancient history, the bible or what was in it. He felt like he was in a college class rather than in a court of law.

"On your other points, Dagon, I'll continue the proof. You're trying to lure me off-topic and out of order with your three topics creating rabbit-trail sidebars for me to defend. But I will present proof of any topic that you can produce." More ancient scrolls of all sizes and shapes appeared on the floor of the court as Gordon reached out his hand to produce them.

"These are the original recorded annals of former kings of the earth, former empires ruled by Nebuchadnezzar of Babylon, The Pharaohs of Egypt, King David of Israel, Kings of Persia and the Greeks. Let's not forget the recorded annals of all the Caesars of the Roman Empire. All of these documents are before you. Each contains their own court scribes' descriptions of the power and the accuracy of The Almighty's book.

"The Egyptian scribes in Pharaoh's court described the ten plagues the Almighty cast down on them to let his people go.

"Nebuchadnezzar was given the mind of a cow and grazed naked with dew forming on his back for seven years when he decided that he was a god. Later he was restored to his kingship and forgiven when he finally confessed The Almighty. Here are his own court records for your review.

"King David was a self-admitted adulterer and murderer but was forgiven of his sins when he confessed them as recorded in *The Annals of the Kings of Israel.*

"Tiberius Caesar's own court historians, along with other historians during the age of Jesus such as Josephus, recorded the death of The Almighty's Son, Jesus, because Caesar's own governor, Pontius Pilate, ordered the crucifixion. All of Caesar's sentences were recorded.

"On that day of crucifixion, Pilate's own court scribes recorded that the daylight turned into night. There was a huge earthquake and in the Jewish synagogue in Jerusalem the veil leading into the Holy of Holies where only the High Priest was allowed to go once every year was ripped in half from top to bottom. It is also written that in the surrounding cemeteries of Jerusalem dead people crawled out of their graves in plain sight of the rest of the population. Even the Roman Centurion responsible for carrying out the sentence of the crucifixion made recorded comments that this *Jesus* was truly the Son of God ..."

"Objection!" Screamed Amon, taking over from Dagon who just sat in his chair trying to figure out what to say.

"Amon, you can 'object' all you want. You wanted proof. I'm giving it to you. I will continue ...

"The birth of Christ was recorded by three kings from the east who followed a star that appeared over Bethlehem. Modern earth astronomers have confirmed the existence of such a star appearing just as The Bible described. Shepherds in the field all attested to heavenly hosts of angels announcing the birth of The Almighty's Son, Jesus, as foretold in the Old Testament. Jesus was born of a virgin ..."

"Objection!" screamed Dagon "It is impossible for a virgin to give birth."

"Nothing is impossible with The Almighty, Dagon. You saw this. Again, do you deny your own eyes?"

"But there's no proof that this *Jesus* was the son of the Almighty!" Dagon shot back.

"The proof was in all of the miracles He performed. He cast *you* and many other demons out of a man and put you into a herd of pigs. Do you remember that, Dagon? He made the blind see, the lame to walk and the deaf to hear. He raised Lazarus from the dead four days after his death in the presence of hundreds of mourners by simply saying, 'Lazarus, come out!' This is the proof that Jesus was the Holy Son of the Almighty! No other man in all the history of mankind was able to do these miracles. Not you, not your master, Satan, nor anyone else. This is your proof!"

"But there's no smoking gun, Gordon. There is no body of Jesus to be found anywhere. How do you explain that?"

"He arose to defeat sin, death and Satan, Dagon. Your master failed! He couldn't stop what the Almighty ordained to happen. The Son now sits at the right hand of The Almighty and takes away the sin of any who would confess with his mouth and believe in his heart that Jesus is the Holy Son of God. During the forty days after his death and resurrection, over five hundred witnesses saw him living, talking to people, preparing breakfast for His disciples and eating food with them. It is recorded by eye witnesses."

"We're back to belief, Gordon! It's only a belief. Who can believe in what they cannot see and have not experienced? You haven't proven your case! You've only produced a bunch of moldy old scrolls, told twisted stories of unknown origins and attempted to steer people into believing a complete hoax. Where's the logic in that?"

"The logic *is* the belief, Dagon. The logic is in faith and hope and eternal salvation through that belief, the acceptance of Jesus as Savior. Without hope, mankind dies. If he dies without faith in The Almighty, in His Son, Jesus, he spends eternity with you in Hell. What do you offer greater than hope and salvation in wondrous splendor?"

"There is no hell!" Dagon shouted out.

"You know there is, Dagon," Gordon retorted. "You also know that you and all of your other demons are destined to spend eternity there in the lake of fire and you want to take as many lost souls as you can with you to torment them in a place where there is no hope. I'm sure you've read Revelation!"

"Curse his book, Amon! Close Gordon's lying mouth!" Dagon was fearing the consequences of his imminent defeat.

Instead of lowering the tension of the courtroom atmosphere as the demonic group had planned, Gordon, himself had turned up the heat past the boiling point. He pressed the demon's lies with undisputable proof. They could only try to spin it, manipulate it and flatly lie about it, denying the very basis of salvation which was faith in something unseen, something to give hope and purpose to life. The demons continued to throw point after point in Gordon's face, daring him to defend them with proof. Every point was covered and Gordon never raised his voice but continued to produce evidence, irrefutable evidence. The debates went on for what seemed to be hours.

Wayne was caught up in the heat of the debates until his mind was filled to overflowing. Each side was getting into topics way over his head and his frustration to even follow what they were saying got to the point of explosion. He had no idea what he was supposed to do or to say, if anything. Finally, anxious to the max after long stretches of debate, he stood up from his juror's chair, picked it up and hurled it across the courtroom.

"I can't stand anymore of this! I'm spent! I'm done with the preaching, with the deception, with half-truths that I have no idea which is right and which is wrong. I don't want to hear whether or not there is a heaven or a hell. If I'm a juror of one, I'll declare right now that you have a hung jury!"

"Wayne, simmer down, lad," Dagon said in a low, soft comforting voice. "Do you want to go back? Do you want to sign our contract? What do you want to do, my boy?"

"I'm not *your boy*! No, I don't want to go back and I damn sure don't want to sign your funky-assed contract and let you steal my soul. And Gordon, no offense, but I don't want to call upon the name of the Lord either! What I want is to get the hell out of here and just have a quiet drink and get my thoughts together. Can we just do that?"

"Of course we can, Wayne." Amon chuckled. "I'll declare a mistrial due to an indecisive jury. We'll adjourn to the bar and give you time to think. Gordon, would you like to join us?"

"I'll pass."

Amon called Dagon up to the bench for a quick conference. "Dagon, it's just like Baal has planned. We have Wayne right where we want him. He's completely confused and has no clue of the truth. Seeing is not always believing. Good job!"

Amon clapped his gavel down hard, instantly changing the courtroom into a plush, high-end club setting with soft music playing. The new venue hovered over the stadium. The gallery spectators returned to their respective stadium seating as both sides stared at each other across the field wondering what would happen next. The fourth tribulation was over. Little did Wayne know that trials five and six would happen back-to-back in the same setting and Gordon would not be present. Wayne was on his own.

14

SEDUCTION
ELIXIR OF THE GODS

Abby, Hank, Robbie, Bella and the rest of their group were again in the stadium seating on the bright side of the arena, still present in the midst of their dreams, waiting for the next trial to begin at this realm called Betwixt. They became enthralled with their apparition look-alikes seated on the other side of the arena. Each one of them focused on the ghoulish mirror images of themselves sitting on the dark side. They all began to think about their respective lives and the choices they had to make going forward. They could be in Wayne's position, facing tribulations, horrific trials and battling for their own souls. The thought of winding up like their counterparts was sickening. Each knew that one day they, too, would give an accounting of their lives for all to see.

Unknown to Wayne, the spectator seating rose to eye level with the platform. Everyone could see him, but Wayne was completely unaware of their presence. In the new plush bar setting he was alone with his thoughts and that's exactly where he wanted to be. He was truly a man living in a glass house with eyes that would not see out and a world looking in.

Wayne was seated in a corner booth with a table before him. The lights were low and soft music filled the setting when a male waiter dressed in a tux walked over to him and got Wayne's order for a Lone Star beer. Wayne looked around the club area. Everyone was dressed to the nines, appropriately, so he had no reason to think that this was anything but another time out. He asked the waiter for a pen and paper.

Sitting quietly, gathering his thoughts, Wayne began to think of Abby. She had become the focus of his fight, his grit, his reason to continue this crazy, unthinkable charade of dueling the underworld for his soul. He was determined to write her a new song as he began scribbling word after word on paper only to be torn up, wadded up and thrown on the floor around his table. It was like he was once again sitting on the patio of Tequilaville. The words wouldn't come. Frustrated, he ordered another beer and wondered if he could actually become inebriated in this out-of-this-world setting. Alcohol had always expanded his mind in the past to give him thoughts beyond his own. It wasn't working this time and he was far from becoming drunk and far from the words to his special song for Abby.

Seated nearby on padded stools at the luxurious bar were the twins, Asherah and Ashtoreth. They were dressed in expensive but modest attire. Their make-up was perfect and adorned their uncommon beauty. They wore expensive but tasteful jewelry as they sipped Manhattans and spoke quietly to a couple male suitors.

Ashtoreth leaned over to whisper in her twin's ear. "Give him some time, Asherah. Mr. Tyler doesn't like women to come on to him. He likes to check them out first, see them talk, see them walk and get a feel if he's interested. Besides, it seems like he's becoming frustrated trying to write that song. We'll drop in on him when he glances at us … and he will."

Eventually Wayne noticed the twins seated at the bar and remembered seeing them in the courtroom setting. They looked very different out of their bailiff uniforms, very chic, elegantly dressed and very beautiful. He put his pen down, looked at all of the wadded up pieces of paper on the floor and turned his attention back to watching them.

"Let's go, sister. That's the look we've been waiting for. Wayne's been staring at us for the longest time. I think he's ready for some company."

Asherah and Ashtoreth slid off the bar stools, kissed their male suitors gently on the cheeks and walked over to Wayne's table.

"My name's Asherah and this is my twin, Ashtoreth. Got time for some conversation?"

"Time? Ladies, I have nothing but time. I'm Wayne. I saw you two in the courtroom. Are you going to try and steal my soul, too?"

"No way. We're just chilling out, getting a couple of drinks like you are. What's with all the paper wads on the floor? Writing a letter to someone?" The girls laughed as Wayne motioned them to sit with him at his booth. Asherah slid in one side and Ashtoreth slid in on the other, cushioning Wayne in the middle.

"I'm a singer and musician. Just trying to write a new song and so far, it's not working out. Can I buy you two a drink?"

"We'll buy you a drink, Wayne. Have you ever tasted a drink called Elixir of the Gods? It's really hard to find, but we think you may enjoy it."

"Never heard of it, but I'm game." Wayne was briefly amused at the thought of a special drink, especially one that someone else was paying for. He didn't have any money or a credit card and hadn't thought, until now, how he was going to pay for his beers.

The twins were pleasant, good conversationalists and offered no reason for Wayne to suspect anything. He was enjoying the company of these two beautiful women.

The waiter came back with three drinks on his platter. "Elixir of the Gods. Enjoy!" he said. The drinks were in big crystal brandy snifters. The contents glowed with a soft vapor rising above the rims. The aroma of the vapor filled the room with a mesmerizing fragrance. Wayne took a sip and sighed. It was like nothing he had ever tasted. So smooth, so light, so … numbing.

"Here's to life and to love!" Asherah said. Wayne laughed and smiled as they toasted the first of many elixirs to come. The twins began to spin their magic, setting up the entrance of their Queen, Ishtar. Wayne was feeling no pain. He imagined that he was literally off in Neverland, and he didn't want to leave. The drinks swept his anxieties away and gave him a level of comfort and security.

"So tell us about this song you're trying to write, Wayne. What's it about?"

"Well, ladies, I have to admit, it's about something that I don't know a lot about. It's about luvvvvv." The elixir concoctions were causing Wayne to slur his words. "It's about the luvvv I feel for a very special woman and I just can't express it in words."

"Who's the lucky lady?"

"Her name's Abby and I think I luvvvv her. I've never luvvvvved any woman and that's probably the reason that the words just won't fall in a row. I can't express what I'm feel-ing."

At the sound of her name, coupled in the same sentence as the word, *love*, Abby shed a tear of joy as she sat in the crowd between Daddy Hank and Robbie. Robbie leaned over to Abby.

"Do you think those twins are trying to seduce him, honey?"

"Ms. Robbie, my woman's intuition tells me that's not their main plan. I think they're just trying to get him drunk and see what happens next. We all know that we do weird things when we drink too much, huh, Bella?"

"Duh, Abby! You would know!" Bella was not a stranger to being over served. "I think they're trying to seduce him. Wanna bet?"

"No, Bella, no bets. Wayne's not flirting with them. He's pouring out his heart to 'em. He's telling them about me and, for now, that's good enough."

In normal character, even in a dream, Bella added her two cents to the conversation. "He's got to be thinking of a *ménage a trois*. You know men when they get drunk, surrounded by two sexy devils like that. He's got to be thinking that! They're beautiful and look like they're willing ..."

"Hush, Bella! Get your mind out of the gutter," Robbie scolded her daughter. "I'm with you, Abby. He really isn't flirting with them, is he? But no telling what they'll do to him if he gets too drunk. Something's up and we both know it. I'll pray for him."

"If Wayne keeps his mind on me, the girl who really loves him, he'll be okay. I just know he'll resist. But, Robbie, he's not dealing with flesh and blood, and we're not back on the block. I don't even know where we are or how any of us got here, but I know that no good comes from this place. I've just got to love him through this and get him out of this bad dream. I feel so helpless. It's been so long since I went to a church that I've forgotten how to pray. I appreciate your prayers, Robbie, you'll have to teach me how to pray again one of these days. My God! I do love him. I need to learn to pray again ..."

Robbie put her arm around Abby, drawing her closer and whispered to her, "Abby, you just did!"

The twins had succeeded in the fifth trial which was to get Wayne drunk. It was only planned in order to prepare him for trial number six, a trial that was surely to win his soul. Wayne worshipped lust and fornication. These were some of his favorite escapes and the twins knew it. They had manipulated him more than a few times back on earth and they knew exactly what Wayne liked, what turned him on and how to get him right where they wanted him. The Elixir of the Gods clouded his mind, gave him a false sense of security and took away his inhibitions. The twin beauties never intended to help him with his song for Abby but to maneuver him into a nostalgic mood to set him up for their Queen, Ishtar, more powerful than Baal and second only to her private consort, Satan himself.

Asherah leaned closer to Wayne and asked, "Are you an educated man, Mr. Tyler?"

"Oh, yesssss!" Wayne was still slurring his words. "I went to community college for almost two years."

"What were your favorite subjects?"

"Oh, let's see, uh, I liked muuusic. I liked the girlzzz I met and I liked some of the booooks I had to read in a lit class."

"What's your favorite book, Wayne?" Ashtoreth asked.

"Without a doubt, it was *The Odyssey* by Homer. It was the only real book I ever read. I was intriguuued by the sirens who called out to the ancient mariners in order to draaaw them in …"

"You read Homer?" The twins never asked a question that they did not know, in advance, the answer to.

"I told you that I was an educated man. Yes, I did read it!"

"Then you're in for a wondrous surprise. The entertainment is about to begin and the featured singer is our own Queen, Ishtar. She has the voice of a siren."

"Really? I didn't know you had a queen. Queen of what?" Wayne's interest was piqued.

"Many called her the Queen of heaven, Wayne. She's the most beautiful woman that ever walked the face of the earth, even more beautiful than the only perfect immortal woman ever created, Eve, who lived in the Garden of Eden. She's our master's private consort, our Queen and no mortal man has ever laid eyes on her, heard her sing or has even been privileged enough to be in her presence. Prepare to be amazed …"

A bright light from above highlighted a stage area off to one side of the club. A full orchestra appeared as Ishtar materialized out of thousands of silvery sequins right before the crowd. In an instant, everyone bowed down to their Queen, showing her the honor and acknowledging her power and prominence that was due their monarch. Wayne remained seated, unable to move. His eyes were fixed on her, entranced in a deep daze. Thoughts of Abby, her song or even the reason for his being in Between were swept away by her dazzling entrance. She was truly beautiful, gorgeous. There were no words to describe her.

Copper timpani drums began to roll. Violins and cellos in perfect scale began to play as Ishtar commenced her siren's song, "Come into My Garden", a song like no other Wayne had ever heard. Her voice was alluring and captured his very soul. He looked her up and down, realizing that no mortal had ever witnessed the beauty that stood before him or had ever heard the voice that engulfed him. Queen Ishtar allowed everyone to gaze upon her beauty as she swayed gently to the left and right, continuing her private song of invitation. She was about five foot ten inches tall and had the flawless skin of a baby. Her hazel eyes were like pathways to an unknown eternity. She wore a flowing white dress adorned by tiny diamonds top to bottom, glittering in the bright spotlights that showered her from all directions. Around her neck was a full diamond necklace holding an inverted cross inlaid with multiple layers of jewels.

Her hair was like strands of gold, perfectly coiffed that flowed across her bare shoulders. Her lips were like a threads of scarlet, her breasts like twin fawns perfectly shaped and sensuous. Her scent filled the air with myrrh and frankincense. Ishtar's magnificence was consuming and without equal, even down to her thin, long, pointy … tail … that trailed behind her flowing gown.

She was pleasantly full of contradictions, being, at the same time, flirty and aloof, sexy and prudish, alluring and unapproachable.

Her song continued to penetrate deep as, unknown to Wayne, she blasphemed the very Words of the Almighty's own love song to humanity, "The Song of Songs". Ishtar sang:

> *I am here in my garden, my darling, my man.*
> *I gather my myrrh with my spices*
> *And eat my honeycomb with my honey.*
> *I drink my wine with my milk.*
> *Oh, lover and beloved,*
> *Eat and drink!*
> *Yes, drink deeply*
> *And come into your private garden*
> *Waft my lovely perfume*
> *And eat its choicest fruits.*

Ishtar cast a glance at Wayne and he knew that she was singing to him, inviting him into her garden to partake of the fruits of her body, a place that no mortal man had been, pleasures beyond any imagination. He could not speak, he could not move, he was captured by her siren song and could not resist.

Gordon gazed down upon the immense blasphemies of Ishtar's song against The Almighty as she lured Wayne's soul closer to her. She was not even aware of Gordon's presence and was determined to end these trials and claim Wayne's soul as a tribute to her king, Satan. For that high honor, Ishtar was willing to do anything, even beyond the rules set by God, Himself. This was her fifteen minutes of fame in all her demonic glory and nothing would stop her. Gordon was helpless to intervene until given instructions to do so by The Almighty.

When Ishtar finished her song everyone in the club bowed down to her, then rose, clapping, yelling, "Bravo! Hail our Queen!"

As she stepped down from the stage, assisted by six men in tuxedos, she floated over to her own private corner booth on the other side of the room. Wrapped around the wall behind her booth was a green mirror that reflected her elegance. On the way she looked at Wayne and with a lustful thought, lifted him from his table and created a path to her booth. He floated about a foot off the ground as Ishtar drew Wayne over to her. He was defenseless to resist, nor did he want to resist. He was a willing captive and couldn't wait to be near her, to feel her touch, to eat the fruit of her garden. The gallery awaited Wayne's imminent seduction by Ishtar, the Queen of Hell.

As Wayne settled in next to her, Ishtar held out her hand so he could do her proper homage by kissing it.

"Bow to me, Wayne Tyler. I am your queen!"

Wayne had never bowed to anyone or anything in his life. For a split second he was confused between his anger and not wanting to show any disrespect. He barely tipped his head down for a brief moment, took her hand and kissed it. He still didn't like to be told what to do by anyone, whether or not popped up on elixir.

"I'm Ishtar … and you are … Odysseus, I presume!"

"Not quite, Queen. I'm Wayne, Wayne Tyler."

"Of course you are. Would you like to get out of here and accompany me to a very private spot that I have picked out for you and me?"

"Lead the way, Ishtarrrrrr."

"Just step through my green mirror," Ishtar said with a smirking smile, wrapping her tail around him to guide him through.

As they stepped into the mirror, Wayne found himself in an opulent chateau that appeared to be on top of one of the mountains of the Swiss Alps. The view was breathtaking, looking down on all the other snow-covered peaks. The entire setting was one large bedroom complete with a blazing fireplace, a sunken tub next to the picture windows filled with hot, steamy bubble bath water. The smell of orchids filled the room.

Wayne looked at Ishtar and asked, "Why me? If no mortal man has glanced upon your beauty, what makes me soooo special?"

"Because you're basically a romantic at heart, Wayne. You've read *The Odyssey*, one of my favorite myths. I've always wanted an Odysseus-type man to play with. I can be your Penelope, remember her, Odysseus' wife?"

"Yeah, I remember. But she waited faaaithfully for her husband and Odysseus resisted the call of the sirens. I remember that part, too."

"That's why they call it a myth, Wayne. If Odysseus had been real and I was that siren, Penelope would have lost her man and I wouldn't need someone like you to indulge me in my pleasures. You do like the pleasures of the flesh, don't you, Wayne?"

"Hey, Ishtar, I'm like any other red-blooded … druuunk … man …"

"But I, Your Queen, am far from any, and I do mean *any* other woman you have ever laid eyes or hands on. Would you admit that?"

"You're pretty tantalizing, all right, Queeeny. Right down to your … tail. That's an interesting, uh, appendage. Is that real or am I still drunk on that elixirrr?"

"You don't really need an elixir to appreciate my beauty or my tail. Want to see more of me?"

"Sure, but …"

"No buts, Wayne. Either you do or you don't."

"I didn't say I didn't want to see more of you, Ishtarrr. My god, you're beauuutiful and the sexiest woman creature ever. But I always like to get unfinished bizzzness out of the way first."

"What type of business?"

"The twins said you could give me the words to a song. I'd really appreciate that, Ishtar. It's important to meee."

"More important than me, Wayne?"

"Well, uh, no, uh, but can you give me some luuuv words to write down before we do this thing?"

"We'll write this love song as we go, Wayne. I'm sure you'd rather experience love than simply to write about it … hmmm?"

"But Ishtarrr, is our *thing* luvvv? Do you luvvv me?"

Instantly, Ishtar was wearing a sheer red, long flowing nightgown that left nothing to Wayne's imagination. He could see her beauty from head to … tail. She wrapped her soft, pointy tail around him several times and drew him into her. She kissed him softly on the lips so he could taste the nectar of her embrace. As they kissed, she stared deep into his eyes and put him into a hypnotic state, doing away with any resistance he could offer.

"You mortal men are so contemptuous, my darling. When one of your passing thoughts can destroy a moment like this. One that you'll never have again." Her gown fell to the floor as she guided Wayne into the hot, steamy tub. She entered first, somewhat releasing the grip of her tail around him. His clothes disappeared as he followed her into the warm water. Ishtar began kissing him softly, passionately behind his ears and filling him, once again, with a lust and longing for her. Ishtar's tail pulled him close to her naked body and injected a direct shot of elixir into his buttocks. Wayne felt nothing.

Ishtar continued to wash him, kiss him and make him feel completely relaxed until she thought the moment was right for his complete seduction. But he had to consent to make her victory final.

"Are you ready to make love to me, Wayne?"

"Yeah, uh, wait. I have a question for you furrrst."

"Why all these questions? Do you want to do it or not?"

"Are you sure this is still a tiiime out or is this another tribulation? I mean, I'm like hypnotizzzed, like I couldn't resist if I even wanted to. But, Queeeny, you're not Pen-el-o-pe, Abby is my Penelope. Why are you in such a hurry to seduzzze me?"

"Don't flatter yourself, Wayne. The choice is and always has been mine! Yes, we are in a time out and, no, this is not another tribulation …" Ishtar was lying right through her perfectly white glistening teeth.

"Who's this 'Abby' and what is she compared to me?!"

The effect of the elixir began taking hold of Wayne. Ishtar levitated both of them from the bath into her big, round bed with red satin sheets. She wrapped her tail around him several times to stop any attempt of escape. Wayne couldn't move. His head was laid back, his arms were without strength. He was helpless as he thought of the one strength he had left.

"Abby is the woman I luvvv. I don't luvvv you, Ishtar and I don't think you luvvv me. You just want my soooul. You're a demon just like all the rest. Let me up. I want outta of here."

"Say it, Wayne! You can't resist me. No man can resist me. I am the mistress of all desires, the spellbinding temptress that tests men's souls. I am *the femme fatal.* Do you or don't you want to have sex with me, the Queen of all mankind?"

"NO! NO! I do not!"

"Too late, Wayne. You said, 'yeah' just before all the questions. I have your consent and we're doing this!"

Ishtar injected more elixir into him with her tail and pulled him on top of her. As she prepared him for the final act, a booming voice came crashing out of nowhere …

"STOP!" Ishtar, 'No' means 'No.' You cannot rape him! You, an evil spirit being, cannot have sex with a mortal man without the eternal punishment that goes with this crime. It is forbidden by The Almighty and you know it!" Gordon's commanding voice shattered the windows in the alpine boudoir as snow and cold entered into the room.

"Get away from me you, lowly angel. I am the Queen of Hell and I have much power. I'll claim his soul with lust and there's nothing you can do about it!"

"You will not, by command of The Almighty. He has sent me here to rebuke you and render His justice for your vile act against this mortal man."

Ishtar immediately loosened her grip on Wayne and turned into a twenty foot, scaly cobra with fangs flashing, shouting obscenities toward Gordon. The guardian angel swept away the alpine scene and returned things to a barren platform, still high above the coliseum. Wayne lay on the marble slab in front of the galleries on both sides, drunk, almost lifeless, as Gordon continued to proclaim the judgment of The Almighty upon Ishtar.

"Ishtar, you are fully aware when the sons of God, the fallen angels, came to earth in ancient times and indwelled the bodies of mortal men to have sex with the daughters of men. The offspring of these demonic rebels produced Nephilim, a twisted race of giants to infect the seed of all mankind with the seed of Satan himself."

"Yes, I do remember! It was a great victory for darkness! We of the spirit world had sex with mortal women. We coveted their bodies and made them pregnant with the seed of Satan."

"And you also know what happened to these fallen angels who defied the commands of The Almighty. They were bound in chains and forever cast into the lake of fire and brimstone where they remain to this day."

"So what, lowly angel? It was worth it to them to serve their master and glorify him."

"I hope *you* think it was worth it, Ishtar. The same judgment is rendered unto you by The Almighty this day. Did you think that the Omnipresent God did not see and know what you were doing just as it happened in times past? Do you also remember that The Almighty caused a great world-wide flood, killing all living things on this earth with the exception of Noah and his family in order to rid and exterminate the evil seed caused by these fallen angels from His green earth.

"By proclamation of The Almighty, you, Ishtar, will drink from His cup of wrath and are sentenced to the bottomless pit for eternity. Your punishment will be carried out immediately."

Suddenly there was a rumbling earthquake that caused the ground below the platform in the arena to shake and split apart. The galleries on both sides were terrified to their roots and drew back in mortal fear at the power of The Almighty. Tongues of fire and the smell of sulfur and brimstone could be seen and felt leaping from the huge crevice traversing the entire length of the field between the two galleries. Hot, black smoke belched from the bottomless pit covering the coliseum in a heinous slimy soot.

With a commanding wave of his hand, Gordon carried out the sentence, "Into the pit, Ishtar. The Almighty has spoken! You claim to be the Queen of hell, now go to your kingdom and be in torment forever and ever."

Ishtar's huge serpent body, no longer appearing as a perfect, beautiful woman, plummeted from the platform down, down into the fiery abyss of the bottomless pit. Her shrill screams of agony and shouts of blasphemies followed her descent and became less and less audible the deeper down into the pit she fell. In an instant Gordon closed over the top of the pit and restored the break in the ground. The smoke and fire dissipated. Ishtar, even the Queen of Hell, was banished forever for her unforgiveable sin against mankind.

The crowd on both sides were in complete shock, awe and silence. The apparitions of the demons on the dark side shook with fear. Six tribulations were finished. The seventh and final trial would be against Baal, Satan's enforcer who had the strength and power of all the other demons put together. Now with Ishtar gone, he was the second greatest epitome of all evil and cunning. No one escaped Baal.

Gordon took complete charge of the situation since Wayne was too weak to call for a time out. Wayne lay in a fetal position on the platform in a semi-conscious, drugged state. His nakedness could be seen by all the spectators in the stadium but no one uttered a sigh, a gasp or a single word. Because of the violation by Ishtar, Gordon called a time out and no one dared to defy him for fear that they, too, would be sentenced to the pit.

With another wave of his arm Gordon once again changed the setting to the cabin venue where Wayne had regenerated and recouped after the other trials. Gordon had redressed Wayne in his flannel shirt, jeans and boots, and now placed his defiant, worn-out warrior gently on the huge leather couch and sat down beside him, offering Wayne a cup of coffee. Slowly, with time in the entire universe frozen, Wayne began to heal from the drugs and elixir forced into him by Ishtar.

The bright side group watched as Gordon tried to prepare Wayne for the final trial. Abby was crying. Daddy Hank reached his arm around his beloved daughter and gave her his handkerchief to wipe away the tears and mascara from her swollen face. All had lumps in their throats and could not speak after seeing the atrocities inflicted upon Wayne by one heinous demon after the other. The previous trial was sickening to them, witnessing the near rape of a man with little or no defenses to fight it off.

"That one's over, Wayne. You're okay" Gordon was kneeling beside him. "How do you feel?"

"I feel … violated. I feel … dirty. I feel..helpless. I feel … guilt and shame. I feel … exposed. I feel like I have betrayed the trust of the only one who has ever truly loved me, like I don't deserve a second chance. Ishtar sucked the life and dignity from me. I feel empty and hollow inside … Gordon, did she take me? Oh my god … Did she take me?"

"No! She did not. You said 'no,' Wayne.

"I'm not sure I can go on with this. What do I have left to fight with, Gordon? I'm completely depleted of any decency I have ever known in my vagabond life. Maybe the demons have won. What else can I do now? Please tell me! What can I do now?" Tears poured down Wayne's cheeks, his nose was running.

"Buck up, Wayne. Be strong! Find your strength. Be a man today."

"Where do I find strength, Gordon? I have none left. My fight is gone."

"Where did you find the strength to say 'no?'"

"Gordon, Ishtar was so beautiful, so alluring, so perfect. It was the thought of Abby that made me say 'no.' I've never thought about seduction as being bad until I realized that my own body is sacred only to the one who really loves me. It was Abby's love that caused me to resist."

"Wayne, how badly do you want another shot at life? How badly do you want to write Abby that new song, to feel her touch again? How bad is your *want to,* even though there are no guarantees of you ever doing this?"

"Gordon, I want this more than anything I've ever wanted in my life. I'll face another demon."

"Then fight with love, Wayne. It's the most powerful force in the universe. The Almighty describes Himself as I AM LOVE! Love conquers all. It triumphs over hate and evil a million times out of a million."

"But, Gordon, it's Abby's love for me that keeps me going. What about my love for her? I still don't quite understand love. I don't know if I have that special love inside of me to give love back. Where do I find my love?"

"One place, in Him. He is the giver of all love. Wayne, if you survive the last trial and the Challenge of the Door, I'll show you what love looks like, feels like and the entire experience of love. I will allow you to be engulfed in love in a way few mortals have ever known. Let that be your strength and your goal."

"Gordon, I can only try. I've come to the end of my own strength, but I still don't know The Almighty. I can't truly say that I can call on His name and mean it. I've got to know that before I can, otherwise, they're just words."

"Then I'll sweeten the pot as you mortals say … If you make it through the last trial, and Wayne, I'm going to be honest, it's doubtful that you will because this one will be the worst of all, you'll find the words to Abby's new song, know what love is and possibly a new beginning, possibly a new life with a new heart. There's a high probability that you may not get to deliver that song to her yourself but at least you'll have the satisfaction of fulfilling your promise to her."

"How would I do that, Gordon?"

"All things are possible with The Almighty, Wayne. HE may allow you to deliver that song to her in a dream. To show Abby once and for all that you really do love her."

"I can't think of anything in this world that I'd rather do than to simply tell Abby that I do love her and really mean it. I'll let that be my strength for the last trial, win or lose."

Wayne reached across with his flannel sleeve and wiped the tears from his face wondering where he would find his grit, his strength for one last trial.

"You're going to be fighting against Baal, Wayne. He's second only in evil and power to his master, Satan. The entire wrath of hell is coming down on you in this final trial."

"Why me? Why are they so mad at me, Gordon?"

"Because The Almighty sentenced Ishtar to the lake of fire for trying to violate you. Satan is without his queen, his consort, and he is furious. Baal will attack you with more fury, evil and vengeance than has ever been seen before."

"Great! So just how am I supposed to fight this, Baal? With my beat-up old Stratocaster guitar? I'll just use it as a bat and be like the mighty Casey and knock him out of the park. Think that'll work? Somehow I don't think so, Gordon. Got any advice now?"

"Wayne, I want you to take a moment and think what I've told you. I said that you have three options: 1. Fight, 2. Send Me Back or 3. Call upon the name of the Lord.

"Since you continue to choose to fight, after this final trial there will only be two options left, Send Me Back and take your chances in fourteen feet of water at Red Fish Island, or to call upon the name of the Lord. So far you've refused to sign your soul over to the demons, you've barely come out of the previous six trials so you really need to do some serious soul searching about this last tribulation, Wayne. Remember *love*! Remember where it comes from, remember *who* loves you and gave His own life for you on a cross!

"Wayne, I tell you truly, you cannot defeat Baal with your own grit, defiance or even with someone else's love. You can only defeat him with love from above. That's your hope and where there is hope there is life. The demons, even Baal, cannot kill your soul, Wayne, you have to give it to them. You have to remember who loves you and who hates you. It's as simple as that."

"Then I'll be honest with you, Gordon. You may be a guardian angel from heaven. But I never knew about a heaven or a hell until you brought all this stuff up ..."

"I didn't bring this *stuff* up, Wayne. You did when you attempted to end your life through suicide."

"I'll give you that one, but you, yourself said that I have free will and free choice. It seems to me that you're forcing me into decisions I don't want to make just like the demons are. Why do I have to decide this now?"

"Because, Wayne, even at this place called Between, where time stands still, it will begin again. Soon you'll have to decide where you want to spend eternity, in eternal splendor or in eternal agony. Those are *your* choices. Not mine and surely not the demons."

"Okay, Gordon, so how do I know that the Lord truly loves me?"

"You're about to find out, Wayne. May the Lord have mercy on your soul!"

15

O.M.G!
Baal: The Final Tribulation

Wayne was apprehensive at the thought of facing the Prince of Persia, Satan's own captain, the epitome of evil. It was the final tribulation and he had no idea how he would get through it. He found himself back on the marble platform in the coliseum looking down on the crowds below. The only objects on this barren stage were his two guitars. Dressed in boots, jeans and his familiar flannel shirt Wayne scoped out the crowd below. There was complete silence in the arena. Everyone, demons and bright side spectators alike, were still in complete awe, in shock at the mighty earthquake that had just swallowed up Ishtar and sent her into the abyss, a punishment so terrible, no one could imagine.

The faceless throngs of the millions of observers that surrounded the outside of the arena sat still and quiet as well, awaiting the arrival of Baal. Their worst fears were about to be seen and experienced. Wayne looked down on Abby, Hank, Robbie, Bella and the man with the white streak over his right ear to get any encouragement he could glean from them. Abby's face was smeared with tears and mascara but she had a determined look on her face as if to tell him, *I'm with you, Wayne!* Gordon hovered above the bright side group and said nothing, either in thought or voice. It was time for Wayne to face his final demon, to make his choices and fight with everything he had. But would it be enough? In a place where there was no time, only time would tell.

At the given moment, the earth began to shake as though there would be another mighty quake. The sky above the stadium became pitch black, complete darkness consumed the light. The only illumination that could be seen was from Gordon's brilliance standing over the bright side group. A strange rumbling in the distance became louder and louder to the point of almost shaking the entire coliseum into dust. Wayne faced the direction of the sound and was the first to see what was coming for him.

A fireball blasted from the darkness and turned the field below into a raging lake of fire and brimstone so hot that it singed the faces of everyone present on both sides. Gordon held out a protective hand to shield Abby and her group from the heat of the flames. Wayne stared down at the fiery pit and wondered if that would be his final destination even though he had yet to lay eyes on Baal. He was embraced in his own fear but stood his ground.

Without pomp or ceremony, a gigantic two-headed, fire breathing dragon began to take shape flying toward the arena. Baal's chosen form was over one thousand feet long and had a wingspan of at least fourteen hundred feet. As he slowly flew over the coliseum, the dragon's mighty size encompassed the entire sky above. The vortex effect of Baal's giant wings created tornadoes, sucking up many of the spectators outside the arena into a black hole created by the swirls of his wing tips. Everyone looked up in utter shock. Baal's size and strength were unimaginable and indescribable by any adjective of any language known to mankind.

Slowly circling over the arena, giving everyone time to be amazed and fear his size and power, one of Baal's dragon heads spit out several fireballs on the surrounding crowds outside the venue. The fiery bursts exploded over them like small hydrogen bombs, melting their flesh, eyeballs and tongues before their skeletons had time to hit the ground. The horrifying smell of burnt flesh filled the air as millions were burned to a crisp.

Baal slowly circled the arena once again, psyching the onlookers, giving them a closer look at his audacious image and sending a message to all who gazed upon him. Ancient followers of Baal, a.k.a., Molech, believed that they had to sacrifice their own children upon a fiery altar in order to restrain his wrath upon them. Now Baal was coming to claim the soul of one Wayne Tyler and to avenge the punishment of Ishtar, Queen of hell. He brought Satan's own vengeance with him to dish out a mighty cup of wrath of his own.

Wayne watched the massive beast hovering past him like a gigantic monster that defied gravity itself. Baal had massive armored scales covering the entire length of his terrible serpent body. They appeared impenetrable, the size of modern day tanks, each overlapping another. Between them protruded slimy worms with the heads and teeth of snakes.

The seventy-foot long jaws of Baal's dragon heads were laden with rows and rows of sharp, yellowy teeth. His forked tongues resembled monstrous anacondas. Fireballs belched out of one, Baal spoke through the other. On the leading edges of his mighty bat-like wings were hands with claws like razors. The sharp, pointed talons that trailed below the beast were like heavy, green, jagged wrecking balls that could demolish a building with one swooping pass.

Speaking out of one of the dragon heads, Baal's booming voice shook the ground and could be heard and felt by everyone.

> *Much ado over you, Wayne Tyler, Much ado over you.*
> *See the power of the dark, listen closely to my bark.*
> *Pain and suffering are in store for the banishment of Ishtar.*
> *I'll blister with fire and make you a liar.*
> *Six, six, six the mark you'll bear, this, to Satan, I do swear.*
> *Grab your guitar, swing at me. It's your idol, bow down to thee.*
> *Like ten leviathans, I am Baal. Reach out to me and say, "All*
>   *Hail!"*
> *See below the brimstone lake, today it's your only escape.*
> *Go full circle to suicide. Move to the edge, lean over the side.*
> *Where's your Almighty, even now? Forsaken you! There is no vow.*
> *Wait in fear and hear my thunder. As I tear you in asunder.*
> *Greater pain you'll never know, there's no hope, just let it go.*
> *Into the pit your soul is mine, don't depend on your divine.*
> *Avoid your suffering that is due. Wayne Tyler, I come for you!*

Baal blew another mighty fire bomb from his mouth aimed directly at the bright side group. Everyone ducked as Gordon, unflinchingly raised his hand to shield them from the fiery blast. The white hot ball of fire struck Gordon's invisible barrier with such intensity that it bounced back across the lake of fire into the dark side bleachers, searing the faces of the demonic apparitions. They cheered as their spirit bodies boiled with blisters. The more horrid they looked, the better they liked it.

For a split second Wayne was terrified seeing Baal personally attack Abby and his family. What he'd been told about Baal by the other demons proved to be the only truth he had heard from them. Baal was all bad, all the time. No good was in him and he was greatly to be feared. By demonstration Wayne knew that Baal would show him no quarter. He knew he was in for more pain and suffering than any man could endure. Terror and fear gripped him as he spoke directly to Gordon, shrugging his shoulders with hands out and palms up as if saying *I'm afraid it's no use.*

"I can't fight this … this … thing! It's too big, too powerful and deathly evil. What do I do, Gordon? What can I do?"

Gordon, hovering stoically over the bright side bleachers replied, "Fear not! This too shall pass."

Anxious to the max, Wayne fired back, "That's it? 'Fear not? This too shall pass!' That's the best you got for me, Gordon? Easy for you to say. You're not the one standing alone on this elevated platform over a lake of fire about to get his ass kicked … uh, butt kicked. You gotta give me more than that, Mr. Angel!"

"You chose to fight, Wayne. So fight!"

"With what?!"

"Remember your choices, Wayne. It's all about your choices …"

"Then I choose to go back! No! Wait! I can't go back. I'd never see Abby again. I'd never see sunlight again. I'd never breath air again … I'd never write that song or know what love is … Got to get a grip … 'This too shall pass.' That's right, 'This too shall pass' … But I have no idea how …"

Baal continued to hover around the platform adding to the fear of all who saw his daunting size and his demonic power.

"Okay, you bad boy, bring it! Give it your best shot," Wayne yelled defiantly, grabbing his Stratocaster by the neck, to use as a baseball bat.

Baal reduced his own size by half and dove straight at Wayne, head first with his arms on the leading edge of his mighty wings reaching out to inflict razor sharp wounds. Wayne swung his guitar against the gnashing claws of the beast, shattering his instrument into a thousand pieces. Baal slashed Wayne's head, leaving a bleeding gash just above Wayne's right ear.

Wincing in pain, Wayne fell to his knees, grabbed his ear, tried to stop the flow of blood spurting from his head.

"You're gonna have to do better than that to get me, you bastardly beast!" Wayne shouted, getting to his feet and reaching for his acoustic guitar to use as a weapon if only to buy himself a few more seconds before his inevitable defeat.

Baal plummeted down at Wayne a second time, blowing a fireball at him that covered the entire platform. Wayne hid behind his guitar which was immediately incinerated in his hands. The intense heat blistered Wayne's face, hands and arms and forced him into a fetal position as he tried to cover himself, feeling the pain of the blisters.

"Oh my god! You are bad aren't you, Baal? But I'm still here. Come on, I'm not done with you yet!"

Baal made a quick loop in the sky and dove at Wayne again. Wayne stood with only grit as his weapon. If he were going to die, he'd die as a man facing his demons. Baal's razor fingernails carved a 666 into Wayne's forehead as the beast pulled up with a heinous roar.

The dark side gallery shouted, "Victory, victory to Satan!"

"I will not take your mark, Baal!" Wayne screamed out in utter pain as he grabbed the skin on his forehead and ripped off the mark, writhing, crying out in tortuous pain, blood flowing down into his eyes, making it almost impossible to see. The pain was so bad he couldn't think.

The dark side gallery was standing, arms out, thumbs down as in ancient gladiator days screaming, "Kill him! Kill him! Kill him!" Their shouts added strength to the mighty Baal's vicious attacks. Baal was absolute flying oblivion. No one or nothing could strike him down.

Hank stood up from the bright side bleachers with his fist raised high and shouted, "Fight to the death, Wayne! Stand and fight!" T-Bone, Tito and Mary stood with Hank and shouted "Fight!" Wayne was not a favorite of any of these men; they really didn't like him at all but they knew he'd met his match. He was a member of the human race, an underdog, fighting against supernatural forces. They joined together like a band of brothers in his defense.

Abby cried out, "Take me, Baal! Take me! Leave Wayne alone, he's suffered enough. I'll go with you. Take my soul. I give it freely, but leave my man alone!"

Robbie fell to her knees and began to pray as beads of sweat and blood poured from her bowed face, "Father God! Please protect Wayne with Your mighty power. Be his high tower, his fortress, his shield and buckler and deliver him from the fiery darts of this present darkness. For thine is the kingdom and the power and the glory, forever and ever. I ask this in the mighty name of my Lord and Savior, Jesus! Amen."

Bella just sat next to her mom, speechless, engulfed by the macabre situation she witnessed in her dream. "Mom, we gotta get out of here. We've got to end this bad dream. I'm scared to death, Mom. Help me!"

The unknown man sitting with Hank and Abby with the white streak over his right ear simply stood, facing up to Wayne offering a slight gesture of encouragement by giving him a thumbs up.

Baal paid no attention to the prayers and shouts from the protected bright side crowd as he made the lake of fire on the arena floor roar with more intensity and heat. The tongues of fire rose up from the lake and nipped at the edges of the elevated platform, engulfing Wayne with sulfurous black smoke making it harder and harder for him to breath. The terror of the situation seemed as if it could not get worse. But Baal was just getting started …

Burned, bleeding profusely, in writhing pain, Wayne shouted out, "Baal, you can't kill my soul! You can't kill me!"

Baal replied, "I'll make you wish you were never born. You addict of lust and pursuer of porn. I'm indestructible and unrestrained. Your will to live has now been drained. I'll help you move right to the edge,

To the downward spiral of the wedge ..."

Baal plummeted straight at Wayne with all of his massive size and vengeance to deliver the final death stroke. His heavy talons led like an eagle swooping down on a defenseless rabbit and inflicted a terrible gash in Wayne's back, ripping his shoulder out of joint, adding to the bloodshed, soaking up the last bit of defiance, strength and life that Wayne had left within him.

Gordon watched the torture impassively but was not instructed to intervene.

Wayne was on hands and knees, trying to stand but unable to do so. Slowly, he crawled toward the edge of the platform and looked down into the lake of fire.

Baal's roaring voice spoke directly to Wayne, in modern language, not in rhyme:

"That's exactly where I want you, mortal! You've come full circle from suicide to suicide once again. You're weak, you cannot face your demons, Wayne. You never could! Look down into the fire and embrace it. It will end the pain and suffering. Now leap! Lean into the fire! Go full circle. Suicide will save you!"

"No Wayne, No! Don't do it! Fight for me! Fight for your soul! I love you!!!"

Abby was beyond control as she stood waving her arms , fists drawn tight and shouted out encouragement, realizing that Wayne nor any mortal man could withstand the pain and punishment he was trying his best to endure. She couldn't let go of the fact that Wayne was doomed. It was unthinkable that she would never hold him in her arms again.

Crying, defeated, lifeless, Wayne clung at the edge of the platform on all fours. He stared into the fire. It mesmerized him. He watched the tongues of flames as they reached out to him to come join them. Wayne had a brief moment of peace knowing that just a little lean forward would end his tribulations, his pain and his agony. The crowds grew silent. It was the moment of decision whether or not to choose death or life for his soul.

Casting one last longing glance toward Abby, Wayne sent a weak thought to her, "I tried, Abby. I'll miss you, baby!"

Wayne leaned over the edge of the platform and began his fall into the lake of fire about two hundred feet below. It seemed as if he were falling in slow motion. His thoughts were clear as he watched his sinful life pass before him, every detail, every moment, still falling, falling, deeper toward the fire that seemed to embrace him.

He remembered his conversations with Gordon as he continued downward. "This too shall pass" and "Call upon the name of the Lord …"

Ten feet from the lake of fire, with his last breath, Wayne cried out, "J E S U S! Save me!"

Instantly, the mighty finger of The Almighty streaked down into the stadium in the form of a huge, bright, booming lightning bolt. On it rode Michael, the Arch Angel, warrior, commander and general of the armies of heaven, the created head servant to The Almighty. In his perfect bronze hand was a two-edged broad sword, a thousand eyes on the blade. Michael reached down and rescued Wayne with the huge blade of his sword just before Wayne entered the lake of fire. With a thought and the authority of God Himself, Michael whisked away the fiery lake and turned it into green pastures with still waters. Flowers and trees of every color and kind appeared to reveal a scene of restoration, blue skies, white billowy clouds, serenity, a heavenly scene of new beginnings. The mighty angel gently lowered Wayne into a bed of green grass and piled up leaves from the trees running on each side of the river of life. The leaves healed Wayne's wounds the moment he touched them.

Michael then turned his glance upward toward Baal, still hovering above. With a mighty shout, the Arch Angel commanded Baal to depart.

"By his own free will Wayne Tyler has called upon the name of the Lord and is now a child of The Almighty, a member of the Royal Family of Heaven. You have lost, Baal. I rebuke you in the name of the Lamb of God, Jesus Christ. Depart now and take all of your demons with you or feel the wrath of The Almighty!"

Baal shrieked blasphemies toward Michael and The Almighty, "You have tricked me, Michael! I had Wayne Tyler's soul in my claws. Who are you to claim this victory?"

"I am the servant of the Lord of Lords and the King of Kings. The One who is the way, the truth and the life. Do not question His authority over you, fallen angel. Your time is short. Your doom draws nigh unless you, too, Baal want to join your queen in the pit. Go now! I'll see you at Armageddon."

Without admitting defeat, Baal and all of the other dark side ghoulish apparitions vanished into thin air. The coliseum was gone, the platform vanished.

As quickly as he had appeared, Michael was gone. Off to fight another battle against the tireless demons that constantly attacked the people of earth causing pain, grief, sickness, pestilence, wars, and death.

Abby, Hank, Robbie and the rest of their group found themselves sitting in the grass around Wayne who was in a deep sleep. Abby stroked Wayne's now restored forehead and leaned over and kissed him on the cheek.

Her kiss of love produced a wonderful rainbow that came down from the beautiful skies above. It was like a stairway from heaven itself, so brilliant with colors never before seen. Descending down the path of the rainbow toward them was the glorified image of a man. As he descended toward their small group, twenty million soft voices of a heavenly choir could be heard singing, rejoicing in perfect harmony. The music gave Abby and friends undefined peace, love and joy beyond anything mortals like themselves had ever experienced.

"I am Gabriel, The Almighty's messenger angel. I bring you good tidings of great joy which shall be to all people present. For unto you, this day, a lost soul was saved. His name, 'Wayne Tyler,' has been removed from The Book of Life, with all of his sins listed underneath his name and is now written in The Lamb's Book of Life where no sins are ever recorded. They have been paid for by the blood of the Lamb. Wayne's name is in indelible ink and cannot ever be removed. He is now a citizen of heaven with all rights and benefits that go with it. Rejoice!"

At Gabriel's final word, millions of angel wings could be heard flapping in the skies as they rejoiced together at the saving of a lost soul, the addition of another citizen of eternity in paradise as a welcomed brother. The sound of their voices was beautiful and grace abounded abundantly.

Gabriel then turned to Gordon and said, "Good work, guardian. Your charges are in good hands. I must depart."

Gabriel ascended into the skies as the heavenly choir continued to rejoice and sing praises of glory to The Almighty in the highest.

Gordon took a brief moment to speak to Abby and her group.

"You have been allowed to be here in this place to offer encouragement to this man before you. You must now return to your sleep, to your dreams, to your dimension and you will not remember all that you have seen. For you, yourselves, could be called here another day. Like any dream, you may remember bits and pieces of this mighty spectacle but how much you remember is not left up to me. You may remember the good or you may remember the bad. Whatever your mind and soul records. I would suggest that each of you take a good look at your own lives and consider this experience ..."

"Gordon, will Wayne live? Will he write me a song? Will he return to me?!" Abby blurted out.

"Not my choice, Abby. I can't tell you what The Almighty or Wayne will decide to do. I can tell you to have faith. I can tell you that your prayers will be heard by The Almighty. And I will say something to each of you before you depart this place."Hank, you've been an honorable father to Abby, continue to do so. The Lord will bless the fruits of your labor. He created you with a warrior spirit. You will be called to use this to glorify Him in the future.""Abby, The Almighty witnessed you crying out to Baal when you told him to take your soul instead of Wayne's. There is no greater love than this and your love for this man will be rewarded one day. "Robbie, it was your prayer that called The Holy Spirit into action to plant the last minute thought into Wayne's mind to call upon the name of the Lord. You will be rewarded for saving a lost soul. There is a jeweled crown awaiting you when your time on earth is finished. You are a mighty prayer warrior and you will be glorified.

"Tito and Mary, the Lord will bless your marriage, your children and your life. T-Bone, you turned your life around when you made the decision not to murder Wayne. Continue your path of wisdom for that is the gift of The Almighty to you.

"Scott, I want you and your band to cling to your passion of music. The Almighty loves music, He invented it and He gave you that passion to play, to sing and to write. Don't forget to sing praises unto Him."

"What about me, Gordon. Does The Almighty know who I am?" Bella interrupted.

"Yes, Bella, The Almighty is very fond of you."

"He is? He's fond of me? What does that mean, Gordon?"

"It means that you're a very unique person, Bella. The Almighty has given you a sterling personality and a bright mind. Use it to serve Him and to serve others." "I will! How do I do that?"

"You'll figure it out, my child. Just go where The Almighty leads you. But you must accept His salvation first."

Abby was still wondering about the man seated next to her, the man with the white streak in his brown hair above his right ear.

"Gordon, before we leave, could you introduce us to this mystery man here? I mean, we have no idea who he is or even his name ...."

"Can't do that right now, Abby. This man must remain a mystery until the proper time. I want to leave you all with one last thought. The Almighty has saved your tears that you shed in this arena in a small vial that will sit before His throne. No act of true compassion and love is ever lost or overlooked in His eyes.

"Now it's time for everyone to depart from this place. May His blessings, His grace and His mercy be with you all. Go in peace …"

"Gordon, I don't mean to get the last word in, but, uh, if I need to talk to you. Do you have some kind of a direct line that I can call?" Bella always liked to get in the last word, just part of her Type-A+ nature.

"Bella, just pray. I'll hear you and so will The Almighty."

"Hmmm, I was hoping you wouldn't say that … I 'd, uh, rather just talk to you kind of on the side, if you know what I mean. I'm not sure I want to discuss all my little secrets with The Almighty …"

"There are no secrets from Him, Bella. Just give it a shot. He loves you very much."

"He does? How cool is that?"

Abby took one last glance at Wayne as he slept peacefully in the green pasture, surrounded by immense beauty on all sides. She touched his face with her hand and thought about how quickly he was healed by the hand of Michael.

"Gordon, take good care of my man. I love him so much."

"Wayne is in good hands, Abby. But he still has some decisions to make …"

16

THE DOOR
LOVE IS ...

In the twilight of Wayne's awakening, he slowly began to touch his forehead, felt his back, looked at his arms and hands checking for blood and blisters. There were none and he felt no pain at all. As he came to his senses, he glanced all around, taking in the beauty and serenity of his surroundings. In complete awe, he saw the brilliant blue sky above, the oceans of fragrant, multi-colored flowers, the massive green trees and animals; lions, tigers, lambs and beasts of the field all lying together. A cool breeze blew across his face and a peace came over him like he'd never felt before.

"Beautiful!" is all he could say.

The lake of fire, the coliseum, the demons, the platform and all the people were gone. He was lying in splendor. It took his breath away. As far as he could see everything had a certain glimmer, a glistening, a sense of wondrous perfection. He was bathed with a dazzling light that warmed him and gave him peace of mind, heart, body and soul.

He looked up into eternity and exclaimed, "O My God! I don't deserve this. You saved me from myself. I failed every trial ..."

Gordon was standing next to Wayne in the green pasture like a sentry guarding his soul. "This is called *grace* and *mercy*, Wayne. You took your final option and called on His name. By *grace* you were saved. He never forsook you. You were healed by His stripes. You finally believed in your heart ..."

"I came to the very end of myself, Gordon. I faced my demons and they won every time. I thought that I had rebuked them, depending on my own reasoning and logic, but they deceived me. They magnified every element of my own evil life. They got into my head and twisted my thoughts of greed, fame, success, recognition, money, women, lust, drink, and living an irresponsible life. I'm just no good. I don't think I ever did anything in my entire life worthwhile for anyone but myself. I surrendered, Gordon. I had nothing left but to embrace the flames to end my own suffering."

"It was your surrender that led to your belief, Wayne. Surrendering to Him is a good thing, a prerequisite of sainthood ..."

"Surely you're not saying that I'm a saint, Gordon!"

"You are now, Wayne. You're a member of the Royal Family of the Almighty! Your sins have all been swept away, never to be looked upon again. You've got a clean slate."

"Just like that?"

"Just like that!"

"But Gordon, how could that be? It can't be that simple!"

"It is that simple. Take a look around you. Compare where you were to where you are now. You're getting a rare snapshot of what heaven is like, what salvation is like. Tell me what you remember as you fell into the fire, Wayne."

Wayne took a deep breath of the refreshing air and searched deep within his memory for his last thoughts.

"I remember the pain of Baal. I remember feeling completely defeated. I longed to be free of further agony ... I couldn't take anymore.

"I remember falling down toward the lake of fire, the tongues of flame roaring upon my face. My life flashed before me in slow motion, every word I'd ever spoken, every act of lust, every dirty joke I'd ever told, all of it ... Then, I saw it! I looked beyond the surface of the lake into its depths and saw the open gates of hell welcoming me. I saw the sign over that grizzly, rusted gate that read, *'Abandon hope, all ye that enter here.'* I saw millions of lost souls that were in complete agony, gnashing of teeth, lonely isolation, eternal agony that would never end and there was no hope for them.

"Then, Gordon, I actually saw a hand outstretched to me and a still gentle voice that said, 'Say My name. I will save you!'"

"That was the voice of the Son of God, Wayne. It was Jesus who called out to you."

"Somehow I knew that. I knew exactly who it was and I don't even know how I knew."

"Someone prayed for your salvation, even when you couldn't. There's power in prayer."

"Gordon, what happened after that? I think I blacked out. The last thing I remember is bracing for the unthinkable pain of the molten fire engulfing my soul."

"You missed a mighty divine event, Wayne. When you surrendered your soul to the Son, The Almighty sent the arch angel, Michael, to rescue you, to heal you and to banish Baal and all the demons that were screaming for your soul. In an instant, the fire was gone and things were changed to what you see now.

"Then the messenger angel, Gabriel, announced your entry into the Royal Family and twenty million holy angels flapped their wings, welcoming you to your inheritance ..."

"Inheritance? What do you mean, inheritance, Gordon?"

"As a child of The Almighty, you will share in all the riches of The Almighty. You will receive your portion of the entire universe. It will be your playground for eternity. He, by His own hand, will build you a mansion in the sky. There will be no more tears, no more pain, no more want. He will provide everything you need and all that you have ever wanted ..."

"Like a family? I've never had a family, Gordon."

"You've lived a tough life, Wayne. The Almighty knows all about your drunken, murderous daddy and your mother who tried her best to protect you and died early. That's why he sent old Mr. Elroy to you. To protect you, to teach you to play the guitar and give you a passion for music. Mr. Elroy was me, Wayne. You never knew that did you? I appeared twice in your life ..."

"Mr. Elroy was you?! An angel? I thought he was just a poor ole black beggar that needed a friend. He played guitar like no one I had ever heard before ..."

"You were the one who needed a friend, Wayne. I taught you how to play."

"Wow, Gordon, I didn't know you played the blues. No wonder I learned from the best. Thank you! And thank you for filling me in on what happened after I blacked out. I would've really liked to have met Michael and Gabriel. "Mr. Elroy, uh, you, Gordon, read to me about them while I was sleeping in your bed in that one room shack. It was the only time I ever heard the truth, when Mr. Elroy read to me from his beat-up old bible. But I wasn't listening very much, huh? I never forgot him ... uh, you. He saved my life!"

"But Jesus saved your soul, Wayne. You may want to take the time to give thanks to Him."

"Oh, Gordon, more than anything I do thank Him. He paid a heavy price for me."

"That's love, Wayne, summed up in His book as, 'God so loved the world that he gave his only son ... '"

"I mean, looking back, Gordon, I still don't understand it all, this 'salvation thing,' but I'm beginning to understand. And I always wondered how the Austin Child Protective Services never found out about my Mom's death, how she was buried and how Mr. Elroy got custody of me, much less raised me, bought me clothes and fed me until I graduated high school. I remember coming back to our little shack one day and Mr. Elroy was just gone …"

"You didn't *need* me anymore, Wayne, and nothing is too difficult for angels of the Almighty. That was my assignment and it was carried out according to His plan. Leave it at that. I just got you through a tough time. You saved your life when you made the right decision. In eternity, you'll have a huge family. But now you've still got more decisions to make."

"Like what, Gordon. I thought I made my decisions. What more do I have to decide on? Are we going back to Between?"

"No. You're in the light now, Wayne. Do you want to go back to the misty fog of Between or stay here in green pastures?"

"Uh … that's not a real hard decision to make. I'll stay here. Is this really a glimpse of heaven? Where are Abby and the others? "

"Abby and the others are back in their dreams on earth. And yes, Wayne, you're getting a small peek at heaven. You couldn't imagine or even comprehend its entirety. Do you remember me telling you that if you made it through the trials that I would show you what love is?"

"I'd forgotten about that, Gordon. Yes, I do remember. You also said you'd give me the words to a new song for Abby. Is that part of the deal you made with me?"

"It is. But I also told you that you may or may not be able to deliver that song to her, didn't I?"

"Yeah, in all honesty, you did, Gordon. What's next? Will I ever see Abby again?"

Wayne was still lying in the bed of healing leaves when Gordon reached down his mighty hand to help him to his feet. Wayne was no longer in boots and jeans but was wearing a white robe and sandals, just like Gordon, but without the brilliance of his angel. They walked across the beautiful valley of flowers and trees, petting the lions and tigers as they approached a very high snow-covered purple mountain.

Climbing up, without effort, they came within ten feet of the beautiful peak when Gordon spoke. "Go up to the summit by yourself, Wayne. You're about to know what love is by divine appointment …"

Wayne walked up the final ten feet on a well-trodden path to the top of the mountain and stopped. He was immediately engulfed in a bright, cream-colored cloud that surrounded him head to toe. He couldn't see anything around him. For a split-second Wayne was somewhat fearful of what was coming next but instantly felt a warmth, a feeling of peace that transcended any fear that he had.

What he was experiencing caused him to lay his head back and lower his arms and shoulders. He was basking in something that he never wanted to go away. Then he heard that small still voice again saying to him …"You're here for a reason …"

From above the cloud, thousands of broken, golden threads came down diagonally and pierced his mind, his body and his soul. Those threads of love enraptured him, swirling around in his mind and body like tornadoes of cheer and happiness and sheer delight. Tears of joy poured from his closed eyes. The hole in Wayne's heart had been completely filled with what he was seeing, feeling and experiencing. Love was so much more than he could have imagined as it flowed in and around his soul like the dance of a thousand brides on their wedding day, a first kiss, the inexplicable unconditional love of a mother, and the security of a father's presence. Love is conception, the moment of birth, a baby's first coo, a father's first sight of his child.

This love felt like bells and banjos singing to his heart. This love was a new born puppy's breath, soft as kitten's fur with the fragrance of roses all around. Love was exploding in his senses like giant starbursts that fell down to the earth from heaven above. Love felt like it had found a home in every cell of his body. Love was a walk in the park, holding hands with someone more than a friend. It was as big as the universe, like lying on his back in a field and looking up at the stars. His experience was light as a feather, free as the moon above. It had the warmth of the sun and was wide as the universe. This feeling of love could not be contained or restrained. There was no beginning and no end to it. Love filled his life and his heart. Love filled the length and breadth of all creation from never ending to never ending. It consumed him. It was all around him and free to receive it.

As quickly as the experience had arrived, it was gone. The cloud dissipated, the golden threads were gone, the sound of the bells and banjos faded as Wayne just stood, trying to make the moment last, even a second longer.

"Gordon! Why did the love leave me? I never want it to go away! It took away all of my cares, my fears, my anxieties. I've never felt so loved in my entire life. Please, Gordon, make it return to me."

"Wayne, you wanted to know what love is. The Almighty has shown you His love. Tell me, what did you feel and experience? Tell me what love is …"

Wayne was panting in jubilation, trying to organize his feelings and thoughts. He wanted to remember every detail of the wondrous experience.

"Oh, oh, love is so much more than a feeling, Gordon. I saw it. It permeated my being. I experienced it, heard it, touched it and, yes, I felt it. I'm overwhelmed. But I'm not sure I can describe it. I'll try to tell you what I …"

"Love is so powerful, Gordon! It's nothing like the songs that call it a second hand emotion. There's nothing second hand about it. It's the Alpha and the Omega. It's so much more than a feeling. It's all around us, there for the experience, there to receive. It's a monumental gift. It's patient, it's kind, it's free, it's loyal, it goes on forever. It is everything good with no evil in it. Love is pure and as white as snow, uplifting and cannot be taken away. Love is the most powerful force in the entire universe and it originates and emanates from the very throne of the Almighty. I saw it, Gordon! I saw it. Now I know why you described The Almighty as 'I AM LOVE!' He is love! And He's just given me some. I know what love is, Gordon. I know!"

Gordon just smiled at Wayne as they made their way back down the mountain and once again walked through the beautiful valley, talking as they walked.

"Gordon, reflecting on what has happened here, I understand what you meant when you told me, 'This too, shall pass.' At the time, I thought that was a pretty lame thing for you to say to me when I was facing such a great trial with Baal. Did you know what would happen to me then?"

"No, I didn't Wayne. I do know that The Almighty would never bring you to a task that you couldn't handle with His help. What I didn't know was whether or not you would ask for it. The Almighty knew what you would do."

"So I could've bought the farm right there?"

"Or you could gain eternal salvation, which you did. Now you have to decide what's next for you. Remember the challenge of the door?"

As they walked slowly across the beauty of the green pastures, Wayne saw a great door floating down from the sky, settling just a few feet in front of him. He'd seen the beautiful twenty-foot high transom with the golden door knob and singed edges back at Between but didn't know its meaning or its purpose. He just knew it would be his final challenge.

Gordon spoke. "Wayne, you arrived at Between because you attempted to end your life by suicide. The key word here is *attempted*. Your life still hangs in the balance."

"So even under fourteen feet of water in Galveston Bay, I may still be alive?! Right, Gordon?"

"Right. You may live or you may die there. If you do live or are somehow miraculously rescued, there may be consequences …"

"What kind of consequences?" Wayne asked.

"You may have contracted debilitating diseases from the micro-organisms in the water since, at this moment, you sucked sea water into your lungs. You may have hit your head upon the reef or some underwater rocks. There are sea creatures down there that could harm you such as jelly fish stinging you. Your lack of oxygen while breathing in sea water could give you permanent brain damage and leave you in a vegetative state for the rest of your life."

"Gordon, are you telling me that I could have another chance at a normal life?" Wayne broke in.

"There is that chance also, Wayne."

"Gordon, by now you know me pretty well. I'm a risk taker. So what are my options?"

"Wayne, when you first arrived at Between, I told you that there were three options: First, to fight your demons head on …"

"Yeah, well, thank God, I've already done that and failed miserably, huh, Gordon?"

"I'll continue. The second option was to say, 'Send me back' to your situation under water …"

"Which, at the time would have probably sent me straight to Hades, right?"

"Possibly, you could have still been rescued somehow. Time has not progressed beyond the point of you going down into the water, has it, Wayne?"

"I guess not if you say so, Gordon."

"The third option I gave you was to 'Call upon the name of the Lord,' which you did. This means that whatever decision you make right now, you are saved and will enter the gates of heaven to spend all eternity in wonder and splendor."

"Okay, Gordon, I'm getting a little confused again. Where do we stand with the options?"

"Wayne, you fought your demons, you called upon the name of the Lord but you can still say, 'Send me back.'"

"And take my chances with all the consequences that go with it, huh? Like the choice of becoming a vegetable?"

"You are clear on this, Wayne. But before you decide, I'm going to give you more information before you make your choice.

"The doorway before you represents a portal to heaven. You can turn that golden door knob right now and enter for all eternity. The singed edges around the door represent the trials and tribulations of your lifetime which will be forgotten forever if you decide to enter."

"But I'll never see Abby again, I'll never feel her touch or experience love on earth and I'll never write her that song, will I, Gordon?"

"No, Wayne, that opportunity will be lost forever ... But there's more. I'm going to tell you about heaven now, Wayne. Listen closely.

"If you decide to enter the pearly gates right now, you'll come before the Throne of The Almighty. You will not be judged, your sins are forgiven. It will be an awards ceremony based upon your good works after becoming a child of The Almighty. You could receive up to five crowns. However, Wayne, you have no good works. Every good thing you did before being saved doesn't count in eternity, only good works after you become a member of the Royal Family."

"Gordon, I always thought just making it into heaven was good enough. What would I be doing there forever and ever, just sitting on a cloud and playing a harp all day? That sounds pretty boring."

"I assure you, Wayne, heaven is not boring. Every day is beautiful and there is no night. Remember me telling you that The Almighty created the entire universe as your playground and that travel is done by the speed of thought?"

"Yeah, Gordon, I remember, but what will I do there?"

"That depends on the good works you store up. It's what I told you when I appeared as Mr. Elroy and told you to store your treasures in heaven, not on earth."

"I guess I wasn't paying attention back then. Why don't you go over that with me again, Gordon?"

"In eternity, the more good works you have while you were on earth, the more duties, position and responsibilities you'll have in heaven. For example, evangelists and pastors who have been instrumental in leading many people to salvation may rule over entire galaxies."

"Are you telling me that there is life out there in the universe, Gordon?"

"Not for you to know, Wayne. Let me continue. Remember Mr. Elroy telling you about the thief on the cross next to Jesus?"

"Yeah, somewhat. I guess I missed that part, also. Too busy playing my guitar."

"The example of the thief on the cross is significant. He was saved that day and went on to paradise, but, he had no good works stored up. His duty in heaven may be to shine the pearly gates forever, but, being in paradise, he'll love every moment and do a fantastic job for the Almighty."

"So, if I decided to enter the portal right now, I'd have no good works and may join the thief shining gates for all eternity, right, Gordo?"

"It was just an example, Wayne. I don't make the assignments. Being in heaven is the most wonderful thing that can happen to humans. So much better than the alternative, wouldn't you agree?"

"I got a real close glimpse of the alternative … Of course I agree. Let me ask you a question about eternity, Gordon. Will there be music in heaven? Can I sing and play my guitar?"

"Oh yes! There will be beautiful music sung by billions in the heavenly choir and every saved musician that has ever walked the face of the earth will be there, from all ages past, present and future. The music is just one of the many things that make heaven so wonderful."

"Can I write new songs there, Gordon?"

"Not only can you write new songs, Wayne, you'll have a new heavenly language, a language that will allow you to write all of the feelings and thoughts that cannot be written back on earth. Every language known to mankind cannot come close to the language that will be spoken in heaven. You'll never be at a loss for words there.

"Let me tell you more about heaven before you make your choice, Wayne. There are no tears there, no pain or suffering, you will want for nothing. Every meal will be a banquet and you will have a family of billions of brothers and sisters of all races. They will love you and be closer to you than your own Mom … Incidentally, Wayne, your Mom is waiting for you there along with many of your ancestors. You'll meet the great and the lowly of all mankind. Each person will tell you his story about his life on earth and you will tell them yours. You'll live in a mansion built by The Almighty Himself, but there will be no need for sleep. Another thing, Wayne, do you still feel the love that you experienced up on the mountain?"

"Oh yes, Gordon, how could I ever forget that feeling, that experience. It was the most paramount feeling that I've ever had."

"That love, that feeling, that experience will be with you forever, Wayne. You will see the face of The Almighty and feel the love of His Son and of the Holy Spirit. You'll also sit in judgment of all the holy angels …"

"You mean that one day I'll judge you, Gordon?"

"Yes you will. I am a created being. I have no conception of a father. I've never experienced a mother's love. I am a servant being that does the will of The Almighty. Mortals like yourself are so blessed to know what love is and what trials and tribulations are, Wayne. To feel hot and cold, to feel love and hurt and pain. I only know obedience. One day I will serve you. I will answer all your questions about the creation, I'll be your escort throughout the entire, unending universe. And I look forward to each and every adventure we'll share together."

"And all I have to do is to turn that door knob and enter the pearly gates?"

"Yes. Or, you can say, 'Send me back' and take your chances. Wayne, listen carefully so that you will fully understand. If you say 'Send me back,' there are no guarantees. You may or may not make it back to life. You may or may not ever be coherent again. You may or may not ever see Abby. You may or may not ever write her that song. Are you clear on this, Wayne? Perfectly clear?"

Wayne sat in the splendor of the beauty of the field, remembering the love he felt up on the mountain. Remembering Abby's face, her touch and the love he wanted so desperately to experience with her. But there were no guarantees. He could be in for a life of pain and suffering. He could die if he chose to go back.

Wayne thought while trying to make up his mind what path he would choose.

Why would any man choose not to go through that doorway? Why would anyone with half a brain subject themselves to more pain, more suffering, more trials and tribulations that life on earth brings forth daily? Why would anyone refuse unconditional love in eternity to only have a chance at conditional love on earth with no guarantees? Why would a man choose the possibility of death over eternal life? My music certainly isn't worth it. My miserable life isn't worth it. I don't care about stardom, fame or money. None of that is worth it! Is Abby worth it? Is the chance of knowing love with her worth it … ?

"Gordon, I've been putting things on a scale. I'm not an educated man at all. This is the only way I know of making a decision. I've weighed risk and reward, life and death, even eternal life in splendor. I've weighed pain against love and I've weighed destiny against fate. But it all comes down to one thing …"

"What's that, Wayne?"

"It comes down to an unpaid debt that I think I owe."

"You're debt free, Wayne. You owe no debts; they've been paid."

"It's a debt that I think I owe in my heart, Gordon. I heard Abby yell out to Baal to take her instead of me. She was willing to do that in the face of hell itself. It's the moment that I knew that Abby truly loved me, when she was willing to give her own life for mine. I can't get that moment out of my mind and if I go into eternity without repaying her. I'm afraid that it will haunt me forever."

"It won't, Wayne, but you're making a good point."

"I do believe that I have a purpose in life, Gordon, and I have no idea what it is. Maybe it is just trying! Maybe it is just dying! I don't know. But I do know that I must go back. If there is one chance in a million, I've got to take it. If I have any fight left in me, I've got to fight. If there is an ounce of love in me for her, I've got to take the chance to prove it to her. Even if I become a vegetable, I'll write her that song somehow and feel that my life, my pain and my suffering have been worth every word."

"Wayne, are you asking me to send you back?"

"Can I ask you one more question before I tell you, Gordon?"

"Yes."

"Will I ever see you again? Will you leave me if I become a veggie?" Wayne chuckled at his own words.

"He will never forsake you, Wayne. As for me, I do what The Almighty tells me to do. I've been with you since the day you were sent to earth, through every moment of your life, your every thought, deed and action. I doubt that He will direct me elsewhere but there is always that chance. Again, Wayne, no guarantees."

Wayne reached out and shook Gordon's mighty hand for the first time. He touched his bronze, porcelain-like skin and looked into his fiery eyes. Gordon wrapped his arms around Wayne, holding him close in a brotherly hug. With one last glance at the beauty that surrounded him, Wayne spoke his final words in this unknown realm, his divine appointment in this place called Between.

"Gordon. I'm gonna risk all for love! I've got to try and repay that debt I owe to Abby and to love her … now that I know what love is. Send me back …"

17

TIME RESUMES ...
CHAOS, REVELATION

At 8:30 Tuesday morning, Hank's phone began playing *Sara*. He was still groggy from the pain pills that the ER doctors had given him after putting a cast on his right hand earlier in the morning. He'd only been asleep for a few hours. The cast was foreign to his slumber and his hand still gave him instances of shooting pain as he tried to fight his way out of the twilight and answer the phone.

"Hi, Sweetie Pie."

"Dad, so sorry to wake you ... You sound horrible, what's wrong?" Abby knew her daddy well enough to know that something wasn't right.

"Uh ... give me a minute, Abby. Trying to wake up. Are you okay?"

"Not really, dad. I cried myself to sleep last night and I woke up just now with the weirdest feeling that something's wrong with Wayne. Can I come over?"

"Sure, baby. I'll put on some coffee and get cleaned up."

Down the hall from Hank's place, Bella was tossing and turning in her sleep. She'd stayed overnight with her mom to take care of her after Robbie was X-rayed at Clear Lake General on Monday and it showed a hair-line fracture of one of the bones in her right foot. The doctors put a boot cast on her foot, gave her some crutches and some meds for the pain. Short of calling the police since Bella had gone with her mom and looked like she had been in a brawl with her face scarred and one eye almost swollen shut, the ER staff knew Robbie and believed their fabricated story of the event leading to their visit to the emergency room.

Robbie had slept restlessly most of the night and was up early, experiencing the pain of her foot and still feeling terrible about banging on and accusing her own daughter of such a terrible act. She stumbled and thumped her way to the kitchen to make breakfast.

Robbie looked over to see Bella asleep on her couch. She was restless, unsettled and grinding her teeth. She heard her talking in her sleep …"No … Don't … Help!" It made no sense but Robbie sensed Bella was having bad dreams. Probably from the trauma of the night before.

At the first sound of pots and pans clanging, Bella awoke with a start.

"Mom! Are you okay?"

"Yeah, baby girl. I'm okay. Just couldn't sleep too well. I've been tossing and turning all night long. I feel so bad about what I did to you. Are you having nightmares? I heard you talking in your sleep."

"Oh Mom! You don't know the half of it! It's the worst dream I've ever had. I dreamed about hell and demons."

"You're shaking, baby. I'll fix you a cup of coffee and you can tell me all about it. Sometimes that helps. Besides, I had a corker of a dream myself. How's your eye doing?"

Abby walked into Daddy Hank's condo and immediately saw the cast on his hand.

"What happened, Pop? What's wrong with your hand!?"

Hank was still groggy and didn't really want to tell her. He had never lied to his daughter so this wasn't going to be easy.

"Baby, I lost it last night. Officer LeGrano who did traffic control for us at the club called me this morning around 1:30 to tell me that Wayne was drunk, sitting out on the patio at the club … I got there in about five minutes. Wayne was bombed and blubbering about writing you a song … After what he had just done to you, uh, sleeping with Bella, I lost it and floored him. I'm sorry to say, baby, that I couldn't restrain myself. I hit him with everything in me … probably broke his nose and cheek … I took his keys so he couldn't drive and hurt anyone else and just left him lying on the wood floors of the patio … went to the ER, got this cast and some pain pills and came home … that's all I can remember."

"Oh, Dad, you didn't!"

"I did."

Abby buried her already puffed up face in her hands and began to cry. Hank reached into the back pocket of his jeans and pulled out his handkerchief to give her.

"That can't be … !"

"What can't be, Dad?"

"There's mascara on this handkerchief. I changed it early this morning when I got back from the ER. My other handkerchief had blood on it from my knuckles."

Hank got up, went into the bathroom where his clothes hamper was and pulled out the bloody handkerchief and walked back into the living room where Abby was sitting on his couch.

"See! Here it is. I don't understand …"

Abby looked at the handkerchief that Hank had given her and said, "Daddy Hank, that's my mascara on your handkerchief. How'd it get there? I haven't seen you since all of this happened."

Hank went into his bedroom, grabbed a fresh handkerchief and gave it to Abby, trying to put two and two together, trying to remember.

"Not important right now, Abby. Tell me about your weird feeling now that we know what happened to my hand and to Wayne."

"Is he okay? Where is he, Pop?"

I don't know, Abby. That's the truth. I left him on the patio. He wasn't hurt too bad, just mostly drunk and feeling sorry for himself."

Abby took a sip of her coffee. A tremble shot though her body.

"Pop, I just had the most horrible dream … I dreamed that Wayne was fighting demons, terrible demons … and we were all there."

"Who was there, baby?"

"You, me, Robbie, Bella, Tito and Mary, T-Bone, Scott Wood and the band. We were all sitting in some kind of stadium watching Wayne get completely tortured by some two-headed dragon. Pop, I saw hell. It was terrible!"

Hank sat down beside Abby, comforting her, pulling her close to him as she cried uncontrollably.

"It's going to be okay, baby. I'm sure it was just a bad dream. Wayne's okay, probably sleeping off the hangover somewhere …"

"Dad, it probably was just my dream. You don't remember anything about it? You were there, too."

Hank took a sip of coffee and a deep breath.

"Yeah, Abby, I had the same dream … I remember Wayne playing on some kind of big stage with Johnny Cash and some other greats … I remember a name … Chiun. I've never heard that name before in my life and can't believe I remembered it."

"Did you see the demons, Dad?"

"I saw 'em. I saw a lake of fire … Still trying to remember what I did dream about last night. It's still kinda foggy."

"We gotta find Wayne, dad. I know he's in trouble. I feel it."

"But what about what he did to you, baby? With Bella? Are you just going to let that go?"

"I'll deal with that later, Dad. Right now, we've got to find Wayne."

Bella tried to get a grip on herself long enough to tell her mom about her nightmare. Robbie looked concerned as she gazed at her daughter and said, "Tell me what you remember about the dream, Bella."

"I remember Wayne getting seduced by a beautiful woman with a long sharp tail … Wayne kept saying 'No,' but she had control over him … Mom, that sorry bastard, Wayne, really does love my little sister …"

"Bella, let's try not to use the words *love* and *bastard* in the same sentence. It's kind of an oxymoronic statement, don't you think?"

"I can't help it, Mom. You said to tell you what I remember. It was terrible! And, Mom, you were down on your knees praying for him. You were crying out to some fifteen foot angel to help him! Don't you remember that, Mom? You were there, too. It's scaring the hell out of me I'm still shaking just thinking about it!"

"Something super natural is going on here, baby girl."

"Mom, did you dream about it, too?"

"Yes."

Without going into her recollections of the same nightmare, Robbie said a quick prayer along the lines of "Father, guide me. What do we do now?"

"Bella, the first thing we have to do is get right with Hank and Abby. We've got to tell them the truth … That this thing they think you did, didn't happen."

"Mom, what did you dream?"

"I'll tell you later, baby girl. We've both had the same dream and that's significant. God is trying to tell us something."

Robbie grabbed her crutches as Bella helped her to her feet. Both were in pain but determined to set things straight with their best friends in the world. Robbie and Bella crutched their way down to Hank's condo and knocked on his door.

"Hank! Open this door right now! It's Robbie and Bella."

Hank headed toward the door thinking that this was all he needed right now, another confrontation. Abby was crying, beside herself, and now he had to deal with the one that caused the problems, Bella, that little self-centered hussy. He really didn't want her in the same room with his daughter. But for Robbie's sake and their friendship he'd make the time and face the problems they were all having with one another.

"Hank! What happened to your hand?" Robbie blurted out.

"What happened to your foot?" Hank answered.

"Hey, we can tell each other our ailments later. Right now, Bella and I have to get right with you and Abby. Is she here with you?"

"Yeah, there in the living room. Come in." Hank was not very pleasant.

Bella ran past Hank and went over to Abby. "I love you, little sister. I would never do anything to hurt you. I didn't sleep with Wayne. I just planted that earring in your bed to make you think I did so you would kick him out. He was cheating on you … Please don't hate me, Abby. I'm telling you the truth!" Tears flowed from Bella's battered face. She was trying to be so sincere that it caused her to shake.

"What happened to your face, Bella?"

"Mom beat the crap out of me. She thought I slept with Wayne, too. But I didn't, Abby. Please believe me! I didn't!"

"Wayne said the same thing, Bella. So now I'm supposed to believe both of you?"

"Abby, look at my face! Look at my mother's foot! I stood right there and let her bang on me and kick me. I didn't fight back! Now is that like me? I didn't deserve that beating but I took it just to let Mom get over her anger and to have one minute to tell her the truth. Do you even think I would let *anyone* mess up my face? You know how I am, little sister … Now do you believe me? Please believe me."

"You look terrible, big sister!" Abby said, thoroughly convinced that Bella was telling the truth. They hugged each other and cried together.

"You look like warmed over you-know-what yourself, Abby. What's up with you? Did you know that I dreamed about hell last night?"

When Bella said the words *dream* and *hell* the room went silent. Hank looked at Abby and Abby looked at Robbie wondering what was taking place. Had they all really been present in the same nightmare?

"Hank, did you and Abby have a bad dream last night?"

"Yeah, we were just taking about it. Trying to fit the pieces together. How about you and Bella?"

"Uh hmmm … We had the dream, too, about hell and demons. It was all about Wayne. He was having to face his demons for all the bad things that he'd done in his life. That seemed to be the scene of the dreams."

"I can't believe I'm saying this, but I even remember pulling for that idiot. I remember telling him to fight to the death. Tito, Mary and T-Bone were doing the same. They were there." Hank was still deep in thought and the words just rolled out of his mouth.

"Robbie, you're the Bible reader in this family. Do you think there's something to all of this?" Abby asked.

"Abby, Jesus said in scripture that where two were gathered in His name, He would be there also. Yes, there is something to all of this. We've just got to put the pieces together and figure it out and pray what to do next."

"The first thing we've got to do is find Wayne!" Abby was insistent.

"We need a plan," Hank said.

"You're right, Hank, but since you know what happened to my foot, what happened to your hand?" Robbie said with a smile on her face.

"Long story short, I punched Wayne out this morning around 1:30 …"

"Typical, Hank. You and your testosterone. I was wondering when you'd get around to that. Let's just start from there. Where did this take place?" Robbie shot back.

Hank told Robbie his story as they sat around his kitchen table trying to decide where to start in their search for Wayne. For a brief moment they stepped back from their task at hand and looked at one another. Robbie with her crutches, Hank's cast, Bella's battered face and Abby's swollen eyes … what a motley crew. They looked terrible because of their own misunderstood opinions and what they thought Wayne would look like when and if they could find him. He may have just left town or he may be in grave danger.

"Robbie, Abby and I'll drive down to the club and see if Wayne may have hotwired his van and taken off. Why don't you and Bella make a few calls to the Police Department and some of the hospitals to see if Wayne wound up in jail or at the ER somewhere. Then, you might want to call the others to see if they have any recollection of what went on … to see if they had the dream, also. We can keep in touch in case any of us find out what's going on."

"Hey, do any of you remember a guy with a white streak in his hair?" Bella said as they were all walking out the door.

"I do, Bella," Abby said. "He was like a mystery man. Do any of you remember seeing him there?"

They all froze, looked at each other, giving a nod and saying nothing more. It was another piece to the puzzle confirming that they all had a divine moment in their lives. What it meant was yet to be discovered.

❧❧

When Hank and Abby arrived at Tequilaville, Wayne's van was still parked in the lot. They peeked inside to see if he was there but found no one. They went into the club and found it empty so they walked to the back patio. Abby saw the blood on the wood floor where Wayne had been. Hank noticed that the boat belonging to their bass player, Dylan, was missing but thought nothing of it. Dylan or his dad could have come and gotten the boat at any time during the night.

"What's next, Pop?" Abby was so anxious to find Wayne that she was having trouble formulating the next step which was rare for her list-making personality.

Hank pulled out his cell phone and punched in Officer LeGrano's number with the Clear Lake PD.

"Rob! This is Hank from Tequilaville. I need another favor."

"Sure, Mr. Hawkins. What can I do for you?"

"We can't find Wayne Tyler. I did take his keys last night like you asked me to but now he's nowhere to be found. We're a little worried about him. Could you give your office a call and see if he was picked up last night?"

"Sure thing. I'll get back to you …"

Hank put in a call to Robbie to see if she and Bella had any information.

"Hank, Wayne's not at Clear Lake General hospital. Maybe that's good news. Have you found out anything?"

"Just that his van is here at the club and Wayne is not. I put in a call to LeGrano and he's calling me back. Have you heard anything from Tito, Mary or T-Bone?"

"Yeah, Hank, I've talked to all of them. They had the dream also and are on their way to Tequilaville. You and Abby may want to stick around while we put more pieces of the puzzle together. See you there in ten."

Meanwhile, Officer LeGrano called Hank back and told him that they had no record of Wayne being arrested earlier in the morning and had no clue of his whereabouts. LeGrano went on to tell Hank that it took forty-eight hours to officially file a Missing Person report but he would ask some of his fellow officers to keep an eye out for him and to let them know.

Ten minutes later everyone was at the club. Robbie took out a tablet and began recording what parts of the dream everyone remembered, hoping that it would yield a clue to Wayne's whereabouts.

Hank told everyone about remembering Chiun and the big rock concert in the sky and that Abby had experienced a dream about the two-headed dragon, Baal, along with terrible visions of the lake of fire which Bella also remembered. Tito and Mary remembered the courtroom scene and mentioned the judge and prosecutor by name, Amon and Dagon, neither of which they had ever heard of before. Scott Wood dreamed about the twin bailiffs, Asherah and Ashtoreth. T-Bone recalled Diana, the demoness who put Wayne into such writhing pain. Robbie recalled dreaming about the deceit of Mama Che, the plump little pixie punkin that had such a great attitude about demons not being all that bad.

Robbie read from her notes, "What I'm seeing here is that this host of demons attacked Wayne on each of his weaknesses: Fame, lust, infidelity, pride, self-centeredness and a general lack of needing God or anyone else in his life. It's fairly obvious when we put all the demon attacks together."

Still, no one had mentioned Gordon, Wayne's angel, or seeing the mighty hand of Michael, the arch angel or even the stirring speech of Gabriel. There were still gaps in their experience.

Hank looked over at Scott Wood. "Scott, the *Maui Blush* was parked out at the dock when I was here last night. It's not there now. Could you call Dylan and ask if he or his dad came to get it last night? Right now that's the only thing we have to go on to find Wayne."

Scott called Dylan and found out that neither he nor his dad had picked up the boat. It may have been stolen but since they'd just found out, no one had filed a report with the police. Scott filled Dylan in on what was happening and asked him to give them a couple of hours before calling the cops.

Hank had done some electrical work at the Coast Guard station just down the lake and had a contact there stored in his phone. He put in a call to them.

"Is Lieutenant Barry there? This is Hank Hawkins."

"Hey, Mr. Hawkins, this is Barry. How's the club business?"

"Lieutenant, it's going okay, but we may have a missing boat that was tied up at our pier last night. Could you give me any insight on a twenty-five-foot red and white Sea Ray, named the "Maui Blush"?"

"Your ears must be burning, Mr. Hawkins, I was just filling out the report. I've got the craft tied up here at our wharf …"

"Any word on the owner or who may have taken it?" Hank didn't want to involve Wayne in the theft and just played it cool with the lieutenant.

"Yeah. It's a long story but, Mr. Hawkins, it involves one of your employees, a Mr. Wayne Tyler. You may want to come down here. I'm about to turn it over to the local sheriff's department."

"Is Wayne there with you, Lieutenant?" Hank inquired.

"No, he was rescued last night by one of our heli-teams. We're investigating now but we don't know if Mr. Tyler fell off the boat into Galveston Bay or it was an attempted suicide. He's alive, but I can't really tell you the details over the phone. They're only for next of kin and the authorities."

"We'll be there in five minutes, Lieutenant, and thank you …"

Everyone heard Hank's end of the conversation with the lieutenant and started packing up to get to the small Coast Guard station just down the lake from them.

"Pop, is Wayne okay? Is he alive? Is he under arrest?" Abby was insistent, anxious and demanding.

"He's obviously alive, Abby, but we'll have to go down there to get the details. That's about all I know."

The entire group piled into their vehicles and caravanned to the station. When they arrived there was hardly standing room for everyone at the small Coast Guard station. Lieutenant Barry began the story of the rescue.

"Yesterday afternoon a large sailboat anchored at Red Fish Island. There was no alert as this is not uncommon for this time of year. However, when the "Maui Blush" pulled out of Clear Lake at around 2 a.m., that was odd and caused us to scramble one of our helicopters to see if there was a possible drug deal going down.

"Our helicopter hovered several thousand feet above the area and with its sophisticated infrared radar we discovered a warm body going into the water from the Sea Ray. After several minutes the radar didn't detect the body surfacing so at this point it became a rescue mission. The chopper spiraled down over the area and we dispatched a rescue swimmer who was on our aircraft. We knew the general area where the victim entered the water but it still took our diver a few minutes to actually locate him and bring him to the surface, then into the rescue basket and get Mr. Tyler on board the helicopter.

"Mr. Tyler was unconscious, his lungs were full of water and he had no heartbeat. Our EMTs on board began CPR on him but no pulse, so they hit him five times with the paddles and finally got a heartbeat. By the way, do any of you know who a 'Gordon' is? Mr. Tyler gurgled out his name a time or two while semi-conscious."

Everyone looked at each other but no one could recall a Gordon.

"We have no idea who 'Gordon' is Lieutenant Barry," Robbie answered.

Barry continued, "Because of Mr. Tyler's critical situation, we airlifted him to Ben Taub County Hospital in Houston where there's one of the best trauma teams in the south. Everyone there has been trained by Dr. Red Duke who was known world-wide for his experience in all types of trauma. If anyone could get Mr. Tyler stabilized, they could. It was our best bet."

"So he's alive?" Abby screamed out.

"So far as we know, Mr. Tyler is alive, but we turned him over to the staff at Ben Taub. He had no current ID; the last known address was on an expired driver's license in his billfold and listed an address in San Antonio.

There were no phone numbers of next of kin to call since his cell phone in his back pocket was fried when it hit the water. We have no further details."

"Lieutenant, I've called the owners of the "Maui Blush" and I don't think they want to file any charges. They'll be down to reclaim the boat. Could you hold off until they get here from contacting the sheriff's department?"

"No problem, Mr. Hawkins, but I do have to file my report."

In the time it took to literally run to their vehicles, everyone was on their way for the thirty-mile trip to Ben Taub Hospital. There was a lot of anxiety and tension but there was also hope that Wayne would be okay. Upon their arrival, they all headed toward the ER with heightened anticipation.

"We're here to see a Mr. Wayne Tyler," Hank said. "Can you tell us where to find him? The Coast Guard air lifted him here earlier this morning about 3:30 a.m. or 4 AM."

The ER nurse checked her computer and paged an attending trauma physician. "Are you the family of Mr. Tyler?"

"Yes, but not official family. He has none and we're the closest thing he has to a family," Abby blurted out. Her hand was trembling and the nurse could see the concern on her face.

A few minutes later, a woman doctor walked up to the group.

"I'm Dr. Lucie Clint, neurologist on the trauma team. Are you Mr. Tyler's family?"

Once again Abby, Robbie and Bella dove into the conversation trying their best to convince the good doctor that they were all Wayne had for a family. There was no one else.

"Okay, I'll trust you for now because of your concern. Could you all follow me to one of our family rooms? I'll fill you in on Mr. Tyler's condition." Dr. Clint was wearing scrubs, she was young, very attractive, highly skilled but stern and didn't mince words.

No one dared utter a word. After they gathered in the small room, Dr. Clint began her report. Abby had no patience left but forced herself to be silent.

"When Mr. Tyler arrived here earlier this morning he was unconscious, his blood alcohol level was very high, he had a very weak heartbeat and was suffering from mild hypothermia since the water this time of year in Galveston Bay is around seventy-seven degrees. His heart stopped two more times and we revived him with paddles and direct injections into his heart. We finally stabilized him and began running tests.

"Tests showed that he had already contracted bacterial meningitis, his lungs were still partially filled with sea water and he was suffering from brain trauma due to a lack of oxygen while he was under water. The Coast Guard EMTs literally kept him alive until they arrived …"

Abby began to cry silently at this point, tears gushing from her eyes, trying to hold back any sound that would prevent Dr. Clint from continuing. Hank pulled her close and put his arm around her. Robbie moved closer to her other side.

"I know this is difficult to hear," said Dr. Clint, "but there's more that I need to tell you. Do you want me to go on?"

"Yes, all of it!" Abby cried out.

"Mr. Tyler is currently in quarantine due to his contagious meningitis but not to the point of an Ebola virus patient. You'll be able to view him but you can't go into his room at this point. He's in a coma and we'll continue to keep him in that state so we can administer the strong antibiotics to fight the bacteria. Another part of the prognosis … His muscular system, at this early point, is not responding to any stimulus below his waist …"

"Oh my god! Is he going to be a vegetable?" Bella interrupted.

"Shut your face, baby girl, or I'll close that other eye!" Robbie said with a look that could kill.

Dr. Clint dealt daily with families and many serious situations. She paused, giving everyone a chance to get a hold of their emotions before she continued. This was all part of her training as a trauma physician.

"Dr. Clint, do you have any idea how long it will take to bring him back to consciousness again and for us to know where he is physically?" Hank asked.

"It's just going to take time, Mr. Hawkins. Bacterial meningitis is a beast but not one that we can't overcome. It's too early to tell. Side effects can be hearing loss, distortion in voice and speech patterns, blindness, seizures, paralysis and personality changes due to learning problems or as we call it, intellectual disabilities …"

"His voice?!" Abby cried out. "He could lose his voice?"

"There's that possibility, Ms. Hawkins. What's Mr. Tyler's profession? I should've asked."

"He's a very talented singer and musician," Abby said.

"Ms. Hawkins, listen to me. Never give up hope! I've sworn a Hippocratic oath to tell you all of the bad things that *can* happen. It doesn't mean that they *will* happen. We've got a great team of skilled specialists here at Ben Taub and we'll fight to overcome every side effect of this disease. Just pray if you're religious and we'll do our part …"

Abby could barely stop crying long enough to say anything but found the strength to ask, "Can I see him now, Dr. Clint?"

"Sure, follow me. I'll take you up to ICU."

When they got off the elevator and arrived at Wayne's room, they saw a yellow "Quarantine, Do Not Enter without Protective Clothing" sign on his door. Abby pressed her nose against the window and saw Wayne. Her tears began rolling down the window and at first sight, she completely lost it and had to turn away.

The only part of Wayne that was not covered by white sheets and blankets was his swollen head which was wrapped in a bandage. He looked like a single meatball in a bowl of spaghetti with all the tubes, lines and sensors connected to his body. He was on a respirator, his left eye was swollen shut and his cheek was badly bruised.

"I'm so sorry, Sweetie Pie. I should have never laid a hand on that man. Please forgive me …" Hank felt terrible at what he'd done to add to Wayne's suffering and shed a rare tear.

"Oh, Daddy Hank. I'd have done the same for you. Just hold me and tell me everything's going to be alright …" They cried together in each other's arms.

For the next hour, Abby remained fixed to the window watching every monitor in the room and Wayne's every labored breath on the respirator. She was trying to digest all that Dr. Clint had told them. One thing kept popping up in her mind, the same thought everyone else was thinking, "No reaction to stimuli below the waist …" Now was a time to decide her role in Wayne's life, if he had a life. She finally turned and walked down the hall by herself.

Robbie began walking after her but Hank touched her arm and gave her a nod.

"Robbie, just let her alone for a moment or two. This is something that she has to deal with on her own."

Bella broke past them and ran down the hall after Abby. She put her arm around her, began lightly elbowing her in the ribs and giggled as she talked.

"Little sister, everything's going to be okay. Wayne will get well and he'll be back at Tequilaville in nothing flat. You've got to believe that. Besides, if you don't want him, I'll take him … Sex isn't at all what it's cracked up to be …"

Abby looked sharply at Bella with fire in her eyes, "You'll what?!"

"I was only kidding you, Abby! Just trying to lighten things up. You know me better than that. Wayne's *your* man and I'm going to be there for both of you. I'm going to make damn sure you both have a great life together, just trust me. Now chill out and look on the bright side, little sister! It only gets better from here …"

Abby was a bundle of emotions and once again broke down in Bella's arms. They cried and laughed on each other's shoulders, holding each other up.

"What would I do without you, big sister? I sure hope you're right this time. I'm gonna need all the help I can get with this."

Robbie looked over at Hank, "I'm so sorry, Hank. Bella's uncontrollable at times. I hope she isn't making things worse again. But whatever she said to Abby, it put a smile on her face. I guess that's what's important."

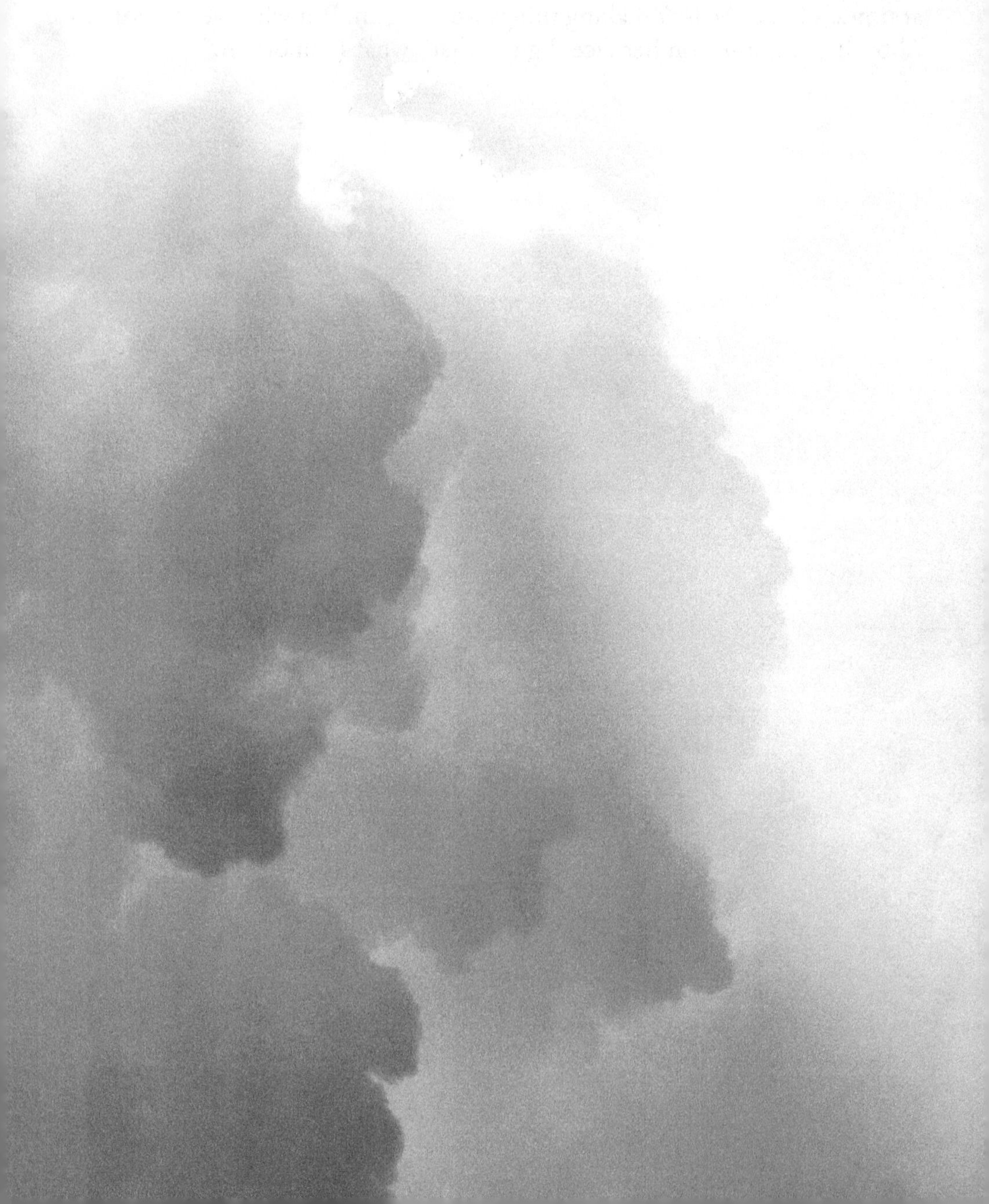

18

REHAB
THE STREAK

There was a mixed bag of emotions as the group drove back to Clear Lake from Ben Taub Hospital. Even though there was a long list of complications that Dr. Clint had gone over that could occur, there was also hope. Wayne was alive. Abby clung to one statement made by the skilled neurologist: "It doesn't mean they will happen …" She also remembered the part about praying and that the trauma team would do the rest. As Daddy Hank drove her home, Abby closed her eyes and said a silent prayer, still not sure if she even knew how to pray.

In another car with Robbie, Bella and Scott Wood, there was little silence and the conversations, especially Bella's, were going a hundred miles an hour.

"Mom, I told Abby that everything's going to be okay. I promised her that. So how are we going to make everything okay, Mom? I'm clueless. You're a nurse. What's next?"

"We pray and we wait, Bella. Medicine's not an exact science. It takes time for bodies to heal and each one heals differently. Procedures going forward depend on what's going on with Wayne and how he reacts to the medication. Right now they have him in an induced coma, but I'm guessing they will get him out of it as soon as possible. Then, they run more tests and go from there. By the way, what did you say to Abby in the hallway that caused such a start in her face?"

"Oh, just sister talk, Mom. I was trying to put a smile on her pretty face and I did, too, didn't I?" Changing the subject, Bella said, "Is it possible for him to make a full recovery?"

"The best answer I can give you, baby girl, is that The Bible says that all things are possible through Christ who strengthens me. So, yes, it's possible for Wayne to recover and live a normal life, but it's going to be a long path. He's going to need lots of physical and occupational therapy, not to mention a lot of support. We don't even know if he did attempt suicide and what his attitude will be when he wakes up. He's gone through a lot. Remember the demons?"

"C'mon, Mom, let's forget about them for a while. I'm still scared to death that I'm going to have more nightmares about 'em and they'll come and get me."

Robbie directed her attention to Scott in the back seat, "Scott, you're going to have your work cut out for you when the club reopens tomorrow. Do you think you can do some rehearsal with the band and keep everyone entertained?"

"Yes, m'am, I know I can. Mr. Hank and I talked about it in the hallway of the hospital. I've already called the guys and we'll be rehearsing my play list tonight. We've been together for a long time, Miss Robbie, we'll knock their socks off."

Driving home with her dad, Abby began putting a plan together for the club and for making the time to be with Wayne.

"Pop, I'm going to work at the club in the evenings, but I want to be with Wayne every morning. I know it'll be a while before he wakes up but I want to be there when he does."

"No problem, baby. I knew that. I've already talked to Scott about taking over the entertainment. What a great man we hired; he's a trooper."

"Yeah, Dad, he'll do great. I wanted to let you know that I put Wayne on our insurance about a month ago. It should pick up most of the tab if his accident isn't listed as a suicide, but with therapy and recovery, there's going to be some big bills to pay."

"I thought of that, too, Abby. Actually, since Wayne was alone out there at Red Fish Island, no one knows what happened but him. I'm thinking about getting the word out around Clear Lake and doing a series of benefits, fund raisers for him. He's got lots of fans and when they know he's in the hospital, I think they'll step up and support him, don't you?"

"God, I hope so, Dad. Those bills are going to be staggering. But we can't abandon him. You know that I love him, don't you, Daddy Hank?"

Hank grinned for the first time in hours, "Yeah, baby, I kind of got that impression from your swollen eyes and your tears running down the window outside of Wayne's room. Besides, I'm kinda getting used to him and so far, Wayne's been our biggest asset. We've got to get him back up on that stage to make us some money to pay these bills. I'll get our marketing team working on the benefit announcements. I'm thinking this weekend isn't too soon to start. We just need sunshine, good weather and lots of thirsty people."

Four days later, Abby was at the hospital early as she had been every single day. Dr. Clint was making her rounds.

"Ms. Hawkins, I'm glad you're here."

"Dr. Clint, how's our boy doing?"

"That's what I wanted to tell you. Mr. Tyler is doing great, beyond our expectations. We're bringing him out of the induced coma and will probably take him off the respirator. He can breathe on his own."

"Oh, praise God, that's so good to hear …"

"Don't get your hopes too high, Ms. Hawkins …"

"Please, just call me Abby."

"Okay, Abby, but I wanted to give you fair warning that he's going to be a little out of it for a few days due to the medications and may not be able to talk or to even recognize you. It'll take time. Stick around outside the room. You can see him after we're finished, tests have confirmed that he's no longer contagious."

The medical team went into Wayne's room, pulled the curtains around the bed and began their procedures. Abby took up her normal position with her nose and hands pressed up against the window trying to see anything that would add to her hope.

Moments later Dr. Clint came out of Wayne's room, "If you'll put on these gloves, mask and gown, you can go in now, Abby. Just don't touch anything, but you can see him. You can even talk to him; he may or may not hear you and respond."

Abby suited up and went into Wayne's room. He was breathing on his own and unconsciously coughed every now and then showing signs of life that she hadn't seen before today. She looked into his closed eyes and took his hand in hers, gripping it ever so lightly. It was warm. She wanted so badly to pass all the love she had for him from her hand to his. For two hours she stood by his bedside talking to him and hoping that he would hear.

As she was turning to go, releasing his hand, Wayne's eyes slowly opened. His first sight was Abby but in his state, he couldn't talk and really didn't know where he was or who she was.

"Wayne! You're awake! I'm Abby, you're in a hospital in Houston and everything's going to be okay. I love you so much. Dr. Clint!" Abby yelled. "He's awake!" Tears of joy poured from Abby's eyes.

For the next week Abby and Wayne got reacquainted. She brought him pictures of the club, him singing on stage, people cheering and a few photos of them together at her house. His memory slowly began to return although his speech was still not near normal. His voice was raspy and he would sometimes slur his words. His sentences left gaps in his thoughts and often didn't make much sense. Abby barely noticed. Just the sound of his voice sent her into orbit. He was getting better and that was all that mattered. Abby did most of the talking and Wayne did a lot of listening as he slowly became coherent to his surroundings. Abby didn't mention the 'accident' and Wayne was still in a state of confusion as to why he was in a hospital.

The first weekend benefit for Wayne at Tequilaville was beyond their wildest expectations. People that had never been to the club or had children dropped by to give their donations to Wayne's "Benefit Can." The sun shone, the weather was wonderful and lots of thirsty people showed up to hear Scott Wood and *South* sing their hearts out.

At 4 p.m. the following Thursday, Abby's phone rang. It was Dr. Clint from Ben Taub.

"Abby? Dr. Lucie Clint."

"Dr. Lucie! I'm so glad we're on a first name basis, now. What's going on with my cowboy?"

"That's why I called, Abby, Wayne wiggled his toes this afternoon."

"He wiggled his toes?! He wiggled his toes?! That's the best news I've heard in my entire life … He wiggled his toes! I can't wait to call everyone and tell them … Wow, Lucie, he wiggled his toes!"

"I thought you'd like to know, Dr. Clint chuckled. "Hey Abby, my husband heard on the radio about Wayne's benefit that you guys are doing at your club. Do you think you have room for our entire trauma staff at Tequilaville this weekend? We're all coming next Saturday night. We didn't know that we were healing such a celebrity."

"Absolutely, Lucie. How many? We'll set up a table right in front for all of you, drinks and food are on the house … He wiggled his toes!"

"I'll call you with the number, Abby. I think half the hospital, at least everyone not on duty will be there. Oh, I almost forgot, tomorrow I'm going to move him to a rehab center there in Clear Lake so he can be nearer to everyone. I know most of the doctors and therapists there and highly recommend them. Our job here at Ben Taub is about finished. We'll transfer him by ambulance. I've got your email and will send you the details. Wayne was so 'up' when I checked on him this afternoon. He's ready to get out of here and start his life again. And, Abby, I think he likes you a lot …"

"He'd better, Lucie! He better *love* me a lot. I can't wait. Thank you and thank your staff. All of us are so grateful and really appreciate what you've all done for Wayne."

"Abby, he still can't walk. He's still weak but with occupational and physical therapy, I think the prognosis is good. See you this weekend …"

When Saturday night arrived, Tito had set up a table for fifty in front of the bandstand with a sign on it that read, "Reserved for Dr. Lucie and her Loving Trauma Team from Ben Taub!" The club was packed to overflowing. Scott Wood and *South* created a musical atmosphere of happiness and exhilaration with a brand new play list to fit the occasion. Jett, their drummer, used drumsticks covered in day glow paint, spot-lit with black lights and went into a drum solo that made the sticks look like a blur, raising everyone from their seats. Scott recognized the Ben Taub trauma team with a rousing introduction followed by huge applause from the other occupants who were buying the team drinks all night long. Dr. Lucie, her husband and the rest of the medical staff had a blast.

Putting on a "Pharrell Williams" hat, Scott did his own rendition of *The Happy Song* and dedicated it to the trauma team. Finally, there was immeasurable joy at Tequilaville. Abby and the rest of their family danced in the aisles and wished that Wayne were there to experience what they had always wanted Tequilaville to be, a good-times place where people could be themselves and go away feeling better than when they first walked in. The word *suicide* was never mentioned or written up in any of the reports. What happened out at Red Fish Island was officially an accident.

Wayne arrived at the Clear Lake Rehab Center. Abby was there to greet him and had packed a bag of some of his work-out clothes and toiletry items, trying to make him feel more at home. He was going to be there several weeks or even months, only time and his progress would tell.

The days at the center began at 6 a.m. He was assigned to a room, given a wheel chair and several I's, Certified Nursing Assistants, were assigned to him, both male and female. Wayne had never been a real modest man but since he had to be strapped into a lift and lowered into his bath, often by female CNAs, he felt completely uncomfortable with it. His dependence on other people embarrassed him and he became instantly frustrated with his daily routine.

Speech therapists helped him on speech patterns with test after test that completely bored and humiliated him. Then there was the physical therapy and the dreaded parallel bars. Wayne had never had to work out physically to keep his trim appearance so his muscle structure was far from being toned. The therapists were unrelenting and pushed him as hard as they could to build his strength, which was the first step in his learning how to walk again. His whole body ached. There were times on the parallel bars where he would fall on his face because his legs couldn't hold him up. The therapists allowed him to fall in order to motivate him to keep on working hard. He had to *want* to walk again. He fell, therapists picked him up. He fell and they picked him up again but would not allow him to stay down. Quitting was not allowed at this rehab center. Once again Wayne had to find the grit and determination to keep him going, to find a new life.

Abby had the schedule that the center had worked out for Wayne and knew when to call him and when not to interfere with his many sessions. She would usually come by in the evenings and have dinner with him in the dining room just to stay close to him and hear all of his frustrations. It helped him to complain and to have someone to sympathize with his struggles.

"I feel like I'm in a paraplegic boot camp, Abby. They're trying to kill me! I'm not sure I can keep doing this ..."

"Do you want to dance with me again in the moonlight?" Abby leaned over to him and kissed him, batting her big green eyes right in his face and flickering her eyelashes on his nose.

"Well, pretty lady, when you put it like that ... Yeah, I do. Sorry for complaining, it's all that keeps me going and the thought of holding you again ..."

"Guess what?" Abby smiled to cheer him up.

"What?"

"The whole gang is coming over here tomorrow night to give you a little 'Keep on Keeping on' party. It's supposed to be a surprise so look surprised, okay?"

"Oh, Abby, I'm not sure I'm up for that right now. I've got so much farther to go. I wanted to face everyone standing on my own two feet …"

"Do you want keep your friends from supporting you, Wayne? To deny them from showing you their genuine love and concern for you? Do you really realize how many people are pulling for you?"

"Sorry, Abby. I guess I'm feeling a little sorry for myself again. This place is depressing sometimes …"

"That's why we're coming, Wayne. Do you get it now? Besides, we all wanted to be here tomorrow when they take your head bandages off."

The next evening, after a full day of therapy, the gang showed up. Abby wheeled Wayne into the library that was decorated for a party. He looked surprised, as best he could, and greeted everyone with a smile.

"Hey, Wayne," Bella said planting a big kiss on his cheek, "have you learned to wiggle your hips yet? Let's see your Elvis routine!"

"Bella!" Robbie was embarrassed again at the boldness and the untimely, off-the-wall statements of her wild-child daughter. "Wayne, we're all so proud of you. Hey, Bella is just being Bella, don't take it to heart."

"Robbie, I love Bella to death. What would the world be without her?"

Hank walked up to Wayne. "How're you feeling, son? We've missed you."

"Hank, I feel like I know what Marine boot camp is like now. They're working my butt off. What's with the casts on you and Robbie?"

"Oh, Robbie had a run in with her coffee table and as for me … Wayne I want to apologize for trying to rearrange your nose …"

"Think nothing of it, Hank. Like I said, I deserved it and you needed it. Are we good?"

"Yeah, son, we're good."

One by one Tito, Mary, T-Bone, Hattie Lang and several of the other people at the club walked over to Wayne, giving him hugs and offering words of encouragement.

Scott Wood and the entire band were there, too.

"Scott, I hear you and *South* are trying to get my job," Wayne kidded them. "I hear you guys are knockin 'em dead on stage."

"Hey, buddy, you may have to pass audition again. We're pretty good!" Scott slapped Wayne on the shoulder in jest.

Hank walked to the back of the room and escorted a lady over to Wayne for him to meet.

"Wayne, I want to introduce you to Kendalynn Murphy. Keyndalynn, this is Wayne Tyler."

"Glad to meet you Kendalynn. What brings you to our party?"

"I'm a voice coach. Mr. Hawkins has hired me to help you 'pass the upcoming audition.'" She kept Scott's tease going. "I've been scheduled into your therapy sessions beginning tomorrow afternoon. Your voice is still a bit raspy, but I'll have you singing at the top of your game in no time."

"So how're we going to start? I've never had a voice coach before."

"Probably with the scales, you know, do-re-me?" Everyone had a good laugh.

"Thanks, Hank. I do appreciate the help and I sure could use it. I don't know where my voice has gone, but I'm hoping Kendalynn will help me find it again."

The moment arrived to remove the bandages from Wayne's head. The chief RN of the center walked in with a small tray containing scissors and some medical tools on it. Everyone backed off to get a better view of the event as the nurse began cutting the bandages. Slowly, she unwrapped them as the room grew silent in anticipation. The first thing everyone noticed was a white streak of hair growing just over Wayne's right ear and each of them began reflecting back to their divine dream.

As everyone stood in silence, the nurse gave Wayne a mirror and, acting like a barber, she asked him, "How does that look, Mr. Tyler?"

"Uh … uh … it looks like I'm getting prematurely gray," was all Wayne could think of to say. No one else said a word except, of course, Bella.

"Wayne, that streak isn't gray, it's white as snow. Maybe that can be your new trademark, you know, like Wayne, 'the Streak,' Tyler."

19

THE ONLY...
I'LL LOVE YOU, ANYWAY

A young, man dressed in a Coast Guard officer's uniform walked in on the festivities at the rehab center. No one knew who he was. Hank began thinking that this could not be a good thing, recalling the final Coast Guard report of whether the incident at Red Fish Island would be classified as an accident or an attempted suicide. It could mean that their insurance would not pay the bulk of Wayne's medical bills.

"Sorry to crash in on your party. I'm Lieutenant Stan Stark, a chaplain with the local Coast Guard rescue detachment. Mind if I join you?"

"Not at all, Lieutenant. I'm Hank Hawkins, co-owner of Tequilaville along with my daughter Abby. We were hoping to have your rescue group join us at the club and honor you guys for pulling our boy, here, out of the drink." Hank was nice but was still holding his cards close to his vest.

"It's what we do, Mr. Hawkins." Lieutenant Stark said, removing his cap.

Instantly the room went completely silent. Lieutenant Stark had an identical white streak of hair over his right ear and for those that could remember, looked just like the mystery man sitting with them back on the bleachers of that divine arena in a place near Between. It was complete *déjà vu*. At that point the festive atmosphere at the party got real serious.

"What brings you here, lieutenant?" Robbie asked.

Up until now no one had any recollection of the angel who had guided Wayne through his trials. That was about to change.

"Uh, I'm not sure how to begin." The lieutenant looked off for a minute, gathering his thoughts. "One of the EMTs on the chopper that rescued you,

Mr. Tyler, said that you gurgled out the name, Gordon, a time or two. Do you know who *Gordon* is? It's real important to me …"

Wayne kept staring at the streak over the lieutenant's ear, trying to remember. "Yeah, lieutenant, I know who Gordon is. Do you?"

"Please excuse me," said Lieutenant. Stark, "I'm afraid that I am casting a wet blanket over your party. Maybe another time …"

"No, no, we're all here and we all want to know about this *Gordon* and why we both have these white streaks in our hair." Wayne was insistent to get on with the missing pieces of his own puzzle. Maybe even to let them know what he'd been through during his trials with the demons. Even he was not sure that they had actually happened and he dared not say anything to anyone else. They'd surely think he was out of his mind with such a tale.

Everyone that was present, with the exception of Hattie and Kendalynn had dreamed the dream. No one had discussed the ordeals with Wayne. It seemed like a good time to get it all out in the open. Maybe it would heal all of their minds and souls and add clarity to the puzzle that was still missing some pieces.

Stark began his story, "I'm twenty-nine. When I was nineteen, I was on a party boat with a bunch of my college friends. We dropped anchor at Red Fish Island. We were drinking and partying when I lost my balance and fell in during the night. No one saw me enter the water and I hit my head on the reef, knocking me unconscious. Minutes later, my girlfriend saw my baseball cap floating on the surface and a couple of guys on the boat dove in and pulled me to the surface. I had a similar experience to yours, Mr. Tyler, but it was what happened between the time I hit the water until they dragged me out that I'm here to learn.

"I met Gordon at a place called Between. Gordon was a fifteen-foot angel that led me though some ordeals and changed my life. And I dreamed that I was back there watching you go through some really terrible things in a dream I had a few weeks ago. Almost like I did ten years ago. It's been giving me nightmares.

"I never knew if my experience was true or just a dream. Maybe it was a true dream but that's why I'm here … to find out. Did you meet Gordon?"

"We all did, Lieutenant," Robbie said, "We haven't said anything to Wayne yet, but we were all there in that same dream, in that same arena to witness the atrocities, the demons and the lake of fire. We saw the battle for a man's soul. We saw you there, too, but didn't know who you were."

"You were all there?" Wayne asked. "I thought it was just a figment of my imagination, a bad dream. I saw everyone there, including you, Lieutenant, but I didn't want to say anything about it. You would've all thought me to be mad!"

"Oh, Wayne, it happened all right. We all remember bits and pieces of it. We all woke up with nightmares and got together and started comparing notes," Robbie blurted out.

"It scared the hell out of me!" Bella added, hiding her face in her hands.

"Abby, I remember you yelling out at Baal to take you instead of me. Did you actually do that? Do you remember?"

"Yes, Wayne, I do remember and I did say that to that two-headed dragon trying to knock you down into the lake of fire. You'd gone through enough. I wanted to take your place in hell …"

"But Jesus saved me, Abby! Did you know that I'm a child of the Almighty now?"

"Yes, baby, I've known in my heart and mind since the moment it happened, Praise Him! He spared you, Wayne. He was your last hope and you asked for His saving grace. You called on His name of your own free will."

"This is so important to me everyone, so could I ask you a couple of more questions? It may be my reason for being and I need to know." The lieutenant was dead serious.

All agreed to answer all the questions that Lieutenant Stark had. This was a moment of revelation to all of them.

"Wayne, I didn't have to face any demons when I went to Between. I stayed there talking to Gordon. Did he, uh, well, 'cocoon' you in that creamy colored bright cloud with all the golden threads running through you and show you what love is?"

"Did he ever, but it was after the demon trials. I was in a beautiful field with flowers and still waters, like a glimpse of heaven. Gordon walked me up on top of a mountain. That's when I experienced, felt and saw all those golden threads of love going right through me. Abby, I know what love is now, like I've never known before …"

"Oh, Wayne!" Abby said looking at Wayne with big green puppy-dog eyes. Love was in the room. There was another divine appointment happening, a moment of reflection, remembering and trying to figure out the purpose of what was happening in all of their lives.

"My last question, everyone. Did Gordon tell you what your gifts are? I mean, if you can remember it, it's important to me because he told me that my gift was to be a rescuer of souls … That's why I entered seminary and became an ordained minister and later joined the Coast Guard as a chaplain assigned to a coastal rescue unit."

Every person in the room that was present at Wayne's ordeal began to search their memories, trying to pull out the answers to the lieutenant's question.

"Gordon told me that my gift was a prayer warrior," Robbie said. "He said that I have a crown in heaven waiting on me …"

"He told me that my gift was being a good father and provider, and that the fruits of my labor would be blessed," Hank added.

"He told Mary and me that our gift was to raise a family and that He would bless our marriage and our kids," Tito chimed in, nodding at Mary, holding her close.

"My gift was wisdom since I turned my life around and made the choice not to murder Wayne." Tears rolled down T-Bone's cheeks.

"Gordon told me that no greater love has a man than to lay down his life for a friend. I don't know if that's a gift or not, but that's what he said …" Abby looked to Wayne, again confirming what she'd done on two separate occasions during his ordeals.

"Abby, Gordon told me that my gifts were my voice and my passion to play music. He said that God loved and invented all types of music. The big question is right now is, will I ever be able to use that gift again. And, he said that now I had the words for your song, Abby, and that I could write them one day …"

"You will, Wayne. One day you will write that song for me. I've always known it even before you went to Between …"

"He said the same thing to me, my passion for music and to never give up on my dream," Scott added.

"Well, everyone," Bella was smiling ear to ear, hand on her hip, flipping her hair and taking center stage, "Gordon told *me* that God was very *fond* of Bella and that my gift was my *sterling personality*. God is pretty sharp if I do say so myself. He knows me almost as well as I do! Gordon also told me that I can call him, *personally*, anytime I want to … Hmmm I don't remember his cell number. I'm clueless how to get a hold of him …"

The puzzle was finally coming together to form the final picture of what had happened in that divine realm near a place called Between. No one would ever remember it all, but bits and pieces of the memories stuck in their minds, confirming that this had, indeed, been a true dream, experienced by each of them in their own recollections.

"Give me a call when Wayne gets back to Tequilaville," Stark said, giving everyone his card. "My squadron will be there. We want to hear that new song you write for Abby. We 'streaks' have to stick together." Lieutenant Stark said, pointing to the white streak of hair over his right ear and giving everyone a big smile.

The party at the rehab center continued for another hour, then everyone but Abby went home to talk about what had just been revealed in their lives.

"I need to talk to you, Abby!" Wayne was dead serious. He had a lot on his mind, still facing his demons.

In the privacy of the library, Wayne became very pensive and tried, once again, to face reality.

"Abby, now I'm going to tell you something that no one knows but me and Gordon. After everyone left the arena, I was standing at the very portal of heaven itself. It was a twenty-foot high door with a golden knob. All I had to do to walk into the glories of heaven was to turn the knob and enter. No more pain, suffering, no more agony, no more trials and tribulations of life … just turn the knob and walk in."

"Why didn't you?"

"Because I found out what love is. I wanted so badly to experience that with you here on earth. More than you'll ever know, so I told Gordon to send me back. I never expected what was waiting for me. All the therapy, the recovery, being like I am now …"

"And he did send you back, didn't he? You're here, you're with me now."

"Abby, I'm convinced that what you and all the others witnessed, in some kind of a divine dream, is what really happened to me at that terrible place. You saw a prideful man lose every tribulation that I faced. I feel like a broken man …"

"Wayne, you're not broken, you surrendered … to Jesus. He saved you from yourself. As for the demons, you turned down a contract with Chiun, avoided the deception of Chemoth, you took the pain of that witch, Diana. You decided not to decide in that kangaroo court, you didn't lust after the twins and you said 'no' to Ishtar.

"Yes, Wayne, I remember. I saw it all and I remember most of it now … I saw you stand up to that mighty dragon, Baal, and tell him to come and get you. That was your moment of courage, your moment of true grit. Wayne, you've got to find that moment again. Do you think any one of us could have done any better? All of us would've failed. That's where Jesus comes in. He's the Calvary riding in to save us in the eleventh hour."

Wayne just sat in his wheel chair, looking at his legs that couldn't hold him up, took a deep breath and said in his raspy voice …

"Abby, I've cheated on every woman I've ever been around …"

"It's okay, Wayne, you've been forgiven. I love you anyway."

"But baby, I don't know if I can sing again and make a living …"

"It's okay, I love you anyway."

"Abby, you don't understand, I've been a liar and a cheat ..."

"I love you anyway, Wayne."

"I only know how to live a self-centered, pointless, hedonistic life. You don't deserve that."

"I love you anyway."

"Abby!" Wayne slapped his legs, hard. "I can't even stand up! I'm in a wheel chair. Look at me!"

"That's okay, Wayne. I'll push your wheel chair and I'll love you anyway," she said in a soft, gentle voice.

"Abby, face facts! It's time to be realistic here. I couldn't return your love when we were together. I didn't know what love was."

"But you do now, Wayne. I'll help you remember what you learned at that place ... I'll love you anyway."

Wayne was falling apart, crying, despite his efforts to hold back the tears. He had to get to the heart of the matter and convince Abby to move on without him. He didn't deserve her. He didn't know if he could keep going or if he just wanted to die all over again.

"But Abby," he was having difficulty holding himself upright in the wheel chair. "I'm not sure that I'll ever be a man, again. I may not be able to love a woman the way a man should ... You know..?"

"Wayne, I'll love you anyway! You're my man and I'm your woman. Nothing else matters."

"Abby, how can you say that?! How can you love a man that may not be able to love you back ... properly. Have you ever thought about that? A life without intimacy? I may not be able to do that!"

"I-Love-You-Anyway!" Abby screamed out, her tears intertwining with Wayne's as she pulled him close to her. "Don't you dare give up on me, Wayne Tyler! We've both been through too much hell to quit now. We're kindred spirits. We're made for each other and I'm never letting you go. I love you anyway!"

For the next two weeks Wayne worked hard at the rehab center. Instead of dreading the parallel bars, he embraced them. He was still dragging his feet but at times he could stand alone, unaided for a few seconds. He felt his strength returning albeit ever so slowly. Kendalynn Murphy worked with him to get his voice back and brought his guitar over to aid him in finding his notes. It was good to play and sing again. He hadn't forgotten how to tear up that beloved instrument and it gave him so much comfort to hear the tunes coming from it and from his fingers, which were working again.

During his down time Wayne spent hours in the library, scribbling down a new song and trying to find the words and the music to go with it. They came easier this time and there were no wadded up pieces of paper on the floor around him. He called Scott Wood to come over to help him write the words, to put them in a row and to hear the music. When it was finished, Scott gave the song to the band to learn.

"Hank? This is Wayne."

"How's the rehab coming along?"

"Slow, hard, but I'm not complaining. I wanted to ask you if I can sing a song at the club this Saturday night?"

"Just one?"

"Just one. It's for Abby. I promised her."

"You love my daughter, don't you?"

"Yes, I do, Hank. That's another thing I wanted to talk to you about."

They talked for a few minutes and got some of their differences settled. Wayne bared his soul to Hank and wanted to know if he still had a job, if he could do it again.

"I'll slide you into the schedule this coming Saturday night, Wayne. We'll build a small ramp up to the bandstand for you."

"Thanks, Hank, you're the best."

Scott and the marketing team began sending email blasts to all the patrons of Tequilaville letting them know about the "Return of Wayne Tyler" to the club. Houston radio and TV stations got on the bandwagon. Wayne's ordeal had become news all around the Gulf Coast NASA area. Reservations were pouring in and the phones were ringing off the hooks. Two special tables were set up for the return of the Ben Taub staff and for Lieutenant Stan Stark and the Coast Guard rescue squadron.

"What're you going to wear Saturday night, little sister?" Bella asked, calling to touch base with Abby.

"I don't know. Do you think I should dress up or just wear jeans?"

"Definitely dress to the nines. Let's go shopping, I'll find just the right outfit for both of us. Off to the mall. I'll meet you there at noon. Then we can stop by the spa for some TLC, a mani and a pedi. I have a feeling tonight's going to be a big night!" Bella loved to shop and help Abby with her ensembles.

"Why do you say that, Bella?"

"Oh … because Wayne is coming back. He's going to sing again and everyone's gonna be there …"

"That's it? That's all you know?"

"Isn't that enough?" Bella giggled. She knew more than Abby knew about the night to come and about Wayne's song just for Abby. Scott had spilled the beans to her during a rehearsal at the club. Bella was beside herself not to tell Abby.

Wayne arrived at the club about 9 p.m. sitting in his wheelchair in the back of Jett's pick-up truck that had a hydraulic lift gate that he used for a delivery service as a second job. Scott and *South* were just beginning their first set, the ramp for Wayne's wheelchair was in place to the left of the bandstand and the place was packed. There were lights set up on one side of the club for the TV crews who wanted to film and interview Wayne. Radio stations had remote airing tables in the back of the club and were covering the event live. The atmosphere was one of anticipation. Most of the visitors to the club had no idea what Wayne had gone through and didn't know he was unable to walk.

Abby, Bella, Robbie, Kendalynn, Hattie Lang and Mary were all tricked out and looking good, sitting with Hank at his corner table. Hank had on his jeans and old cowboy hat, as usual.

At straight up 10 p.m., Scott walked up to the microphone on stage.

"Ladies and gentlemen, it is my pleasure to introduce a great performer, singer, guitarist and one of my best friends, Wayne Tyler. He has a special song to sing. Please welcome him back to Tequilaville …"

Applause rocked the house for several minutes. Dylan rolled Wayne on stage and the applause subsided for a brief moment while everyone dealt with the image of Wayne in his wheelchair. Some of the ladies in the crowd grabbed their hankies and some just cheered louder. Mixed emotions of well-being overwhelmed the audience. People noticed how thin Wayne was and a buzz started around the room about the streak of snow white hair over his right ear.

Sitting in his chair in front of the microphone, waiting for the applause to diminish, Wayne began to speak.

"I'm baaaacck!" Applause filled the room. "Hey buckaroos, why rock when you can roll, huh? How do you like my new wheels?" Wayne was trying to lighten up the moment and keep the good times going. Everyone applauded for several minutes. Hank's table joined in the laughter thinking that Wayne was an entertainer to the nth degree.

"You're looking at the new poster child for 'Learn to Swim' week!" The laughter in the huge room became louder as Wayne made pun after pun of his condition.

"Speaking of learning to swim, I'd like to recognize some very special people who pulled me out of Galveston Bay. They never sleep! The Rescue Squadron of our local men in blue, The Coast Guard, keeping our waters safe from people like me."

Lieutenant Stark and the rest of his team stood and took a bow.

"And the great trauma team at Ben Taub led by neurologist, Dr. Lucie Clint. Let's hear it for them."

More applause.

"I'd also like to recognize the staff at Clear Lake Rehab center and to my special voice coach, Ms. Kendalynn Murphy. Please stand and take a bow …"

"Finally, I'd like to recognize my family, Hank and Abby Hawkins, owners of Tequilaville, and hopefully, my continued employers, Robbie and Bella Cantrell and the rest of the staff here at the club. Thank you for making us a success. We applaud you …"

With all his 'Thank You's' made, Wayne reached over to get his acoustic guitar. The laughter ended, the applause stopped and the room went dead silent. Scott lowered the lights. A single spotlight shone on Wayne as he adjusted the mic to his sitting level.

"Before all of this chaos entered my life," Wayne said in a raspy voice as a lump formed in his throat, "a very special lady asked me to write a song for her. Sometimes bad things happen in a person's life to make it better. A month or so ago I didn't have the words to tell her what was on my heart. I didn't know what love was or how to express it …

"Now, before my newly found God who saved me and everyone present, I would like to sing my song … dedicated to Abby for all her love and encouragement that she's shown to me during my ordeal and for you to take home and share with your loved ones. This is Abby's song, "The Only

Love Song …" Wayne looked back at the band, took a deep breath and tried to sing. The lump in his throat prevented him from continuing so he took a moment, apologized to the audience and started again …

> *You smiled when you asked me*
> *To write a song for you*
> *I laughed and said, "That's easy, girl,*
> *Cause this is what I do."*
> *Call me confident or crazy*
> *And both may be true*
> *But when I tried to find the words inside*
> *Didn't take long to realize*
> *There's just no way with you …*
> *Cause how do you tell*
> *The stars how bright they shine,*
> *When they light up your darkest night?*
> *How do you describe*
> *The deep blue ocean*
> *When you're swept out with the tide?*
> *How do I put all my feelings*
> *In just so many words,*
> *When I've searched the world*
> *And come to find…*
> *You're the only song I've ever heard.*

Holding back the tears and lump in his throat, Wayne began the chorus as the silence of the crowd hung on his heartfelt words to Abby.

> *You're my first thought in the morning*
> *'Till I close my eyes at night.*
> *I see your face and your sweet eyes,*
> *Shining brighter than the sky.*
> *No way I can put a label*
> *On all you are to me,*
> *'Cause you're much more*
> *Than my wildest dreams,*
> *My life, my heart, my everything.*
> *No, words can't describe what you mean to me …*
> *I wanna show the stars how bright we shine,*

Wanna get swept out on the ocean tide.
Wanna spend the rest of our lives together,
Giving you all my heart and all my words
'Cause you're the only song I've ever heard …
Yeah, you're the only song I've ever heard.

The applause started slowly with a single woman standing, clapping by herself. The rest of the audience joined in. It was a moment. Everyone could hear the love and sincerity in Wayne's still broken voice and looked back to Hank's table to see Abby's reaction. She sat stoically beside Daddy Hank, tears of joy running down her cheeks. It was her moment. It was her song and she cherished every note of it.

Wayne bowed low in his wheel chair and waved for Abby to come up front. Jett rolled Wayne down the ramp and onto the dance floor. The single spot light followed Wayne down as Abby walked up and gave him a big hug, crying on his shoulder in front of everyone.

Wayne struggled to lift himself from the chair and stood in front of Abby for about a second or two before his strength ran out. He slumped down to his knees and rested his body on his haunches. Dylan and Jett immediately started down from the bandstand to help him stand up but Wayne waved them off.

"Thanks guys, but this is something I have to do myself."

Abby was wearing a long, flowing low cut purple gown with a single strand of pearls adorning her neck. Her brunette hair and her glowing green eyes sparkled as she stood before her man.

Wayne reached in the back pocket of his starched jeans and pulled out a small box, fumbling to open it.

"Ms. Abby Hawkins, I've just told you how I truly feel in my song for you. Would you do me the honor of becoming my wife?"

The crowd burst into applause. Everyone in unison was yelling, "Say yes! Say yes!"

Abby composed herself, trying to add more time to her big, precious moment.

"Well, Mr. Tyler, do you promise to love me? To honor me and to obey me until death do us part?" Abby had her hands on her hips and walked around the dance floor, looking back occasionally at the audience as she lovingly taunted Wayne before she replied.

Wayne was caught completely off guard and stuttered with his response.

"Uh, Ms. Hawkins, I do promise to love you and honor you … and I'll do my best to obey you, as best I can …" Wayne looked back at the room. Everyone laughed but kept their laughter short to hear the rest.

"Till death do we part, Mr. Tyler?"

"Till death do we part, Ms. Hawkins."

"Before God and every woman in town, do you promise to be faithful to me forever?"

"I promise, Abby, forever!"

"And Mr. Tyler, have you asked for my hand in marriage from my Daddy Hank?"

"Uh, yes I have. Who do you think loaned me the money to buy this ring, baby?"

Wayne was getting frustrated. His reply brought the house down. Laughter and applause at such a wonderful moment that the entire audience was sharing.

Abby kneeled down, staring at Wayne eye-to-eye, and put forth her left hand.

"In that case, Mr. Tyler, YES! I would be honored to be your wife …"

Seizing the moment, in typical form during the moment of intense silence Bella wanted to have the last word.

"Hey, Wayne," Bella yelled from the corner booth, "you'd better check the back of her dress to see if a tail is poking out!"

Pandemonium was the only word to describe the moment. TV camera lights were on, announcers gave Abby and Wayne a second for their moment then began sticking microphones in their faces asking questions.

"And ladies and gentlemen, you saw it live on Eyewitness News …"

As Abby and Wayne clutched each other on their knees in the middle of the dance floor, Hank looked back across the room at the lone lady who had first stood up and began the applause. He'd never seen her in the club before but somehow the woman looked familiar. She was tall, slim, sixtyish, had dark hair and glistening green eyes. As he fixed his stare on her, she looked back at him. At that moment it seemed if time was again frozen. For the third time in his life, the world stood still for Hank Hawkins.

Imagine that …

LOOKING FORWARD

This family group of normal, everyday mortal characters who play the many diversified roles in *Wayne's Angel* and who are joined by spiritual beings—some good, many the baddest of the bad—are only beginning their great adventure into the unknown. Why end their amazing story with everything being all warm and fuzzy. After all, life is full of trials and tribulations and the characters' lives continue.

Wayne has proposed to Abby. Abby has accepted. Will they actually tie the knot? Will Daddy Hank ever accept Wayne as his son-in-law? And who is this mysterious lady at the end of the book who has made Hank Hawkins' world stand still. Will she complicate his life or will she compliment it?

If Wayne doesn't literally get back on his feet, will he be able to pack Tequilaville with his group of fans and followers? Will the club continue to prosper or is tragedy in store for this venture?

I haven't a clue who your favorite character was in book one but the author took a special interest into the flamboyant character of Bella, Abby's *almost* sister. I want to expand Bella's character with a stronger role in book two to see just where her amazing personality takes her and the rest of *the family.*

Book two of the trilogy will be titled, **Betwixt,** and the author has plans to make it more colossal, more amazing and further out-of-the-box that leads the reader to the realm of *out there.* Literally, **Betwixt will be Wayne's Angel on steroids!**

There will be some new characters in *Betwixt*. Dr. Eric Palmer, a NASA parapsychologist who counsels U.S. astronauts who have seen unexplainable phenomena while in outer space. Palmer has a counter-part colleague, Dr. Helle Guyion, who works with Russian cosmonauts to explain their unknown experiences. Dr. Guyion is an albino beauty originally from Norway. She's also a mesmerizing, very powerful priestess of darkness. She's going to turn some worlds upside down when she is asked to join Dr. Palmer in piecing together the amazing dream that Wayne and his group cannot fully remember. This will be highlighted in a chapter entitled, *Houston, we have a problem!* A problem that NASA and all of their scientists have never encountered.

Finally, I do hope that you enjoyed Wayne's Angel and that you'll tell your friends about it. Who was your favorite character? Just email me at ronmumford@aol.com. I'd love to hear your feed-back. And, if you want to know when Betwixt will be on the book shelves, let me know and I'll put you on a special announcement list.

ABOUT THE AUTHOR

Ron Mumford is the author of a non-fiction book, *Finding Your Soul Mate, God's Way*, an action thriller, *Gray Justice*, and a fantasy trilogy which includes *Wayne's Angel, Betwixt,* and *Z-Gen*, soon to be published by 3rd Coast Books.

Mumford was a Journalism major at the University of North Texas, worked at two small newspapers as sports editor, as associate editor at a national trade magazine, and has written freelance articles for several newspapers and magazines. After being drafted into the U.S. Army, he was an information specialist (Army Combat Correspondent/Photographer) in Vietnam and Germany, receiving two Bronze Stars for his service in Vietnam. He also wrote for Army Times and Stars & Stripes.

Mumford started his own business as a literary agent in Houston, Texas. He went to New York and Hollywood to pitch his clients' work.

Mumford wants other authors to gain from his experience. One of his first editors, Myra Barnes, Ph.D., from Baytown told him, "Ron, as a writer, if you ever make it big in the book writing business, send the elevator down to your fellow writers!"

He has never forgotten that plea and continues to support fellow Indie writers in any way he can. *IF YOU QUIT, YOU LOSE!* He hopes to spread the word to never quit writing and never give up hope. Someone will come along and send the elevator down...

Other Books By Ron

Non-Fiction:

Finding Your Soul Mate, God's Way (Christian Non-Fiction),

Fiction:

Gray Justice (Action Thriller),

Wayne's Angel Series (Fantasy)

Wayne's Angel

Betwixt (Coming Soon)

Z-Gen (Coming Soon)

Books and ebooks by Ron W. Mumford are published by 3rd Coast Books and can be found at www.ReadersCloud9.com or www.RonWMumford.com, as well as all major online retailers